Welcome to the Mayhem

Astraea Long

Welcome to the Mayhem

Paperback edition ISBN: 979-8-9888946-2-9

E-Book ISBN: 979-8-9888946-3-6

This is a work of fiction. Names, places, and incidents are products of the author's imagination. Any resemblance to actual persons, living or dead, or events that occur in real life, is entirely coincidental.

Astraea Long asserts the moral right to be identified as the author of this work.

Copyright © 2025 by Astraea Long

All rights reserved.

No portion of this book may be reproduced in any form without written permission from the publisher or author, except as permitted by U.S. copyright law.

To every child who was forced to grow up too fast.

Contents

Note to Readers

This book includes alcoholism, mentions of abuse, blood and gore, mental illness, murder, mind-control, self-harm, suicidal ideation, mentions of suicide and suicide attempt, and violence.

Thank you!
Astraea Long

Beginning of the End

Glazed eyes remain unperturbed when lightning strikes through the umber irises, like a timeless stretch of calm ocean water, too apathetic to feel a ripple, too deep to ever reach the bottom.

"So, what's your plan?"

Zero doesn't answer for a moment, blinking through the haze of her thoughts, curled up at the bay window of her room in the Wraith Tower. The fog of the mountains sets a dreary cloak over the mansion, the distant lights from the city cold and extrinsic like the stars.

It's been three months since Tal left the Aconites. The heaviness in her chest hasn't lifted, nor has the struggle to get up every morning left her body, even after she fought off the fever. She hasn't spoken to Rovis in eleven weeks. In her defense, the man hasn't spoken to anyone since that night in Tal's room. The Scavenger's footprints in the desert have long faded in the sand, and if it weren't for Zero's nonstop meetings with the inner circle of the Aconites, the organization would be in shambles.

While they're managing to stay intact in the depths of crumbling mountains, the city of Dyvris continues its descent into chaos. Once lively with curious tourists and overly enthusiastic vendors, the streets have become as desolate as abandoned research facilities. The Purity Syndicate must have known the instability within the Aconites, if the appearance of hundreds of them two days after Tal's departure indicated anything. They destroyed thirteen Aconite fronts and trashed all the shops in between. Every innocent civilian who was in the wrong place at the wrong time was killed, and every unprepared member of the Aconites who tried to stand in their way was critically injured.

For a month following the attack, none of the Aconites could walk on the streets without spoiled milk and rotten vegetables raining down on them. Zero couldn't blame them. They failed to protect their city, after all.

Yet she will never forget the time she almost got lynched downtown, her hair torn right off her scalp, her clothes ripped off her body. She had to resort to breaking bones to get away, knowing that she'd become the villain in all their stories no matter what choices she made.

Even though her money is what's keeping a roof over their heads, when she drained her bank account to invest in public housing. Not that anyone would care or believe her. She doesn't even care to defend herself.

Now, the streets are quiet again, a cemetery for everything the Scavenger has ever built. The targeted violence has fizzled out not because they are forgiven, but because the gnawing chokehold of poverty and doomsday's approach has drained the hatred away. In its current state of economic depression and political vulnerability, Dyvris looks nothing like it used to. Unemployment is at an all-time high, and even the business owners, whom the Scavenger saved when they had nowhere else to go, blame their bankruptcy on the Aconites, all history forgotten.

Where the Aconites used to stride on the streets like royalty, they now float through the city like ghosts, hiding behind gas masks and beneath shadows of large hoods. Constructed from neuron-sensitive nanotechnology, the Tech Hall has upgraded their headgear to protect them from angry Dyvrians, less flaunting than their formerly shiny helmets for obscurity.

Most importantly, the Mechs built in new filtration systems for nature's newest attempts to purge itself of mankind.

The rising global temperatures crossed a certain threshold that caused a methane eruption and released hydrogen sulfide from the bottom of the oceans, contaminating the air with toxic gasses. Most of the working class, a third of the population, is either bedfast or six feet under, while the upper and middle classes carry on by replacing them with machines and codes.

Such is the world they live in. Survive the game, or become nothing.

"Zero," her therapist prods.

Fingers twitch around a steaming mug of black coffee when Zero turns her stare back to the holographic projection in the center of her bedroom, where a middle-aged Avyrian woman holds her own mug and gazes back at Zero, open and unwavering. Zero has been seeing Cacia Ttean since she was a fledgling, when she thought starting her new chapter in life with the right decisions could make a difference.

Trusted by the Aconites, Cacia values doctor-patient confidentiality more than her own life, with her own history of trauma and violence and morally ambiguous choices. The most twisted and broken criminals of Dyvris don't believe in her words because she's a saint; they listen to her because she's grounded, brutally honest, and accepts their histories without a blink of an eye. She's not here to make them better people, to lead them to their inevitable demise in this callous world with the illusion of a moral high ground. Selective with her clients, Cacia only takes in those who want to save themselves from themselves, to guide them out of the labyrinth when they spiral in vicious cycles of self-destruction, to suggest paths of logic that make waking up the next morning less dreadful.

Too bad Zero is a lost cause.

"I think I want to get out of this city for a while," she answers, voice soft and higher in pitch than normal, an illusion of sweet serenity with subtly upturned lips.

She tried. She really did. But it's not just a single battle. Every single day is a war against her own mind, and she's been losing her grip. Again.

And this time, she doesn't know if there will be a swerve to save her.

Objects in motion stay in motion unless acted upon by an unbalanced force, according to laws of physics. Zero thinks she's already used up her miracle force in this lifetime. Maybe there's no stopping it this time.

The peace in her chest isn't false, though. It's like looking up from the bottom of a swimming pool. It's like nothing at all.

"A vacation would be good for you," Cacia agrees, as if Zero didn't misinterpret her question on purpose. "Where would you like to go?"

Zero looks past her projection. "I'm not sure."

"Well, that's not necessarily a bad thing. Sometimes it's good to not have a plan. You've been making plans after plans since the day you decided to find the Aconites. Perhaps it's time to give your brain a break."

"Perhaps," Zero says, noncommittal.

"Will you talk to Rovis before you leave?"

"No."

Cacia isn't deterred by her apparent decisiveness. "You've spoken even less about him than usual these past three months. Are you avoiding each other?"

"No," Zero says again. It may be a lie, or it may be true. Cacia isn't stupid; she's not really asking. She wants Zero to think about it, to determine reality before making rash decisions. But Zero's thought about it more than enough, every time the inner circle held a meeting to organize damage control and Rovis didn't show up.

Even if they are avoiding each other, there's nothing to avoid. They are simply nothing now, not even coworkers.

"Okay, what about Tal?"

"Tal made his decision," she says, indifferent. It's not the first time they've had this conversation. Cacia only knows that Zero kept a secret from him, not the size of the secret. If she knew, she'd understand why Zero doesn't care to go after Tal. Except, Zero still cannot tell anyone about Saige.

"Yes, he has, but you haven't," Cacia pointed out.

"I have. We're done."

"Are you? You've given Rovis all the tools to find Tal."

Irritation creeps in Zero's voice. "That's between the two of them. I don't want anything to do with either of them. I just want to leave this city and be alone for a while."

"You want a break," Cacia deduces. "And that's understandable. But are you punishing yourself for what happened three months ago?"

"No, I'm not. I'm not sorry for what I did."

"I didn't say you were."

Zero blinks, slightly frowning. "Then why would I be punishing myself?"

The corners of Cacia's lips twitch. "Just checking. You look tired."

"I'm always tired."

"I know." Cacia checks her watch. "Time's up, if you don't have anything else you want to talk about. Will I see you next week or after you get back?"

"After."

"Okay. Have a good vacation."

"Thanks," Zero says without the amount of politeness that she definitely should speak with.

"Zero," Cacia calls out before Zero could hang up. "I know you're doing what you need to. You've kept the Aconites together during these trying times, and I'm glad that you're taking some time for yourself now. But remember that avoidance is not truly moving on, even if it feels like it. You're not really done. You, Rovis, and Tal. The three of you are each taking time away from the others to figure things out on your own, and that's more than fine. Except you don't have forever. You will need to face what happened that night and what led to it, and you will have to figure out how to move on together."

Zero takes in her words, sees the logic, then promptly dismisses it. Still, she says softly, "Okay."

"Call me if you need anything," Cacia says, voice firm.

"I know," Zero says with an imperceptible smile.

She waves the hologram away to end the session. With a heavy sigh, she uncrosses her legs and stands. She tips her head back and finishes the coffee with one gulp, then saunters over to her kitchen to clean out the mug. She wipes it dry with a towel and sets it neatly into a wall cabinet. She folds the towel into a perfect rectangle and places it next to the sink, parallel to the short edge. With all the counters clean and empty, the kitchen looks as though it's ready to be on a real estate website.

Soft steps bring Zero back to her bedroom, where she shoves her feet into the only pair of boots she has left, and throws on the only black jacket hanging by her door. With dim eyes, she looks to her desk.

Five envelopes sit on the surface. Three of them contain longer letters, written for Rovis, Tal, and Raven. She doesn't know when Raven will resurface from hiding, but Zero knows that when the time comes, Rovis will find a way to get the letter to her. The two shorter ones are for Saige and her favorite cousin, Dziye.

Of course, Zero does have a plan. Just not one Cacia would approve of.

She picks up the envelopes and spreads them out over her pillows, on her bed made so carefully there isn't a single wrinkle.

Zero pulls open empty drawers and closes them, swings open closet doors and shuts them, brushes her fingers over dusty counters. Finally, she steps into the elevator without looking back.

1

break;

A black ball of fur appears at Zero's feet when she steps off the elevator. She almost smiles, looking down at Starlight weaving through and around her legs.

Laughter draws her attention to the lounge, and she follows the familiar sound to find her Heartless gathered around an incoherent mess of board games, cards, casino chips, a roulette wheel, and files of their targets floating above them in holographic display. All of which, she knows, is one big, complicated game that the fledglings have just made up while intoxicated.

"Off to vacation?" Rivka yells when she sees Zero, swaying only slightly as she gets up but manages to walk in a straight line to the door.

Zero nods. "I trust you know what you're doing?"

"The Heartless will be fine, as always," Rivka answers, speaking a bit slower than usual. Zero's olfactory receptors are assaulted by the scent of vodka when Rivka envelops her into a hug. "Have so much fun, my lovely!"

The others echo her sentiment, and Zero finds herself trapped in a massive group hug, drowning in the smell of alcohol and flavored nicotine. Someone starts singing an awful pop song, and to Zero's dismay, all the Heartless join in, bodies swaying in every direction at different frequencies like a dysfunctional accordion. Taking advantage of the fact that she's the only sober person here, she slips out of Rivka's arms and slithers her way out of the clump. Before anyone can see and start chasing her, Zero escapes the Tower and strides to the Poison Core. She doesn't notice Starlight trailing after her until she catches the cat in the reflection of the glass doors, zir sharp eyes watching her every move.

Summer and Daleyza notice Zero the moment she enters the training room, the two of them covered in sweat from their boxing match. She waits for them to snake out of the ring with uncharacteristic patience.

"No suitcase?" Summer asks, raising a brow as she towels down her face and neck.

"Redoing my closet," Zero lies with ease. She ignores Daleyza narrowing her eyes, arms crossed.

"Ah, that explains all the giveaways." She smirks. "You'll have to give everyone a fashion show with all the new clothes you bring back."

"Only if you can hire models."

"How long are you gone for?" Daleyza asks.

Zero shrugs. "However long it takes for me to stop feeling this exhausted. So forever, probably."

Summer laughs and slings an arm over Zero's shoulder. "Good. You deserve it."

"Would you two feel comfortable about dealing with Rovis for me?" Zero asks, glancing between Summer and Daleyza.

Daleyza nods, still assessing Zero's blank expression. "If Boss comes out of his cave before your return, I'll explain things to him. In the meantime, I'll keep everything running as you've suggested. With our resources, the Tech Hall won't have any trouble keeping up with the changing climate, and we've kept the Purity Syndicate away. We've got it. You have nothing to worry about."

Zero smiles then. "That's why I nominated you to be interim underboss."

Daleyza says nothing, only ruffles her hair with silent affection, and Zero doesn't miss the questions and concern in Daleyza's lingering gaze. But Daleyza doesn't ask, and Zero doesn't want to answer. She gives each of them a squeeze on the arm before she's off to do the last thing she needs to do before she leaves Dyvris. As she walks out of the gym, she notices with a frown that Starlight is nowhere to be seen.

The circle of walls surrounding the wolfsbane garden at the center of the Core is lined with thousands of vials of the poison produced from the flowers that the organization exclusively grows. Glass windows whoosh open as Zero approaches one of the panels. With an inexplicable sense of peace and finality, she reaches up a hand, covered in black leather.

Something small but dense knocks Zero's hand away.

She whirls around to see a rubber ball bounce into Kagiso's hand. He chuckles as she lifts her chin to glare at him, while she shakes out her fingers by her side.

"I never took you for a thief, Zero," he drawls, casually tossing the rubber ball down into the concrete, letting it rebound up to his tilted smirk, then catching it without breaking eye contact with Zero.

A traitorous lump of black fur is purring at his feet, nuzzling against his shin.

Zero narrows her eyes at Starlight, but the cat ignores her.

"The poison is free for all members to take," she says to Kagiso.

"Technically, yes." He continues playing with the rubber ball as he walks forward, until he stops in front of Zero. "There aren't any official rules on this. *But* the unspoken rule is that the poison is for Reapers only."

"What if the rest of us have people to kill?"

Kagiso tilts his head and narrows his eyes. "Who are you trying to kill? If you want someone dead, I'm sure Daleyza would be happy to make your wishes come true. You are a Heartless. You are the Ace of Crowns."

Zero rolls her eyes at his poor attempt at a motivational speech. "Do you have a point, Kagiso?"

Frowning at her reaction, Kagiso steps closer and lowers his voice, all mirth dissipated.

"But you are not a Reaper," he insists. "We are all monsters, yes, but we are different breeds. Reapers do the worst of the dirty work for a reason. You are not a killer, Zero. What, exactly, do you think you'll be doing with a vial of aconitine?"

Zero snorts, crossing her arms. "That's for me to know, and for you to not find out."

Kagiso stares, jaw clenched.

She doesn't back down, jutting out her chin.

"Fine." Kagiso smiles, showing too many teeth, and steps back.

Zero rolls her eyes again and snatches a vial before turning to leave.

Without warning, she jerks her head to one side, narrowly avoiding the expected blow from behind.

"Kagiso," she growls as she spins around, seething.

"Not bad," Kagiso comments with a smirk. "Now, do you want to tell me why you're taking that vial, or do you want to fight, just for me to beat you and find out the answer anyway? You know you can't win against me."

Zero's blood feels like lava in her veins as she contemplates smothering him in his sleep before she leaves.

When she says nothing, Kagiso shrugs. "Your choice."

He takes another swing, and Zero barely catches it with a grunt. But she doesn't have time to pause or fix her balance when the assault doesn't stop there. While blocking attacks, she has to shift back on the defense, and with the poison still in her hand, she struggles to redirect Kagiso's fists. Zero takes several hits, arguably in the worst fight she's ever taken part of, though Kagiso is clearly pulling his punches.

As if finally bored, Kagiso kicks the back of her knee and takes her wrist easily, twisting her arm behind her back as Zero falls to the ground. The vial falls out of her grip, before she gets yanked up and stumbles back into Kagiso's chest.

A thick arm comes around her neck, not tight enough to choke, but solid enough to trap.

The unwelcome contact and Kagiso's body heat makes Zero want to vomit, but she clamps her jaw shut and focuses on breathing.

"I win," Kagiso whispers in her ear, his triumphant smile too close to her face as he shakes the vial in front of her eyes.

"Give it," Zero grits out, forcing the bile in her throat to stay down.

"Tell me who you want dead."

"It's personal." Involuntary tears form at the corners of her eyes as she stops herself from retching.

"Not good enough."

Acid is relentlessly climbing up her chest, and Zero claws at Kagiso's arm when a traitorous tear rolls down her face, brows creased and desperate to get away from the misery of her deteriorating body. "Let me go. Right now."

"You—"

The vial disappears, and Zero squeezes her eyes shut, head spinning and stomach churning. Then her eyes shoot open when Kagiso tugs her glove off her hand with harsh fingers and pulls her sleeve up to her elbow, revealing faintly glowing white veins crawling up halfway. Heart pounding, Zero thrashes in his grip, only to make the nausea worse. Unable to keep it back anymore, her body curls up as she retches, acid hot in her throat and bitter on her tongue.

Kagiso's hold finally slackens. With weak legs, Zero takes the opportunity to slip out underneath his arm and put some distance between them. But not without a feeble punch to his stomach, because no amount of words could describe her fury, even through her illness. Kagiso barely reacts, only stares at her like he's never met her before.

"You're not taking Wright's antiretroviral," he says, brows furrowed.

She scoffs while catching her breath and putting her glove back on, still indignant. "Wright's dead."

The news is still broadcasted in holographic form all over plazas across Pureland. It was not a clean assassination, swift and silent; it was a long cat-and-mouse game, modern guerilla warfare, and a horror movie all combined and intertwined into a ruthless assault on a rich family that had too many skeletons in the closet.

"Are you stupid?" Kagiso's irritated words rudely interrupt Zero's mental replay of what should have been a hit reality show. "We stole the formulas of the antiretroviral a long time ago."

Shaking her head, Zero grabs another vial from the wall behind her and tucks it inside her jacket. "We had a deal, Kagiso. You do not ask me about the disease."

"No, your conditions were to not tell anyone you got it from Didier Whiston, to steal a test from Ofir's office for you, and to not ask you about the result afterwards. It's not my problem that I know you have it because you were being painfully obvious about it. Wait." Kagiso crosses his arms. "You don't want to be treated. Why?"

Zero turns to leave, a scowl on her face.

"You've been giving away all your stuff," he calls after her. "I keep track of everything that goes on in the House, you know. *Zero.*"

She stops, almost at the entrance. Kagiso appears in front of her.

"I can't let you leave with that vial," he says, voice low. "I know what you're going to do."

"And you care?"

"No." Kagiso's eye twitches.

Zero sighs and rolls her eyes. "That's what I thought. How much do I have to pay you?"

"To keep my mouth shut about this? You can't. This is serious. It doesn't matter that I can't care less about you as a person. If Boss finds out that I knew and didn't stop you — and he always finds a way to know everything — the Scavenger will have my head. If Tal comes back, he'd scrape the skin off my bones, tear my limbs off, rip the organs out of my body, and feed it all to hungry dogs on the street."

"You are so dramatic," she mutters. "They will have no proof. With your status in the organization, they can't touch you unless you confess. Tal and I are no longer acquainted, and Rovis is busy looking for him. I have a vacation to catch, so stop wasting my time. Do you or do you not want to get paid for your silence?"

Kagiso stares at her. "You've really made up your mind about this."

"You don't care," Zero reminds him.

"Right." He looks away, at the wolfsbane flowers, at the glass walls, at the scarlet sky of a late afternoon, at Zero's gloves. Finally, Kagiso clears his throat. "I'll take your ring."

Without a word, she tugs off her left glove and hands him the ring, as if it's nothing, as if it wasn't a gift from Enyo for protection in the dreadful world of the Damned.

"Give me your word," Zero says.

"You have my word that I will not stop you or inform anyone else of your plans." Kagiso's tone almost sounds somber.

"Live well, Kagiso."

"Wait."

Zero almost growls and considers stabbing him in the leg, but Kagiso ignores her and pulls something out of her hair. She flinches back, not at all a fan of his touch, though he's already holding a leaf that seems to have somehow fallen onto her head. He crushes it in his hand and gives her a long look. Then he turns and walks away without another word.

Zero has no more interruptions leaving this time. With a frown, she pats the sleeve of her jacket and finds that the vial is still there. Kagiso didn't steal it from her.

And Starlight is gone again.

Shaking her head, Zero takes a motorbike and sets the coordinates as the west subway station of Dyvris. When she leaves the mansion, she taps on the small circle behind her left ear, a house of nanoparticles that sprouts into a helmet with the new filtration system. She lets herself enjoy the feeling of flying through the city on her bike, knowing it will be the last time. Once she reaches her destination, Zero leaves the bike by an Aconite front in western Dyvris before descending into the underground station and slumping down onto the plastic seats of a subway car.

The next stop is Lime Gateway. She wonders if Raven will ever return to the place they grew up in. Now that the Purish government has wrestled back control, they've pushed out a new wave of mind-control drugs that thankfully failed but permanently damaged their victims minds. They've squashed all Faceless sympathizers, after tear gassing protests and bringing out war machines. This means that whatever revolution that Raven's Descendants are hoping for will not be happening any time soon. Especially when Pureland's economy is booming once again so that the government can bolster up the military, with Ezclovia slowly making its way back into the global trade network. The former empire drafted millions from Lasantirk to shake off the grip of Riyssolx, becoming Pureland's greatest ally in the world war that's coming for all of them.

There are too many pieces on this board, and Zero has already forfeited the game.

I'm sorry I can't stay long enough to help you, Zero sends a silent message to Raven, knowing it will never reach its destination.

The subway takes two hours to reach Ferrisque, the city of false nature. It's supposedly designed to look like what cities from a century ago did, with genetically enhanced trees lining the streets beside skyscrapers that disappear into the black clouds. Zero thinks it looks nice, but the leaves are too green, the flowers too pink.

A large garden with an unimaginable catalog of genetically modified flowers extends from the center of Ferrisque to its southeastern border with Aurodus. Zero takes her time walking through it, soaking up the last moments of this life. Steady fingers brush through petals, and quiet footsteps meander around every single exhibit.

When she reaches the border, barely any other tourists are around as the sun begins to set. Zero climbs up to the roof of an abandoned factory right outside the garden, the metal stairs vibrating beneath her heavy boots. The gray scale of the complex is both dreary and comforting. It's dull, neutral, and forgettable. Zero's even steps stomp on, almost mechanically, like a metronome, until she reaches the top. On the windy rooftop, she can see all of Ferrisque in one direction, and all of Aurodus in the other.

Zero trudges to the edge, gazing out at the shades of orange and purple. Gingerly, she sits down and swings her legs over the edge.

The vial of wolfsbane poison glints between her gloved fingers.

She doesn't look down as she brings it up to her lips outside the mask, keeping her eyes on the horizon. Between the hydrogen sulfide and methane in the air, she can't hesitate once the mask disappears. Taking one last deep breath of filtered air, she prepares herself for the acrid smell of rotten eggs the instant the nanoparticles retract and reveal her face. Her eyes tear up already upon contact with the toxic gases, and she grimaces as her head spins.

Without another thought, she pops off the top of the vial and tips her head back.

A sharp, obnoxious tone from her communication device shocks her ears, so much that she flinches and almost drops the vial to the side. She catches it before it tilts too far and caps it again. The annoying tone repeats itself in a pattern, drilling into her brain like an Agency torture method, though Zero's head is too hazy to determine the pattern and who it belongs to in her contacts.

"The fuck," she breathes, then chokes on the swear, twisting her body to fall onto her elbows. Her lungs feel as though a hundred needles have shot through them.

The nanotech mask closes over her face again, immediately pumping amyl and sodium nitrates and oxygen into her system. She gasps and wheezes from the effects of the poison, eyes wet from the irritation.

When her head finally clears, she says, "N.A.D.E., who called me?"

Rovis's contact information flashes before her eyes. Before she can even start seething about it, he's calling her again.

"What?" she grits out when she picks up.

"I heard you're on vacation," Rovis ignores her rude greeting and says casually, as if they haven't gone radio silent on each other for months.

"You heard correctly."

"Funny how I'm your boss, and I knew nothing about this vacation of yours."

Her chest still heaves from fighting against the poison. She tries to keep her voice even when she answers, "You've been busy."

"Yes." The sound of his office chair shifting brushes her ear. "I think I'm almost done solving it. I just need to figure out the keys. You knew Saige. Did she tell you much about her and Tal before?"

Zero runs her thumb over the surface of the vial in her grip. After a moment, she regains control over her breathing and says, "She was nine when he left home. Tal was twelve. His parents kicked him out when he came back in the middle of the night, bloody and missing an arm. Saige wanted to go with him, but Tal told her it was safer for her to stay. That's pretty much all I know about their relationship."

"Okay."

"Saige likes coffee more than tea. She reads almost as many books as I do. She watches cute animal videos when she's bored." Her mind digs up more memories from middle school, thinking back to all those conversations she used to have with Saige in art class. Zero adds, "Tal used to call her 'little bunny' in Lasan."

"*Koneighxta?*"

"Yeah. She painted bunnies a lot. Won a couple competitions. She wrote, too, and entered contests but never got anything. They were rigged. There was one story about the two of them in a fantasy universe without their parents, with time travel and magic spells. It was really good. Tal would ask her to read it to him almost every day. It was titled Twin Crowns, I think."

"Anything else?"

Zero pauses, searching in her head. She has patches of lost memories, probably due to trauma, so there's likely more, but none that she can think of at the moment.

"I don't remember much else."

"I have enough to work with. Where are you?"

"West," she answers vaguely.

Rovis waits, but Zero does not elaborate. When he gets the message, he says, "Alright. Enjoy your time off. Be care—"

Zero hangs up before he could finish.

She lets out a long breath and attempts to drink the poison for the second time. When she lifts it up to study through the dark lenses of the mask, however, her neck and her arm turn to stone. No matter how hard she tries to move, to follow through with her plan, her body refuses.

"Damn it," she breathes, dropping her hand into her lap and closing her eyes. "Damn you, Rovis."

She flicks her wrist and returns the vial to her sleeve, the movement jerky with irritation.

Pacing around, Zero decides to get dinner at a nearby restaurant. Food always helps, right? Maybe once she eats, she'll feel more fulfilled, thus more prepared to leave this life.

She notices eyes on her when she walks in, but dismisses it when the stares don't linger. When she's halfway through her meal, however, Zero notices that most of the customers have cleared out. The restaurant has gone mostly quiet, some metal clanging in the kitchen, employees walking back and forth. Sitting on the ground floor, she thinks she hears both the front and back doors lock.

Then it becomes eerily silent.

She pretends to stare at her phone, but a glance out the corner of her eye tells her that only three Purish men remain in a booth across from her, no workers to be seen.

Her thumb scrolls through her contacts.

Zero sneaks another look at the men, who begin to stand. One of them has a torch tattoo.

Purity Syndicate.

Her fingers tighten around her phone, and her eyes narrow.

Well, now I don't want to die, her brain tells her helpfully.

The Syndicate men have isolated her in an enclosed area. Either they recognized her as the Ace, or they were in the mood to torment a vulnerable-looking Avyrian girl.

Although the men approaching her look heavily built, more than twice her size, Zero refuses to go down without a fight. Three against one is difficult, not impossible.

Without thinking too deeply, Zero opens up Tal's contact information. She taps on the call button but turns off the sound on her phone, so that he can listen in on whatever happens next, but no one here will hear him. Zero watches the call go through, sees the moment Tal picks up, when the numbers start counting the length of the call.

She looks up with feigned cluelessness and tucks her phone in the deepest pocket of her black pants.

"Hello, boys." She smiles sharply. "Can I help you?"

"It's time for you to go back to hell," one of them snarls, "*parasite.*"

Zero slides beneath the table as a knife digs into the seat where she was just sitting. Her own knife appears between her fingers when she swipes out at a leg and twists the blade right above the knee, through the quadriceps tendon. A yowl pierces her ears as she rolls out between brown boots.

She barely reacts fast enough to activate an energy shield when the bullets start flying.

Slamming her right wrist against the ground, she activates the electromagnets on her forearm guard, which Zero holds up in front of her face to snatch the carbon steel guns with an induced energy current as she deactivates the shield. Her fingers slide into shooting position as though practiced millions of times. Unfortunately, her shooting accuracy is less practiced, so it takes her firing all of the ammunition to catch one of the men in the gut.

The other two march closer to swing punches at Zero, but she rolls and hops onto the table, kicking up a tray to throw into one loathsome face, while the bowl of unfinished soup flies into the other. In their moment of distraction, Zero crouches down to avoid a bullet and digs out a blaster from her boots. She flies onto another table and stuns the man whose leg she already incapacitated. His back hits the wall from the force, and he lands on his front side with a groan.

"You'll regret that," he growls, getting up on his knees.

Six throwing stars fly at her, and she's not fast enough to dodge all of them. She stumbles off the table and rolls on the floor to soften the fall. Zero clutches her left arm, hissing and letting out a pained gasp.

The energy shield goes up again when more stars soar in the air.

"Cultural appropriation," Zero grumbles at the Avyrian weapons crashing into the wall of pure energy inches before her eyes.

As soon as the attack wavers, she gets up and hurls out eight of her own stars, crackling with electricity.

Zero's back suddenly flares up in pain, a burning stripe across as she stumbles forward, narrowly missing a freezing blast from her side. She didn't notice one of the men sneaking up behind her, preoccupied with the throwing stars. Her body starts to feel lethargic from that blow, but Zero gathers all her energy to lean back and avoid the electric stick swung at her, while her black war fan slides into her hand. She flicks it open and flings it at the man with the ice blaster, but her aim is so terrible it completely misses him and instead blinds the man next to him with the stick as it returns to her grip.

The roar of pain almost brings a smile to her face as she slides on the floor to swipe his legs out from under him, and the assault of knives, blasts, and bullets raining down on Zero lands on him instead.

"Enough!" A booming voice thunders.

Something stings Zero's right leg, and her knee gives out. She looks down to see a syringe sticking out, her blood beginning to feel cold, her muscles growing numb.

"Shit," she breathes, fighting to stay standing as she sees bulky figures emerge from the kitchen.

Two more men join the scuffle.

"Little girl, you're quite the trouble," one of them drawls, gun pointed at her. The other holds the projectile launcher that must have shot the syringe.

Zero slams her wrist again on the table, so hard that she thinks she probably bruised herself. The gun becomes hers, but not before a bullet grazes her shoulder. She tries shooting at all of them, but barely any of her shots make damaging hits.

Another knife flies at her, and she pushes off her one functioning leg and hauls up her useless one to leap over the table. For a moment, all her weight is supported by one arm, before she lands shakily on the other side.

Her head jerks back when a laser weapon slices the painting behind her in half.

Someone grabs her from behind and tries to cover her nose with a piece of cloth soaked in a compound she definitely does not want in her lungs. Zero thrusts back to jostle the hold and shoves a knife in the attacker's gut.

She hops out of the loosened grip, just for a stun gun to shoot squarely in her abdomen. Air rushes out of her lungs as she wobbles from the shock, just barely keeping herself from falling to her knees.

"*Fuck*," Zero growls, though she can barely hear herself.

The cloth comes at her again when one of the men restrains her arms.

"No," she snarls. She jumps up to kick away the man in front of her with her good leg, but the one that's been tranquilized has become deadweight.

Her muffled shouts weaken the longer her nostrils take in the sickly sweet smell. Her vision blurs as the room tilts.

A rough hand grabs the top of her hair, almost tearing it off her scalp, and slams her head against the floor.

Something sharp jabs into her neck, and she hisses while thrashing.

Her dizzy mind lurches, and her vision goes dark when her left hip explodes with blinding pain.

Her fingertips sting, but she can't feel her arms.

Her throat burns, the taste of iron thick in the air. It infects her lungs and her eyes, choking her while she can feel blood rushing out of her veins.

She tries to stay awake, nails digging into her own palms.

But she slips away, like damp fingers slipping off the edge of a cliff.

2

Restart Kernel and Run

G reen text on a black screen stare back at Rovis like a stubborn enemy in a stalemate.

TWO JOBS SUBMITTED.

DECRYPT_KONEIGHXTA — 32 NODES RUNNING

DECRYPT_TWINCROWNS — 32 NODES RUNNING

He sits back and waits for the supercomputer to finish the decryption process, rolling his head back and forth to shake out the stiffness. Holed up in his office like a nocturnal animal, Rovis spent the last three months relearning programming languages with his neglected coding skills. Not only did he have to solve the ten-link cipher, he had to figure out Saige's invented original language from Zero's deciphering of the first few lines. Each of that took all of his brain power, brute forcing his way out of mazes of logic, and over twenty days of nonstop staring at his screen.

He shouldn't have been surprised that Saige's work would put him through this much hell, given that she's Tal's sister and Zero's friend. But that didn't stop him from breaking four punching bags brought to his office and destroying the skin across his knuckles.

When he figured out a potential logic to do what he needs to do, with no sense of whether he's on the right track, he realized he had to translate that into lines of code. That was, right before he ran into a million warning messages just from building the environment because some software packages were outdated, and others simply did not exist. With the help of members from the Tech Hall, the build finally worked. But then he clumsily wrote out a mess of classes and functions that gave him a new error every time he tried to compile them, which meant weeks of debugging and rewriting.

Finally, these couple of days, his program runs without screaming red text at him, but he has no idea if it actually works, because the test keys still give him gibberish results. If his logic was wrong from the beginning, then he might as well say goodbye to the sun for the rest of the year. If his programming still has bugs, he's going to be very embarrassed explaining to Avery why everything in his office is broken. He can only hope that the possible keys that he got from Zero might return something that actually makes sense.

Rovis frowns as the sound of her voice from the phone call echoes in his head. It fell between her dead, unfeeling default tone and her sharp, exaggerated false cheer. She sounded too calm, too neutral. She answered his questions like a robot, gave him information about her friend without a price, without playing any games. Certainly not out of the goodness of her heart. But that's where Rovis is lost. She is a Heartless. She portrays emotion as a mean of redirection, to distract her targets from her real goal. He knows she uses that on him on a daily basis. Except this time, there was nothing. No direction, no aim, no purpose.

Or perhaps he's overthinking it.

Sighing, Rovis shuts his eyes and rubs out the crease between his brows. Even when Rovis devotes all his time and energy into finding Tal, she pops into his mind like an annoying little fly that he can't bring himself to kill. He'd blame it on that promise he made all those years ago, but he's finally starting to come to terms with the fact that she doesn't need him anymore. She's made that more than clear, with all the missions she accomplished and people she fooled. She's one of the strongest people he knows, he has to admit. Growing up, she never had to rely on anyone. So why does he keep worrying?

His fingertips find the comforting curve of the golden hoop hanging from his ear.

He just can't shake the feeling that something's wrong. *Vacation*, she says. The girl doesn't even know how to take a five-minute break. Of course he knows she's lying. He just doesn't know what she's up to this time.

Maybe Rovis should have paid more attention to Zero over the past few months. But he can only do so much when she keeps shutting him out again. He may have forgotten to seek her out, trapped in his programming loops and errors, but she never came to see him, either. Nine out of ten odds that she did so on purpose.

Rovis pushes himself out of his chair before his train of thought goes down the inevitable path of pointless anxieties, stretching out his stiff muscles and cracking his neck an unhealthy amount of times as he stands.

Finding Tal is top priority, before the trail goes cold. He may not even be at the coordinates that Saige sent anymore, but Rovis still has to try. He needs to focus and work faster. Relationship issues with Zero isn't something that can be fixed in one day; it's going to take time, and they have a whole lifetime to work on it. He shoves down the uneasy feeling in his chest, because he can't afford to spiral in paranoia.

There's nothing to do except to wait for the decryption results, so he wanders over to the Tech Hall instead of pacing around his office. He finds Vanneza Otieno, lead of the Digitals, sitting in the lounge and drinking what looks like a pisco sour, so Rovis settles down across from her. More addicted to the screen than even Tal, he scarcely sees the woman, but she's been on standby ever since Rovis asked for the Tech Hall's help. Unlike some people, Rovis isn't a genius, nor is he too proud to admit it.

"You look like shit." Vanneza raises a brow at him when she sees him walk in.

"Thanks," he says, voice flat. He's sure that he looks like a ghoul right now, shadows beneath his eyes and cheeks sunken from malnourishment. With Saige fake-dead and Tal off-the-grid, Rovis is basically trying to rob a grave anyway.

"Don't you dare go out looking like that." Vanneza points at him. "With our nearing bankruptcy and extreme lack of popularity right now, our good looks is all we have left."

"I didn't realize my organization was a modeling agency," Rovis retorts dryly, pouring himself a drink.

"It is now," she claims with a smirk. "Yeah, Zero even started a new fashion line."

Rovis chokes on the straight pisco, grimacing at the fire in his throat.

Unbothered by his graceless drinking skills, Vanneza tosses her hair back to reveal an iridescent hummingbird dangling from her ear. "See? I got her earrings."

"I—" Rovis blinks several times, at a loss of words. He has no idea what goes on in his organization anymore. He decides to drop it and change the topic. "Did Zero ever mention where she's going for vacation?"

At that, Vanneza frowns, leaning back and crossing her legs. "No, I don't think so. At least not to me. Rivka probably knows more."

His phone buzzes when he nods, unsurprised. The screen flashes a mail notification for the end of the decryption for 'twin crowns' as the key.

"That was fast," he mutters. "Way too fast."

And he was right. Much to Rovis's chagrin, the program only returned a whole page of numbers, with absolutely no spaces, letters of any language, or special characters. He deflates, pinching his nose and resisting the urge to throw his glass at a wall. Instead, he drinks every drop in it, ignoring Vanneza's raised brow, and pours himself another one. Then another.

Three drinks in, and all he can see is Damian's cold stares after Griffin's death, Zero's sharp grin when she's going on a mission, and Tal's bloodshot eyes when Saige was announced dead.

"What am I doing?" Rovis mutters. "He clearly doesn't want to be found."

"Look," Vanneza interrupts his thoughts, taking pity on him. "I'm sure Tal had a reason to go. We all are. Maybe Saige Harlow was someone important to him. But he'll come back for you, if not for the Aconites. Meanwhile, Zero made sure that all of us would step up to fill in the gap until Tal comes back. So you just take care of yourself, okay? We know you're having a hard time with him gone."

Rovis narrows his eyes at the amber liquid in his glass, head spinning as the alcohol starts to hit. Vanneza's words don't make any sense.

"Zero," he says, looking up at Vanneza to confirm that she's not joking. "And how did she manage that?"

She stares at him, nonplussed. "You didn't get the notifications? The inner circle held meetings almost daily, and she wrote every single agenda."

Frowning, Rovis scrolls through his thousands of unread messages and finds the channel in which Zero sent almost a hundred emotionless lists of notes, with the same amount of thumbs-up reactions on each message.

"She's technically not inner circle anymore," Vanneza continues, "but none of us had a problem with it. She just talked to all of us about splitting the work that you and Tal did, and told everyone to go to Daleyza if any problems come up. I guess she was trying to make the transition smooth for Rivka, since she's not the head of the Heartless anymore. I still don't understand why she resigned; she's insanely good at her job."

And the Scavenger's, she doesn't say, but Rovis hears it anyway, because it's true. Zero has always had a habit of helping people without them knowing and then disappearing, and this time is no different. He doesn't know what Zero's up to now or what the consequences might be. Truthfully, he doesn't care, as long as she's alive and well, but the uncertainty means he won't be able to predict what troubles may show up to his door ne xt.

Rovis thinks back to the day he threw her out of his office, to the night he stopped Tal from attacking her, to the morning she gave him Saige's message, and to the phone call they had earlier.

She was a different person every single time.

The uneasiness returns in his gut, and it takes all the concentration he can muster up while tipsy to push it away again. Rovis shakes his head and asks, "What projects are the teams working on now?"

"Well..." Vanneza pauses to accept another cocktail from a Clockwork. "The city's a mess because the peace between us and the locals have always been a result of fear. It doesn't matter that you've been doing things differently than Bianchi; they gave us free services and information out of fear. But now their anger at our inability to stop Syndicate hate crimes far outweighs that fear, so all the teams are mostly focused on stabilizing everything within our territory. The Digitals and Reapers are trying to find more Syndicate members in the area and getting rid of them. The Mechs are upgrading all of our gear because, you know, poisonous gas in the atmosphere—"

"What poisonous gas?"

She scowls at him and deadpans, "You haven't been watching the news, have you?"

Rovis tenses, almost sheepish. "No."

"Okay, you should do that before you go outside. Do not leave without one of the new masks. Stars, how have you survived this long? Anyway, the Heartless are out searching for information on sightings of the torch mark and patterns of appearances. Rivka is doing great as the new head, by the way. They've helped us dispose of almost fifty Syndicate members in a week. And the Sleightists are our steadiest source of income right now, going on twenty heists per day."

"Twenty," Rovis repeats. "Per day? Do we even have that many rich families to steal from anymore?"

She laughs, mischief glinting in her eyes. "Oh, yes. Avery gave us a list of all the trillionaires, billionaires, and millionaires in the country. The Clockworks are working overtime, truly. It seems like our businesses will be okay, since Zero calmed down the local labor union."

Rovis stares.

At his visible confusion, Vanneza shrugged. "Don't ask me how. She just said she'd handle it. Now almost every shop downtown has opened back up with a bit more of our funding. It's still not the same, because they hate us more than they used to. Most of us keep our masks on even when we're inside, and you should, too."

Rovis opens his mouth to ask another question when his phone flashes with another notification. Attention drawn away, he takes a deep breath and opens the output file for '*koneighxta*' as the key.

One line of numbers and letters stare back at him.

He tosses the phone onto the coffee table in annoyance. His fingers pull at his messy strands as a soft growl escapes his lips.

"May I?" Vanneza gestures at his phone.

Rovis waves her on. "I'm out of ideas."

She glances at the screen and chuckles. "Boss, what do you mean? You did it. These are the coordinates."

"Those aren't coordinates."

"Oh, man, you've really been westernized, haven't you?" Vanneza leans forward and spins the screen right side up for Rovis. "Rovis, this is a system that Lasantirk and Toullifuka used. The early civilizations of those two countries were closely involved, and they used this system. Today, everyone uses what Ezclovia passed down to Pureland, since it's a 'world power' now, but other systems still exist."

"This is why I barely passed world history," Rovis mutters. They're both Toullish, but Vanneza is more connected to their mother culture than he is.

Vanneza ignores him. "These angles are with perspective to the oldest bridge built across the river, at the border between the two countries. The first half tells you that it's west of the bridge for that many radians, and the second half tells you how far south."

Rovis sucks in a breath and holds it, his heart pounding. This can't be real. Part of him thought he might never solve Saige's code. Yet, he's looking at the final step to finding Tal.

"Go get him, Boss," Vanneza says, grinning.

He stands abruptly. "Keep this on the down-low. No one else should know that I found him until he's here and explaining himself to the organization."

"Understood." Then she calls after him, "Get a new mask before you go. I'm going to kill you if you die of gas poisoning."

Brushing off her illogical threat, Rovis rushes to the Mechs lab downstairs, practically storming in to collect a nanoparticle house for his new gas mask, scaring the wits out of the fledglings. After he puts it in place behind his ear, he strides briskly to his car while searching up the coordinates on the Toullish map on his watch. A blinking red dot immediately shows up.

"You've got to be kidding me," he curses.

Tal is in a suburb of Divako.

He's been so close to Rovis this whole time, only two cities away. But then Rovis thinks about it again and it finds it not so surprising after the initial shock, since Saige worked with the Skulls to fake her death. It seems obvious, in hindsight, that she and Tal would be near Divako, because Saige likely works for Damian now in exchange for his help.

Rovis floors the accelerator and follows the automatic navigation.

He remembers Tal's empty room the morning after he walked out on him, all blueprints and sketches gone from his desk and floor. He remembers coldness crawling over his skin as he took in the view. He remembers wondering his lungs might have collapsed. He remembers standing there, paralyzed at the door, for hours.

A week after Tal left Dyvris, the Wrights' youngest child went missing. Tracking devices told them that their son was taken across the ocean to Ezclovia, and just when they sent people to find him, their daughter disappeared, too. Her phone pinged from a red-light district, turning the Wright family's crisis from an uninteresting cry for help to a fascinating scandal. When Jeremy Wright's people got to the phone's location, however, it suddenly pinged from a different red-light district across the country. They chased after it, of course, until it happened again, and it became obvious that they're being toyed with.

And that's when the older son disappeared, despite being locked in at home, under the watch of twenty guards. Three kids in three days. No one saw who did it, and no one could find where the children really were. Their trackers went haywire on the satellite grids, appearing in too many places at once, changing every minute, driving the entire nation mad with confusion until it settled into two words written across the map of Pureland.

START

GAME

In the week after those words formed on the grid, the Wrights' company went bankrupt, with investors pulling out and customers turned away. Overnight, every single Wright property went up in flames, due to different causes, from fried electric wires to overheated dryers to leaked gas. Even more petrifying was the Wrights' main house becoming an entity of its own. It started with flickering lights and slamming doors. Then machines started turning on and off at random. Then blood started streaming out from all the faucets.

Jeremy and Skylar Wright tried to run. They made plans, contacted people they trusted, and got on armored vehicles. Except they always ended up back in their house, in their bed, not knowing how they got there or why they failed. They made four attempts to run, sanity unraveling with each time they ended up where they started.

The last time they woke up, their house was bathed in blue lights. They crept down the stairs, and opened their front door to hundreds of holographic tombstones on their lawn.

The names on those phantom tombstones were of every single victim of the Agency's experiment during the Moon Festival, across the country. Not that the Wrights had the time to find out. They were dragged back into the house from behind by an unseen monster, door slammed shut to muffle the agonized screams.

In the morning, before the front door were two scarecrows impaled into the grass among the tombstones.

Except they weren't scarecrows.

They were, indeed, Jeremy and Skylar Wright. With their faces scratched off, blood dripping onto their clothes and into the dirt.

To the entirety of Pureland, the psychotic killer behind the scenes remains a mystery.

To the Aconites, however, the claw marks were like fingerprints they all knew by heart.

It was Tal telling them, *I did it. I avenged our family.*

It's all hitting Rovis now, the possibility of seeing Tal again, after these grueling months of guilt and yearning.

What will he say? What will Tal say? Does he still hate him?

Saige is going to be there, so what will she think of Rovis? Would she hate him, too? Does she know what he said to Tal that drove him away that night? How did the reunion go between brother and sister? How much has Tal told her about the Aconites? Does she even know who Rovis is? Is he still relevant to Tal, or is he dead with the past?

The questions whirl in his mind, swallowing all his other thoughts as he drives out the mountains, through Dyvris, and across the desert.

He doesn't notice he's being followed until he's switching highways near Metloxcy.

"N.A.D.E., scan the truck behind me," he orders.

"Scanning." After three seconds, the AI responds, "Five members of the Purity Syndicate detected."

Just as expected. Rovis scowls and takes the next exit, changing route to go through Torch City instead of directly going to Divako. He leads the truck into Torch City, the skyscrapers a blur on both sides. He feigns taking a couple exits, and the truck follows him but manages to get back in lane every time.

Once he reaches the heart of the capital, approaching another exit, he says, "N.A.D.E., operate sequence 17-02-0031."

Right as he passes the exit, metal spider legs shoot out from beneath the Shapeshifter, one side faster than the other. The uneven forces push the vehicle into the air and flip over the side of the highway. It falls and spins once, the legs retracting halfway, while a claw shoots out from the roof and hooks onto the bridge. The moment swings the car beneath the bridge, and the spider legs soften the landing right between the back and front ends of two cars. As soon as the wheels touch the ground, the Shapeshifter transforms into a smaller model, narrowly avoiding a pile-up collision.

The car behind him honks furiously, and the police sirens start blaring right on cue. A smile tugs at his lips. He's done this countless times on Aconite heists when he was working as a Sleightist for Bianchi. The tunnels are bright from pink and purple lights, but it flickers with the remote voltage manipulator lining the top of his car.

One moment the police car is almost about to run him down; the next they can no longer find the silver micro car.

Rovis watches them drive past him from the slow lane, sitting in a black sports utility vehicle.

"Every time." He smirks.

But his pleased expression slips off his face when he exits the tunnel and sees gigantic mechanical bulldogs prowling the streets of the city. One in particular stands guard at the end of the tunnel. Its eyes glare red as it scans the passing cars.

"Silver micro model 504 with license plate FU17-487," the enforcement bulldog's robotic announcement booms over them, "you are being arrested for unlawful driving. Turn yourself over to the police or face severe consequences."

"What the hell is this," Rovis breathes.

He drives past the bulldogs without a problem, thanks to the brilliant Mechs who designed the Shapeshifter, but he's bewildered by the new additions of law enforcement. Colossus robots mimicking animals is generally produced underground for the tournaments in Drokklo's Playground; never have they been above ground to disturb the lives of people outside of the country's most secure prison.

"Since the mysterious death of business tycoon Jeremy Wright's family," N.A.D.E. answers, likely reciting the news that Rovis obviously have not read, "Purish citizens have demanded an improvement in surveillance and peacekeeping. Effective six weeks ago, the Purish government launched a new series of standard law enforcing robot models, inspired by the success of Drokklo's Playground."

"Called it," Rovis mutters as he gets on the southbound highway route to downtown Divako, leaving behind the bulldogs towering over bridges and watching cars pass by like insignificant ants.

The familiar glittering city disappears as he follows N.A.D.E.'s navigation, where dim buildings welcome Rovis into dark neighborhoods. The car comes to a stop in an expansive lot filled with stacks of old shipping containers. He doesn't quite process the sheer size of this lot until he walks out into the maze of diverse containers, hundreds of rows of different orientations.

"They're living here?" Rovis wonders, almost disbelieving.

It's not completely unexpected for someone who's supposed to be dead. He has been in worse conditions, during longer and more dangerous missions that the Reapers assigned him to. But shipping containers are not ideal in the long run, and Rovis thinks he last saw a grocery store an hour ago on the drive. Even instant foods need to be bought somewhere, unless Tal has figured out how to spawn matter out of nothing.

As he looks around, Rovis scowls at the realization that he has no idea which one they might be in, and that's assuming his program actually correctly decrypted the codes and he used the right key. The output file could quite possibly have just returned a random line that happens to look like Lasan-Toullish coordinates, and he showed up to this lot for no reason.

Rovis takes out a stunning blaster and holds it by his side, grip loose but solid, as he walks through the maze. Walls and walls of graffiti with infinite shades of glow-in-the-dark spray paint glimmer under the red haze of the night sky.

A graphic image of wolves burning alive in a firestorm jumps at him. The blood spatters dotting the torn flesh of the wolves look as though someone was actually shot in front of this container. A closer look confirms his theory when he realizes one of the beady eyes is a bullet hole.

Rovis drags his attention away to the next set, where a portrait of Damian mocks him. Those silver eyes pierce into him, as if his old friend were right in front of him and taunting the fact that he's come running after another person that he betrayed. His gray coat rests over his shoulders like a cloak, his arms poised with arrogance beneath the open lapels. Blood drips from the corner of his smirk and dots the collar of his white button-up. The portrait must be relatively new, given that Damian hasn't been the boss of the Rose Skull for very long. The artist is skilled, Rovis can see from the way bold colors almost seem carelessly painted on, giving the portrait power and pride. In a tilted line of scribbled writing, someone sprayed the words:

HAIL ETERNAL RULE OF THE ROSE SKULLS

He briefly wonders who would visit this industrial wasteland, and who takes the time to paint over rusted containers. The Skulls don't come here often, otherwise they wouldn't have put Saige here. That would bring the attention of too many enemies while they're harboring a not-so-dead national prisoner. Yet they seem to have many fans.

Tearing his gaze away, Rovis rounds the corner and studies the mural that stretches across long containers stacked directly on top of each other. It's a portrait of downtown Divako, not unlike the quick sketch Rovis did of downtown Dyvris before the Moon Festival. Although, Rovis's work was more realistic, and this artist takes a different approach with the method and color choices. Every block of color seems to result from one spray, taking different shapes that make no sense up close, but contribute to the overall depiction of the city. It gives Divako a more simplistic look and captures the livelihood with bright shades, in stark contrast to Rovis's forbidding vision of Dyvris.

He keeps moving until something freezes him to his spot.

An uneven stack forms a sort of nook on the bottom layer, with two containers protruding out on either side of a hidden, dark one in between.

A light but distinct outline of a crown glows softly on the smallest wall of each outer container, almost too faint to the eye when surrounded by loud murals.

"Twin crowns," Rovis breathes.

He moves through the two symbols to the container concealed by the shadows.

The door is locked, as expected.

His lock picks appear in his gloved fingers, and he easily jostles the archaic deadbolt until it clicks. When he walks in, the door slams shut behind him. Rovis narrows his eyes at the hinges, which don't seem to have the imbalance that would cause the door to shut on its own.

He takes a step forward, except the floor has disappeared.

Rovis is falling into the darkness, his breath caught in his chest. Completely off guard, his blaster gun has slipped out of his hands the moment gravity became his enemy.

He lands with a grunt, one fist digging into uneven concrete, and he silently thanks Tal for upgrading everyone's combat boots to protect their joints before he left. Lines of nanoparticle material light up purple along his legs in his lunge from the energy absorption, and his forearm guard fizzles with electricity.

Rovis brings out a small orb that fits in the palm of his hand and lights it up. He walks around, finding his blaster and hits a solidly black wall. His fingertips brush the smooth metal as he tests the perimeters, searching for a crack.

When he finally hits a frame, the white glow of the orb shows him a heavily bolted iron door with no knob. It doesn't seem to have a stainless steel coating. Rovis feels around the edges and finds that the entire thing is sealed in.

"Well, that's not good," he mutters.

Even if Rovis had water and frozen oxygen and a chemical catalyst to corrode the edges, it would take ages to get through the thick door.

He tilts his head back to try to see where he fell from, but the ceiling has closed up again. Rovis has no obvious way out, and he has no idea if he's following the correct clues. He definitely should have brought backup. And his phone predictably doesn't have any service.

Who would he have called anyway?

His first choice has always been Tal, but Tal never picked up any of his calls after leaving.

And Zero's on vacation. Besides, her greatest strength is tricking people to get her what she wants, and there's no living, breathing being in sight.

Daleyza would have been the smart choice, though Rovis's pride might have to take a hit. She would get him out and tease him with dry remarks about coming to Divako alone for the next year.

Rovis sighs. There's no use thinking about that if he can't even call anyone.

He looks around again, considering where the weak spots might be. This entire land is pretty poorly maintained; there's no way he can't brute force his way out.

A drop of water splattering on the ground catches his attention.

His footsteps echo as he follows the source of the sound, and he finds a rusty corner of the ceiling.

"Aha." Rovis switches out his stunning blaster for a freezing one and shoots the spot three times, then takes out his regular gun to shoot it with lead-alloy bullets.

Debris showers down as he shields his eyes with his arm.

A decent sized hole reveals itself when the dust settles. Rovis just needs to keep making it bigger, then he can pull himself up and worry about getting out when he's on the ground level again.

Abrupt cranking of metal reverberates behind him. He whirls around and holds up both weapons as the sealed, iron door unlatches.

With a heavy bang, the door unlocks. It's slowly dragged open from the other side.

Thin fingers wrap around the edge when the crack is large enough and shoves it over the rest of the way.

A girl with white hair and blue eyes scans over Rovis, her loose strands swaying with the air rushing into the dark room he's trapped in.

Saige Gierkas, it seems, has cut and bleached her hair, and changed the color of her contacts since she faked her death.

"You must be Rovis," she says, a bright smile tugging at her lips, and he sees the resemblance in the mischief lurking in her eyes.

Rovis stares. Then he remembers to speak, "Miss Gierkas."

"Oh, drop the formalities." Saige turns, and her eyes look like she's making fun of him, but she gestures for Rovis to follow. "And drop the guns. You're welcome here."

She shuts the door with all the weight of her lean body once he crosses over, and Rovis rushes to help, before Saige locks it again.

"My brother said you might be coming," she continues. "You are early though. He thought it'd take you at least two more months to figure everything out."

Rovis barely processes her words. He's too busy gawking at the massive underground house powered by crystals when they descend the spiral staircase. On a long table, the mess of gadgets and parts have Tal written all over them.

Saige follows his gaze, chuckles, and says, "He's not here."

He looks back at her, forgetting to hide the puzzlement on his face.

She shrugs. "I don't know where he went. He got a call earlier. He seemed very annoyed about it, but as soon as he picked up, he bolted. It must have been an emergency."

"Oh, so he was ignoring me on purpose," Rovis says without thinking.

Saige laughs. "I did try to tell him to work things out with you, but he's always running away from his problems. I do apologize for the bad timing, since you're looking for him. But it's just me right now. Sorry to disappoint."

"No, no," Rovis says quickly, trying to gather himself. He studies her for a moment, then adds honestly, "I'm curious about you, too. All I know about you is that you're Tal's sister, you were friends with Zero at some point, you somehow landed with the Faceless, and then you worked with the Skulls to fake your death when the government found you."

"Ah, yes. Zero. It's such an odd name she picked out." Saige takes out a glowing blue stone hanging on a thin silver chain from underneath her white hoodie and gray jacket. Her hand closes over the stone and her eyes gloss over for a second before she shakes her head, chuckling. "I guess her self-deprecation issues have only gone downhill since I last saw her in person."

Rovis tenses, surprised by how well Saige knows Zero. "And when was that?"

"Last day of eighth grade." She smiles at him. "Yes, I was also at Lime Gateway. I had been introduced to the Faceless already, so when I decided I wanted to join them, Zero was the only person I told. We weren't even close back then, but there was just something about her, every time I talked to her in class. I just trusted her. And I was acquainted with her whole friend group, before Lila died. I was shocked to hear that Jacek was killed, too.

"I'm still not sure why I said goodbye to Zero when I left Lime Gateway, other than feeling the need to say goodbye to someone. Anyway, a year and a half later, she somehow got word to me that she may have found my brother. So the Faceless gave me a burner phone and very strict rules so that I could keep in touch with her."

"What about Tal?" Rovis asks, mentally taking note of the similarities between her and her brother as he watches her speak.

"I kept tabs on him through Zero. He couldn't know where I was or what I was doing. He would have wanted to pull me out and tuck me away somewhere safe."

Rovis nods. "That sounds like him."

Saige huffs. "So I made Zero promise that she would keep me a secret. I was doing what I needed to do with the Faceless. But when the government started a witch hunt for us, I reached out to the most powerful Lasan criminal organization. It was a gamble, but Damian Narvaez came through. A Skull disguised herself as a guard and gave me a drug that would make it seem like I was dead. As soon as the Purish shipped me off to cremate my body, the Skulls gave me the reverse drug and sent me here. I knew what was going to happen, so I got a message out to Zero before I let myself get captured, and bought the other Faceless some time to get away."

A deep breath fills his lungs as Rovis processes. He lets out a long sigh.

"Zero had no idea until after," he says, not quite a question.

"I didn't want to involve her in dealing with the government," Saige confirms.

"Because you knew she was in the Agency, and she couldn't risk getting caught," Rovis guesses, the pieces starting to fall together.

"That, and because she would have torn herself apart in case I didn't make it out."

Rovis nods. "And Tal? How did he take the news when he found you?"

"He didn't react much. I think he was just happy to see me alive." Saige stares at the workstation, a far away look on her face. "It makes me wonder why he didn't come back for me when he became Lithium."

"He didn't talk much about you, so I can't answer that for you." Rovis admits. "Did you ask him?"

Saige shakes her head, lips curved into a sad smile. "Not yet. We have a lot to unpack."

Buzzing against his thigh drags Rovis's attention away from Saige. He raises a brow as he reaches for his phone. Wherever Tal goes, there's cell service and electricity, apparently. When he checks the screen, though, it nearly tumbles out of his grip when he sees who's calling.

He hurries to pick up, heart pounding and blood rushing to his ears.

"Zero's in trouble," Tal says before Rovis opens his mouth. "She had help, and I'm with her now, but..."

Rovis's fingers go cold, head spinning. The words barely make any sense, yet the gnawing feeling from before he left Dyvris returns tenfold. His stomach twists, wondering what kind of mistake he made ignoring his instincts.

"Where?" he demands.

As reliable as always, despite months apart and radio silence, Tal says, "I'm sending you the location now."

3

Synapses

The muscles in Tal's arm slacken when he hangs up the phone, like a marionette puppet when the string's cut.

His hand still shakes when he shoves it back into his pocket, missing the opening twice.

Zero lies unconscious on the bed in front of him, unused blankets crumpled on the floor. Now that most of the blood has been cleaned off her face and body, she looks like she passed away in her sleep, heavy shadows beneath her eyes. But Tal would die before letting that happen to her, the image of her bathing in her own blood etched into his brain. He watches her chest shift with her breathing, weak but even, surrounded by people protecting her on the top floor in this safe house.

Not an Aconite safe house, but a Starcatcher safe house. Another formidable organization of the Damned, the Starcatchers dominate the northern city of Jinnoska. Alongside the Water Lords, they possess the most advanced technology in the country. If it weren't for the brutal competition between the two organizations, and Enyo Zhao's widespread history with both that make them each more suspicious of the other, they could probably take over Pureland by combining forces.

When Tal tracked down Zero's phone, anxiously driving faster than ever with the call still connected, he got to Ferrisque just in time to watch around twenty Riyssolans break into the restaurant and start shooting. He leapt out of the car and ran after them, forgetting to shut the door. He didn't even make it to the main entrance when the gunfire ceased after mere seconds.

In that moment, he thought she was dead.

His heart stopped beating, and he was frozen in time. His limbs suddenly felt weak, the urge to throw up whirling in his stomach.

He never saw this coming.

Then something inside him cracked, like a switch being flipped, but the electric current is overloaded, buzzing dangerously with high voltage.

His metal fingers flexed to unsheathe his claws as an ugly feeling burned in his chest, marching towards the Riyssolans blocking the door. Some widened their eyes when they saw him, and he would've been proud of his reputation if he weren't feeling so vengeful then. He didn't give them any time to prepare, a knife already swinging toward a throat.

An electric baton blocked him from making the kill, but his claws already cut through the ligaments of someone's arm. And the bloody fight began.

In hindsight, that was not the smartest thing Tal has ever done.

He had no plan, other than 'Kill everyone in sight,' like an indiscriminate war machine with no capacity for logic or even a bit of intelligence. Until someone slammed the pause button on his death script.

"Lithium," a gravelly voice called through his rage.

All the Riyssolans stepped back, while Tal's flexed metal hand slashed through the air, his whole body twisting with it when it caught nothing. Then his gut burned as sparks shot through his spine. He fell to the ground before he even realized he got tased, and the force of it had blown him back several paces. Grunting, he stood up through the fried veins in his body, ready to go again, until he saw a boy watching him, giving him a slow once ov er.

"Your Ace is safe now," the boy said, before Tal could decide to choke him to death for the interruption.

"Your words mean nothing to me," Tal hissed. "Let me through."

"You came alone," the boy noted, not quite a question, yet giving away a hint of surprise. "And so did she. What have the Aconites come to, if even you two are making such stupid decisions?"

Tal fought the urge to tear out his throat. "None of your business. Let me *through*."

Something flickered in the boy's green eyes, and he said, "She wouldn't want you to see her like this."

Tal flinched then, not only because of the words, but also because the boy spoke to him in Lasan. He demanded, "Who are you?"

"My name is Vasily Golubev," the boy said, switching back to Purish. "I'm a lieutenant of the Starcatchers."

"Riyssolan mafia of Jinnoska, city of ice," Tal remembered, dropping his arms by his side but not fully letting his guard down.

Everyone knew a large population of Riyssolans live in the northernmost city on land, where meteor showers frequently glimmer against the crimson sky, hence the name of their organization.

Tal didn't think he'd ever meet them, as long as he never went to Jinnoska. Their skill in technological development was beyond even him.

Vasily nodded, sharp eyes pinning him in place. "The Ace of Crowns... Zero, is it now? My sister is currently tending to her injuries. We owe her a debt. Consider it paid."

"I don't care," Tal snapped then, unable to process the boys words until he could see the truth with his own eyes. "Get out of my way, or I will remove you."

But the boy didn't even blink at his threat. Vasily only studied him, apathetic. "Very well."

He stepped aside, and Tal hesitated only for a moment, surprised. Then he shoved through the broken frames before the Riyssolans could change their mind.

His head spun at the sight of two girls in a pool of blood, heart pounding as panic rose again. The room reeked with violence, shattered tableware everywhere, and his shoes stuck to the floor where more blood was spilt.

"Katina Golubeva, Mender of the Starcatchers," the Riyssolan girl introduced herself without looking up, fingers working a spider where the skinny limbs were stitching up a deep gash ran down Zero's leg, the fabric of her pants sliced open. "Do not touch me. Don't move Zero, either. I'm going to stop the bleeding, but when she's stable again I'm going to need to fit her with prosthetics."

Sliding and slipping through the blood separating them, Tal collapsed to his knees next to Zero without much grace. Her head was turned to the side, eyes squeezed shut, brows knitted, and face splattered in red. His mind flashed back to the Purish mob that maimed his arm when he was a child as he scanned his eyes over her visible injuries.

Tal's voice trembled when he asked, "Prosthetics?"

"Correct," Katina told him. "Those shitheads tore out all the tendons and ligaments in her left leg."

A shaky breath fell out between Tal's lips. Shallow cuts marked her arms, and he suspected the leg would look much worse if Katina peeled back the fabric.

"You better have left me someone to torture," Tal said without looking away, a soft but dark demand.

Zero stirred, blinking sluggishly. Her face contorted, and her breathing quickened. When glossy brown eyes found Tal, confusion clouded her expression.

"Tal?" she croaked.

He shifted forward, gingerly brushing back messy, sweaty strands of hair, now darkened with black and red dye, a bit longer than her previously pink lob.

"Hey," he said softly, and hoped that she couldn't hear the way his voice cracked. "I'm here."

She looked like she tried to process that, but her eyes rolled back as she lost consciousness again.

"She's in pain," Tal looked at Katina, his hand still hovering over Zero's face. "Can't you do anything?"

"She has a concussion; I have to give her a specific kind of sedative that I don't have right now." Katina shifted up to work on Zero's arm. "Don't worry, I did a scan. No internal bleeding in the brain, but she does have a linear skull fracture. And yes, we kept some of the men alive. You can have them once we're done with Starcatcher business."

Katina carefully tugged off the sleeve of Zero's jacket.

Breath caught in his chest, Tal fell back onto one hand, skin almost skidding through the layer of blood on the floor. White veins crawled up Zero's arm, a sickly glow through her skin, like a dormant parasite waiting to feast.

"Well, that's new," Katina commented next to him. She tilted her head at Tal. "Is Dyvris so poor that you couldn't get her antiretrovirals?"

He couldn't hear the girl at first over the roaring in his ears. His brain tried to do the math, counting back the days when Zero could have gotten the disease. At that point, his heart might as well just spasmed and failed with the amount of shock he went through in that hour. Tal, underboss of the Aconites, was blindsided again, because Ofir was supposed to report every fatal injury or disease of their members to him and Rovis.

"Oh." Katina resumed cleaning Zero's wounds and stitching them up. "You didn't know. I was wondering why she would have joined such a useless organization instead of contacting me or my brother when she fell in with the Damned."

"The fever," Tal muttered, ignoring her callous comments. It made so much more sense, knowing that a fever caused her delirium right before he left.

Zero must have known. Why didn't she tell him? Rovis, Tal knew Zero wouldn't have confided in. But she knew Tal would have helped, didn't she? Or did she find out after Tal left? Surely she got tested, and Ofir would have to report it. Then Rovis must know.

Except she wouldn't have been in Ferrisque alone, if he knew. So she never got tested, which meant Zero knew exactly what was happening to her, and decided to keep it a secret.

Tal's fingers clenched into fists.

How typical.

"Save the breakdown for later," Katina said with a disinterested tone. "I'm done for now. We need to take her to the closest safe house. You can make yourself useful by carrying her."

And that's how Tal is now slumped in an uncomfortable chair by the bed where Katina is standing over Zero, who's finally on anesthesia and looks more at peace. He himself is still in a hoodie and cargo pants from tinkering with Saige before he got the call, with an oversized tech wear jacket hastily thrown on top.

He's watched the Riyssolan girl work for hours on machines he has never seen before, treating the cracked skull, healing the stitched cuts, and currently putting in nanotechnological prosthetics in Zero's mangled leg. He stays on the side with the covered leg to give her some privacy while Katina prods at the other one, exposed from the deformed hip joint to the lacerated ankle.

He only remembered to call Rovis when he started wondering how he's going to explain finding Zero like this after ghosting him for months.

I'll deal with that later, Tal reminds himself.

Shaking his head, he picks up Zero's jacket from the floor. A shiny yet small object falls out from the sleeve, and Tal catches it out of reflex. He frowns at the familiar vial, black with golden patterns, the Aconite mark etched on the cap.

Why would Zero have aconitine?

"How did you know Zero was in danger?" Tal asks.

"We didn't," Katina answers without tearing her gaze away from her work. "We're here for business matters. You know as well as the rest of us that the Syndicate is becoming quite the problem. It was only when we took down the Purish that Vasya realized who they were tormenting."

"So you saved her out of pure luck," he concludes, a heaviness sinking in his chest.

"The timing was luck. Saving her is returning a debt."

"Your brother said that, too. Why do you owe her?"

Katina steps back, and the machine quiets down as it stops, the long mechanical arm retreating to the side. "She should be good now. It will take a while to get used to, but she's a tough one."

Tal doesn't bother thanking her, since it's a repayment.

"Why do you owe her?" he repeats.

Katina picks up the comforter from the floor and settles it over Zero. "My brother and I ran into some problems when we were nine. Zero saved our lives. She was seven."

Tal wants to ask more, like how the hell that happened and what did Zero do, but Katina's stony face makes it clear that she will not answer. And it is, after all, a strange world where anything can happen.

"Katya," Zero's sleepy voice slurs. Tal snaps his eyes back to her, leaning forward to study her exhausted frown, her half-lidded eyes, her creased brows.

"You woke up early," Katina remarks, clasping Zero's hand with a strong grip to help her sit up. "What idiotic choices have you made this time?"

Zero chokes out a weak laugh. "The usual. Is Vasya here?"

"Yes, he's standing guard. I'll send him in to say hi after we test out your leg."

She shifts her legs beneath the comforter and scowls. "They fucking drugged me."

"Yeah," Tal cuts, tone sharp with irony, "and they fucking tore out your tendons."

"Right," she says absently and pushes the comforter down, hand grazing over the glow of the prosthetic joint at the sides of her knee. Then she looks over, her brows once again furrowing in confusion.

"You called me," he reminds her.

"Yes, but how are you here?"

"I flew." At Zero's unimpressed frown, Tal adds, "Built a flying car. It's a prototype."

"That doesn't sound safe."

"I tested it for you," he mocks her words from ages ago, when Tal got drunk on the roof after Levi's death and Zero deliberately gave him a heart attack by jumping off the roof with his unfinished version of an energy shield. "It works great. Good job, Tal."

Zero only blinks at him. Then she turns back to Katina. "I thought you were in Jinnoska."

"And we thought you were in Dyvris," Katina returns.

"Vacation."

"Business."

"Bullshit," Tal snaps at Zero. "Nothing you do is a coincidence. You did not take a 'vacation' and magically end up where the Purity Syndicate and Starcatchers are having some kind of showdown. And by the way, friends in the Riyssolan mafia? The white vein virus? What else aren't you telling me? Would it kill you to harbor a couple less life-changing secrets?"

Zero looks down again, stretching out her fingers, no longer gloved, her arms no longer covered by black sleeves.

Katina rounds the bed and lifts her chin at Tal. "Your services aren't required at the moment. You may now walk yourself to the door."

"You—"

"I what?" She challenges him. "*I* need to give my patient here a new set of clothes and test out her new prosthetics. *You* are disturbing her peace, when she needs rest and emotional security."

Tal clenches his jaw, but he can't argue. "I'll wait outside the door. I will see her when you're finished."

"You will see her when you revise your bedside manners."

He narrows his eyes. Katina doesn't back down. Scoffing, he turns and steps out. Vasily flicks him an indifferent glance before going back to watching the hall. The safe house is three stories tall, and Tal can hear the six Starcatchers milling about downstairs speaking in rapid Riyssolan. Then he wonders how long Zero has been fluent in the language, given her history with the Golubev twins.

"How does a seven-year-old save the lives of two nine-year-olds?" Tal questions without pretense, slanting a look at Vasily.

The boy doesn't answer. He doesn't even look Tal's way.

"I mean," Tal continues, "how could it have been so significant that you two still remember what happened — let's see — ten years ago?"

"Did she not save you?" comes Vasily's disinterested reply.

Tal opens his mouth to say 'no,' but he suddenly remembers that Zero admitted to have secretly steered him clear of a mind-control drug failure.

"Exactly," Vasily says when Tal is too slow to answer. He thinks he might hear a hint of bitterness in his blank tone. "That is her problem. She will save anyone but herself. We told her to come to us when she started asking questions about the Damned and planning to drop out of school. Instead, she chose the most disorganized criminal group this country has ever seen. If we knew she was here, she wouldn't be in this situation. Joining the Aconites is her downfall."

"She's seventeen." Tal crosses his arms, feeling defensive of the Aconites. "She can make her own choices. When she came to me, she knew what she was doing, and she knew the consequences. Zero is as self-sufficient as she can be; someone is supposed to do the rest of the work and take care of her."

"Self-sufficient," Vasily repeats, almost derisively. "If you say that, then you do not know her at all. And are you that 'someone'? Because you are doing a wonderful job."

"I—"

Tal cuts himself off, the words dying on his tongue. Vasily's biting remark reminds him of Saige, how she had similarly cryptic comments about Zero when Tal tried to justify losing his temper with her before he left Dyvris.

Saige.

He reaches for his phone to check on his sister.

Your boyfriend came by, she texted Tal not long after he called Rovis. *I like him. He's smart. Looks scary but is actually soft like a puppy.*

Tal scoffs at the last comment.

He left, Saige added. *Seemed like an emergency. Same as when you left earlier. Is he with you now or was it something different?*

Not yet, he texts back. *I found something he needed to see. I'll be back soon.*

Okay, comes the fast response. *I'll be right here. Not that there's anywhere I can go, being dead and all.*

Tal huffs softly. *Good. And he's not my boyfriend.*

Whatever you say.

The screen goes dark, and Tal puts away his phone again.

When he found Saige in that depressing lot of shipping containers, after a month of unleashing his vengeance for Levi on the Wrights, she just hugged him and refused to let go. Even though she definitely knew what he's done, what he continues to do, she acted like everything was normal. Since their reunion, he can't find any proof that she holds any resentment towards him for leaving, but he knows that can't be the case. Yet she just welcomed him back as her older brother, like the past eight years were nothing.

The door cracks open behind him.

"Vasya." Katina says something in Riyssolan and jerks her head toward the room. A Starcatcher climbs up the stairs and arrives just in time with a bag of food.

Vasily takes the bag, slips in the room, and shuts the door behind him.

Katina looks Tal up and down before she nods. "You can go in after him. I found something odd about Zero's blood sample, so I need to go check with someone about this."

Tal frowns. "Is it serious?"

"Possibly." Katina takes off her medical gloves. "Stay here until Vasily comes out."

Tal curls his fingers around the vial in his pocket as Katina leaves. His head starts to spin with theories about Zero's possession of the poison. It's not for killing anyone, because Zero can't care less about wasting energy on other people unless they mess with someone she cares about, and even then she prefers breaking her victim's heart and destroying their mind. Usually Tal would be the one who cleans up after her and actually strikes the killing blow.

Yet the dosage is enough to kill someone three times over.

He has a suspicion, but he doesn't want to believe it.

Vasily walks out, leaving the door open for Tal but without acknowledging him. Tal elects to ignore the disrespect in favor of seeing Zero awake and safe.

She's sitting on the bay window, leaning her head against the glass. All the blood on her body has been cleaned off, her veins extra visible against the black of her tank top and the Aconite tattoo. Her fox necklace dangles around her neck, and her short hair has been washed and dried, still somewhat messy. A brown nylon ripstop overall covers her legs, presumably given to her by the Starcatchers. The top half piles at her waist, unclasped. A blood pressure monitor wraps around her bicep. Her right boot rests over her stiff left leg, a half-eaten takeout box sitting in her lap.

Zero flicks her eyes at Tal before staring out the window again.

"You didn't expect me to come," Tal says.

He doesn't get an answer, but he doesn't need to. Zero's puzzled expressions both times when she first saw Tal after waking up already tell him everything. And it hurts, more than anything that has happened to him since he joined the Aconites when he was fourteen.

Tal scoffs to cover up the hitch in his breath. "So what was the point of calling?"

Again, nothing.

"Answer me," he demands softly.

"Where are Jeremy Wright's kids?" she asks without looking at him.

Tal's brow twitches, taken by surprise. "Does it matter to you?"

"No."

"Then why ask?"

She lifts one shoulder in a minuscule shrug. "Just curious what your punishment for them was."

"I permanently altered their faces with chemicals and sent them to juvenile labor camps, then made sure they'd all do terribly on their psych evals so that no one would ever believe a word they say. I forget who's who, but one's in Loveias, one's in Aurodus, and one's in Jinnoska." He tilts his head. "Are you satisfied with my answer, or will you start judging me for my cruelty now, after all these years?"

Zero only closes her eyes and nods. "Good work."

"You haven't answered me. What was the point of calling me, if you didn't expect me to show up?"

Zero's head slowly turns against the glass to the left, then to the right. "I don't know."

For once, Tal believes her.

"I guess," she adds quietly. "I just wanted someone to know I didn't make it easy for them to kill me."

"You made me listen." His voice wavers on the last word, just a bit, with lingering fear, with fury, with restrained volume. "You made me listen to what they did to you. You made me listen to your screams."

Zero breathes a deep sigh, the takeout box shifting in her lap. "You could have hung up. No one forced you to pick up."

"It was *you*," Tal says, stepping closer. "Of course I picked up. Of course I ran after you. How can I not, no matter how upset I am with you, knowing that you only ever call during emergencies? You really don't understand, do you? In case you forgot, I have an eidetic memory. I don't just know what happened; I'll never forget it." He tugs at her watch, gesturing at the white veins. His chest hurts at the sight of it. "Were you ever going to tell me?"

"*Naslata*," Zero says softly.

No.

Her fingers fumble next to her, and Tal realizes she's patting around her black jacket.

"Looking for this?" Tal pulls out the vial.

Zero stops moving. She still refuses to look at him. Tal's jaw slacks, a grim understanding weighing heavily in his limbs.

And he knows. He *knows.*

She will save anyone but herself, Vasily said.

Her sense of self-worth has been tossed into the pits of hell, Saige said.

She was traumatized, but she wasn't self-destructive yet, Rovis said.

The Aconites have the resources to treat the white vein disease, yet she clearly left it unattended for months. She was alone in an unfamiliar city. She didn't — she *doesn't* — think Tal still cares.

"Why?" Tal whispers, his eyes stinging.

Zero's fingers twitch. She knows that he knows. "You should go."

"Rovis doesn't know you're dying, does he?"

"Leave."

"*No,*" Tal snarls, suddenly furious. "You don't get to do this. You don't get to call me, then expect the worst from me. You don't get to lie there, half-dead in a pool of blood, then turn me away when you wake up. You want to burn your bridges? Fine. But I figured out a way to fly, so you're not getting rid of me. Look at me."

Zero does not budge.

"Look at me," he growls, putting so much force into those words that his claws slide out. She finally turns her head, and Tal shoves his hand behind his body. He is not a saint, and he can't control his emotions, but he could never allow himself to turn against this girl again. Especially not with all the information he has now. "You are going to tell Rovis, and you are going to fix this. There are solutions out there, and you're not picking the aconitine. You've done enough breaking him with your words; you will destroy him if you go through with this. Do you understand? You'll destroy him."

"No."

"What did you just say?"

"It wasn't supposed to be like this."

Tal scoffs, disbelieving. "Oh, you weren't supposed to catch the white vein virus and have your tendons torn out by sadists while you were planning to commit suicide? Yeah, that happens."

"I was never supposed to live," she whispers.

A shaky breath rips out of Tal's chest as he staggers back. He looks down and takes a deep breath to regain composure, then stores the vial inside his metal arm, before he looks at her with watery eyes. "Who did this to you?"

"I already told you."

Zero did, when she was delirious with the fever from what Tal knows now is the white vein disease. Tal didn't think she'd remember saying it.

"Your mother's been dead for years," Tal says.

"It's not a spell that lifts when the evil witch is dead." Zero shakes her head. "It doesn't matter anyway."

"It does to me," he hisses. "Why won't you fight?"

"Why does it matter to you?" she shoots back without any heat. "We don't work together anymore, and we are not friends."

"Because I invested too much in your survival for you to do this to yourself," he snaps. "All I ever wanted for you was—"

"Listen," she interrupts, lifting her gaze to look Tal dead in the eyes. "When you ran away from home, Saige trusted me for some mysterious reason that neither of us can explain still. So when the universe rolled its dice, and I found her brother, I told her. I respected her wishes not to inform you of our connection. Because she needed to protect you and herself. I'm not sorry about keeping that secret from you, but I'm sorry that I'm not sorry. I'm sorry that someone turned my head, my heart, my soul, inside out, and made me into a monster."

"You're not—"

"I'm sorry that I'm not strong enough to reverse that. I did try, Tal. I did fight. I've been fighting since I was five, but I can't change what I am. I never meant to choose between you or Saige, between two people that hold weight in my empty heart, but it just happened. And I'm too tired to care. If you mistook me for a fallen angel, then that's on you."

Tal's open mouth struggles to close. He tries to speak, but the words choke and die in his throat. He feels as though someone reached into his lungs and punctured it.

Zero suddenly lifts her head up from the window, turning it so that her ear points to the door. Her narrow eyes tell him that she's calculating someone's footsteps again.

"Rovis is going to enter in about forty-five seconds," she estimates. "If you wish to go back to Saige without any more conflicts, now is the time."

Tal stays rooted to his spot.

"Forty," Zero counts down.

He's not ready to see Rovis again, and she knows it.

"Thirty-five."

Tal hurries to take off his jacket and covers up Zero's arms. "You owe me for this. Tell Rovis. Live. You're not going to take yourself out. I won't allow it. We'll figure everything out. You are not worthless, remember these words until you believe them."

Zero turns her head away, though her fingers curl around the edges of Tal's jacket. "Twenty-five."

"We are not done here," he says, backing away to the open window on the other side of the room.

"I've heard that one before."

Tal jumps out the window and lands solidly in a lunge on the ground. His metal arm and his boots glow red for a moment, charging up with electricity from the impact. A shadow falls over him, and Tal lifts his head.

Katina peers down at him, unamused.

He stands and grins, sharper than his finest knife. The adrenaline from the jump is enough to bring back Lithium once again. "Where are these men you promised me?"

"What will you do?"

"I'm going to make them suffer," he promises. "And I'm going to erase them off the face of the planet."

Katina nods with a faint air of approval, and leads him across the street, down the basement of another house. She dismisses two Starcatchers who were standing guard in the room. The low lighting is truly banal, but luckily Tal has always been one for the theatrics. Three men are groaning in pain, hung low by chains around their wrists, almost kneeling when their broken legs are deadweight dragging them down. Serves them right, for what they did to Zero.

Tal saunters up to one of the men, while Katina stays by the door. He slips on a brass knuckle covered in diamond spikes, gifted by Damian Narvaez when he swore in as an associate with the Skulls, in return for helping Saige.

In a flash, diamonds catching the sick lighting of the basement, Tal backhands the man across the face. The room resounds with a satisfying crack. The Purish spits out a tooth before he glares up at Tal, four deep cuts growing redder with blood seeping out across his cheek.

"Go to hell," he snarls, hatred and disgust blazing in his eyes.

"You know—" Tal drawls. The fingertips of his metal hand sharpen into claws. "I really would love to."

He plunges the claws into the man's chest and rakes down, slicing through fabric and flesh. Tal grins, relishing the shriek of agony.

If only this sweet sound could write over his memories of Zero's screams.

Tal's vision goes red.

"But Drokklo and I are in a tough spot right now," he hisses as his claws dig deeper, blood coating his metal fingers like fresh paint.

4

Operator Overloading

Zero keeps her eyes closed when Rovis walks in, her labored breathing scraping against her throat. She hears him pause, before proceeding more quietly.

"I know you're awake," he says when he's next to her.

She cracks one eye open. Rovis stares at her, though his gaze briefly flickers down at Tal's jacket, which she's now wearing properly, after she found her gloves in her own torn jacket.

"You just missed him," Zero says, looking out the window again. "If you ask one of the twins to show you where they're keeping the Syndicate guys, you'll probably find him there."

In this pathetic state, crippled and confronted by Tal, avoidance is Zero's best move. She's using Tal and Rovis against each other so they can leave her alone, and she does not feel a single bit guilty about it. Her throat and lungs burn, yet her arms still tremble beneath the black fabric of Tal's jacket. She wants to close her eyes and lie down, in a permanent way. She wants to sleep and never wake up again.

Through the reflection of the glass, Zero sees Rovis clench his jaw at her taunt, eyes darting between Zero and the door.

Unfortunately, he pulls a chair over to sit next to her, and Zero has to swallow back a sigh.

"How are you feeling?" he asks softly.

Zero huffs. "I don't. You know that already."

"I'm not playing along with that anymore," Rovis says. "Does anything hurt?"

"Even if it does, there's nothing you can do about it."

He sighs. "Do you have to keep pushing me away all the time? Do you not get tired of it? Why aren't you letting me in this time?"

"What do you want me to say, Rovis?" Zero closes her eyes. "They shot at me, threw blades at me, tranquilized my right leg, mutilated the left one, drugged me, cracked my skull." She frowns, rubbing her fingers on the spot in her neck where she thought a needle pricked. "What are you going to do about it? Tal's got the revenge part covered."

"How about just being here?" he counters. "You keep throwing the fact that I left you in Lime Gateway back in my face, so how about I stay?"

"Do whatever you want," she grumbles, failing to find the fault in his logic.

"How's your head?"

If Zero had the strength and energy, she'd strangle him. With as much derision as she can muster up right now, she snaps, "Is this an interrogation? It's fine. Katya sewed it up nicely with her fancy Riyssolan machines."

"And your leg?"

Zero sighs, more irritated than exhausted. She reaches for the hem of the pant leg, careful to keep her arms hidden under the sleeves. Then she pauses to flick her eyes at him. "Don't you dare react."

Cautiously, she rolls the fabric up to her knee, revealing the web of liquid metal buried in her muscles to support her bones. The fine structure starts from her achilles, follows intricate lines up her calves, circles around right below her knee with extra support curling down the front, then sweeps up into thicker bars through her thighs. Parts of her flesh has grown over silver structure, tinges of red visible where the light passes through deeper tissue. Every segment of the metal has an indicator light that currently shines blue to declare it's working properly.

Rovis stays silent, but Zero doesn't need to see his face to hear his breathing hitch.

"It goes up to the hipbone," she says, apathetic.

After a tense moment passes, Zero pulls the edge down to tuck in her boot again. Her heart speeds up as she drags her gaze to meet Rovis's intense stare. She watches him work his jaw, struggling to keep his expression blank.

Eventually he grits out, "You don't deserve this."

Zero scoffs, settling back against the wall and crossing her arms. "There's no such thing as 'deserve.'"

"*Rena.*"

Everything in Zero's body goes cold. Her blood, her fingers, her heart, her eyes. Slowly, she turns her head. Her dead stare lands on Rovis's crestfallen face.

"Why," she seethes, voice so harsh it's just barely above a whisper.

"You called me 'Rozzie' first," he says calmly, lifting his chin.

"I was eight."

"During your fever," Rovis clarifies. "You said it. You said it twice."

Zero leans away from him, trying to dredge up the memories from that day. All she remembers is losing half her mind in Rovis's office, drunk on her own insanity. Then she remembers the cool, wet cloths wiping down her arms and pressing against her forehead in Ofir's office. She might have dreamt afterwards, but she can never recall what her brain makes up when she's asleep.

"I was giving you medicine," Rovis adds, interrupting her whirling fragments of memories.

It takes her a second to process his words. It takes her another five to understand them.

A breath escapes her chest in a mix of disbelief, exasperation, and incomprehension.

"And why," Zero hisses, "exactly, did you come into my room in the first place?"

His face shutters. "Tal said you were sick. I went to check on you."

"After everything I said?" She huffs in outrage, even feeling a bit insulted. This man is even more one-track minded than a machine. "Have you learned nothing? Do you not remember me stabbing all your weak spots until you threw me out? Or is Tal's eidetic memory so good that you've decided you don't need any memory retention at all?"

"Of course I remember," he shoots back. "Why are you bringing Tal into this? No, don't throw me off track. Tell me, what makes you think I wouldn't care for you when you're down? No matter how much you try to hurt me, I'm not going to turn my back on you."

Zero's chest heaves as she curls then uncurls her fingers, repeating the process several times before she twists her body and punches the window.

The impact against the glass sparks pain through her knuckles, across her metacarpals, crashing into her scaphoid and dancing up her radius, even though the gloves.

Rovis is so stubborn, it's giving her a headache. Her temples feel as though a metal bar is sticking through them.

"That defeats the purpose," Zero says through her teeth.

"Purpose of what?" Rovis asks quietly, anger deflated, just like that.

Taking a deep breath, Zero regains her composure and crosses her arms with her back against the wall again. "Nothing."

"Purpose of *what*?"

She shakes her head and curls in on herself. She's drowning, suffocating. All of it chokes the life out of her; Rovis's incessant questions, the toxic gas in the air, the never-ending violence it takes to survive. But if she takes a step back, it all goes away. None of this matters, after all. This is just one moment of a long, arduous life on a dying planet that's a speck of nothing in the bigger universe. This conversation will pass by, and Rovis will forget it or let it drop, and he'll never have to know.

"I didn't come here to fight," he sighs. "I just needed to see if you were—"

"I'm great," Zero says flatly. "I'm alive."

Rovis looks away, raking a hand through his hair. She knows she's being difficult; *that* is the point. She's making it hard, because Rovis cannot handle everything Zero's going to make him go through when she dies, when she chooses to let herself die. And there's no such thing as 'deserve,' but Rovis really drew the shortest end of all sticks when he wound up in Zero's orbit.

Just like the card games, like Keepers and Thieves, luck cannot be chosen or manipulated. Winning with a bad hand takes observation, strategy, and risk. Rovis has a stupid card that he's too attached to, and will ultimately destroy him in the end if Zero doesn't take it out of his hand.

Zero has been living comfortably in her sinking ship, but she will not drown before Rovis grows a brain and gets on a dinghy heading to the shore.

"Why didn't you call me?" Rovis interrupts her internal monologue.

She looks him in the eyes. "I called Tal."

His fists tighten until they start to tremble. "Why didn't you call *me*?"

"Did you find Saige?" Zero says, not really asking.

Rovis narrows his eyes. She can see the gears turning in his head. He works his jaw, and smoke's practically coming out from his ears when he says, "You've known where Tal has been all along."

"I vaguely guessed when he started destroying the Wrights." Zero shrugs. "So Tal was closer to Ferrisque than you were."

In truth, she absolutely did not have time to reason through that when the Syndicate men were closing in on her. She didn't really think about it. Even though she told Tal that she didn't want to die alone and in silence, she still has yet to process why her fingers pressed on Tal's number, rather than anyone else's. It's not like Rovis and Tal were her only choices.

You made me listen.

Zero's mind flashes back to Tal's miserable expression, his eyes shiny with unshed tears and his lips twisted in unspoken pain.

Maybe that's why, she wonders. Not that she wants Tal to suffer, but she would do anything to keep Rovis from looking like that. Right now, he's worried, he's angry, but he didn't come soon enough to get second-hand trauma.

Then again, it's not fair that Zero did exactly that to Tal. Zero could laugh at herself. With the story of how he lost his arm, she's truly a monster for making him relive that through her. The worst kind, when she would use people close to her without hesitation.

"But would you have called me if I were closer?" Rovis asks quietly.

She sighs. "It doesn't matter."

"I don't understand," his voice cracks, rough like splinters from a tree bark. "You're old enough to know why I left. I was doing my best, Rena. I sent you money every month. I sent you birthday gifts every year. I know it wasn't the same as me being there, but you know it was the only way for us to survive. Will you never forgive me for leaving?"

Something in Zero's chest twitches, but she stomps away the feeling. She cannot move backwards on her plan, and the number one rule was to kill what should be dead and buried, and detach herself from everything. Rovis is her weakness, and she is his. One of them has to be strong enough to break this cycle.

"You're so stupid," she grits out.

"What?"

"The past is dead. How long will it take for that to get through your thick skull?"

Rovis stares, stunned.

"Why do you look so surprised?" Zero snarls. "You must know by now that I'm not kind. I'm not *sweet*, or innocent, or naive anymore. I'm a liar, a spy, a schemer, a manipulator. I'm a villain more despicable than even you. There's no going back, no salvation for people like you and me."

"But this is *us*," he argues, standing. The chair topples over behind him. "I know that our parents—"

"Our parents are dead," she snaps, swinging her legs over the edge of the bay window. "Let it go. There's nothing tying us together anymore."

"But—"

"*Stop it*," she growls and stands, too. Or at least she tries to.

Her left leg gives out, unaccustomed to the metal nanoparticles connecting to her nerves.

Rovis catches her before she can crumple to the floor. Out of reflex, her hands clutch at his bulky shoulders. Her lungs struggle to take in air as he sets her back onto the soft cushions on the bay.

She remembers the knives digging into her muscles and bones. She remembers not being able to tell what exactly they were cutting out of her body, because all of it was just white-hot torment, so unbearable that she lost consciousness. She remembers her last thought, filled with rage and spite, because she didn't even get the chance to end her pain before the torture started.

Zero doesn't let go when Rovis tries to move away.

Fuck. Fuck, she's so, so tired.

"I can't do this anymore," she breathes, feeling heat pressuring at her eyes. "I can't, I can't do this. I don't want to."

The Syndicate laughed when they held her down, surrounding her like opossums feasting on roadkill. And this world is full of people like them. The twins saved Zero's life, but what for? To carry the humiliation and trauma with her for the rest of her very short life, destined to end in her veins burning her to death from inside out? She survived, yet the road in front of her doesn't look any less desolate. She's alive, but even nature wants to exterminate every last one of them.

"Do what?" she hears Rovis ask, his solid grip unwavering.

She shakes her head, and the movement rubs her forehead against his shirt. If she told him every hopeless thought that passes through her mind, he'd crumble. Yet he's the one person she'd want to tell everything to. And she hates it. Because Rovis became her home eleven years ago, and that will never change, no matter how much she tries to deny it. Before everything went to hell, he was her haven, the hidden corner of a bookstore, an unexpected umbrella in a storm, family that she never thought she'd find. He keeps derailing all her plans by feeding her hope that things can go back to the way they used to be, but she knows better. She knows nothing can ever return to the past.

Perhaps it's the lingering shock of the ambush, or maybe it's the cold awakening that even her body is altered forever, that prompts her to carefully choose a slice of truth to surrender.

"I don't want to fight you, either," she admits.

The words burn her throat and choke her. Her chest aches from how much she's shaking, and cold sweat forms on her forehead. Her eyes are begging to close, to rest for a long, long time.

"Then don't," Rovis whispers, "for your sake and mine."

It sounds so simple, so easy, yet Zero cannot see a way out. She's trapped in a cycle of abuse that runs in her family for generations, and she already let it bleed into her when she turned the knife of her tongue to point at Rovis, thinking it'd make him give up on her.

"You're so stupid," she repeats, though the fragile sound of her voice takes away the heat from the insult. "Why can't you give up? Why won't you let me go?"

"I made you a promise." He combs through her messy hair with a hand, the movement as effortless as his words.

She sighs. "And I told you to make a new one. Everything you've ever done has been for someone else. Your father, your friends, Griffin, me, Tal. When are you going to do something for yourself?"

"You are still young," he says gently. "You're right, I am stupid. I thought you've grown up so much that you don't need me anymore. And you don't, not in the way that you used to. But I am so sick and tired of watching you run yourself to the ground, keeping everything to yourself. When you knowingly took Damian's drug, when you lashed out at me because of the fever, and now. I'm not going to stand to the side anymore; I'm not letting you do this alone."

Zero shakes her head violently. "You have to."

"No, I don't. Your mind is your own poison, and it's not your fault, but you need to let me help you. Talk to me."

"No," Zero grits out through the needles in her head.

"Whatever you've been doing, whatever you think you've been doing, it clearly isn't working. What good would it do to keep doing the same thing?" Rovis shakes her lightly. "Who's the stupid one now?"

"I can't. It's not possible."

"What's not possible?"

Words struggle to form in her mouth. Her lungs grapple for air, but each time her chest feels smaller and her throat feels raw. The room is too small, and the lights are too bright. She needs to leave, to run, to get out, but she's frozen in place as the walls close in on her. Everything around her is too hot, suffocating and imposing.

A warm hand covers the back of her neck.

Her eyes soften, and the panicking thoughts in her head start to slow down.

She hears counting.

One, two, three, four, five.

Six, seven, eight, nine, ten, eleven, twelve.

Rovis mumbles with his soothing voice as he taps his fingers with the numbers on her wrist. Zero tries to follow, like the way Rovis taught her to when he was sitting on the floor in his kitchen, just turned thirteen, and he needed someone to count for him.

After several minutes, maybe several hours, Zero shudders and deflates. Her eyes are clear again, though she didn't notice when she started to lose her vision to black dots. Her nostrils feel like an icy winter while her throat feels like a blazing summer. Zero tries to rub the soreness out of her chest, but at least she can breathe properly now. A headache lingers, like a shadow of claws clutching her brain. She feels as though she's recovering from a cold, when her body's won the fight but remains weakened.

"I haven't had an anxiety attack in three years," Zero mutters, voice scratchy and head still resting on Rovis's shoulder. "That was embarrassing."

He squeezes her wrist lightly. "Don't worry, I've seen worse."

Zero huffs. "I'm sure Vasya heard everything."

"No, he didn't. I sent him away before I came in." His hand returns to the back of her head. Light fingertips brush against her hair. "I couldn't keep you safe, but I won't hurt you again."

"I hurt you more," she rasps. The truth chafes her heart and makes her unfurl more than all the lost tendons and ligaments in her leg. Once spoken out loud, she can't bury it anymore,

"It's not a competition," Rovis chides softly.

"All those things I said were meant to hurt you, so you'd walk away from me."

"I know."

"It wasn't okay. It still isn't."

"It's not," he agrees. "But you are not your mother."

Zero nearly forgets how to breathe, again. But one anxiety attack is enough for the day, so she forces herself through it, counting the same patterns.

"Even if I'm not," she chokes out, "she already turned me into this. I cannot be fixed, Rov. These shards will only cut you again."

"Only if you keep bottling things up." Rovis leans his head on top of hers. "Don't you see? Your mother still haunts you. It's not your fault, any of it. But the moment you let your mind twist your perception of reality, you shut down, and you turn all your fears about being an awful person into a weapon against everyone else, against me. And you hate yourself even more because of it, once you realize what you've done; I see it now."

One meltdown, and Rovis can see right through her again.

Zero's head spins, still aching.

"I'm so tired," she breathes, the words drifting out like a sigh.

"I know," Rovis says again. "Just try one more thing for me, okay? I don't need anything else from you. I don't need you to be perfect; I don't need you to be a saint. We are the Damned, after all. Our lives are messy, violent, and ugly, and sometimes we are that to each other. It stings, but I'll live, as long as you try what I'm going to ask of you. You can keep calling yourself broken, if that's what you want, but I don't need you to be fixed. I don't need you to be sweet or kind. I don't need you to be what you once were. Times have changed, and it wouldn't be fair to ask you to fight that. I don't need you to fight."

The hand on her wrist slides down to squeeze her fingers.

"Whenever something bothers you," he continues, "when there's an itch in your chest or a darkness in your head, I need you to tell me. That's my one request. It doesn't need to be big or small; it's just whatever comes across your mind. It doesn't need to be soft words and calm tones; it just needs to be the truth. Will you try that?"

Zero straightens and looks at Rovis, who shifts to gaze right back at her.

A shaky breath escapes her wearied lungs.

She should be fighting him on this. She really, really should not give in, because everything inside of her is far too rotten to be good to anyone else.

But Zero is weak.

Tal took the vial, and Rovis was the reason why Zero couldn't drink the poison in the first place. After two aborted attempts to spare Rovis from more of her cruelty, she knows now that she's never going to be able to do it. Just the thought of it seems to choke her, because what the hell is she holding on for? She's exhausted, from everything and every game she plays, yet she's still here, and for what?

Zero is too weak to follow through with her own plan, so she has to listen to Rovis. Every word that he's said is true, and all he asks is to try. Suddenly she's six again, when she first met him, and she could finally take a break and lean on him. Survival was much more bearable when he came into her life. Zero resolutely does not want to go back, to relying on others and to growing attached, but what other choice is there, when it seems like she has to go on?

"Sure," she rasps, reluctant.

The corners of Rovis's lips twitch, and he pulls her into a real hug. Zero tightens her grip around his shoulders.

Her headache starts to pound now. Her brows knit together, and her frown deepens.

One of her hands falls onto her knee and rests there, while the pounding eases as she digs her forehead into Rovis's shoulder.

The hand drops to the edges of her boot and fidgets with the material.

Zero counts the numbers again to get through the waves of pain.

One, two, three, four, five.

Six, seven, eight, nine, ten, eleven, twelve.

Her fingers curl around the hilt of a knife.

The hammers in her brain eases, though it still beats at her skull, as if driving her to keep going.

She pulls out the weapon and switches it into a reverse grip.

The movement fills her chest with elation.

The unfamiliar feeling makes her pause, frowning as her brain slowly catches up with the rest of the body.

When did she take out the knife hidden in the side of her boot?

Her arm wavers, and the headache intensifies once again. Zero blinks, brows twitching in confusion.

Then her heart nearly jumps out from her ribcage when she realizes what she's doing.

She shoves the knife back into her boot so fast she almost slices her calf.

Dark spots start to fill her vision, and Zero feels like someone took a giant nutcracker and put her skull in between the jaws. She tries not to sway, so that Rovis doesn't notice something's wrong.

Has she seriously lost her mind tonight?

Zero abruptly pulls back. Rovis scans her face with that soft look still, completely unaware of her attempt to... To what, stab him?

"Can you, um, get me some water?" she asks and clears her throat.

"Yeah." He squeezes her shoulder and walks to the hot and cold dispenser across the room.

The grip on her brain lightens up enough for her to start panicking.

What just happened?

Was she...

Was she about to *kill* Rovis?

That thought alone makes her limbs weak, so much that they begin to tingle and feel numb as her heart races. Her fingers are freezing underneath the leather of her gloves. Goosebumps quake her entire body in a violent shiver. The knife burns against her leg, but she's too scared to put her hand anywhere near it. Her breathing grows harsh as she scrambles for an explanation for this torture.

It was like her arm grew a mind of its own.

"What's wrong?" Rovis's concerned face appears in front of her. A warm cup lands in her hand. "You look really pale."

"Nothing, I just..." Zero exhales, a sharp sound that grates against the noise in her head. "I don't feel well."

"You should lie down. Do you need help getting back to the bed?"

She lifts up the cup and gulps down half the water. When the headache doesn't ease up, she drops her hands back into her lap and says, "I think I'd rather stay here."

Rovis moves away again, and Zero almost falls over from how much the pain level drops.

This is not natural, that quiet part of her mind supplies.

Zero squeezes her eyes shut, heart running faster than her foggy brain.

What is happening? Where did that come from, the thought to hurt Rovis? There wasn't even a thought, though; it just happened. It was like her fingers developed their own mind. But how could that be? Why, out of all things to do in this forsaken universe, did they decide to take out the knife?

Could she really be that cruel? Right after promising Rovis she'd try to do things his way, to rectify her wrongs and hope to move on, she'd... literally stab him in the back? Why?

And why does her head hurt so much? Zero knows that Katya is a highly skilled Mender, but maybe she didn't completely fix the skull fracture? That doesn't seem like her, but Zero can't think of any other reason. It could be an aftermath of an anxiety attack, but it usually isn't this strong and inconsistent.

Another wave of pain splits her mind like pieces of a shattered mirror.

She blinks open her eyes and watches Rovis take the mug out of her grasp, set it to the side, then help her lie back onto a pile of pillows he must have gathered from around the room. He drapes a soft blanket over her and pulls at the edges.

"I think you should sleep." His voice sounds galaxies away. "You've had a really long day."

Sleep? She can't sleep like this; she needs answers. She has no idea what's going on with her mind or her body, and it's driving her insane. Everything that Zero has done in her life has been a calculated choice, and never a mindless impulse. Even her call for help to Tal, it was deliberate, even if she's not sure of the reason at the moment. She doesn't understand her hand is itching for her knife. She doesn't know where it wants the blade to be buried into.

Zero frowns as a split-second memory blinks in her mind. Her hand reaches up to rub the spot on her neck again.

The tides of pain and happiness seem proportional to her distance from Rovis and how close her knife was to him.

Could it be...?

Katya opens the door, glancing at Zero and Rovis. She looks the same as usual, cold and the opposite of empathetic, though her shoulders carry a tension that tells Zero might be coming to the right conclusion.

"The blood sample," Katya says.

Rovis straightens, matching Katya's posture. "And?"

"It's the government's newest edition of the mind-control drugs," she says, and Zero recognizes the grim undertone. "Our Zero here is this version's first victim."

"Oh," Zero mutters, closing her eyes. "So that's what that was."

5

Overwritten

Rovis stares at Katina, his mind replaying her words over and over again.

Another round of drug experiments, this soon?

The last one, he's heard, was only a week ago, and a couple hundred people across the country fell ill. The drug made them vomit day and night, burned through their stomach lining, and somehow had a component that acted like a brain-eating amoeba.

His limbs suddenly feel weak.

Levi's bloody face, Jacek's limp body, and Ayssa's empty eyes are still ingrained in his memories.

Yet he just can't wrap his brain around the fact that Zero's next. That their new twisted concoction is going to tear her apart even more than what they've already done to her. That she may not survive the night.

Rovis can't let this happen. He can't.

"Fortunately," Katina says through his racing thoughts, "they've managed to stabilize the drug, so it won't kill her."

Relief flood through Rovis's body and escapes through his mouth as a soft sigh.

"Not so fortunately," she continues, "the injected nanoparticles into her bloodstream can mimic neurotransmitters."

His chest tightens once again. "Does this mean...?"

"That the government has successfully created a mind-control drug? Yes," Katina answers his unfinished question. She pads over to Zero and picks up one of her gloved hands. "You are quite the handful, old friend."

Zero lets out a weak laugh. "I think an Agent has been watching me."

"I second your prediction," Katina says. "Every experiment requires observation, which means there must be an Agent still around to record the results of the drug. I've already sent some of my people to hunt them down."

"You're doing so many favors for me today," Zero croaks.

"Don't be ridiculous. Vasya and I owed you for a decade. Besides, the Syndicate and the Agency have become everyone's problem, so working through this with you will help us help more people in the future."

"*Svachee erd Kruluu zvaghess.*" Zero's Riyssolan flows like a calm stream meandering around pebbles. Rovis assumes it's some expression of gratitude. Katina only nods, and her emotionless demeanor is starting to get on Rovis's nerves.

"Is there a way to get it out of her?" he demands.

"Blood transfusion, of course." Katina tilts her head at Zero. "Your blood type is O-negative. Do you know anyone else with type O-negative?"

Rovis turns away, breathing harshly as he rubs his furrowed brows in frustration, and the floor starts moving like the sole of a ship. It never once occurred to him that their blood types are incompatible, even though they've known each other for over a decade. Now in a dire case of emergency, he can't help her. Zero has been through too much; he refuses to let her suffer any more today.

"I already checked the database of the Starcatchers I have around the area," he hears Katina saying. "None of them match."

He digs out his phone to contact Ofir and Avery. The Aconites may have a better chance for a match given their diversity, and it shouldn't take long to go through their database. If they find a match, Zero will just have to hold on until they get back to Dyvris.

Unless Tal hasn't left yet. Rovis taps the edge of his phone, thinking. If Tal's a match, that would be even better, because he's already here.

"Where are you keeping the Syndicates?" Rovis asks.

Katina turns to study him. "House across the street to the left, down in the basement."

Rovis strides out before she even finishes the last word. He ignores the stares from the Starcatchers as he stomps down the stairs and yanks open the front door with more force than necessary, his nanotech mask closing over his face. He should stop making such a ruckus in someone else's territory, really. But he's struggling to contain the fear and agitation and worry and rage from this night.

The other house is locked when he gets there, though he easily thrusts the door open after scrambling the configuration of the keyless pad with a standard Sleightist electromagnet.

Blue electricity sparks in his face as three blasters point at him.

Vasily comes up the stairs behind his Starcatchers and raises a brow at Rovis. He puts a hand on one of their shoulders, signaling them to stand down.

"You could have knocked," he says.

Rovis sets his jaw. "Is Lithium still downstairs?"

"He is."

Vasily steps aside for Rovis to pass through. He descends into a shadowy yellow haze, and the smell of blood slams into his nose. Whimpers echo along with his footsteps.

When he reaches the bottom, however, the sight before him makes him forget how to walk. His feet are frozen midstep, and even his fury over what the Purish did to Zero wavers in his burning chest.

Tal's hair has grown longer, curlier. The gray sleeves of his hoodie, stained with dried blood, are rolled up to his elbows, and coats of fresh blood replace his usual gloves. He holds up a gasping man by the neck with his metal arm, melted crimson dripping down the shiny silver. His other hand, equally slick with blood, grasps an electric whip that buzzes a bright p urple.

He looks like the king of demons, a force that even Drokklo fears.

And Rovis is weak for it.

Claws tighten around crunching bones. The man's head tilts at an un-natural angle, and blood oozes out of the hollows where the eyes have been carved out.

Tal tosses the corpse to the side, broken chains clanking on the concrete floor, in front of two other men, still hung by the wrists with their limbs intact and eyes attached to their heads. Though their horrified stares are so wide that Rovis thinks Tal won't need to carve their eyes out with a knife; they'd just pop right out themselves.

Lithium turns and looks right at him, and Rovis swears the wrath burns in his glare so brightly that it would set Rovis's heart ablaze if he were any closer.

"Scavenger," Tal greets him, voice rough.

Rovis's mouth goes dry.

He can only gaze at the blood splatters on Tal's face, the slight tilt to his lips as he studies Rovis as well, the lean muscles of his forearms, and the familiar posture that feigns carelessness yet screams danger at the same time.

"Would you like to take a turn?" Tal asks, the whip striking the ground before the men's feet, which causes more wails of terror to grace their ears.

As sweet as vengeance fused with a reunion with his right-hand man sounds, Rovis forces himself to remember why he came here.

"What's your blood type?"

Tal blinks, brows twitching in confusion. "A-positive. Why?"

Rovis lets out a frustrated sigh and looks away, clenching his jaw. Without another thought, he throws his arm to the side, and a double-edged sword made of pure energy and violet photons appears in his grip.

"Which one of you did it?" he hisses at the pathetic men. "Which one of you had the Agency's drug?"

His only response is weak whimpers.

The image of liquid metal embedded in Zero's leg flashes in his mind, and suddenly Rovis isn't so patient or merciful.

With three quick swings, Rovis slices through one of the legs by the ankle, knee, and hip.

That's for Rena, his livid mind whispers.

Agonized screams reverberate around the dark basement.

Blood pours out like a faucet at full capacity, splattering onto the grimy floor and spreads across the room. Bits of it land on Rovis's clothes, but he can't care less. He keeps his eyes on the Purish, demanding an answer, though he can feel Tal's intrigued stare burning into the side of his head. While he's seen Rovis's worst side before, it's a rare occurrence.

"Neither of us," the man, now down a leg and miraculously still conscious, screeches. "Neither of us had it! The Riyssolans already killed him."

"The Agency?" Tal asks Rovis. Then he lowers his voice. "Her?"

Rovis turns to see that his face has paled, and the electric whip is starting to slip out of his fingers. Tal must have put it together.

"She's alive," Rovis promises. "This is the newest version, and it won't kill her."

"But it's in her."

"Yes."

"Does it work?"

Rovis clenches his jaw. "I think so."

Tal's face shutters. His eyes harden again. His claws shoot out to dig into the last, untouched man's chest.

"Is there a cure?" Tal asks through the shrieks of pain, his Lithium smile stretching his lips unnaturally. He leans in and says into the man's ear. "You will answer truthfully, if you'd like to die with your heart in your body."

"I don't know! I don't know!"

"So you're useless," he growls, burying the claws even deeper.

"They just came up to us! Offered a lot of money!"

"Ah. You Purish and your money."

Tal sinks the metal all the way through the rib bones.

Rovis has to lean back to avoid getting assaulted in the face by a slimy heart.

It instead hits the wall with a thud and splats onto the floor, painting a growing cloud of red on the dirty concrete.

Rovis hears clamoring and harsh Riyssolan words before he sees another man shoved down the stairs, who falls right into the fresh pool blood, his face a breath away from the dismembered heart. He gasps and scrambles back, but Vasily kicks him onto his knees towards Rovis and Tal.

"I must request that you two refrain from killing this man at the pace that you're currently taking," Vasily says. "This is the Agent that is in charge of the experiment that our dear friend Zero has been forced into. I, for one, would like some answers before you render him useless."

"Where is the cure?" Tal takes a threatening step towards him.

"There isn't one," he rushes to say, shrinking back. "Why would we make one? The drug either kills them or controls them. We don't need to reverse it in either case."

"How do the nanoparticles work?" Vasily interrupts.

"It copies the way neurotransmitters work. The program ties a motive to emotional chemical levels so it would guide the way for the subject to reach our objective."

"And what is the objective of this current experiment?"

The Agent's wild eyes dart between Vasily and Rovis. When Tal strikes his whip again, the Agent flinches back and trembles.

"To..." He gulps and glances at Rovis again. "To kill him."

Rovis feels the color drain out of his face.

The Agency is making Zero kill him?

But he's still here.

"Well, clearly it didn't work," Tal says, voice flat.

"It was," the Agent insists, a sick gleam of excitement flashes in his eyes. "It was working. That annoying little bitch was close to doing it, but then she fought it off, no matter how much I increased the pain levels. I could see it. If I could just break her threshold, I can make her kill him."

"Turn it off," Tal demands.

"He destroyed the source terminal, and the particles will regenerate," Vasily says. "She can't get rid of it naturally. You'll have to put her through a blood transfusion."

Rovis seethes, "Do I get to kill him now?"

"Just one moment." Vasily stalks up to the man and grips his hair, pulling his head back so their eyes meet. "What was the last experiment you worked on?"

"Version 38.4." He tries to back away, but Vasily's hold is too strong.

"You made the drug."

"Yes."

"When was this?"

"I don't know. It was some Avyrian holiday."

"No," Rovis hears Tal say, as realization dawns on both of them.

"The Moon Festival?"

"Right!" The Agent perks up. "There were a lot of red paper light things."

"Are you aware that you killed thousands across all major cities?"

"Well..."

Teeth fly out of his mouth as Vasily walks away, hands held behind his back, as if he didn't punch the Agent to oblivion. The only sign of emotion from the boy is in his clenched fist, trembling just slightly.

Before he takes the first step up the stairs, he half-turns to Rovis and Tal. "Now you may fulfill your wishes, Aconites."

The Starcatchers leave, and it's just the two of them, with two terrified Purish men and two rotting corpses.

"You can do the honors," Tal suggests in Lasan, "And I'll look for some-one to help Zero. What's her blood type?"

"No," Rovis rejects, "you stay. I'm not in the mood for this. This is your specialty anyways. I already asked Ofir and Avery to search the database for someone in Dyvris with O-negative blood and hope to get her back in the city safely. You didn't see how much pain she was in before I came to look for you. I wish there was a closer option."

"Be glad you weren't there when I found her. Wait. O-negative?" Tal widens his eyes, dropping his hands to his sides.

Rovis straightens. "You know someone?"

Tal lowers his gaze and works his jaw.

"Talon," Rovis presses.

"My sister," Tal mumbles.

Rovis leans back. Saige was the whole reason why Tal left him and Zero. Rovis can't make Tal choose between the two girls, not again.

He shakes his head and turns to leave. "I'm calling Ofir."

"Wait."

Rovis hears two sharp sounds of a knife slicing through flesh. He turns to see both bodies crumple to the ground. Tal carelessly collects his dirty weapons and tucks them in his sleeves and pants without cleaning the blood off.

"That can't be sanitary," Rovis comments.

"I'll wash it off later." Tal grins, a ridiculous expression rather than a threat.

Rovis rolls his eyes and exits the basement, pulling out his phone to scroll for Ofir's number. Tal wraps his fingers around Rovis's wrist, an instinctive move.

They both freeze at the heat of the contact.

Rovis looks up from his wrist to Tal's face, resisting the urge to use his hold to pull him into his own arms.

Tal keeps his stare on his hand to avoid Rovis's stare.

"Let me ask my sister," Tal pushes through the moment.

"You don't need to." Rovis jerks his arm out of Tal's hold and presses the call button, bringing his phone up to his ear.

"Hello, Boss," Ofir picks up immediately. "I just saw your text."

"Give me a list of Aconites with type O-negative blood, now."

"Five minutes," they promise.

Without another word, Rovis hangs up. He looks over at Tal again to see him typing away at his phone. Switching into Lasan, he says, "She can't even leave that place. What exactly do you think you're contributing?"

Tal shoots Rovis an annoyed look. "Helping. If my sister finds out she can help Zero, and that I kept that from her, she'd skin me alive."

"You don't want her to do this," Rovis points out the obvious.

"You're right, I don't. But she would." Tal glances down, then flashes his phone at Rovis. "See? She said yes."

What Saige actually wrote was:

Of fucking course, why didn't you ask sooner?

"So do we have a candidate?" Katina interrupts, appearing out of nowhere. Her white and pink hair sways where it falls over her shoulders.

Tal jumps, and Rovis berates himself for not noticing her standing down the hallway in the shadows.

"Yes," Tal answers. "We just need to get Zero across Aurodus."

"That would not be advised," Katina says. "I attempted to give Zero a sedative due to the amount of pain she feels from resisting the algorithm, but the nanoparticles reacted terribly with the chemicals, which has only made matters worse. I apologize for my inexperience."

"I'd be concerned if you had experience with this fucked up drug," Tal mutters, and Rovis glares at him.

"Zero's immune system fought off the reactions, but she has significantly weakened from the energy it took. And she was already in poor shape from the torturing and then the surgery. I fear that transporting her through a city now would destabilize her even more. There is also the matter of equipment. I must perform the transfusion here in order to do it safely." Katina crosses her arms. "What is the issue with this sister of yours?"

"She can't be seen," Tal answers.

"That can be arranged." Katina pulls out a clear mask that can cover an entire face, and a small remote from a pocket inside of her thick black jacket with a hood. "You can configure what she'll look like. She should wear something that covers her hair and loosely hangs on her frame so her figure isn't too defined. Make sure you aren't being followed."

Tal takes the mask, studying the structure with a calculating look. He must be wondering why he didn't come up with something like it.

"I'll get her," Tal promises Rovis.

They watch him leave, the filtration helmet closing over his head as the door shuts. Rovis ignores the pang of Tal walking away from him again, knowing that this is what's necessary.

Katina looks at Rovis. "What would you like to do now, Scavenger?"

"I'll stay with Zero."

She tilts her head. "That is unwise. Vasya has informed me that the Agency set Zero's objective to killing you."

"She won't do it," Rovis asserts. "She's in pain either way because she's not going to kill me. I'd rather be there with her."

"The proximity gives her access to completing the job."

"Are you underestimating my strength? Or are you underestimating Zero's pain tolerance?"

"Your confidence is strange," Katina remarks. "But this is not my business. Do as you wish, Scavenger."

Rovis nods at her, before crossing the street to return to Zero.

Back in the room, her face is contorted with pain, cold sweat dripping from her face, curled up against the window, but she still seems aware of her surroundings.

"You should stay away from me," she grits out when she registers his presence.

"I think I can take you," Rovis responds dryly.

Zero huffs. "Are you calling me weak?"

"Never." He sits down in the chair again. "But I am a Reaper, and you're not."

She hums.

"Is there anything I can do?" Rovis asks softly.

"I don't know. Read the news, or something."

"Okay." He grimaces at the odd request, but he swipes through his watch anyways. "Let's see."

The news, however, is more of a chaotic mess than it has ever been.

TOULLIFUKA FIGHTS OFF RIYSSOLAN INVASION ATTEMPT

BARREN COUNTRY REVEALS UNPARALLELED TECHNOLO-
GY?

CRYSTAL CAVES HIDDEN BENEATH SURFACE OF TOULLIFU-
KA

TOULLIFUKA ENDS BLOCKADE ON AVYRIA
RIYSSOLAN-TOULLISH TREATY SIGNED
TWO UNLIKELY COUNTRIES TO JOIN FORCES AGAINST
PURELAND

"Um," Rovis starts. His brows twitch at the headache that the headlines are giving him, and he decides that Zero doesn't need any more of that. "How about a book?"

Zero, ever so attuned to Rovis, frowns and turns her head to squint at him. "What's happened?"

"I'll tell you later," he promises.

"What?" She attempts to sit up. "How bad is it? Are we at war?"

"No." Rovis rushes to push Zero back down. "We're safe, for now. I'm not lying. There are just some world politics you might want to process later, when your mind isn't being torn apart by the Agency."

She coughs, "Rude."

Rovis snorts, looking back down to search for books to read to her. He skips all the romance recommendations, skims the fantasy titles, then settles on an Avyrian folklore. Zero closes her eyes as he begins reading, speaking about a supernatural world of martial arts and shapeshifting foxes.

"I didn't know how to tell you," Zero says unexpectedly, cutting him off mid-sentence hours later.

"Tell me what?"

"That I was... That something wasn't right in my head. I guessed that it was the Agency's drug only a moment before Katya came to say so."

"Okay," Rovis says, leaning forward to wipe off the beads of sweat on her face with his sleeve.

"I don't know how— How am I supposed to—" Zero sighs, brows creased. She presses her knuckles against her forehead. "I never—"

"It's okay," he says softly.

"I almost stabbed you," Zero says, blunt and void of emotion.

Rovis hides his flinch by reaching up to rub the golden hoop at his ear. He hardly believed the Agent when he claimed that he successfully turned Zero against Rovis. Hearing from Zero herself is like getting doused in cold water.

"How was I supposed to say that?" she rasps, tilting her head to finally meet his eyes.

My request, Rovis remembers. *To tell me the truth when something's wrong.*

Realization hits him slowly, like an explosion under water. He's so used to Zero shoving him away that he can't fathom the meaning behind her words.

She's trying, even though it hurts. For the first time in five years, she's listening to him. Hope stirs in his chest like a hibernating animal waking up when the ice starts to melt. Rovis knows that she's tired, that she's giving up control to trust him again, even just a little bit.

"Just like that was fine," he answers and tucks a strand of hair behind her ear. "Don't worry about it too much. I've only just asked that of you a couple hours ago; of course it's hard for you. Don't forget that you have an experimental drug in you right now."

But then Rovis frowns, thinking. What does it mean, now that the government has successfully created a drug that can manipulate people into carrying out tasks that they give them? What will happen now? Will they dump it in their water sources? Contaminate their food? Release it into the air they breathe?

"Your brain is too loud," Zero complains, voice weak.

"That's rich, coming from you," Rovis retorts, though he dutifully clears away his worries about the drug and returns his attention to the book.

She sighs. "I don't like that you can read me."

"Well, now you know how everyone else feels. There's a reason why people are more scared of the Heartless than, say, Sleightists."

"I'm not technically a Heartless anymore."

"And you never should have been. You were way too young. You still are. I wish you never joined the organization." Rovis clenches his jaw. "But there's no use wishing to change the past. My point is that it's only fair that someone can understand you when you can understand practically everyone else. And you may not be a Heartless, but the Ace of Crowns will definitely be haunting the Damned for at least a century."

"If the planet survives until then," Zero mutters.

"What do you want to do when we get back?" Rovis asks.

"I don't know. What do you want me to do?"

"It's up to you," Rovis says. "You can work whatever you want. I'd prefer if you don't go back out into the field, but even Sleightist is better than Heartless. Actually, you don't even have to work. It's not real work, and we both have enough money."

She says nothing, so Rovis goes back to reading the book out loud.

After a few chapters, he stops, thinking that Zero has fallen asleep, but she stares at the ceiling as if it held all the answers to the universe's mysteries.

"Rovis," Zero starts, but she hesitates.

He watches her struggle with words. For a moment, she looks as though she hasn't slept in years. The sight is a pinch to his heart, when he's the one who watched her grow up and start carrying the weight of the world on her shoulders. Rovis wishes Zero would stop being this 'Zero' that she insisted on becoming when she joined the Damned, and come back to him. He wishes she'd let him in and let him help. He just wishes all her suffering would cease.

"What is it?" he prods, when minutes pass by.

Zero frowns. Her brows furrow with either pain or confusion. Rovis waits for her to gather her thoughts.

"Tal's coming back," she tells him.

Rovis stills. He often forgets that Zero has wicked hearing abilities. It's only a small part of why she makes such a great spy and information gatherer for the Aconites.

"And?" he asks.

"He brought someone. Someone smaller than him." More shifting beneath the blanket. "But not one of the Starcatchers."

"I forgot to tell you." Rovis takes her hand. "We're going to get that thing out of you soon. Tal found someone to give you blood."

"Who?"

He gazes at Zero steadily without speaking, hoping she'd hear the answer from what he can't say. And she's smart, so of course she does, despite having been thoroughly beaten up by the Purish and put through several wringers tonight.

"No," she answers, disbelieving. Her cloudy eyes blink widely at him. "Is it safe for her to come out here?"

"Your friend Katina found a way to make it happen."

"I didn't think I'd see her again." She squeezes his hand. "Rovis, you should go."

Rovis shakes his head. "I'm not going anywhere."

"No, there's something else I haven't told you." Zero pauses, gathering her thoughts. When he waits patiently, instead of scolding her like he usually does, she says, "It hurts more when you're closer."

His heart drops. Rovis stumbles out of the chair and staggers back. "What?"

"I don't know how it works, but I'm guessing it's to motivate the victim into completing their mission. It's fine. I wanted you to stay."

"But you're in so much more pain because of it," he points out, nonplussed.

"I wanted you to stay," Zero repeats, slower this time.

Rovis lets those words sink in. Taking a few more steps back, he nods. He has to respect the amount of vulnerability she's showing him, after everything she's been through with the Purish. She's allowing herself to lean on him again, like when they were younger, just for tonight.

He can trust Katina to do the blood transfusion, and he doesn't even need to question the fact that Tal would make sure everything works out.

But right now, he needs to go for a drive.

6

Almost

Tal frowns in confusion when Rovis hurries out of the room Zero's staying in.

"Where are you going?" he calls after him.

Rovis pauses long enough to say, "Call me when it's done."

Then he disappears down the stairs.

"Is this really the way you two communicate with each other?" Saige asks, unimpressed.

Her short, white hair swings beneath the oversized hood as she comes to a stop in front of the shut door, the large black cloak engulfing her small frame. With the rest of her body covered in baggy pants and a turtleneck top, Tal decided to set the mask as pale as possible. In this country, the lighter the skin color, the safer.

"What about it?" Tal says.

Saige turns to check if he's serious, then snorts. "No wonder you haven't slept together yet."

Tal's jaw drops, affronted. "*Koneighxta.*"

"What?" She shrugs innocently. "So do I get to take off the mask when we go in or not? I would like my reunion with Zero to happen with my real face. It has been years."

Sighing, Tal crosses his arms and taps his fingers.

This entire operation is a huge risk for Saige already. Even if Tal has checked if they were being followed a million times, taken different routes between cities every time, and hacked into all camera feeds in the area, it's never one-hundred-percent foolproof. She hasn't left that secret base since she faked her death. Leaving was dangerous enough; showing her face outside, where anyone might walk in, or where secret cameras that N.A.D.E. can't detect might be watching, can be a costly mistake.

And he hates that she has to give blood. She probably has fifteen drops of blood in her body at most. Why couldn't it have been Tal?

But he knows what needs to be done. After the long, awful night Zero has been having, he can't possibly draw it out longer because of his over-protective instincts for Saige. Even though his relationship with Saige seems fine, he feels like he's on thin ice. If he meddles with her friendships, the ice will crack without a doubt. The younger generation seems to always find a way to know everything, too, so keeping Zero away from Saige was never an option.

Of course, there's also Rovis.

The man is rightfully cross with Tal. He left things on bad terms when he set out to look for Saige. So when Rovis rejected his help earlier, he had no right to be surprised. But after years of working side by side, that was the first time it's ever happened. And Tal does not want to get used that feeling. He's on the outside now, and he despises it. Tal hopes, just maybe, that taking a step back and letting Saige help Zero would chip away at the wall between him and Rovis.

"Fine," Tal eventually answers. "But let me make sure it's safe first."

Saige nods and lets him enter first. He shuts the blinds to cut off the light from the rising sun, scans for cameras, and deactivates the two bugs he finds. Zero attempts to sit up, face as white as a sheet.

"It's alright," Tal says. "Do you trust me?"

She watches him, squinting through the pain. Feeling self-conscious, Tal touches his face, but thanks to Saige, he remembered to wash off all the blood and change into a clean crimson button-up before returning.

"Do you trust me?" he asks again.

"What are you on about?" Zero says weakly, brows knitted. "I know who she is."

"Oh. Well, then." Tal gestures at Saige, who steps into the room, and he shuts the door behind her, lingering to stand guard.

His sister slowly approaches Zero. The mask detaches from her face, and she peels it off when she's standing in front of her old friend.

Zero's chapped lips twitch, an imitation of a small smile.

She glances at Tal before staring at Saige again, yet no words come out of her mouth. Even when her physical and mental wellbeing are compromised, she's perceptive enough to know not to risk uttering Saige's name.

Saige holds out a hand.

Zero grabs it and tugs Saige down to sit next to her, the two girls facing each other. Saige gently puts a hand on Zero's neck and presses her lips firmly on her cheek. Zero pulls Saige again, and they collapse into a tight hug.

Tal stands there, watching them, and suddenly understanding how uncomfortable it is to be a third wheel.

He doesn't look away though. Not just because he's guarding them, but also because this is the happiest he's seen either of them.

"It's been so long," Zero murmurs.

"I know."

She pulls back to narrow her eyes at Saige. "Don't fucking do that again."

Saige laughs softly. "Which part? The disappearing act or the fake death?"

"What do you think?" Zero retorts.

Saige pouts at her, playing with Zero's fingers, as though they can't even bear to separate their hands. The girls are looking at each other like they're memorizing everything, afraid that the end of the world will be tomorrow, and that they'll never get a chance again.

At that point, Tal's had enough.

He tears his gaze away from them and stares at the floor, studying the patterns on the carpet. He almost envies their soft reunion. Tal, on the other hand, was choking a man to death when Rovis first saw him again after months of ghosting on Tal's part.

A knock on the door snatches his attention.

Tal shoots Saige a warning glance, and she dutifully puts the mask back on. When she looks absolutely nothing like herself, he cracks open the door.

"Is everyone ready?" Katina asks with her characteristic apathetic tone.

Tal steps aside, allowing her through. Katina tweaks the settings on another machine in the room. Tal briefly wonders exactly how much more technologically advanced the Starcatchers are compared to the Aconites, to the rest of the Damned, and what their bases look like if their safe houses are this equipped.

"Arms," Katina says.

Saige takes off her cloak, while Zero hesitates before she pulls off one sleeve of Tal's jacket. Goosebumps run over her arm from the lost layer, but she doesn't twitch at the drop in warmth. Saige's gaze catches on the white veins wrapping up Zero's arms and gasps before she can help it. Katina only looks over for a moment, likely just to check nothing new has come up with Zero's condition, then goes back to work. Saige looks back and forth between Zero and Tal with wide eyes, bewildered.

When she settles on a staring contest with Zero, all she receives is a head shake.

Saige deflates. She takes out the extra jacket Tal told her to pack from the inside of her cloak and sets it on Zero's lap. She chides, "You are not my favorite person right now. At least my secret was good news."

"Tell me about it," Tal grumbles.

Rovis would never forgive Tal if he finds out that Zero's dying, that Tal kept it from him, and that even Saige knew before him. Not to mention the vial of aconitine in his possession at the moment. This girl is not giving him a break.

And the odds of Zero actually making the right decision is lower than that of the planet magically cooling down, in spite of all the human activities burning it up like an insatiable beast.

Maybe Tal should just tell Rovis. And deal with Zero's cold shoulder afterwards, but the truth will be out. Or, at least, find a way to pressure Zero into talking to Rovis. Because, surely, this isn't sustainable.

Zero jerks her gaze over to Tal, and he freezes, caught guilty in his thoughts. Her focus falters for a moment, and Tal fights the urge to reach out to her as she works through another wave of pain, grinding her teeth. When her jaw relaxes and she regains clarity, she rasps in Lasan, "I know what you're thinking. I'm working on it. Don't force my hand, Tal. *Biv'ye nu wanotai.*"

His breath catches. The Toullish phrase is only ever used by Rovis and Zero for each other. He understands it more than any other outsider. He values it in his heart as much as they do, because they gave the words a new level of meaning that encompasses everything they've been through, whether together or separately.

Tal swallows down the lump in his throat, fingers curling into fists. Betraying her request now would be disregarding all of that. It's the same as telling Zero her words mean nothing to him.

"Fine," he yields, the word so soft that he can barely hear himself. "I won't."

Katina pulls the bed closer to the bay window. "Mystery girl, help Zero onto the bed. I'm going to need room to draw out the nanoparticles. Zero, I apologize that you will need to stay awake for this."

Zero waves a dismissing hand, leaning against Saige as they trudge across the small distance to the bed. "I'd rather stay awake than feel my blood cells hosting a chemical war against an incompatible sedative in my body."

"Not funny," Saige mutters, though her lips twitch fondly.

"Lithium," Katina continues. "Do refrain from triggering any acute emotional responses from either of them."

He scowls and glares, but he doesn't verbally protest.

The girls settle down side by side, Zero in the bed and propped up by pillows, Saige on the bay window with a comfortable amount of cushions. Katina wipes their arms with disinfectants, and the needles pierce through their skin. Saige's blood goes into a glass ball, and the sight of it makes Tal want to faint. A tube on the top of the glass sphere sucks it into another tube that goes into Zero, to keep her blood level even. In her other arm, the tube goes into an almost identical sphere, but it's much larger, and there's a different plating at the top.

Tiny specks begin to gather at the top of the second sphere, as the blood level rises at the bottom. Tal narrows his eyes, taking a step closer to study the tiny particles. Katina keeps a gentle hand on Zero's arm as she studies multiple screens.

"Are those dots the Agency's drug?" Tal asks.

"Yes." Katina frowns at one of the screens. "There are quite a lot of them. The regeneration process must have already begun. If we weren't doing this, I suspect that this could have clogged her arteries, because it seems that the Agent overestimated her metabolism rate."

Almost a third of the sphere is covered in nanoparticles.

Tal realizes he's holding his breath, so he looks away and recollects himself. In stark contrast, Saige and Zero start gossiping about people they went to school with. Unsurprisingly, there were a lot of people that Zero disliked, which overlapped with a lot of people that Saige liked. Then they talk about books they've read since they last saw each other, discussing their favorite tropes and 'unpopular opinions,' whatever that is.

He wonders what it would have been like if they could have a regular life like Purish kids do.

A tinge of inexplicable grief pinches his chest.

If Tal's parents never kicked him out after he got ambushed, he would have stayed in school with Saige. And if they actually accepted and treated him as a human individual, rather than an extension of them to use and exploit, he would have had a real relationship with his sister. He would have met Zero under very different circumstances, void of crime and depravity. She would have been his sister's friend who liked to come over to their apartment sometimes to read books together. He probably would have knocked on Saige's door to remind them to do homework. Maybe he would have cooked dinner for them after school, too.

And maybe Tal would have met Rovis. From pieces of information he's gathered from cryptic conversations, he guesses that Rovis was living near Zero, and that they were close. Maybe he would have met him through Zero. Or maybe they would have eventually run into each other in high school.

It's a thought, a fantasy he's never allowed himself to indulge in. It's like a black hole of temptation; once he crosses the event horizon, he wouldn't even know he's pulled in for eternity, trapped in the realm of unreality.

Because he knows it's selfish, to wonder if Rovis would return his feelings in a world where Griffin is still alive.

In every alternate universe, Tal thinks, *I would have fallen for him.*

Tal hasn't told Rovis that he's also from Lime Gateway, because he scarcely has any good memories of that place. They were in different social circles, so they never met. While Purish teenagers avoided Rovis and his crew of wrestlers in the hallways, Tal avoided everyone else by hiding in the science wing. While Rovis and his friends were heavily built, unapologetic, and never alone, Tal was scrawny, antisocial, and always trying to keep his head down.

Perhaps Tal should just appreciate the fact that he did meet Rovis in this universe.

Suddenly his heart aches a thousand times worse.

How could he waste this life running away from the best thing that's ever happened to him? Even if he can't bring himself to tell Rovis the truth, how can he take what they already have for granted?

His palms begin to sweat as his heart races.

He needs to talk to Rovis.

"It's done," Katina's announcement snaps him out of his thoughts.

A glance at his watch tells him that the transfusion only took half an hour.

She closes up the punctures from the needles with an ordinary medical spider bot, and Vasily comes in with water and more food. Saige looks fine but tired; Zero's face is pale, but the space between her brows has smoothed out.

"Water first," Katina orders. "Then eat, then sleep."

Tal walks up to the space between Saige and Zero, then takes each of their hands.

"How are we feeling?"

Saige gives him a sleepy thumbs-up.

Zero nods. "No harrowing urges to commit murder without reason."

Tal snorts at her choice for a dramatic answer. "Good. I'll call Rovis."

He leaves, shutting the door quietly behind him, and pulls out his phone. His steps falter on the front porch when Rovis's contact profile glares up at him. Rovis doesn't like having pictures taken of him — though it's unavoidable as the Scavenger and king of Dyvris — so the profile photo is one of Rovis's paintings. It's a realistic piece, focusing on a wolfsbane flower, and other purple flowers fill in the background, such as sages and salvias.

A memory of Zero handing him a bundle of sages grown in her apartment in the Tower floats into his mind.

Tal sighs at the realization, dragging a hand down his face. The secret was laid out in the open, right in front of him. He doubts Zero was trying to communicate her secret to him, but he knows she chose those flowers deliberately. How did he never even suspect that Zero knew about Saige? She is a spy, after all.

Sometimes, he resents the fact that his genius is only limited to lines of code and building new technology. If he'd known the puzzle pieces were in his hands, he'd have put it together in a second. So much of the pain between him and Zero, and between him and Rovis, could have been spared under different circumstances. If he'd been smarter, he would've found out the truth without forcing Zero to break her promise.

Shaking his head, Tal hits the call button before his thoughts can spiral even more.

"Tal," Rovis answers immediately.

Tal flinches at the sound of Rovis saying his name again. He takes a deep breath and says, "They finished. It was successful."

"I'll head back now."

Rovis hangs up without another word, and Tal drops his phone from his ear, staring at the screen. His legs are begging him to run before Rovis comes back and before Zero wakes up, but he decides to stay outside. He abruptly realizes he forgot to activate the filtration helmet. Yet none of the Starcatchers wear theirs around this area, now that he thinks about it. Frowning, he switches the mode of his contacts to infrared, and he discovers that this whole neighborhood has a shield of some sort that rejects methane and hydrogen sulfide. They're essentially in a protective bubble that can somehow hold its shape without destabilizing.

"How are the Riyssolans so far ahead of us?" Tal grumbles.

He sits down on the steps and tries to figure out the engineering of it to pass time, until Rovis eventually pulls up on the driveway.

Rovis approaches Tal, though he hesitates once he's standing right in front of Tal.

"They're still upstairs," Tal says.

After a moment with a searching look, Rovis nods and steps past Tal and into the house. When the door shuts again, Tal drops his head into his hands.

"Stars, tell me what to say to him," he mutters.

Tal debates with himself, trying to come up with excuses to speak to Rovis. He does not do apologies, but he might start with one for leaving Rovis without a goodbye and then ghosting all of his calls. Or should he begin with reasons why Rovis is important to him, to set the ground?

The door opens behind Tal again. He recognizes the footsteps, so he doesn't need to turn around or draw a weapon. When Rovis settles down next to him, Tal tilts his head back to gaze at the faint stars at the dawn of a new day.

"They're both asleep now," Rovis breaks the silence, his helmet also deactivated, showing his face.

"I'm surprised you left Zero's side earlier," Tal remarks.

Rovis heaves a sigh. "She very belatedly revealed to me that the pain was worse the closer I was to her."

"That, I'm not surprised about."

A soft amused huff turns Tal's head, but Rovis's tired expression causes the words to crawl back down Tal's throat.

Eventually, Rovis speaks softly, voice thick with something Tal can't name.

"Why did you never answer?"

Tal looks down, picking at the torn leather of his boots.

Because the sound of your voice would have me running right back to you, he wants to say. *Because I couldn't bear the consequences of my actions.*

But what comes out of his mouth is, "You would have texted if it was an emergency."

Rovis works his jaw. Then, "So our partnership has been strictly business."

"No," Tal denies quickly. "I..."

Shit. He can translate actions to programming languages, but he can't translate his own heart into words. He should add that as a function for N.A.D.E., so he'll never say the wrong thing again.

When he fails to finish his sentence, too busy panicking, Rovis shakes his head. "No need to spin it around, Tal. I misinterpreted things between us; that's on me. Turns out, we're not even friends."

"Rovis," Tal starts, reaching for his gloved hand without thinking.

They both freeze, with Tal's fingers a hair away from Rovis's wrist.

Their erratic breaths fill in the tense pause.

"It was also because," Tal forces himself to say, softly, terrified of breaking the fragile threads keeping them together, "you'd be the reason I leave my sister again."

"What?" Rovis stares at him, voice equally hushed.

Tal immediately regrets the admission. But he can't run again, not this time. Despite the pounding of his heart and the heat creeping up his neck, he allows the words to come out, to say things that he's buried for almost five years.

"You have changed me, Rovis Bozyd-Wei." Tal squeezes his hand, with purpose this time. "For better, or for worse. It's hard to say when we live in the world of the Damned. You know how sometimes, when you're surrounded by forgettable faces in a crowd, you still feel lonely? That's what it's been like for me all my life, at home, at school. Levi was the first person to make me feel like I could be someone. That's why he was the only person I could be around when I became an Aconite. But then you came along. You made me feel like I was already someone, that I was already enough, even without the things I could build or do for someone."

Rovis's eyes shine a soft brown under the first sun rays.

"Of course I wanted to come back," Tal confesses. "Especially after leaving like that. I know I hurt you, Rov. But I couldn't do that to my sister, not again. You understand that, don't you?"

"Yes," Rovis says. "I do. More than you know."

A sad smile tugs at Tal's lips. "Then don't stay angry at me forever, okay?"

Rovis smirks, just a little. "How could I, when you give me that sad kitten face?"

"Are you calling me a clingy fur ball that only wants to cuddle you when it wants food?" Tal demands, affronted.

A soft laugh escapes Rovis's lips, and it breaks through the sorrowful expression like a ray of sunlight dispelling a ceiling of dark clouds.

"I don't know," he teases. "You did spam the Clockworks channel with huge lists of recipes that you approve of."

Tal makes an offended noise. "It was a very important change to make. Food at the mansion was abysmal when Quade was in power."

"Oh, so that's why you helped me kill him."

"Well," Tal copies the sly look on Rovis's face, "it was mostly the sad puppy eyes."

He barks out a laugh when Rovis punches him in the arm and protests, "I do not have sad puppy eyes. You're just saying that to get back at me."

"I am not." Tal shoves him back.

Rovis grins.

And he is so beautiful it hurts.

Tal knows he's staring, but this time, he doesn't stop.

Rovis's smile fades as he gazes back at Tal, too.

The air is cold, so cold that Tal's convinced that time froze with the two of them. Nothing around them breathes, remaining perfectly still like a vintage photograph. Tal exhales, fogging up the space between them. The mist drifts up and disappears in front of Rovis's eyes.

Those warm eyes are Tal's home, and all the anxious nerves in his body drift to a calmness, like leaves falling onto solid ground during autumn.

He doesn't know who starts to lean in first, but the next time he blinks, Tal can count the number of eyelashes fanning out from Rovis's lids.

Their lips are only a breath apart.

Tal feels the heat from Rovis's breath, and it burns in his head, his chest, his soul, like the hellfire in the depths of Drokklo's palace.

He's been waiting for this for so long; he seems to have forgotten how badly he wanted it.

Yet neither of them closes the distance.

Neither of them *can*.

"Are we ever going to talk about this?" Rovis whispers, coming to the same conclusion. He doesn't shift away, and his gaze is glued to Tal's lips.

Tal inclines his head and sighs, the movement blowing into Rovis's chin. Carefully, he wraps a hand around the back of Rovis's neck and presses their foreheads together.

"I thought you were aromantic for the longest time," Tal mutters into the insignificant yet heavy space between them.

"I'm demi," Rovis says. A hand settles above Tal's hip, his thumb brushing over the fabric again and again. "Once I'm here, there's no going back."

"I know I'm not Griffin, but…"

"I want you for you, Tal. I am definitely not Levi."

"I didn't—" Tal exhales sharply, his eyes squeezed shut. He tries again, and he chokes out, "I loved him, but not like this. He was my closest friend, who knew me better than I know myself. He was my teenage sweetheart, and we shared years of stupidity, saturated sun, and sangria. But you made me weak from the beginning, from the moment I saw you. It has always been you, Rov, since the day we met."

"But—"

"Levi will always be in my heart. His dying wish was for me to tell you my truth, and now I have."

Rovis sighs, pained. "He was a really good friend. I wish I spent more time with him."

"Who doesn't?" Tal's fingers twitched. His eyes open, glazed over with memories. "He wanted me to move on. He told me that you reciprocated, and he wanted us to try this. I didn't believe him, but now I do."

Rovis doesn't say anything for a moment. Then he says, "Why are we stuck?"

"You know why."

Rovis doesn't say anything, letting the words sink in. They stay like that for a several heartbeats, breathing and existing, as the sun rises after a sleepless night, after months of agonizing radio silence.

The warmth leaves Tal's hip, and Rovis instead cups Tal's face, shifting up to press a chaste kiss on Tal's forehead.

"Your sister," Rovis says.

"Yours, too," Tal adds.

Rovis does not deny it. Zero is a sister to him. Tal sees it in the way he always runs after her, tries to protect her, and fights to reach her through her damaged mind.

"We can't have this," Rovis sighs. "Not yet."

"It's not a 'never.' I just need to work things out with my sister first. She still hasn't talked to me about what happened after I left, and I have a feeling she's not quite as okay with seeing me again as she's pretending to be. You need to stop holding back with Zero. You are so close to getting through to her, I know it. I saw a shift in her after you came by. We just have to wish upon the stars that nothing sets her back again."

"I know," Rovis says. "You're right. You're always right, Tal."

"I want this," Tal says firmly, "as much as you do. But you and I both know we'd never rest, as long as things stay this messy in our lives, and we wouldn't be giving us a proper chance."

Rovis nods, staring across the street, past the gloomy houses and into the horizon. The crimson sky is starting to fade to ginger where the sun peeks out between skyscrapers, like a cold, distant fire. Tal knows what he's going to paint next.

"Family first." Tal nudges him. "Us next. We'll be right here."

Rovis turns to look at him, and Tal's surprised to see assessing eyes burning into him. But Rovis only says, "Truth for truth. Did you ever think about me?"

"Rovis," Tal says, voice pained. The man went straight for the kill, didn't he? Tal's tongue is glued to the bottom of his mouth, and his chest heaves with a shaky sigh. When he can finally speak, his voice drops low as he switches to Lasan, "Of course I thought about you. All of the inventions I created in that base were meant for you. I wanted to protect you and keep you safe, even though I was so far from you, even though that was a choice I made. Being away from you has been a nightmare I can't wake up from. So yes, I thought about you. I never stopped thinking about you. I go to sleep every night with your name imprisoned behind my clenched teeth because I have to suffer the consequences of my own actions."

Rovis burns his stare into him, millions of emotions flashing through his brown eyes. His expression says a thousand things, but all that comes out of his mouth is, "Damn."

Tal scoffs and looks away. "Fuck you. Your turn: Why did you want to find me so badly? I expect an answer at least as sappy as mine, preferably more."

"Alright," Rovis says, clearly amused by the challenge. He thinks for a moment, then leans in with his answer in Lasan as well. "I was always chasing you in my dreams. You are a welcome ghost in my subconsciousness. Sometimes I dreamt that you never left, and sometimes you ran away from me. I wake up every morning with your voice echoing in my head, before I remember my own name, where I am, what world I live in. Because the first thing I know when I open my eyes is that you left without saying goodbye, and your ghost has been hovering around me since then. It was like the whole universe was calling me to find you."

Tal's eyes glisten with affection. He echoes, softly, "Damn, okay. I missed you, too."

Rovis laughs then, satisfied, and offers a hand. Tal takes it and threads their fingers together. They watch the sun emerge above the buildings of Ferrisque, the sky now a cozy orange.

"I'm sorry for what I said, before I left," Tal adds.

"I know," Rovis answers softly.

The door creaks open behind them. Tal turns to see Saige poking her head out the door.

"You're awake." He frowns at his watch. "It's only been a few hours."

She gives him a small smile. "Can't sleep."

Rovis stands, stretching out his legs. He stifles a yawn and says, "Come sit next to your brother. I'm going to make some breakfast and check on Zero."

"She's still asleep," Saige says. "We don't know how long she'll be out, after what happened."

"The longer she sleeps, the better." Rovis cracks a few stiff joints. "I'll stay with her for however much time that is."

Saige smiles, and so does Tal.

"What?" Rovis furrows his brows at their expressions.

"You're like a golden retriever," Saige answers cheerfully, beaming.

Rovis grimaces at the comment and goes back into the house. Tal laughs after him and turns back to Saige, eyes glinting with amusement.

"You've done it," he says. "You embarrassed the Scavenger of Dyvris."

"*You've* done it," Saige counters. "Did you kiss?"

"Stars and bloody cities," Tal mutters, looking back at the horizon and away from his annoying little sister, propping his elbows on top of his knees.

"Well, did you?" she asks excitedly, hopping down next to him.

"*No*," Tal growls.

Saige laughs. "Don't worry, you'll get there."

Tal ruffles her hair aggressively, messing up the white strands so much that it almost looks like a cloud when she leans away, doubled over with laughter. Then she tries to do the same to Tal, but he bats her arm to the side. With another chuckle, Saige also turns to watch the horizon, attempting to rearrange her hair.

After a while, she sighs, the brilliant smile waning.

"I didn't know if you'd find me," Saige says. "But I feel silly to have doubted, seeing the way you ran after Zero the moment you realized she was in danger."

"That was about how I reacted when I saw your arrest on the news. And once I got your message, of course I was going to come looking for you." Tal slings an arm around her shoulders. "You're my sister."

Saige hums, distracted by her thoughts.

"And do you want to know a secret?" Tal quiets his voice, leaning slightly forward.

She shrugs, noncommittal.

"We almost did."

It takes her a second to figure out that he's talking about him and Rovis. When she does, she turns her mischievous grin and sparkling eyes on him.

Tal eventually gives in and smiles, too, shaking his head.

7

Hour of Winter

The sky is dark when Zero wakes up. Shades of crimson bleed though the smog, an illusory blanket of the night.

She pushes herself up to sitting and rubs her eyes. Judging by how rested she feels compared to usual, she's slept through at least a whole day.

Rolling her shoulders, she pads across the room in her heavy boots, taking her time to get used to the prosthetics. The cool metal of the structure gives her shivers, but it gives her no pain, only artificial support.

"Vasya," Zero calls softly when she cracks open the door.

The Riyssolan boy stops his pacing in the hallway and turns, his eyes scanning her form.

"It's been a day," he confirms. Then he tilts his head toward the stairs. "Would you like to eat?"

Vasya isn't really asking, so she doesn't answer, letting him lead her downstairs. If she said no, he would have started monologuing in detail about reasons why she should, going into extreme statistical detail about nutrients and energy conversion, with his Riyssolan formality to bore her into eating food.

"Katya?" she asks, cautiously putting her weight on her left leg with every other step, gripping the handrail with one hand.

He offers her an arm from her other side, which she takes. Vasya answers, "Errand."

That can mean anything from destroying another Purity Syndicate base to going out for a cup of coffee, so Zero only nods and focuses on getting down the stairs without falling. The ground floor glows with soft hues of blue and pink, and Zero lets go of Vasya with a squeeze when they reach the kitchen. A Starcatcher sits on the island counter, swinging their legs. They chomp on a carrot and watch Zero like a hawk as soon as she enters.

"Ace of Crowns," they drawl.

"Behave," Vasya scolds as he pulls open the fridge. He passes over a carton of eggs and a bag of tomatoes, which Zero accepts without a word.

"You've more than repaid your debt," the Starcatcher protests. "She is not one of us. Your hospitality is unwarranted and excessive."

"Lyosha," Vasya says harshly.

The nickname triggers a memory. Zero's mind clicks as Enyo's pensive expression, guard let down as she stares at an old photograph, flashes before her eyes. As Zero plucks a couple of eggs out of the carton, she considers the Starcatcher, who has tousled blond hair and piercing brown eyes. She can count up to twenty-eight weapons on them, and that's just where she can see them. They bicker with Vasya, unaware of Zero's observation.

She feels the tug of a smirk on her face.

"Alexei Federov."

Both Starcatchers freeze. Vasya turns and studies her with calculating eyes, while Alexei drops their nonchalant act and glares at Zero with distrust. They look much older than in the picture, but Zero sees the resemblance.

"How do you know my name?" Alexei scowls.

Zero shrugs, turning to crack the eggs against the edge of a bowl. "I know lots of people."

"You must be quite familiar with a Riyssolan, if you recognized me by a nickname."

"I'm friends with the twins."

"We haven't seen you in four years," Vasya interjects, "and we barely speak for more than ten minutes at a time, other than our first meeting."

Zero slants him a look. He's staring at her with a deep frown, evidently displeased. She raises a brow, as she finishes beating the eggs. Zero and Vasya may be acquainted, but they both prioritize their own organizations. If he also wants to know how she got information on one of his people, then she supposes there's no point in deliberately answering the question with an irrelevant answer. Zero looks back to the bowl in front of her and sprinkles salt over the gold liquid.

"Alexei, have you ever been to Loveias?" She switches to Riyssolan, revealing her fluency. She can feel the startled reactions from them as she oils the pan and pours the beaten eggs into it. "It's a beautiful city. I highly recommend visiting."

The confusion is palpable in the wall of silence behind her.

Then she feels the atmosphere shift, a click of understanding.

"Impossible," Alexei hisses.

Zero focuses on finishing her omelet instead of responding. She moves back and forth between the fridge and the stove to add ingredients, enjoying Alexei's silent fuming behind her when he's no doubt spiraling from his memories of the past, of his dead family. When she scoops her cooked breakfast — or dinner — onto a plate, she looks up.

The look in Alexei's eyes is the same one Saige has when Tal comes up in a conversation, and Zero suspects the same that she herself has when it comes to Rovis.

"Think about it. No one has ever heard of the Ace of Crowns until two years ago," Zero says, the Riyssolan words flowing out like a relentless river. "Out of nowhere, I have a reputation that makes the Damned want to either stay away from me or get rid of me. Do you really think I could do that by myself? Who else do you think has the power to do that?"

Pain and betrayal flickers in their glare. "Making a deal with *her* will lead to your death."

"Oh, that's fine. We all die someday anyways." Zero takes a bite of her omelet. "I'm curious, though. Do you speak from experience, or are you repeating rumors?"

"It doesn't matter." Alexei looks away, jaw clenched, a deep frown on their lips.

"Rumor, then."

"What's it to you?" They challenge her with a suspicious stare. "It is not your business."

"Not directly, no. Like I said, I know a lot of people. It's kind of my whole deal, really. Even when I don't mean to, I discover things about them. Everyone has a weakness, Starcatcher, including Enyo Zhao."

She watches Alexei struggle with the information, all while she takes her time finishing the rest of her food and sets the plate in the dishwasher.

Finally, she takes pity on them and adds, "Some stories claim that the Queen of Loveias is ruthless, an ungrateful bitch who killed the entire Riyssolan organization that raised her. Other stories say that the Mistress of the Daggers is a survivor, who turned dark when the Riyssolans killed her parents and kidnapped her, then rightfully took revenge upon them when she was old enough. What most people don't know is that she left one Riyssolan alive when she slaughtered the organization. She spared the one person who was kind to her, a kid who healed her injuries from Riyssolan abuse, who might have even loved her. She sedated that person before she started the killing, took them to the Starcatchers after she was done, then disappeared as soon as they had a new home."

Paler than snow, Alexei jumps off the island counter and stands over Zero, scowling, "How do you know all this?"

"There's a photo of two kids playing marbles on her nightstand in her penthouse. If I were you, I'd book a few days of vacation in Loveias."

Alexei staggers back, eyes wide.

Satisfied, Zero turns and smiles at Vasya, who has been watching this conversation play out apathetically.

"You cannot possibly know this information and live," he says, assessing her. "She would not allow that. Unless..."

"I am one of hers, yes," Zero answers the question he doesn't finish.

"Even with your loyalty to the Aconites?"

She smirks. "It was a special deal."

Vasya shakes his head, clearly at a loss for words. Back when she was doing research on the Damned to hunt down the Aconites, he specifically told her to avoid Enyo Zhao and her Loveias. She smiles at his reaction and reaches up to kiss him on the cheek, which he returns.

"You've grown, old friend," he says when she pulls back.

Zero shrugs. "So have you."

He nods, conceding to her point.

"I'll look for my people and prepare them for departure," Zero says, back to business. "*Svachee erd Kruluu zvaghess*, Vasya. I'm sure Katya told you that I plan to stay with you for a few days."

"For debriefing and deciding the next steps against the Agency's attempt to control the population," he says in confirmation. Then he takes a package wrapped in brown paper off the counter and offers it to Zero. "I nearly forgot. This is for you."

She frowns. "What for?"

"Must I spell it out for you?" The corner of his lips twitches. "My sister and I have grown quite fond of you."

Zero blinks at him, bewildered. "Why?"

Vasya snorts, shaking his head. "They call you the Ace of Crowns, a wild card with no loyalties. Rumors say you have no heart and take anything you want. Little do they know."

She stares at him blankly. "I don't understand."

He pats her shoulder. "You will. Go find your people. If you are going outside, you might want to open that package."

Zero turns to leave the kitchen robotically, nonplussed.

"And who is your weakness, Ace?" Alexei speaks up again, anger faded. "Is it the Scavenger or his right-hand man?"

She huffs, both amused and bitter. "That's the thing about knowing people. I have a lot more weaknesses than everyone else." Zero tilts her head to glance at them with narrowed eyes. "But that just means I'm more easily provoked, when someone is stupid enough to lay a finger on my people."

"That will not be the case with me," they promise. "I was merely curious. To have fought against five Purish men alone, as a non-Reaper, and survived an untested drug with your mind intact, you have the grudging respect of the Starcatchers. Katina insisted that you'd make it when we told her you were a lost cause. Yet here you stand, as if it never happened. We've lost many of our own during the Moon Festival, and we will accept a partnership with you to work against the Agency."

Zero almost rolls her eyes at the amount of words she had to listen to, as if she ever sought their approval. All that, just to say nothing of matter at all.

But Vasya is still standing there, so instead of blatantly disrespecting his friend with a childish reaction, she nods half-heartedly and enters the living room. Her eyes immediately search for Rovis, Tal, or Saige. A few Starcatchers are lounging around in the house still, off duty, but thankfully they leave her alone. They only make brief eye contact and nod to address her.

When she makes her way to the front door, she sees Saige and Tal talking on the front porch. White specks fall gently onto the thin layer of snow accumulated on the ground. Zero understand what Vasya means now, and she guesses that the brown package in her hand is a winter coat. The weather has become so erratic with the warming climate, even aside from major natural disasters, that she finds herself improperly dressed half the time.

Neither of the Gierkas siblings notices her lingering by the window, the curtain pulled back.

Now that she's mostly lucid, seeing Tal brings back an unpleasant itch in her chest. If their falling out happened a year ago, she would've lied to herself and said it didn't matter. She would've reminded herself that people come and go, and that she'd always be fine without someone. But after losing Jacek, sending Raven off to go back to the Descendants, and nearly falling into the hands of the Agency, she can't seem to even try convincing her heart to follow logic anymore.

Without the haze of blood loss and drugs in her system, and much more removed from the traumatic events of the night, Zero finds herself reluctant to be in his presence again.

Tal picked up the phone and rushed to be here with her, but it doesn't overwrite the past. It doesn't change the fact that she betrayed him, crushed all his trust in her, and did all of that deliberately and unapologetically.

She knows that she was never Tal's real sister, and she knows he had the right to be angry that she kept Saige from him.

Yet.

Zero feels cold from the hollowness in her chest. Her fingers are freezing, and all she wants to do is disappear before he notices.

It's stupid, really.

I will lose my temper, he told her, back when they first pulled her out of the Agency and took her back to Dyvris, *but I will never abandon you when you mess up.*

Her fingers slip from the edge of the curtains, and the Gierkas siblings disappear from her view.

Well, Tal? I messed up, and you did abandon me.

Yes, he came for her when she called, but he did leave, just like Rovis did when she was twelve. Just like Rovis, Tal made a promise he couldn't keep. Even though she warned him that she's selfish, calculating, and treats everyone almost as badly as she treats herself. She warned him, and he didn't listen. Zero hates it when people do that. Why can't they leave her alone, and not make stupid promises? She never asks them to do it in the first pla ce.

Zero swivels around to go back upstairs, shaking her head.

"You told him to go," she scolds herself quietly. "You're the fucked up one here. What is there to be bitter about? What was he supposed to do, *not* get mad at you for keeping his own sister a secret?"

Maybe it's more about the probability that Tal would have actually fought her, if she weren't sick. As long as she fought back, he would've fought her. He wouldn't have pulled his punches, but he wouldn't have aimed for anywhere lethal. Zero doesn't think he would have killed her, but it could have been a near thing. And she wouldn't blame him.

She wouldn't blame him at all.

"Then why are you so upset?" Jacek's translucent ghost asks, hovering in front of a ladder at the end of the hall.

Yes, why is she? Tal wanted to save her, despite everything she's done, so she shouldn't be feeling this way, should she? Why can't she shake off the ugly thoughts swimming around her head since the night he turned his metal claws on her? She always knew that this is a violent life with volatile criminals; she wasn't even a single bit surprised when he lashed out at her. They're all dregs at the bottom of society, after all.

Sighing, she rubs her forehead with her knuckles, as if that would clear away the dizzying circles of speculations and doubts.

"Okay," she tells herself under her breath. "You don't want to see Tal right now. Let's go find Rovis."

Her aimless steps falter as she remembers everything they talked about while she was fighting off the Agency's drug.

With another heavy sigh, she buries her face in her hands.

On second thought, she would love to find the nearest subway station and run away.

But Zero also remembers the way his stoic facade broke when he found out that Tal was gone. He didn't leave a message for Rovis, and he didn't answer any of his calls or texts. Just thinking about Rovis's self-isolation and empty art studio makes Zero's fingers twitch.

She remembers wanting to track Tal down only to punch him in the face for that.

"And that was still your fault," Jacek says, the words echoing in her mind.

"I *know*," she growls at the ladder. It was her mess, and she dragged Rovis down with it. She can't hurt him anymore. She can't. He was right when he said her plans to self-destruct aren't working. So if she has to give up on it, she has to do everything to make things right with him again, before the white veins take her.

Wait. Zero blinks then squints her eyes. Her mind processes too slowly that a ladder extends down from the ceiling in the middle of the hallway. Zero approaches it, looking up to see a trapdoor. It must lead to the roof, as she feels whiffs of cold air around the ladder.

She tears the brown packaging with more force than necessary.

Thick black cloth unrolls into a stylish coat.

"Really, Katya?" Zero mutters.

It fits her perfectly, and the bottom sways just above her ankles as she climbs up the ladder. As expected, Rovis is standing by the edge, holding a gloved hand out to catch snowflakes. He's wearing the exact same coat that she just received, fitted to his larger frame, though he has been wearing that one since he came to the safe house.

"You're awake," he says without turning.

He isn't wearing his filtration helmet, so Zero tentatively deactivates hers.

"Apparently they have some kind of bubble that turns away poisonous gasses," Rovis explains. "Or neutralizes. I don't know. Tal tried to figure it out, but he didn't manage to reproduce it."

"I have never bothered to even try to understand their technology." Zero comes to a stop once she reaches his side. She studies his peaceful expression. "Oh, good. You two made up."

But you didn't make out, she doesn't comment. Otherwise, Rovis would be grinning like an idiot right now, Scavenger or not. This is a good first step, though.

"We did." He turns to look at her. "How are you feeling?"

Zero shrugs. "Fine."

Rovis waits for more, yet she doesn't have anything to add. She isn't used to the liquid metal supporting her left leg, but she also could have lost her leg entirely. She feels like a zombie risen from a grave, but she doesn't feel like she's about to fall over from sleep-deprivation. Her head throbs faintly, but she's lucky that she didn't kill anyone before Katya got the drug out of her. Given everything that's happened, she's just fine.

Sometimes she thinks Rovis is insane, for continuously caring for her no matter how hard she fights against it, for believing that both of them can have a happy ending in the shit show that is the world they live in.

She wonders if her father would have loved her this much. This dedication, borderline crazy and downright unreasonable, can't be something ordinary people have. Maybe it's only because Rovis and Zero been through the most fucked-up situations together, where a mother threatens her daughter with a cleaver and shoves her head under a faucet when she doesn't meet her expectations. Where a stepmother whips her stepson until his back is completely covered in blood. Where school is a place of looking over their shoulders and ducking under gunshots. Where they had to drop out because their parents drowned in flooded traffic in the midst of a hurricane, and they had no money to pay the rent to their Purish landlords.

Where survival makes them the Damned.

Zero finds it hilarious that the Purish kids can sail right through high school and have their pick of colleges, while the rest of them can't make it through to graduation without losing everything, and end up having to pick between criminal organizations for protection.

So maybe her father could never have fought for her as much as Rovis does. He didn't live long enough for Zero to find out.

The white veins burn against her skin and bones beneath her coat.

Tal's right. Zero needs to tell him. Because she knows exactly how Rovis will lose himself, if she doesn't. There was never an option to just disappear, not from Rovis.

"Rozzie," she whispers, her gaze still lost in the snow building up at their feet as her thoughts whirl in her restless mind. "There's something I need to tell you."

He looks back at her silently, waiting.

Every attempt of opening her mouth makes her heart beat louder. The words are stuck in her throat, and she thinks she might faint from anxiety before she can say it.

It's not too late to take it back, right?

But her legs are frozen, and the metal buried in her muscles isn't helping. She lets out a shaky breath, which turns into mist then fades away into nothing. She closes her eyes, and panic rushes into her head like lava.

I've already surrendered, she reminds herself. *I lost.*

When she opens her eyes again, Rovis is still watching her, a small wrinkle between his brows betraying his concern.

And Zero is so tired, of fighting, of keeping secrets, of being the monster she is. In many ways, she's already dead. She died over and over again, on the day her father shot himself, on the day Rovis left Lime Gateway, on the day Lila bled out to death from Wyatt Revyxon's rifle, on the day she almost overdosed in that restaurant, on the day she failed to save Jacek and Levi, and on the day Tal walked away from Rovis and the Aconites.

None of it matters anyway, when she can't kill herself and take the truth to the grave before it inevitably comes out in the next five years.

She already lost, and she's surrendering the truth to Rovis.

Before she can change her mind, she steps closer to him. With trembling hands, she tugs at each of the five fingers of one glove. Then, slowly, she pulls the black leather off, exposing the veins that match the snow drifting between her bare fingers.

Rovis's breath hitches. Carefully, he holds her hand with one of his, still gloved, and gingerly pushes up the end of her sleeve with the other. His mouth parts, and a soft sigh of shock fogs up the cold air between them. His face contorts as he processes Zero's condition.

"Who?" he demands, though his soft tone almost blends in with the howling wind.

Considering the line of work that the Heartless get into, it shouldn't come as such a surprise to either of them that Zero would end up here. But she supposes that the youth are reckless by nature, invincible until the universe reminds them that there's no such thing.

"Didier Whiston."

"*Why* were you with him?"

"I made a deal with Enyo Zhao," Zero answers, though she suspects that Rovis already knew. "In exchange for her to use her resources to find out who killed Levi, Jacek, and Ayssa."

Rovis sighs, closing his eyes and bowing his head. "Why did she want information on him?"

"I don't know." Zero pulls her hand out of his grip so she could put her glove back on. "I didn't need to, as long as she held up her end of the deal."

"Did you not know that Whiston was in Hilobis? That his father is Marudas? That he bought his way out of plenty of illnesses?"

"I got sloppy," she admits. "I didn't know until after."

Rovis scowls, rubbing his temples. "Forget it. It's already done. Clearly you're too stupid to get the antiretrovirals, since those veins look like they've been turning white for months, so I'll get them for you when we get back."

"I..." Zero trails off, scared of how he'd react to her next words.

"You what?" Rovis prods when she purses her lips.

She closes her eyes again. The icy wind feels like daggers on her face. Snow lands on her skin and melts. Then she looks Rovis dead in the eyes and grits out, "I don't want you to."

He blinks down at her. "What do you mean? What does that mean? If you don't want me to get medicine for you, maybe you should try getting it yourself."

"I mean," Zero forces herself to confess, "I don't want to be treated."

Rovis takes a step back. His eyes widen like she turned into a stranger right in front his eyes, even though she's been acting like a stranger since she joined the Damned. Harsh breaths rip out of his chest as he stares at Zero, uncomprehending.

"Why?" he asks in Avyrian.

"I still have five years," she tries to soothe him in Toullish.

"Compared to *indefinite* time," Rovis hisses, face hardening. "Compared to probably a *century*. And you want me to be okay with *five years*?"

"*I'm* okay with it." They're still speaking in each other's native tongue, as if it would change each other's minds, as if it would talk more sense into them.

"I'm not!"

"Rovis." Zero tries to grab his hand, but he jerks his arm away.

"I don't want to hear it," he growls.

"You said I could tell you anything," she argues.

"You're talking about throwing away your *life*."

"What is there to throw away?" Zero exclaims.

Rovis freezes. The flames in his eyes fall cold and dead.

"Rovis," she says again.

"*Don't*."

Zero holds out a hand. When he doesn't move, she steps closer.

"Rozzie."

He lets out a long breath and slowly wraps his fingers around hers. His grip is so tense that he may crush her hand into a ball of bone dust. The snow is falling more intensely, a few flakes catching onto their lashes.

"You know what I've been through," she says quietly. "More than anyone else. I'm really, really tired."

"I can—"

"You can't *put* that on yourself. You are not responsible for my happiness."

"Yes, I am," Rovis says stubbornly.

Zero sighs and holds Rovis's fist with her free hand. She whispers, "No, you're not. You have done the best you can to raise me, and I never thanked you."

"You don't need to; you practically raised yourself."

"Listen to me," she insists. "This is a miserable world. The only way we can live the way we do right now, with enough food on the table, clean water, air conditioning, filtration masks, friends all around us— All of it is from us lowering ourselves to the bottom of society, compromising our ethics, and stealing from large corporations and filthy rich families. And it was working fine before, because the Agency wasn't on our radar. But now our friends have died, the Agency's got their drug to work, and the planet is falling apart. It's all closing in on us, and we have nowhere to run. It shouldn't be like this."

Rovis watches her with glossy eyes. Zero takes a shaky breath.

"I don't want to live like this," she whispers.

"Maybe you won't have to for much longer," he says softly, the smallest sliver of hope streaking across his eyes like a dying comet. "A revolution is coming, and it can't be stopped now."

"We can't count on it. We don't know when it'll blow up. You can't protect me from everything. The Agency has *successfully* made mind-control drugs, and it was *in me*, Rovis."

"Rena—"

"You don't know what it was like." Her voice trembles, though she doesn't shed a tear, eyes dry like the desert. "And I hope you never have to. They used operant conditioning, did you know? I almost stabbed you, and if it weren't for the fact that feeling happy was so wrong to me, I would have done it. I'd be grieving at your grave right now, knowing that I was the one who killed you, instead of standing here speaking to you. It's so fucking twisted, and it exists already."

"And how do you think I'd feel," Rovis hisses, and Zero can see the tears quivering over his eyes, "standing in front of your grave?"

"I'd hate for you to go through that, I really would. But you'll be okay," she assures him gently, almost smiling earnestly. "You will still have Tal and the Aconites."

He flinches back. A drop of tear slides down his cheek. "Is that why you keep pushing him in my direction? You think you can be replaced, just like that? You still don't get it, do you? You cannot shake me off, or push me away, or handle me like a child with a shallow obsession. You think you can win every game because you're the Ace of Crowns? Jokes on you, then. Tal and I promised each other that we'd fix things with our sisters first before we could be together. What's your move, then?"

"We can fix things in five years," Zero answers, undeterred. "Think about it, we can live our lives to the fullest, knowing my days are limited. No more games from me, and no more holding back. I don't want to be alive any longer than I have to be; I don't want to *buy* more time to be in this world. My time is up, and I know how long I have left. Now I just want to spend it fixing things with you and pass on in peace. Can't you respect that?"

"I don't want to."

"But can you?" She tugs at his hand. "You know I'm right. This isn't a kind world to live in. After everything I've been through, don't make me stay here any longer. I choose my death, I choose to accept the five years, and I choose to live out my last days by your side. No more lies, no more secrets, no more Ace of Crowns."

Rovis clenches his jaw, his chest shaking from the effort to control the tears falling out of his eyes. In the eleven years that they've known each other, Zero has never seen him in more pain, and it makes her want to take everything back. But she can't.

"Respect my decision." She breathes in until her lungs hurt, closing her eyes. With a pained voice, she whispers, "I beg you."

She doesn't use the Toullish euphemism, nor does she use the Purish word that they refuse to utter. She pleads in her mother tongue, the closest that words can ever translate the feelings trapped in her heart.

When she opens her eyes again, Rovis only stares at her with wet eyes, so full of sorrow and agony. The planet could be exploding right now, and neither of them would look away, as if this were their goodbye.

"You're just so young," he whispers, the words shaking so much they're barely comprehensible.

"Respect my decision," Zero repeats.

"Fine," Rovis relents. His face glistens with snowflakes and tears. "I will."

The strong winds blow Zero's hair away from her face. "Thank you."

Rovis pulls her in, wrapping his arms around her tiny frame, as if afraid that the brewing snowstorm might take her away right in front of him.

"On one condition," he adds.

Zero has already guessed it. She turns her head to the side so her words aren't muffled. "Yes. You can call me Rena again."

Rovis presses his lips against her hair. For the first time in a long time, Zero isn't afraid of letting him in. Her days of hyper-independence are over, and she's allowing herself to lean on him. To let him carry her burdens again, like how he carried her when she was six, and he was ten. Just as Zero's death is her choice, Rovis's love is his choice. She grips Rovis's back and closes her eyes.

There's no one she trusts more than him. There never was.

8

Always A Skeleton

With the snap of a neck, another masked figure crumples to the ground.

"Lurking in *my* territory?" Rovis scoffs, shaking dust off his coat. "Such insolence."

Black boots step over dozens of corpses, arranged with careless and unnatural angles from all the broken bones. Rovis kicks aside a dislocated arm, the torn sleeve revealing a torch tattooed on the inner forearm, to make space for his path out of the alleyway. Shadows of birds circle above him, and he doesn't need to look to know the black vultures are having their next feast behind him, just as the sun begins to rise.

"That's the last of them," Daleyza says when he emerges. She's leaning against the wall, her phone held horizontally in her hands as she obliterates her virtual opponents in the newest pocket game released this morning. A blue screen declaring her victory pops up, and she looks over at Rovis through her gas mask, her blue hair hidden beneath her black hood.

Rovis himself is dressed down, too. He's left behind the suit jackets with gold embroiders in favor of a plain black coat, to blend in as the rest of the Aconites have learned to do while he was on hiatus.

"There will always be more of them," he answers, striding past her, knowing she'd follow.

Dyvris may not consider them akin to dark royalty anymore, but it is still their city. Gone are the days of strolling down the streets like they owned everything, because they did own everything. For now, they still do, but it's no longer a given. Stripped away of the glory, the Aconites have become vigilantes of the night to protect their home, never to be recognized.

It doesn't stop the rumors, though. All their attacks on the Syndicates planted in Dyvris are bound to have witnesses. While no one has proof that the Aconites are the ones restoring peace to the city, but who else could it be?

They are untrustworthy monsters, parasites, criminals. They don't protect the city for each individual resident's wellbeing; they're not heroes, not even close. They protect it because they are predators who enforce boundaries to their territory, and everyone else happens to live in it.

It's a bargain with fickle demons at best.

But no one else is coming to save them.

"Then we'll kill each and every member of the Syndicate that dares to stop by," Daleyza replies simply.

"I still think we should maintain a twelve-percent torture rate," another voice cuts in, new footsteps trailing after him.

Rovis doesn't slow down or turn around. "How did it go?"

"Piece of cake," Summer says. "Do we get cake now?"

"Your sweet tooth will be the death of you," Daleyza mutters.

"Good! It's the most fun way to die in this world, in my personal opinion."

Rovis says nothing and almost rolls his eyes, tuning out the banter. Since he's been back, he's spent every night in the city to deal with the Syndicate, weeding out the rot. With his returned attention, he doubled the Aconites' pace of purging by leading the excursions himself and paid visits to all the major business owners. With proper manners, of course.

His feet walk the familiar path back to Arden's Sunset as his mind roams.

"What do you mean you were playing Messy Messier while Boss did all the work?!" Summer exclaims behind him.

"He had it handled," Dalyeza protests. "Obviously I would've paused the game if we were ambushed."

"Unbelievable. Even I had help. I just took longer because I saved one for recreational purposes and sent everyone else home."

"If you're going to keep being this judgmental, I'm not talking to you anymore. Hey, Boss." Daleyza raises her voice slightly. "When's Zero coming back?"

"Hm?" It takes Rovis a second to process her question. "Today."

Rena called earlier, just before he left for his evening stroll, to say she's arriving back at Dyvris in the afternoon of the next day.

Fortunately, the Starcatchers found that the mind-control drugs are difficult to reproduce, especially if they cut off the source of ingredients to the Agency. Meanewhile, they still have some time to figure out a way to destroy the Agency. Over the past few days, Rena mediated some meetings between the Starcatchers and the Water Lords, and now the two most powerful criminal organizations of the country are collaborating to kill the drug experiments for good. Clearly, the girl has been busy. Even though she's on the brink of death.

No, of course Rovis isn't okay with any of this. He isn't okay with the facts that she caught the disease, that she hid it from him for months, that she doesn't want to be cured, that the world has driven her to this point. He isn't okay with letting her go.

But Rena's hopeless expression on that cold night has been permanently written in his memories. The idea to give her the medication without her knowing only crossed Rovis's mind briefly. As appealing as it sounds, he knows it's wrong, and he does not want to cause another huge rift between them. They cannot afford it, when time is not on their side.

Her mind's already made up, and Rovis can't lie to her and convince her things will get better, because it won't, and it will just keep hurting her. She asked him to respect her decision, and he does.

He respects that she has been through too much to want to keep going on. He respects that she told him that she didn't want the antidote, knowing how he'd react. He respects that she has already made it this far in this twisted world.

But he didn't promise that he wouldn't try to change her mind. Not by convincing her there's something to live for in the world they're currently in, because she was right about all of that. No, Rovis wants to give her a reason to stay by finding them a different world. Whether that's joining the rebellion and burning the Purish government to the ground, or securing tickets to another country.

That was what Rena was going to do with Jacek and Raven in the first place.

Rovis originally wanted to stay in Pureland because of Tal and the benefits of being the Scavenger, and he thought that Rena was in good hands with her friends. Only months ago, she had successfully convinced him that she didn't need or want him in her life.

But so much has changed since then.

Maybe they can go to Avyria. They'd have to hide, and they won't have the power they have now as formidable criminals. They'd become nobodies. But they'd both be home, despite never having been to the islands. The only downside is the heavy surveillance and strict laws, with Avyrian and Purish military submarines hiding in the ocean all around them. If they aren't careful, it might land them right back in Pureland, probably even Drokklo's Playground.

Toullifuka might be better for them, though it'd be harder to get to. Rovis would need to face his past and ask Jordan for help. But he thinks it'll be worth it, if they can get to the Amethyst Cascades. If his mother spoke the truth about where Rovis came from on her side, then he thinks Rena and him would be able to lead a much more peaceful life.

Maybe, then, Rena will let him help her. Maybe he can even convince Tal to bring Saige. Rovis doesn't know how he'll feel if he will have to give up everything with Tal, and he doesn't want to imagine that right now.

He blinks, returning to the present, his nightclub towering over him. Daleyza unlocks the Shapeshifter parked there and gets in the driver's seat, while Summer opens the closest rear door for Rovis. He settles in and opens up reports of the cities' activities as Summer slams the door, gets in the passenger seat, and signals Daleyza to drive off.

The floating mansion remains quiet, a peculiar silhouette against the rising sun. But when he walks into the Poison Core, the Aconites are drinking and laughing around him as they relax in the first-floor lounge. Rovis suddenly remembers the long day of card games before the Moon Festival, when Rena thought she was leaving the country with her friends. A deep pang hits his chest, and all he wants is to see her again.

Rena, with her smart words and mazes of logic, convinced Rovis to come back to Dyvris before her when they were still in Ferrisque.

"Between me and Tal, you've neglected your organization for long enough," she chided, while the Starcatchers were getting ready to head back to Jinnoska. "You need to go back and play boss so I don't have to go back to another coup."

"You're making bold assumptions, after everything you told me on the roof," he shot back. "I'm not leaving your side ever again."

Rena rolled her eyes. "Well, that's just borderline codependency. Who are you, my mother?"

"Oh, don't you use that card on me right now."

"Too late, I just did." She smiled, just a little bit. "We both have things to do, Rovis. Go back to the mansion. I'll be with Katya and Vasya for a few days, then I'm going to North Dew to spend a day or two with Dziye."

Rovis frowned, almost pouting. Jinnoska was close to North Dew, where Dziye was sent to a month ago. He usually worked in the south-western cities of Water Lord territories, but the head of the mob, the Duke, called him north for unknown reasons. Rovis couldn't and wouldn't stop Rena from wanting to visit her cousin.

"Aw, don't look like that." Rena poked his cheek, standing on the tips of her toes. She dropped back onto her heel and added, "How about this? If I don't answer you everyday, you can burn down whichever city you want."

He perked up. "Whichever city?"

She rolled her eyes again and shoved him lightly. "Go."

So here Rovis sits, a bottle of Lasan beer dripping condensation onto his black glove, watching over his organization that was operating perfectly fine even before he came back, and not at all on the brink of removing him from power, thanks to her. Nonetheless, he's spending his time wisely, getting back to the real life. The black fur ball on his lap meows, and he absently rubs his knuckles on the top of Starlight's head.

"*Shit*," someone curses, and Rovis blinks at Vanneza, who's staring wide-eyed at the television screen across from them. Rovis follows her gaze and stands abruptly.

METHANE INCITES FIRESTORM AND DESTROYS DIVAKO

"Tal," he breathes.

His head spins as he staggers out the lounge, tapping on Tal's number on his phone. He listens to the dial tone impatiently as he paces to his office. When it redirects Rovis to voicemail, he nearly smashes his phone.

"Now is *not* the time to ignore me," he mutters, calling Tal again.

Tal finally picks up on the fourth attempt.

"What's wrong?" he says immediately, sounding out of breath.

"The fire," Rovis answers. "Are you hurt?"

"What fire?"

"What do you mean, 'what fire'?" he demands. "Did it get you or not?"

Saige's voice interrupts in the background, and Rovis can barely make out the words. "There was a fire downtown, dumbass."

"Oh," Tal says. "We're safe, Rovis. Really, I was just working on some stuff. You might want to call Narvaez, though."

Damian.

Rovis's heart drops. Tal and Saige live in the outskirts of Divako, but Damian lives in the heart of the city.

"You're right," he says faintly, then hangs up.

His fingers shake as he scrolls through the contacts. He vaguely registers his office door sliding shut behind him. Rovis never ended up calling him to work together, even after the Moon Festival. He doesn't know if it was a matter of pride or fear, or his mind was simply preoccupied with Tal's grief and Rena's sickness.

He takes in a deep breath and slowly lets it out.

The phone blinks as he waits for Damian to answer.

"What?" he snaps as soon as he picks up.

Rovis lets out a sigh. "Damian."

"Rovis," he mocks. "Why are you calling me?"

"I heard about the fire. I just wanted to..." He trails off, unsure of how to continue. Damian still hates him for what happened to Griffin. They are no longer friends, and Rovis didn't accept his offer to work together. So what was he calling to hear?

As if hearing his thoughts, Damian grunts, "I'm alive. Anything else?"

Rovis hesitates. Perhaps the whole partnership matter can wait for another day. Shaking his head, he says, "No."

"Rov," Damian stops him from hanging up. "Spit it out."

"Um." His mind blanks out. "Do you need anything?"

"No, we're moving underground. We have plenty of secret bases to retreat to. But this fire was not natural. Methane did not cause this. Someone — an Agent — must have started it, because the buildings are not flammable. This means they're coming for us, all of us, the Damned, the Faceless, the immigrant communities, anyone who's not Purish. You should watch your back."

"Shit," Rovis mutters, dragging his fingers through his tangled hair. "I know it's late, but I am willing to combine our resources, if you ever need the support."

Damian sighs. "It's been months. Now you give me an answer?"

"I've been busy."

"No, you've always been a procrastinator."

"That's... also not wrong."

"I'm never wrong. I told you what was going to happen."

"I know," Rovis says. "No one has built a time machine yet, so it's not like I can go back in time to redo everything. What do you want to do now?"

"We can go ahead and consider that partnership official. Though I may need you to speak to Jordan. Xe's a bit cross with me at the moment."

Rovis raises a brow. "Trouble in paradise?"

"We weren't in paradise," Damian snarls. "Just like you and Griffin weren't."

"Ah." Rovis understands what Damian isn't saying. "You two fought about me."

"No need to sound so smug."

"I'm not— Forget it. Yes, I'll do it. And send me everything you have on the Agency. I will do the same for you."

"Done."

Damian hangs up.

"Still so dramatic," Rovis mutters, tucking his phone back inside his jacket. He needs to wait for Rena to get back to make sure they have all the information she got from the Agency.

"Boss," N.A.D.E.'s mechanical voice speaks up. "Kagiso is approaching."

"Allow entry." Rovis cracks his neck and paces back and forth.

When the door slides open, Kagiso strolls in, and his usual sly expression glints in his eyes. The chains around his neck jingle with every step.

"Boss." He bows his head slightly. "Congratulations on eradicating the Syndicate. Here's the curated list of major companies in our territory that you ordered from me and Avery. It has links to all their recent contacts and purchases, with potential Syndicate ties highlighted."

Kagiso sets down a disk and twists. It lights up and projects holographic logos of the companies. Rovis picks a random one and swipes up, and the logo expands into more branches of specific information, as Kagiso explained.

"Well done," Rovis says, shutting it down and putting it to the side. "Dismissed."

When Kagiso lingers, Rovis frowns and looks back up at him. But the boy isn't waiting for him. He's staring at the Ace of Crowns card on the desk, which Rovis stole almost a year ago from one of her past targets.

"Where's Zero?" Kagiso asks.

"Out," Rovis answers, voice flat. He studies Kagiso, not bothering to hide the suspicion creeping in his own eyes.

When Kagiso notices the chill turn in Rovis's attitude, he shifts back and laughs, sheepish. "She's ignoring my texts, as always."

Rovis narrows his eyes. "Why does this concern you?"

"I need to consult her with something."

"She's no longer a Heartless." He tilts his head. "Rivka must be around."

"It's not a business matter. It's a personal issue."

"North Dew," Rovis answers his original question. "She should be back in a few hours."

"She said that?" Kagiso's tone sounds off.

"Yes," Rovis says slowly. "She called last night to say so."

"Oh." Something like relief floods over Kagiso's face. "That's great news."

He turns to leave, making it halfway before Rovis flicks his fingers to shut the door. Kagiso freezes midstep, and Rovis can see his shoulders pulling taut with apprehension.

"Kagiso," Rovis warns. "Is there something you're not telling me?"

He doesn't answer.

Rovis takes his time stalking over to the boy, articulating each step with threat. He circles around to Kagiso's front, looking him up and down.

"You've witnessed quite a few of my temper tantrums," Rovis tells him quietly. "How long do you think you can last without telling me what I want to know?"

Kagiso looks down, jaw clenched.

"Did the Ace of Crowns lie to me about where she is?" Rovis bristles.

"No," Kagiso says quickly. "I mean, I don't know. She didn't tell me anything about that. She probably didn't lie to you."

"But she did tell you something."

"Not exactly."

"Kagiso," Rovis snaps, raising his voice.

The boy flinches, taking a step back. Rovis crosses his arms, glowering at him. Kagiso is a Sleightist, not a Reaper. He's not immune to violence; he'll crack eventually.

When Rovis whips out his machete knife, Kagiso staggers back and squeezes his eyes shut.

"Zero didn't intend to come back," he blurts out.

Rovis's blood runs cold.

His heart nearly stops.

He hisses, "What did you just say?"

"She tried to steal a vial of the aconitine before she left," Kagiso rambles on. "I caught her, but she was really determined. She got another one and made me swear not to tell anyone."

"You're lying," Rovis seethes, his hand catching onto the boy's throat, and he slams Kagiso into the nearest wall. "I just don't know why yet."

"I'm not," Kagiso wheezes. "I'm not, Boss. She was giving away all her things. If you check her room, I'm sure everything's gone. I— I also checked her financial account. There's nothing left. If you still don't believe me, I have proof."

His hands scrabble for his pockets, and he holds up a ring.

Rena's dragon ring.

"She tried to buy my silence with it," Kagiso says weakly, face turning purple.

Rovis stares at the ring.

Kagiso must be telling the truth. He's the type of thief who never keeps his act up after getting caught.

But *why*? Why would Rena do this to Rovis?

"Well, it worked," Rovis growls, voice low. "Didn't it?"

"It's not what you think, Boss," Kagiso chokes out, trying and failing to pry out of Rovis's clutch. "I switched out the poison with gin."

"Gin," he repeats, unimpressed..

"It was the only thing I had on me! It's not like I had time to get water. She wanted me to stay quiet, fine, but I wasn't going to let her do what she planned to."

Rovis falters, and his grip loosens slightly. Kagiso gasps for air, and Rovis can only stare at the boy, the greedy head of the Opulent House who only cared for shiny objects. People are like fast fashion to him, superficial and fleeting. Except for Avery, Kagiso would probably sell the entirety of the Aconites to save his skin if the Agency ever got to him. If he didn't stay to ask Rovis where Rena is, he wouldn't be in this situation. His secret would have been safely tucked away, and no one would ever know that he let Rena leave with a vial.

But Kagiso did ask. And he stopped her. The flash of relief earlier makes sense now. The only thing that doesn't make sense is that someone like Kagiso would care.

"You want her," Rovis realizes, and his fingers tighten again.

"No, no, I don't," Kagiso strains to quickly deny.

"Do not lie to my face," Rovis hisses. "Don't ever touch her again. Stay away from her. You want her? You can't have her."

"Want?" The boy chokes out a laugh, tears squeezing out of the corners of his eyes. "Boss, I wish this were as simple as wanting."

Rovis lets go, as if burned.

Kagiso drops to the ground and falls onto his knees, coughing onto Rovis's carpet. He rubs at his neck where the red imprint starts to turn a tinge violet. His eyes are glossy when he looks up at Rovis.

"I swear to you," he rasps. "I never made a move on her."

The poor boy, who sleeps around Dyvris as if trying to win a tally mark competition like his jewelry and clothing collections, has finally learned what love is. Kagiso is notorious for picking up and dropping boys, girls, nonbinary and agender people all around like toys he keeps getting tired of.

Desire is fleeting, but this? This is wanting the best for someone, even if it's not with him.

"She'll never feel the same way," Rovis says.

"I know," Kagiso whispers, voice pained.

Rovis retracts his knife and jerks his head at the door. "Get out before I kill you."

He doesn't watch Kagiso scramble out. It's just a stupid kid having trouble with feelings, after all. Kagiso isn't half the person that Raven and Jacek each were; he's not good enough to be Rena's friend or partner. Luckily, he's either smart enough or scared enough to leave her alone.

Right now, however, Rovis feels his fury rising like hellfire boiling in Drokklo's cauldron. He stomps out of the Core and strides into the Tower, ignoring the baffled stares of Heartless fledglings. When the elevator lets him off on Rena's floor, he storms into her bedroom and rips the door off its hinges at the sight of empty bookshelves and a bed made too neatly.

Did she mean anything she said, about living out her last days by his side?

Or was that a lie, just like every other word that comes out of her mouth?

Rovis clenches his fists. His arms and legs are shaking, and he hasn't felt this livid since the day Rena stumbled into his office with a fever. Everything is too hot. He can even feel sweat sliding down the side of his face.

He makes his way in, toppling everything over out of uncontrolled anger.

Pieces of paper with loopy handwriting on Rena's bed catches his attention. He picks up the one with his name on it. With quivering fingers, he tears open the envelope and pulls out the letter.

Nineteen pages later, his face is wet, and his hand presses over his mouth, trying to stifle the sobs racking his entire body.

He feels hollowed out, reading all the words Rena wanted to say to him but felt like she couldn't. There are four other letters, and Rovis tucks them inside his jacket. He pushes himself up onto his legs, limbs weak and trembling, and stumbles to the dresser.

"No more secrets," he vows.

The lock picks appear in between fingers as he takes apart every lock he can find. A stack of handwritten letters addressed to him sit in the dresser, beneath a false bottom, from the second half of Rena's years alone in Lime Gateway. Rovis once stole from her room the first half of the letters behind the frame of a minimalist painting, back when she disappeared into the Agency for Quade Bianchi. She wrote to him every day when she was twelve, ugly scribbles in a mess of Purish, Avyrian, and Toullish. Then she wrote less and less, but each entry became longer as she grew and matured, and Rovis felt as though he got a window to all the things he missed during those years. He felt guilty enough to not look through any more of her belongings, but not enough to return those letters.

There are three safes worth of books under the floorboards in the closet.

Rovis tosses all of them onto the bed to flip through them, and he finds contacts from all over the world written in code in the margins, as well as detailed information about ghost organizations, spy networks, independent mercenaries, assassins, bounty hunters, and black market listings.

"Okay, we get it."

His fingers freeze around the hard covers of one of the books when the flat words cut through his manic thoughts.

Rovis jerks his head to the doorway.

Rena stands there, arms crossed. "Everyone already knows you can pick locks, *Boss*. You don't need to prove it again."

Her expression says she's unhappy but not entirely surprised. Clenching his jaw, Rovis stands and holds up her suicide note to him without uttering a word. Something flashes in her eyes, as if she had completely forgotten about the letters, before she schools her expression back to indifference.

"You didn't need to be so mean to the books," Rena says, .

"I have a bit of a *temper*," Rovis growls. "You fucking lied. Again."

"Well, obviously, I didn't go through with it, so I don't see why you look like I murdered your entire family."

"You almost did!" he shouts. "Because you're the only family I have left! Did you mean any of it? Or were you just trying to appease me before you inevitably attempt suicide again?"

Rena grimaces, unimpressed by his outburst. "I've survived an attempt before. This isn't anything new."

Rovis steps back, jaw dropping.

"Hey," another voice interjects in Avyrian. "What are you two being so noisy about?"

Dziye steps onto the broken door lying on the floor behind Rena, a cigarette dangling from his lips. His eyes flit over the fallen dresser, the shattered mirrors, the torn sheets, the fragmented closet doors, the scattered books, before they land back on Rovis. He takes out the cigarette with two fingers, blowing out smoke.

"What is the meaning of this?" he demands.

"You want to know?" Rovis twists his lips and pulls out the letter with Dziye's name on it. "Why don't you come here and find out?"

"Rovis, don't," Rena warns.

Dziye looks down at her then at Rovis again. Slowly, he steps over jagged pieces of shelves and reaches Rovis's side, holding out an expectant hand, while Rena deflates and looks away. Rovis drops the envelope into his palm.

"My dear baby cousin," Dziye says, turning to face Rena. "Do you want me to read this?"

"Do whatever you want," she grumbles.

"Do you *want* me to read this?" he repeats.

She sighs, glaring at the ceiling. "No."

"Understood."

Dziye pulls out his lighter and burns the envelope. Rovis watches the paper crumble into ashes, shocked. When it's completely gone, Dziye puts the cigarette back in his mouth and pulls out a box to offer another one to Rovis.

"*No,*" Rovis says, affronted.

Dziye shrugs and puts the box and lighter away. He slings an arm around Rovis's shoulders. "Little brother, you haven't changed a bit."

"I'm not your brother," Rovis says irritably.

"Yo." Dziye tilts his head and peers at Rovis. "Since when did we fuss about the details? Seriously, what's up with you? First you throw a fit in my cousin's room, and now you act like we didn't grow up playing sports together."

"Me?" he snarls. "What about Rena? Has she told you *anything* lately?"

"She will when she wants to," Dziye answers calmly.

Rovis shakes his head. Dziye is different. He may be Rena's favorite cousin, but he hasn't been through all the things Rovis has. He didn't see what went on behind closed doors and shut curtains. He wasn't on that fucking rooftop when Rena told Rovis she didn't want to survive the white vein disease.

"You know exactly why I'm angry," he tells Rena. "Why would you keep this from me?"

"It wasn't relevant anymore," she bites out. "And look how you reacted. How could I have said anything?"

"*This—*" Rovis waves an arm around, gesturing at the trashed room. "This is because you didn't tell me. I had to hear from someone that you don't even like."

Her gaze darkens. "If you're scared, that's fine. This is something you have to work on, because I'm already doing everything on my end, trying to deal with depression and learning to communicate better and accepting your help. I am letting go of every twisted thing that has made me who I am today, so that I can get better. I am giving up a lot, for you. But do not hold it against me when you start digging up the ugly truths about me that you can't handle after you promised to listen."

"That's not what I'm doing," he protests.

Rena shakes her head, looking at him with dim eyes. "I don't want to talk to you about it when you're like this."

A breath escapes Rovis's chest. He bats away Dziye's arm and strides out.

"Rovis," he calls.

Rovis ignores him, stomping on the broken door.

"Rozzie?"

The tinge of wariness bleeding through Rena's voice makes him pause. He half-turns, and a thin layer of guilt pricks beneath his skin. He knows she must be seeing her mother in his storming out. They can both hear the slamming of a door that always comes after.

"I just need some air," he grunts. "I'll be back. We'll talk if I'm calmer."

"Don't go too far," she says quietly. "I have a bad feeling."

He lets out a soft, bitter chuckle, shaking his head. "I wish you felt that way every time you decide to keep another secret from me."

With that, he leaves the Tower, the Aconite mansion, and Dyvris entirely. Rovis flies across highways with the top down, breathing harshly through the filtration helmet. The city spreads out into the suburban landscape, before he's on a bridge crossing a wide but depleted river, an ugly gold under the setting sun. His mind is racing, and his fingers clench and unclench around the steering wheel out of agitation.

A crash against the side of his car has him slamming on the black control to enable the spider legs.

As the car stops skidding to the side, Rovis glances at the truck that's gearing up to slam into him again with creased brows.

Just as he's about to counterattack with a canon blaster, his body jerks forward, his head nearly hitting the wheel.

Rovis looks up at the freight truck in front of him, the container severely dented by front of his car.

With the smaller truck speeding towards him, he reactivates the canon blaster and fires the moment before it slams into him.

The world spins around him in flashes of neon pink and purple.

He only has enough time to activate inner wall protection before the car turns upside down and lands on the roof, the momentum carrying it over the side of the bridge.

And Rovis is falling, too dizzy and shocked and emotionally distressed to think of a way out.

His head hits against the window when the car crashes into the shallow waters.

Slow blinks of dilated pupils struggle to peel open eyelids again every time they slide shut.

Bubbles flow up against the front window and fade into nothing as his vision goes black.

9

Fault Lines

"**B**ut we're underground," Tal hisses into his phone.

The shower is still running in the bathroom, but he's careful to keep his voice low so that Saige wouldn't hear the argument he's having with Damian Narvaez.

"The Agency is turning the entirety of Divako inside out," Narvaez says impatiently. "Either they figured out your sister isn't dead, or they are just in the mood to target my city because it's one of the closest to the capital. It doesn't matter."

"The Rose Skulls have been around for centuries. Why is the Agency trying to get rid of them now?"

"It's not just the Skulls; it's all of the Damned. Especially the large organizations like mine and yours, every group that's had enough of their experiments and started fighting back by massacring the Syndicate. Government branch or not, the Agency and the Purity Syndicate are on the same side. Plus, need I remind you of their witch hunt on the Faceless?"

Tal shuts his eyes, blowing out a long sigh. Ever since Saige 'died,' the Faceless have been slamming the media with more dirty secrets they dug up about the Agency and the Purish government in general. The lower- and middle-class populations have grown more agitated, and the Purish are desperately trying to regain their control. Torch City's streets are blocked by protestors and overrun by those weird bulldog giants. Every time the Agency catches a member of the Faceless, the punishment is aggressively broadcasted on television channels, city square billboards, and market plaza holograms.

"Gierkas," Narvaez warns. "You need to go. If it looks like they can't snatch anyone for Drokklo's Playground, they will just blow the place up. In both cases, you and your sister will die. Some of us are heading to Aurodus to join forces with the Ring, if you want to come with us."

"Aurodus is the same distance from Torch City as Divako!" Tal throws his hand up, leaning farther into the corner.

"Do we need to go?" Saige's voice turns his head. She stands outside the door of the bathroom in all black, as if ready for a fight any minute now, her white hair dripping water onto the floor.

"They're being thorough with Divako," Narvaez explains. "If Aurodus is their next destination, we still have a few days, maybe a week. After that, if you have any Riyssolan or Avyrian connections, find the Starcatchers or Water Lords. Those are the most powerful mobs, so the Agency can't touch them yet."

Tal works his jaw, considering.

"There's an underground convention in Aurodus," Saige adds, seeing Tal's hesitation even though she can't hear Narvaez. "If we have to leave this base, we might as well go."

"But once the Agency figures out how to mass produce and distribute the drugs," he tells both of them, making eye contact with Saige, "it's over. No matter how far we go."

"Cross that bridge when you get to it," Narvaez snaps. "I made a deal with your sister, and you are Lasan. You are one of us, under Skull protection. Not to mention Rov's second. You two get somewhere safe, and we'll discuss the rest. Fight or run, you can't do either if you're dead."

"We'll go," Tal promises. "I'll stay in touch."

He hangs up, gazing at Saige with resignation. She looks back steadily, jutting out a chin, and she has that same look that Zero has when she's already orchestrated a whole game in her head, waiting for everything to play out just as she planned in real life.

The younger generation, so fierce and fed up.

Tal can't begin to understand what happened to Saige after he ran from home, but their parents definitely did not coddle or spoil her. Or they did, but Saige knew better. She's not a princess anymore; she's a warrior. Whatever it was that changed her, she won't tell him about it, which is frustratingly a mirror image of Zero.

He thinks he might understand Rovis a little better now.

Rovis.

Tal prays to the stars that the Aconites are safe, and that Rovis hasn't gotten himself into any trouble. Or Zero, since that girl harbors too many secrets for her own good, while Rovis always tries to deal with her mess.

"Where's this convention?" he asks Saige warily.

"Outskirts of the Aurodus," she answers. "Closer to the border with Loveias."

"Great," Tal mutters.

Choose between a corrupt government trying to exterminate him and his people, or a drug empire where the Daggers lurk in the shadows and tourists lie around injecting colorful hallucinogens into themselves. Just another day.

He swings his jacket around his shoulders.

"Let's go to that convention."

Saige follows him, stuffing food and water in a bag.

"The Agency isn't that big," she says. "If they're distracted with destroying Divako, they can't keep their eyes on Aurodus. I doubt they've even heard about this conference."

"Is this a Faceless event?" he asks, closing up all his blueprints floating around and storing them into his watch.

"Yes, but some of the Damned will be there, too." She attempts to squeeze out the water in her hair, leaving a puddle by Tal's workstation. "At least that's what I heard. And there will apparently be a special appearance. I don't know."

Tal snorts, climbing up the stairs. "It almost sounds like a music concert."

"It does," Saige agrees. "Unfortunately, that is not our life. We get secret rebellion meetings and run for our lives instead."

He pauses and turns. Saige glances at him and shrugs.

"It is what it is," she says. "We deal with what we have."

"You've changed."

"You keep saying that." Saige chuckles and rolls her eyes. "But you don't hear me commenting about the blood on your shirt or the ashes on your face every time you go out to reap some souls."

"No, I just..." He brings up a hand and slowly smooths her hair down with his gloved palm. "I missed out on so much."

Saige's gaze softens. "We're here now."

Tal nods and leads her to the Shapeshifter parked inside one of the connecting containers on ground level. He switches the mode in his contacts to X-ray, scanning their surroundings before opening up the hatch. When it looks like the coast is clear, he breaks the chains with his metal arm and shoves open the metal doors one last time.

The lot is just as dreary as it always has been, but Tal has grown used to the desolate and empty environment. He wasn't a people person before becoming an Aconite, since he always kept to himself in school, tinkering in the robotics room. Then, when he passed the tests from the Ezclovese Aconites as a fledgling and later met Rovis, he learned that loyalty is power, and loyalty is a sort of dependence on others. To use it, he had to give up something for others, and that 'something' turned out to be his brain work. After he established himself as an unfeeling Reaper, he even started enjoying being around other people. Even if he didn't completely trust everyone, the drinking and partying was undeniably fun when they were terrified of Lithium.

And Levi, Tal berates himself. Levi was a true friend, irreplaceable and unforgettable. Tal's biggest regret is allowing them to drift apart, without even noticing, and realizing too late. His juvenile obsession with Rovis caused him to neglect his closest friend, and it's his fault that they barely spent any time together before Levi died. Levi would want him to forgive himself, he knows. Tal doesn't know if he can ever reach that point, but he's trying not to remain shackled by the past, by making things right with Saige, Rovis, and Zero. He only hopes Levi can rest easier now that the Wright family is dealt with.

They all vowed to protect each other when they joined the organization, but very few people became family to Tal. After Levi, he'd say he trusts the inner circle with his life, enjoys drinking games with them a little too much, and knows more about them than he ever intended to.

Yet this quiet scene, far away from people, from conflict, calls out to the child in Tal.

He always preferred being alone. His parents made sure of that.

"*Koneixghta*," Tal says after they settle into the car and shut the doors. He fires up the engine and weaving around containers to exit the expansive lot. "What happened to our parents?"

Saige freezes mid-bite, and the banana in her hand drops slightly.

"I was wondering when you were going to ask," she says, looking out the window. "I don't know what happened to our parents."

"You don't know?" Tal frowns, accelerating towards the main road.

"No." He hears an edge to Saige's voice.

"Didn't you leave after eighth grade? So they were still alive back then? But you didn't care enough to keep tabs on them when you were with the Faceless?"

"Did you care enough?" she shoots back.

"No," he admits. "But they practically kicked me out the door. It's different for you. They loved you, I thought."

"It was not love, Tal," Saige says, raising her voice slightly.

The angry tone catches his attention, and he steals a glance at his sister, who has crushed the banana into a yellow and brown pulp and glares at the road in front of them.

A bullet bounces off the window.

Tal accidentally drifts the car and jerks his eyes back to the road, hurrying to reactivate N.A.D.E. to help him scan his surroundings while he's driving.

"Three Agency cars ahead," her mechanical voice reports.

"Shit," he curses.

"Language," Saige says, pulling out the holographic weapons panel and tossing the mashed banana into his lap.

"Hey! Really?" Tal throws the trash into the cupholder, then tries and fails to wipe the pulp off his pants.

"Serves you right," Saige mutters.

"We've been discovered by the Agency, and you're telling me not to say bad words?"

"You've been in car chases before, haven't you?" she snaps. "Because that's what you were doing for the past eight years, without ever looking back, right?"

"Hold on." Tal floors the accelerator just as she hooks her fingers on the grab handle. "ood to know you are actually furious with me for leaving. I was starting to buy your calm act from before."

"I'm not—"

A blue energy shield materializes in front of the window as bullets and lasers fly at them. Three black trucks have barricaded their path to the highway.

Tal really needs to increase the radius of vision in his contacts.

"I'm not furious," Saige grits out.

"You sure don't sound like it," he remarks as he approaches the Agency cars at full speed. When he's close enough, he can see figures in brown and red clothing, a sad attempt at reflecting the color scheme of a torch, lined up in front of their cars. The Agents scatter and fall back when they notice that Tal isn't slowing down. Just before the Shapeshifter might crash into their cars, he slams the button for the jet thrusts beneath the floor of the vehicle.

They soar in the air above the Agents, nearly rocking the hood into their cars, before the nanotech spider legs poke out from the sides and secure their landing onto the highway. The legs retract quickly, and Tal makes a sharp right to drive west.

"It doesn't matter anymore. What happened happened," Saige says, turning to check if the Agents are following. "They're getting on the highway. I've made my peace with you leaving, but don't you dare tell me that I had it easy."

Tal scoffs. "Easier than I did, at least. Forgive me for getting that impression when our parents treated you like you were their whole entire world."

He swerves left to avoid getting blasted by tiny tracking missiles. Saige taps a few buttons on the weapons panel and sends a wave of photon wall behind them, distracting the Agents for a moment, enough for Tal to trick the missiles into crashing into each other. Two explosions sprinkle down metal debris in the air as the Shapeshifter flies away from the chaos.

"Huh," Tal says, impressed, "You learn fast."

"I was their trophy," Saige seethes, ignoring his compliment.

Tal huffs. "Then what was I? I was trash."

"Oh," she laughs sarcastically. "Very nice to know your true feelings back then. I thought you cared about me, but turns out you did that with a knife held to your neck by our parents. Stressful situations really do reveal the deepest, darkest secrets."

"Saige—"

The Shapeshifter skids as the Agents take out one of the wheels with a small dose of antimatter.

"Ah, fuck it," Tal grumbles and pulls the antigravity trigger.

They leave the ground, and the energy conversion of the vehicle transfers the source directory to solar power. It's a sunny day; they have a reliable source. Even if the sun disappears, he has stored enough energy by using the antigravity engines sparingly for them to make ten trips to Aurodus.

Tal just needs to get rid of the Agents.

They've reached the borders, but Tal takes a left lane to go south into Loveias. A shadow flies above them, but it's too high up for him or N.A.D.E. to determine what it is.

"Where do you think we're going?" Saige demands.

"I figured we wouldn't want to lead the Agency right into a pool of revolutionaries and criminals, would we?" he answers irritably.

"That's—" she deflates, pouting. "That's smart."

"I *am* smart. That's my whole deal. But, you know, it was still not good enough for your parents." Tal knows he's being petty, but he can't seem to stop.

"Oh, they're *my* parents now," Saige mocks. "Do you know how many times they've told me that you're nothing compared to me, and that I shouldn't be so attached to you so I could thrive on my own? Do you know how many times I defended you? But they'd always manipulate me and make it about how they gave birth to me, fed me, housed me. I was their perfect creation, so I owed them my life. Everything I did needed to fulfill their dreams, because they gave me opportunities they never had. I was their doll to play with, so who was I to have my own opinions? Every time I said or did something they didn't like, I was a defective product that needed to be fixed. They told me I needed to be grateful, to be a good fucking girl."

She spits out the last three words, and Tal's eyes dart over to see her face fuming red. Then her eyes widen, and she types in a sequence to shoot out an electric web to stop a giant robot eagle from getting close to them. The massive bird crashes into the wastelands to the side of the road.

"What the hell," Saige breathes.

"Government's new law enforcement bots," Tal explains.

"I *assumed*," she growls, and he only briefly feels guilty about mansplaining before remembering their main argument.

"Okay, you're right," Tal concedes. "I have no idea what it was like for you. But I suffered years of verbal abuse, and when I came home missing an arm because some sadist Purish gangsters felt like having fun torturing me on the streets before Dakota Etienam decided to save me, our parents called me a demon that crawled out of hell. I tried to keep you away from all the yelling, but I'm sure you remember it was not a civil conversation, least of all concern. They didn't ask me if I was okay, if I needed medical help, like normal parents. No, they took out the kitchen knives and told me to get out."

"And you didn't take me with you!" Saige punches the dashboard, and Tal flinches from the unexpected violence. "I thought you'd come back eventually, because you were *everything* to me, but you never did!"

"Do you see how shitty the world is?" Tal gestures at the windows wildly, then jerks the wheel, narrowly missing another energy blast. "It was much safer for you to stay with them."

"Why do you think I joined the Faceless? You knew what kind of monsters our parents were, yet you left me alone with them. It was a shitty world out there and at home, and I much rather live in freedom than a gilded cage."

Tal takes the next exit and enters a suburb on the outskirts of Loveias.

"They weren't monsters to you, *koneighxta*." He flicks his eyes toward the rearview mirror. "You weren't old enough to be out here when I left."

"Here we go again," Saige says bitterly. "You think you're protecting me, but all you're doing is walking on eggshells."

She punches the roof of the car. A panel slides open, and her helmet closes over her head. She pushes open the top hatch, and Tal's helmet shuts over his face before the vicious winds could poison him.

"What are you doing?" he demands.

Saige doesn't answer, only twisting her body to stand and peek her head out the top, rifle in hand. Tal's heart skips a beat when he realizes that she's going to manually shoot at the Agents.

"Get down!" he orders urgently.

Still, she ignores him and aims. With five quick successive fires, she takes down two of the three cars before the third starts shooting back. Saige slides back into her seat as the top hatch falls shut and bullets bounce off of the roof.

When the internal filtration system gets rid of the poisonous gasses, their helmets disappear.

"I didn't need a savior," Saige says. "I just wanted a brother."

Tal purses his lips as the scene around them becomes more colorful and more populated. Neon lights of blue and purple shine on his face as he lowers the Shapeshifter closer to the ground and shifts between cars in an attempt to shake off the last Agency car.

"Even if you were doing what you thought was best for me," she adds, "why did you never reach out to me? You had enough resources to do it. Rovis may have had more of a choice than you did to leave home, but at least he was sending Zero money. I didn't even know if you were still alive until Zero pressured the Faceless to tell me that she found you."

A streak of black and purple flashes in front of them.

"Uh, what was that?" Saige asks, apprehensive.

Tal grits his teeth, trying to focus on the road. "Not sure."

Moments later, a long spear, fizzling with violet electricity, buries itself into the Agency's last car behind them, and it explodes in brilliant shades of orange and red.

"Stars and bloody cities," Saige curses, watching the scene with her body half-turned towards the back. "That's kind of hot, actually."

"What—"

"Oh," Saige drags out the syllable, sitting properly again. "They're coming for us."

Tal slows down to match the traffic speed, no longer desperate to lose a tail. He peers through the windows and freezes at what he sees.

Two women with black hooded tops and long slitted skirts hover on either side of Tal's Shapeshifter, standing on antigravity discs that fly through the air at the matching speed to his driving. They're pointing bulky blasters that can probably destroy a whole building at him, and the red glow of accumulating energy is beaming against their faces.

"The Daggers," Tal breathes, putting up the energy shield again.

They're in the city of Loveias now, and they are definitely trespassing on Enyo Zhao's territory. Tal probably should have thought twice about bringing the Agency into Loveias. A few years ago, he might be activating every sequence of weaponry on this car and declaring war on the Daggers. But he doesn't have that luxury anymore, to recklessly start a feud with another organization of the Damned, especially when a revolution is coming.

"N.A.D.E.," Tal orders, "autopilot mode. Keep going straight."

"Automatic operation activated."

Tal releases a breath and pries his fingers off the steering wheel. Then he lifts his hands up by his head, which Saige immediately copies. They wait, flying past hundreds of sparkling buildings on the high-speed road.

Someone must be giving the Daggers orders, because the blasters power down, and they lower their arms. The girl to the right holds up one finger, which Tal guesses must be warning that this is the one time they'd let him go

.

He nods.

They readjust their stance and fly away, black skirts billowing after them.

"N.A.D.E.," Tal says, putting his hands back on the wheel. "Revert to manual and reroute to original destination."

"Take the next right," she responds, "then an immediate left."

He follows her directions, and when they're going through a narrow alley that he determines to be a blindspot for cameras, the Shapeshifter transitions into a different car model, as well as replacing the tire that the Agent annihilated earlier.

When they finally make it out of the city without being followed, Tal sighs in relief, sinking back in the driver's seat. He turns north.

"Rovis is a better man than I am," he says quietly, though his heart still pounds from the adrenaline. "Zero is a better friend. I was too much of a coward to come back for you all those years ago. You were unfortunate to be related to me, rather than one of them."

"You and your self-esteem issues," Saige mutters. "That's our parents' fault. But letting it get in the way of our relationship? I can't meet you halfway unless you stop treating yourself like you're worthless."

"It's not me," he argues. "I've never been good enough for you. It's just a fact."

"Because you keep telling yourself that. You've resigned yourself to being a disappointment before you even try. You think I don't know about your period of alcoholism? What did Rovis always tell you? You need to want to get better, otherwise the rest of us can't help you. I still want you to be my brother, but you won't let yourself be."

"That's not true. I found you when you sent that message to Zero, didn't I?"

"Yet you even walk like you're apologizing," she snaps.

"What do you want from me, Saige? You're still angry with me, so I'm sorry, but you don't want me to be sorry. I'm just trying to do better."

"Yes, I see that." She sighs, crossing her arms and looking out the window. "I don't care that you became a Damned. I don't care that you've killed and tortured people. I don't even care that you *like* killing and torturing people. Most of the time, I don't care that you left, because we were both young. You were fourteen, and you had no choice. I meant it when I said I made my peace with you leaving. It hurts that you never sent a message back, but I forgive you for that, too. But now that we're both here, we can't try to be the brother and sister we would have been if you got to stay. We have to start where we are."

"A revolutionary and a criminal," Tal deadpans.

"And what's wrong with that?" Saige asks. "All we're trying to do is survive. It's not our fault that someone wrote laws that make living impossible, and it's not our fault that we lost eight years because we happened to have awful parents."

N.A.D.E. directs Tal into a tunnel, and he has to turn on the night vision mode in his contacts to see. Even with the headlights on, everything is too black.

"There." Saige points to some obscure hole that looks barely large enough to fit the car to the side up ahead.

Tal follows, and they speed through a steep tunnel barely lit with green semiconductors arranged in geometric patterns, then land in a garage filled with other cars.

"How do we know it's the right place?" he asks, staring at the interesting choice of venue.

Saige nods at a carving on a thick column. Five strokes form a character that Tal can't recognize. It's neither Avyrian nor Riyssolan.

"It's Zessroan," she explains. "It means 'calibrated.'"

"I'm assuming every secret Faceless meeting is marked like this." When Saige nods, Tal tilts his head. "The meaning is oddly specific."

She shrugs. "I've only been a part of it for a few years."

Tal nods. Then, he says quietly, "I'm sorry I thought our parents were safe for you."

Saige shakes her head. "I didn't understand until much later, either. Abuse is hard to identify when it's so far into your mind that you don't know what's reality and what's not anymore. Especially if it's not physical. I wasn't supposed to be your responsibility anyway, even though you're my older brother. We were supposed to have real parents. I just wish you came back for me."

Tal reaches over to hold her hand, and Saige grabs onto his fingers and squeezes.

"Well, you still turned out okay," he half-jokes.

"I don't know about that," she says, looking away.

"You're better than me. You always have been. The bar is very low, but it's true."

Saige says nothing. Tal hesitates, wondering if he said something wrong again. Not really knowing what to do or say, he runs a thumb over her hand. Her eyes turn dark, lost in memories. Tal feels a pang of guilt and grief, for not being there when she needed him.

"You don't know what it was like," she says quietly, gaze far away, "to have your head turned inside out, conditioned and caged, then try to break out of it all by yourself."

"I'm sorry," Tal says again.

"I know you suffered. Trust me, I know." Saige's voice shakes, just once. "I even told myself that what they did to me was nothing compared to what they did to you. But when I learned about all the signs of psychological abuse, and slowly figured out that it was happening to me, it felt like my mind was crumbling. I didn't know what to believe anymore, and you weren't there."

Tal tightens his grip on her hand. "I should've been there. I will never make the mistake of thinking or saying that you had it easy again."

She nods, her absent stare still pointed away from him. He waits, because there's nothing else he can do. He can't rewrite the past or erase all the bad things that have happened to her. He couldn't even protect her from their parents, when he thought he was doing exactly that.

"I did think about killing them," Saige whispers.

He flinches at the dark turn in the conversation. "What?"

"Our parents. After what they did to you, I wanted to kill them. Stage a car accident or start a fire or fake an overdose."

"*Koneighxta...*" His face contorts. "You were eleven."

"Yet, all through middle school, I thought more about murder than romance."

"You—"

"And what about you?" Saige cuts him off, slanting him a look with a cold fire dancing in her eyes. "You were fourteen. You said it yourself. You came home, after you survived a violent hate crime, with the help of a supposed monster that we were told to fear. They looked at your bloody shoulder and missing arm, and they chased you out with knives in their hands. I was eleven, but I knew then who the real monsters were. What else did you expect, Tal? If you're such a genius, shouldn't I have at least some percent of the smart genes?"

Tal sighed, bowing his head. "I didn't know how much you knew. And I certainly didn't know you felt that way. I thought you loved them. Sometimes I thought you didn't care about me because you were too young to understand some things."

"You," she says deliberately, "are my brother. And they took you from me. When I was planning to disappear, I almost did it. I had a plan, with a gas leak in the kitchen. But then I thought, it would be much, much more painful for them if I left them alive, and left without saying a thing. They thought they loved me? I wanted them to know what it felt like when I lost the person I loved the most."

Tal's eyes sting, and his vision blurs.

"You must have been lonely," he whispers.

"I was." Saige smiles. "Now I'm far from it."

She leans to kiss him on the cheek and opens the door.

"Let's go," she says. "We're already late."

Saige leads him through a hidden door, and a sea of activists are chanting. Tal notes that the sound-proofing in this place is alarmingly effective. Thousands of body are crammed together in this abandoned bunker, revolutionary slogans echoing against the walls, combining and blending thousands of voices. Despite having no interest in protests, Tal feels goosebumps running down his arms, power coursing through his veins.

He follows Saige and joins the edge of the crowd, which surprisingly includes recognizable members of the Damned and hundreds of cyborgs. His sister cranes her neck next to him, bouncing on her toes. He considers carrying her on his shoulders when something catches his eye.

A woman stands on a raised platform in the middle of the abandoned bunker, barely visible above the sea of heads. Behind her stands a familiar girl, still wearing the same green bomber jacket that she wore everyday as an Aconite. Tal widens his eyes.

"Raven?"

10

Reboot Siren

Rain patters on tinted glass, blurring the ominous view of the Aconite mansion, and soft rumblings of thunder drum through all the walls of the Wraith Tower.

Dziye offers Zero a mug, standing over where she sits on the bay window of her room.

She takes it and breathes in the familiar scent of Avyrian tea. Her cousin sits down across from her and holds out his hand.

Zero's dragon ring glints in his palm.

"How did you get that?" She takes it and tucks it into her pocket, frowning.

"Rov had it." Dziye shrugs.

"You Sleightists," Zero mutters.

Kagiso must have given it to Rovis when he snitched on her, or Rovis stole it from him. Then Dziye stole it from Rovis. Somehow, through a chain of thieves, Enyo's gift landed right back in Zero's hands.

"Has he always been like this," Dziye switches back to Avyrian, gesturing at the state of her bedroom, "and I didn't notice, or was this a recent development?"

"Recent," Zero answers in her mother tongue with a sigh, then sips on her tea. "It's my fault. I started making a huge mess between us over the last two years, and now I have to undo all of it. But it's like when you crumple up a piece of paper then try to smooth it out. The fibers are permanently fractured, and no amount of ironing will heal it. It'll never be the same again."

"Same is overrated. People are always changing, whether you like it or not."

"And me?" she asks quietly. "Am I starting to look like your least favorite aunt?"

"She's still in your head?" Dziye puts down his mug and leans forward, tapping Zero's forehead. "Rena, your mother is gone. It's been, what, five years now? She already ruined the first twelve years of your life. Are you going to let that continue?"

"I'm trying," she insists. "I'm even trying not to think too much about whether all these horrible things I do are just part of my nature, the output of my DNA, permanently defined by the environment I grew up in. I'm just trying to do better. For him. Because he's too good for this world, and I hate that I'm causing him so much pain."

"Rovis is a big boy. He just needs some time and space to process, but he'll come around. You know this." Dziye sighs and shakes out another cigarette. "Secrets are a poison, little sister. Why would you write a letter for him to find, if you weren't ready for him to read it?"

Zero stares out the window, chewing over her answer.

Her heart speeds up, and her hands sweat beneath her gloves.

"It was a suicide letter," she whispers, watching her breath fog up the window on this cold evening in the mountains.

Dziye stays silent for a moment, then two, before he lights up the cigarette and takes a deep drag. Smoke hangs in the air and fades, as if it were never there. The smell lingers only a few seconds longer, before that, too, is filtered out by the Tower.

"What changed your mind?" he asks, voice rough from the nicotine.

Tilting her head, Zero scans his blank face, and she finds herself comforted by the indifference. It's always been one of her favorite things about Dziye. He cares, but he's more detached than Rovis is. He only knows about her childhood trauma from a distance, from the other side of a filtered screen. He can't be shaken by every bad thing that happens to Zero, because he didn't have to live through it.

"Rozzie, of course," she answers. Zero looks back at the view of the Poison Core, its violet spiral on the outside glowing brilliantly against the crimson night sky. "He called me when I was about to do it. Hearing his voice made me weak. I couldn't go through with it. Then this whole thing—" She waves a careless hand at the liquid metal snaking up her left leg. "—happened. And now I just don't want to. He has always protected me, from my mother, from the outside world, from myself."

"You should tell him that," Dziye says softly.

Zero sighs heavily, leaning her head against the glass. "When he comes back."

A light smack on the back of her skull makes her slip forward.

"Oh, the sighing and wailing," Dziye chides. "You're not even eighteen, and you're acting like a grandma. If you're old, then I should be rotting in a grave already."

She rolls her eyes and holds up her free hand. "You said that, not me."

"You child—"

"Vanneza is requesting entrance," N.A.D.E. interrupts him. Both the robotic voice and the Purish are jarring against their Avyrian conversation, where their voices round the edges of words like weathered rocks in a river from decades of fluency.

"Approved," she answers, draining the rest of her tea in one gulp.

She hears the elevator open, and Vanneza strides in, heels clicking on the floor like a fast metronome. Her shoulders are stiff with tension, lips pursed and furrow between her brows.

Zero stands. "What happened?"

Vanneza opens her mouth to answer, but her eyes dart back and forth between Zero and Dziye. Understanding the concern, Zero turns to her cousin.

"Go hangout on the ground floor."

Dziye nods, patting the top of her head, and leaves with the cigarette hanging from his lips. She holds up a hand when Vanneza tries to speak again. Only after the elevator has descended at least ten floors does Zero wave for Vanneza to talk.

"Boss has been taken."

The words don't make sense at first. When it finally hits, Zero feels her heart turn to stone. "What?"

"We keep track of the statuses of all our cars, right?" Vanneza explains impatiently. "Other than Tal's, obviously, because he disabled everything on his. But one of the cars apparently crashed an hour ago in the outermost ring of Dyvris, so Daleyza sent Reapers out to check what happened, and I ordered the Digitals to go back through the camera footage."

"It was Rovis's car," Zero guesses, feeling faint.

"He's not there anymore. And the car has been wrecked. In the footage, there were three different trucks after him. I don't know how Boss didn't see them. But it was a well-planned ambush, because our cars are designed to withstand ten times that impact."

"I know that," she snaps, her fingers digging into her hair as she stares wildly at the floor.

Shards of broken glass twinkle under her chandelier, a cruel and mocking reminder that Rovis only drove out because Zero upset him. Again.

"Fuck," she breathes. She can't decide if she wants to nuke the entire world or set herself on fire. She knew something was going to happen, but she still didn't stop him. He wouldn't have listened even if she tried to, because she screwed up.

"Zero—"

"It's the Agency," she grits out, a wave of nausea choking her. Her mouth tastes like salt, and the acid in her stomachache might as well be a tsunami. "Who else would have the resources to brutally demolish Tal's work when the criminal organizations aren't warring with each other anymore? They must have been waiting, within the boundaries of our territory, because Rovis wasn't even supposed to go out earlier. Fucking hell, they did this right under our nose."

Vanneza puts a hand on her shoulder, and the touch sends goosebumps running all over Zero's limbs. Her body shudders violently to shake off the feeling as she shrinks away, and she barely holds back the bile threatening to burst out of her throat.

"Zero. We're going to track him down," Vanneza says through the ringing in her ears.

Zero clamps a hand over her mouth as her stomach rebels against her body, tears stinging her eyes. Everything inside of her is boiling hot, but her limbs shiver like she's naked in the snow. Vanneza tries to hold her up, but she bats the arm away, curling in on herself when she starts retching. She feels as though her throat is inverting itself, her stomach is trying to crawl out through her mouth, and her face is flipping itself inside out.

Deep breaths, deep breaths, she reminds herself as another wave of convulsion rolls out from her chest, and hot tears burn the inner corners of her eyes.

She counts and counts, until her digestive system settles down like a sea monster diving back beneath the surface after inciting a wild storm.

A sharp sigh escapes her mouth, and she straightens her spine gingerly, sniffling.

"Why did you come running to me?" Zero rasps, still panting. She wipes away the mist from her lashes. "Daleyza is the acting underboss."

When Vanneza doesn't answer right away, Zero looks up to see Vanneza staring at her, eyes grim yet determined.

"You are the Ace of Crowns," she says, as though it's obvious. "You have resources the rest of the Aconites don't. We need eyes everywhere in this country if we want to find him. Now, if you're done feeling sick, we need you to do your thing and help us get the Scavenger back."

Zero's fingers curl against the wall. She realizes she's fallen onto one knee by the bathroom door.

"Zero," Vanneza calls softly. "Get up."

Her eyes squeeze shut, and her mind flashes back to Rovis's angry exit earlier. His expression makes her dizzy and sick all over again. For all the times Zero was ready to say goodbye to him, she'd never expected that today could have been the day.

No.

She shoves the premature grieving away and takes a deep breath. Today is not the day. Wherever the Agency took him, she will find them and destroy them.

Zero plants one hand on her metal knee and stands on her trembling legs.

"That's my girl," Vanneza says, a hand hovering by Zero's elbow, as if worried she'll fall again. Vanneza's watch buzzes, and she taps on it to project Avery's holographic form. She asks them, "Did you find anything?"

"We found him."

"Where?"

Avery hesitates, for so long that Zero almost thought the call was lagging. But Tal has perfected instantaneous communication across all Aconite devices with his quantum entanglement experiments when he was sixteen, so it can only mean one thing.

Zero clenches her jaw, too afraid to open her mouth.

She hears the answer before it even comes out of Vanneza's watch.

It's like deja vu, like a prison trap in hell looping her worst fears over and over again, when Avery says, defeated, "Drokklo's Playground."

Her feet trip over cold ceramic tiles. Zero loses her balance, collapses onto the toilet seat, and throws up into the bowl.

Someone rubs her back, and Zero can't even tell them that she does not want to be touched right now. Snot and tears and saliva and bile run down her face as she empties her stomach. Misery and hopelessness envelope her body like a coat of frost.

Because Rovis is in the worst place that exists on the planet.

Rovis is in Drokklo's Playground. The Purish, with their supremacist ideology and twisted sense of humor, created a branch of hell in the human world under their capital thousands of years ago, and they made it a tribute to the god of death.

It's never hard to find someone if they end up there, because the government adores flaunting their tragic and savage deaths on television in the form of modernized gladiator tournaments, where their prisoners' chances to win are essentially nonexistent.

It's impossible to save someone the moment they enter Drokklo's Playground.

"Can you get a hold of Tal?" Zero hears Vanneza ask, likely speaking to Avery rather than the frail girl throwing up into the toilet right now. "If you can't, we need to regroup and elect a second for Daleyza."

"No," Zero growls, spitting out the last slops of her dinner.

"Zero, this is protocol. If Tal comes back, he will be the new head of the Aconites, but if he doesn't, it should be Daleyza. You made that choice, remember?"

With trembling arms, Zero pushes herself onto her feet. She stumbles to the sink and rinses her mouth, running wet hands over her face. Water drips from her chin when she turns to glare at Vanneza.

"The Scavenger will return," she asserts.

"Even the strongest people can't last more than three days there," Vanneza says as gently as possible, her eyes dimming with sympathy.

"I don't care." Zero strides out, and Vanneza follows. "Get me Damian Narvaez's location now."

"Narvaez? The Skull boss?"

Zero slams the down button for the elevator.

"The Agency burned Divako to the ground. The Rose Skulls have evacuated." She whirls around and tilts her head at Vanneza. "You wanted me to do my thing? Congratulations. My final game begins now. Track down the Skull boss and give me his location."

"Zero..."

"I'm not even asking you to break Rovis out," she says, voice clipped. "I'll deal with that part. All I'm asking is for your Digitals to tell me the whereabouts of one man."

Vanneza doesn't relent. "There's no way you can get through that level of security by yourself. There's no way *we* can get through all that, even with every ounce of energy that the Aconites have. Zero, you're a kid. Let him go. He's gone. None of us want you to get yourself killed."

"*One man's location,*" Zero repeats stubbornly, this time in Toullish.

Vanneza leans back and stares. Zero refuses to look away. This woman is ten years older than her, but she doesn't care.

Finally, Vanneza shakes her head and pushes Zero into the elevator, then presses the button for ground floor.

"Your generation is so damn vicious," Vanneza mutters when the doors close. As the elevator descends, she taps her watch and holds up her wrist in front of her mouth. She orders, "Digitals, half of you reach out to Tal, the other half track down Damian Narvaez. The second you find either of them, report."

Zero nods once when Vanneza looks at her again, a gesture of silent gratitude.

The metal doors slide open again, and Zero doesn't waste a single second before marching up to her cousin. Dziye raises a brow at her, taking a half burnt cigarette out of his mouth as he waits for her to speak.

"Where do the Water Lords stand on the matter of taking down the Agency?"

Dziye chuckles and tilts his head, danger flashing in his eyes. "My dear cousin, did you not hear? We lost more members than any other organization during the Moon Festival because of the Agency. It strangely correlated with the average rate of hate crimes by the Syndicate against our elders versus senior members of other immigrant communities every month. The Agency wants Avyrians gone, and they started the extermination with the Moon Festival. What do you think happened to your favorite uncle?"

Zero stares at him, her body going cold. "Your father's gone?"

"Indeed." Dziye takes another drag.

"You... You never told me," she says weakly. Dziye's father spoiled her every time they had family gatherings. He may have been from her mother's side, but he'd never been anything but kind. Hand in pocket, Zero fidgets with her dragon ring. "He made the best meatball soup."

"He did. He was waiting for you to visit us when you joined the Damned so he could make it for you."

Zero sighs, covering her face. She hasn't seen him since her parents' funeral. And when she tracked down the Aconites, she was too busy chasing after things that were dead and gone. She didn't even think about the family she had that was still alive.

"You never told me," Zero says again, feeling stupid.

"Because Rovis said you were already taking it really hard when your friends died that same night. To answer your previous question simply, the Lords would like to see that depraved sector of the government crumble to ash, if not the whole Purish government." He leans in, lowering his voice. "In fact, we discovered that the Agency of Justice and the Purity Syndicate are both run by the same man."

"Emery Marudas is the head of the Syndicate?" Zero asks, though she doesn't feel entirely surprised. Grief for her uncle pulls her down and suffocates her, but she tightens her grip on the anger she needs to save Rovis. "The Purish are really one lovely revelation after another, aren't they?"

"Guess you don't know everything, after all, baby Ace."

Zero frowns at the nickname. Enyo calls her that sometimes, in varying languages, but this is the first time she's heard it from Dziye.

"Did you ever mention a girlfriend?" she asks suspiciously.

"Did I?" Dziye smirks. "You're getting sloppy, Rena."

"Well, you know, constantly thinking about killing myself does that, occasionally." Zero narrows her eyes, trying to connect the dots. "Wait. Is that why the Duke— Why are you looking at me like that?"

"I've never witnessed the dark side of your humor," Dziye says dryly. "Yes, the Duke called me to North Dew to come up with strategies in retaliation against the Agency when they kept rolling out more of their drugs. The Lords have already started plotting, even before you connected us with the Starcatchers. But now that the Agency has found a working formula, we need to work faster."

Zero thinks about international relations, about the treaty between Riyssola and Toullifuka. The two countries have made a deal to take Pureland together, then split the rewards. But what does that mean for the other countries? Surely the Avyrian islands aren't going to sit on the sidelines with the largest power struggle since the fall of the Ezclovese Empire.

"Have you tried appealing to mainland Avyria?" she asks.

Dziye grimaces at her suggestion. "Why would we do that? They reject us for running away from our mother country. And, obviously, the smuggling."

"Try it," Zero requests. "Actually, try it until they say yes. Go back to North Dew right now, and make all the Lords send out appeals for military assistance."

"Yo." Dziye grabs her shoulders. "Listen, you are my favorite cousin, but this is the one thing I cannot do for you. This is beyond me, and I know you hate it when people make promises they can't keep."

"Rovis is in Drokklo's Playground," she hisses, voice low.

At those words, Dziye's eyes turn cold. His fingers tighten into fists over her jacket, and his jaw clenches.

"It's not your fault," he says, though his words sound like they've been rubbed on sandpaper.

"Don't you dare start that with me," Zero warns.

He drops his head, regaining his composure. Dziye knows better than to slow her down with useless emotions when she's in problem-solving mode. When her cousin looks up again, he has corrected the look in his eyes to calm and calculating, rather than anguished.

"How is this connected with the Avyrian military?" he asks.

Zero lifts her chin. "You'll see."

"Rena," Dziye emphasizes. "What's our play?"

"You know my playing style," she says, referring to all the games of Keepers and Thieves they've played. "Carry out my request, and you'll be giving me my closing cards. You have a week, maybe two. This country is going to look very different in a few days, and when that time comes, you need to do whatever it takes to get the mainland Avyrians on our side. You're more connected to our culture and homeland than I am; you'll know what we'll need to sacrifice."

"And if I fail?"

"You are one of the three major Marquesses of the Water Lords. Almost half the Lords have connections on the islands, and you have influence over them. If you can't do it, then so be it. We tried to escape a dictator, only to fall into the trap of Purish lies."

"And Rovis? You still haven't said how this would help. Taking down the Agency now can't bring him back; Drokklo's Playground is practically its own self-sufficient circus."

"It strips away a thick layer of reinforcements." Zero takes hold of one of his wrists. "Leave the rest to me."

"Zero," Rivka's voice turns her head. The lead Heartless strides towards her from the entrance of the Tower, lightning flashing behind her before the door closes. "We followed a lead and figured out what the Agency's next move is. Once they can figure out mass production and a central control base of all samples, they're going to distribute the first wave of the new drugs through the filtration masks made by the Whiston Company."

Zero deflates with exhaustion at the news, thinking back to all the jumbotron advertisements for Didier Whiston's fresh line of masks that will 'a hundred percent prevent the inhalation of poisonous gases and convert to oxygen for reasonable price.'

Thousands of people will get those masks, thinking they received a miraculous act of kindness from a Purish philanthropist, only to have their bodily autonomy taken away from them.

Zero has about a million errands to run, setting all the pieces in motion, for the slim chance of getting Rovis out of Drokklo's Playground. She may not be able to start or run a revolution, but she knows enough people who can. They are all running out of time, and everyone needs to stop hesitating before they lose to the Agency forever.

Unfortunately, she does not have time to warn Dyvrian residents of Whiston's masks, nor does she think they will believe her. Once the first round of drugs get out, every single city will sink into a civil war, tearing apart families and turning friends against each other. Then it'll be too easy for the Agency to gain control of the entire country.

Clenching her jaw, Zero thinks that maybe she'll pay Didier Whiston a visit.

Sighing, she tilts her head at Dziye. "See? Deal with the Lords for me, if I'm really your favorite."

"Alright." He drops his hands and steps back. "I hope you know what you're doing."

Dziye strides out, cigarette between his lips, while Zero thinks grimly, *My brain isn't even done developing. I never know what I'm doing.*

She's just gotten really good at gambling, since the day Rovis left Lime Gateway. But this is a death match, with millions of lives on the table. She cannot lose, not before getting Rovis back, and not before telling him the truth.

"What do we do?" Rivka asks.

"Send out teams of Heartless and Sleightists to find manufacturing plants for those masks, and propose to Daleyza about demolishing them. It'll have to be bombs, probably," she answers absently. "I'm trusting you with this. I have to go."

"Where—"

Zero hurries out, pulling the black hood of her new coat over her head. She pushes through the door, and her watch buzzes as her feet splash through puddles. She projects the message to one of the lenses in her gas mask and sees that Vanneza has sent her Narvaez's location.

Be careful, she writes at the bottom.

Taking a deep breath, Zero jogs to the garage and takes her bike, flying out in the pouring rain for the Skulls' safe house in Aurodus. She takes the shortest route, a straight highway that draws the border between Torch City and Divako, both cities taken over by the Agency.

Since Divako is gone, it makes sense that the Skulls would retreat into Ring territory, given how close the bosses are. While Aurodus has the most lackluster architecture of all the major cities, it's known for the live music and nightlife. This city is the only place that still appreciates physical instruments, regardless of how modernized, rather than shoving soundtracks into a blender and blasting it through speakers. Even in this awful weather, several groups of musicians would be playing under the security of tents.

Despite her heavy mood, a faint thrill buzzes in Zero's chest at the thought of seeing Jordan Faal again, after she finishes the first two tasks on her list. She much prefers xem over Damian Narvaez.

When Zero reaches the town in suburban Aurodus, however, her tire suddenly explodes, and the force of it throws her off the bike. She tucks into a roll when she hits a giant puddle on the wet ground, the movement clunky and less graceful than usual due to her prosthetics. Her soggy clothes make her scowl as she pushes herself up. A strong grip yanks on her hood and tosses her through a door, but Zero is quick enough to land on her feet and spins out of it, her helmet disappearing as soon as the door shuts to see better. Blue electricity flashes before her eyes.

Her back hits a wall inside some antique shop, dim lights flickering.

The attacker pulls off his hood, his nanotech mask disappearing.

"You again?" she exclaims, irritated.

Zeke Reyyez snarls at her. "Funny. I was thinking the same thing."

"You might be having fun, but I'm bored," she snarks. "Take me to your boss."

"Why the hell would I do that?" he growls. "You Aconites think you're all so high and mighty, ghosting the Skulls for months then pretending to be our savior in the aftermath of a catastrophe. Your boss has at last agreed to a partnership with Damian, but he does not have the right to send you over without a warning. Again."

Zero narrows her eyes, disguising her new information processing as calculation. She did not realize that Rovis had put off calling Narvaez for so long since their meeting in Metloxcy, and she definitely didn't know he offered help to the Skulls when Divako was on fire.

"My boss," she says slowly, "has been compromised."

As expected, Reyyez's eyes widen, and the bony arm against her neck slackens. A few drops of rain run down their faces, and a blinding flash of lightning washes over them through the window.

"You're lying," he accuses, though he doesn't make any moves against her.

"Bitch, why would I lie about this?" Zero pushes him back a few steps, annoyed. "What is with men and their obsession to get on my nerves?"

"But if you're not lying, then..." Reyyez's face suddenly turns smug. "You need our help."

"Stars and bloody cities," Zero mutters, rolling her eyes. Louder, she says, long-suffering, "Yes. We do. Oh, Zeke Reyyez, underboss of the Rose Skulls, king of reaping souls, will you do me the great, wonderful favor of shutting the fuck up and taking me to see someone useful?"

He clenches his fists. "You—"

"I what?" She crosses her arms. "Stop wasting my time. I promise you, if your boss finds out that you delayed my message to him, he will not be happy with you."

"And how would I know if you're playing me for a fool again?" Reyyez demands. "I refuse to fall for this a second time. No Heartless can be trusted, let alone the Ace of Crowns. Go back to Dyvris or whichever hell you came from before I carve the skin off your devious face."

A laugh escapes Zero before she can stop it, thoroughly fed up with his drama. Reyyez falters, uncertainty creeping into his stony expression.

Screw it, she thinks, before she walks into his space, and he stumbles back with wide eyes. His brass knuckles meet her chin as a warning to stay away, but Zero merely tilts her head and runs her fingers over his fist.

Reyyez yelps and stumbles back several paces. "What are you doing?"

"Can you keep a secret, Reyyez?" she asks, voice like honey, her even steps drawing closer to him.

"Whatever game you're playing, I'm not interested," he says through his teeth, his back hitting the nearest cabinet.

"So you'll take me to Narvaez?"

He whips out a knife and holds it out. "No. Come any closer, and I'll kill you."

Zero chuckles and keeps walking anyway, catching the blade of his knife with two gloved fingers. "We established this last time. You can't kill me. And I'm not afraid of bleeding. You can't win against me."

"Fine," Reyyez grits out. "What do you want with my boss?"

She flings the knife out of his grip and into a desk with a tut. "I can't tell you. I can, however, trade you a secret of mine for a meeting with him. It's worth it, I promise. It's something you can use against me."

Reyyez scowls, but he relents, "What is it?"

With a smirk, Zero shrugs off her coat and lets it fall onto the floor behind her. Reyyez shrinks and whips his head to the side, eyes on the floor, no doubt misinterpreting her intentions.

"Zeke, honey, don't be scared," Zero taunts. She holds up her arm, where the white veins crawling up to her bicep faintly glow in the dark. Slowly, Zeke slides his stare over to her. She watches him process, watching his features morph from wary to flabbergasted.

"You're dying," he breathes, gaping at the veins.

"Good job, you figured it out," she answers, words flat with sarcasm, dropping her arm and ridiculous facade. "Now, seriously, a dying girl really hates having her time wasted. Take. Me. To Narvaez."

Reyyez doesn't move, staring at her like she grew a second head. When Zero frowns, though, he flinches and licks his dry lips. Then, finally, he nods and leads her out.

Zero bought an audience with Damian with the deadly secret that she's no longer a threat among the Damned, but she can't bring herself to care at this point.

As long as it takes her a step closer to saving Rovis, she'll pay whatever price.

None of it matters to her anyways.

Her helmet disappears when Reyyez takes her underground, beneath a crematory building. Narvaez is speaking to a few Skulls, hovering around some holographic maps at a shabby table when they descend the stairs. When she drops onto the ground at the last step, the worn leather of wet boots squeaking loudly, they all look up.

Zero watches recognition light up Narvaez's eyes as he straightens.

"Hi," she greets with an exaggerated smile.

His stare flicks over to Reyyez. "What is the meaning of this?"

"Aconite trouble."

Narvaez frowns, turning his attention back on Zero. He studies her, and she merely gazes back with an unimpressed brow raised.

He eventually jerks his head to one of the many doors. Zero follows him into a pathetic attempt of a makeshift office. Before he can turn around to ask, she drops the bomb.

"Rovis is in Drokklo's Playground."

Same words as before, when she told Dziye, but in a much more controlled tone.

Narvaez, in contrast, whirls around with wide eyes, all the color drained out of his face. He visibly swallows. "And you're here because...?"

Zero smiles.

It's time that she stops treating herself as nothing, as the number zero, and embraces the twisted puppet master that she has always been. Because to get Rovis out of Drokklo's Playground, he needs the Ace of Crowns, both the notorious spy among the Damned and the reckless teenager who loves dancing with death. He needs everything she's known for, and everything she's hidden in the shadows.

It's time to play all of her deadliest cards.

11

The Devil's Circus

Warm fluid drips from Rovis's burning and stinging cheek when he gasps awake.

He fights the heaviness in his lids as he blinks slowly, brows knitted, and tries to open his eyes.

His entire body feels as though it's made of lead, and sweat drips onto his lashes when he blinks through the pounding in his head. His arms strain above his head, numb from the loss of blood circulation. His chin rests against his chest, and he finds his knees resting on a ground covered in dried blood.

Another lash slices through his middle, ripping out a groan of pain.

Panting, Rovis rolls his head up to glare at a blurry figure standing over him. He forces his eyes to focus through the aching in his brain and sees an ugly brown bodysuit and a red mask. The Agent, he can guess, raises the whip again.

A door opens, and the light from outside almost blinds him. He jerks his head away before he can remember to not show any weakness. Once his eyes adjust, he turns his chin back just slightly to side eye the glaring entrance.

Rovis squints when a Purish man in a three-piece suit walks in, and the Agent steps back, dropping the weapon.

"Hello, Scavenger," the man says, and Rovis feels as though he's seen him before.

His brows twitch as he tries to recall images, from all the times he went through the Aconites' database. Something inside him recoils at the sight of this man, but his brain is too hazy to offer an explanation.

If only Tal were here to tell him.

The man only watches Rovis, as though waiting for him to figure out who stands before him. His confidence rouses something unpleasant within Rovis, something between repulsion and scorn.

Foggy memories flash across his mind as he runs it back through every file he's read in the mansion. A nagging image lingers as he faintly remembers pacing around his office in the Poison Core with Tal, showing each other clues they've found about Levi's murderer. Rovis stares at the ground, stained with his own blood, replaying those days over and over again. His fingers twitch above him when a crucial detail finally fades in to complete the image. One profile always hovered over Rovis's desk during those sleepless weeks.

"Marudas," Rovis growls when the pieces click together, the repulsive name scratching his throat.

"Ah." Emery Marudas grins, and everything about that expression makes Rovis sick. "You know who I am."

He walks closer and leans down, gripping Rovis's chin. Rovis tries to move away, but the chains holding up his arms diagonally outward pull taut. Marudas tuts.

"Toullish," he comments. His other hand tugs on the black strands dangling in front of Rovis's eyes as he inspects the hair. "And Avyrian. How exotic. I would have loved to keep you as a pet. Such a shame that you had to become a problem for my country."

"Your country?" Rovis hisses.

"Why, yes." Marudas straightens, dropping his arms.

Rovis internally thanks all the stars of the night sky that the vile touch leaves his skin, though he wishes he could burn the feeling away just as easily.

"You see," Marudas continues. "I've been watching you. You must be proud. So many roaches crawl around the cities, yet *you*... You've managed to catch my attention. Quade was a good friend of mine, and a wonderful business partner, so don't blame me for being curious about why my largest source of poison weapons suddenly disappeared. Turns out a little brute killed him!"

Marudas waves a hand, and an assistant brings him a glass of red wine, eyes casted down. He takes a sip, watching Rovis with an intrigued stare.

"Of course, you earned yourself a spot on my blacklist when you not only threw off my business, but also made your city some kind of sanctuary with an economy running even better than Torch City. You did this on purpose, didn't you? Redlining worked perfectly before you killed Quade. Now you've ruined things, with so many immigrant social climbers roaming around inland. You animals are supposed to leave each other to die, not save each other. It really would have helped depopulate this crowded land. No matter. You have successfully caught my attention and fascination. Well, there's also that Lasan snake from Divako who messed up that Faceless girl's execution, but he was easily dealt with."

Rovis chuckles darkly. The long monologuing bores him, so he has to interrupt, "The fire didn't kill him."

"You're right, it didn't. But the foundations were so weak, my Agents leveled the entire area, city and suburbs, with a just few explosives."

A cruel delight glints in Marudas's eyes, while Rovis tries to hide his shock. How long has he been unconscious? It feels as though it's only been a couple minutes since he crashed off that bridge. He thought Damian was safe when he got away from the fire, too naive to consider that the Agency wasn't done.

Rovis clenches his jaw as his thoughts spiral, ignoring the sting of cuts made by his teeth when the Agent must have punched him in the mouth. Did Tal and Saige escape? They were safe from the fire, so what if they were too complacent and stayed? Tal was so entangled with his work that he didn't even know there was a fire. Rovis has been working with Tal for years; he knows the man is a genius, but he can be ridiculously foolish outside the lab. Surely Saige would carry the remaining brain cells and get them out, right?

Then again, Marudas could be lying. He never mentioned a body. And Rovis never believes someone's gone unless he sees the body. Maybe all of them were long gone by the time they finished off Divako.

"My apologies, Scavenger." Marudas smiles unkindly. "I know you were friends. Or were you? Nothing was ever the same again between you two when your boyfriend died, was it?"

"Shut up," Rovis snarls, jerking against his restraints. He briefly considers breaking out of them right now, but he knows it's not the time. Not yet.

"Aw, did I hit a sore spot? Young love is truly something. Griffin Faal was a pretty one, I'll give you that." He tilts his head at Rovis's spiteful scowl. "I know everything about you, Scavenger. I know every place you've been, every person you've seen, every crime you've committed. You are a nuisance, and I am going to tear out every piece of you until you are nothing but a hollow shell."

Rovis smiled at him, feeling the blood slipping out the corner of his lips. "You can try."

"Oh, I will," Marudas promises. "It took one of my teams one year to find every existing information about you, from cameras and school records in Lime Gateway dating back over twenty years, to spies I've planted in Dyvris after I found out Quade was dead. Yes, that means four missing years, when the Aconites taught you how to hide, but I have a feeling the past is what haunts you the most."

Rovis clenches his jaw. He has nothing to say.

"Great," Marudas says too cheerfully. "Now that we're on the same page, let's begin."

Rough fingers grip Rovis's hair and pull so hard that he thinks he's going to have an early case of a receding hairline. Marudas steps aside, and a grainy image is projected onto the wall in front of Rovis.

His lungs cave in when he recognizes the boy in the video.

Griffin was still a kid, just beginning high school, and he was stomping out of his apartment building, away from Rovis, Damian, and Jordan. It was the day of the tournament.

Instead of following the trio to the high school, the footage shows Griffin wandering around the town center, where street vendors wave at him to buy something. Eventually, he stops at a dessert stand, where a hooded person offers Griffin a small cake.

Rovis tries to turn his head away, realizing that Marudas is making him watch Griffin's death, but the blade of a knife next to his eye nudges his face to stay put.

In the disk that Rena gave him months ago, this video came along with the observation notes of the experiment, but he couldn't bring himself to watch it. Rovis knew he couldn't handle the truth, but now he's forced to see that Griffin started to lose his mind hours after eating the cake. The Agency bugged his house, documenting every second of his reaction to the drug.

Griffin cried for hours when he got home, unable to stop, and his nails dug deep scratches in his arms and his face before he smashes a jagged hole through a window. With a bloody hand, he tore open all the cabinets, stumbling around his kitchen with tears streaming down his face, and pulled out everything to smash into the floor. Dozens of ceramic plates, bowls, and mugs crash and break into shards. He tripped over the pieces and fell twice, cutting up his hands and legs. Then he crashed into the counter and scrambled for the knife block.

A tear rolls into the cut on Rovis's cheek, and he winces at the sting.

The steak knife plunged into Griffin's heart. Blood spurted out over his hands, wrapped tightly around the black handle. He collapsed onto the floor, and a dark pool of red spread out beneath his still body. Just as how Rovis found him later that day.

The video starts over.

"Stop," he rasps.

Surprisingly, Marudas grants him that apparent mercy. The image disappears, and the Agent lets Rovis slump forward.

"Your high school sweetheart was just a guinea pig," Marudas says. "Too bad he couldn't stay alive to see you under the influence of our finished product."

A hand clamps around Rovis's neck, and a needle pierces through his skin.

"No," the word slips out as he tries to get away. But he can feel the drug flowing into his bloodstream, and the energy drains out of his already heavy limbs. Dark spots dance before his eyes as he struggles to stay conscious, deep breaths ragged in his chest. He almost blacks out, but he pushes through it until color returns to his vision, and the colors morph into shapes, the shapes sharpen into Marudas's despicable face.

"Not to worry," he's saying. "I haven't decided what to make of your first objective, so your mind is still yours, for now." Marudas taps his chin.

"On the topic of your love life, how *is* your second-in-command? Have you told him you want to fuck him yet?"

"Fuck you," Rovis spits out.

"Wrong man, Scavenger." Marudas tuts, looking smug. "Don't lose your wits before I take them from you."

Rovis curls his lips, his entire body filled with loathing. "You won't. I won't let you win."

"Oh, you must be thinking about how valiantly your little Ace fought against my drug." Marudas tilts his head. "Yes, she was quite impressive, but I would have had her eventually, if those vexing Starcatchers hadn't decided to meddle. Unfortunately for you, women have a much higher pain tolerance than men. You won't last nearly as long as your stepsister."

Rovis freezes.

"That's right," Marudas says, grinning. "I know about the freak show that was your family. Your pathetic father remarried after your Toullish mother died. The universe must despise you as much as I do, because he fell in love with an evil hag that beat you senseless every night. She punished you because you weren't full Avyrian, didn't she? And her little clone did nothing to help you. At school, the two of you don't even acknowledge each other. It's a wonder that you let the Ace of Crowns live in a mansion with you, after everything her mother did to you."

Rena's tight expression, from when he left the Tower in a rage, flashes before Rovis's eyes. She tried to keep her face blank, but the fingers twisting the fabric of her pants by her side and the slight frown belied her calmness.

Don't go too far, she said. *I have a bad feeling.*

If she could see him now, he could hear her saying angrily, "What did I tell you?"

Rovis needs to get out of here. His breathing quickens as he regrets leaving things the way he did. He was wrong to throw Rena's words back in her face; he simply had no right to judge her for the battles she struggles with alone and in the dark.

He promised he'd work through anything with her.

"There you are," Marudas says, mistaking Rovis's rising panic for hatred. "Don't worry, I have plans for the girl, too."

"*Don't touch her*," Rovis seethes, thrashing against his chains. His metal finger struggles to maintain its form, the nanoparticles itching to deform and slither up his hand like vines. The Agency took away his gloves but left his prosthetic finger intact, an oversight that speaks volumes about how little experience they have with the world of the Damned.

Undeterred, Marudas continues, "You want your revenge, I know. Sadly, I'll be taking that from you as well. You see, my Agents spread a false rumor to your Heartless team that my son is distributing the first round of drugs through his mask production line. But actually, why bother with masks, when we can just drop it in the water supply? The rural areas are overrun with filth, so we'll start by gaining control over them. Then when I want to get rid of them, all it takes is one command."

"Are you stupid?" Rovis seethes. "Do you know anything about the agricultural sector?"

"That's nothing technology can't solve," Marudas says, so unbothered that Rovis thinks he missed all of his secondary education. "Anyway, I'm sure your awful stepsister will be looking for Didier, and he'll be ready for her."

"Why her?" Rovis demands. "What will he do to her?"

"Because she failed to kill you," Marudas says plainly. "I specifically ordered the Syndicate to find her and make her mine. She had one job, and she failed. It must have taken a lot of energy to resist the urge. She probably feels guilty about your past together, a stupid development in character. Currently, I don't have a version of the drug that will work on her, so she's of no use to exist on my land."

"So you ordered your son to kill her when she goes looking for him?"

"Of course, I can add in a little bit of torture, as a favor to you. You will become one of my greatest puppets, after all."

Rovis clamps his jaw shut, reining in his fury. Maybe it's better that Marudas thinks he hates Rena. It wouldn't matter either way, because he's going to free himself and find her before Whiston can get his hands on her. He just hopes that, for once in her life, Rena doesn't make any rash decisions, and that she doesn't receive the news of Rovis's capture too soon.

Once she does, he has no idea if she would implode or explode.

The odds are, unfortunately, never in his favor.

Marudas checks his watch and claps his hands. "Well, it's time for me to go. I've wasted enough time with a roach. Now that you know you've lost, I'll leave you to it."

A drone shaped like a bee floats in as Marudas leaves. Green light blinks at Rovis, and it's almost overstimulating after being on the receiving end of an interrogation in a room built for sensory deprivation. He squints at the device, but he can't quite figure out its purpose yet. It's not an execution drone, Rovis knows. There wouldn't be a point to kill him if the mind-control drug is in his system.

Before the cell door closes, Marudas calls back, "Your father drowned in a hurricane, didn't he? I'm sure you'll appreciate what comes next."

The Agents follow Marudas out, and the room goes dark again. Any cracks around the doorframe seal shut. Rovis shifts on his knees, studying the ceiling. Only faint lights glow red above his head, but he can see the outline of a trapdoor if he stares long enough.

A strong odor hits his nose. Rovis grimaces, then jerks back when a hole opens up in the wall, and sewage water starts pouring out. His knees are immediately stained, but his arms are so tired that he isn't able to stand.

"Shit," he swears under his breath.

The murky water reaches his waist within seconds.

With a determined growl, Rovis pulls himself up with every last bit of his energy. His wrists feel raw, rubbing against the metal cuffs. He barely catches himself, feet splashing in the rising pool.

The nanoparticles melt and reform into his lock picks between his fingers, and he leans over to grab them with his teeth. He takes one in hand and switches the direction of the other in his teeth so that the long bar sticks out. His fingers and his neck strain to wiggle the short ends in the key hole until the double lock clicks open.

Rovis almost loses his balance when his left arm falls to his side.

The sewage goes up to his chest now, but freeing his right arm is much easier with his other arm released. He kicks down in the water once he's out of the shackles, keeping himself afloat until his hands can touch the ceiling.

Without much energy to begin with, Rovis feels the exhaustion pulling at his consciousness. His wounds flare with pain, and he knows they're definitely going to be infected once he makes it out.

But he refuses to give in. Rovis's hands shake as he picks the lock on the trapdoor, but he manages to shove the heavy board upward with his shoulder after lowering and raising himself in the water a couple times. His fingers catch onto the edge of the gap, almost drawing blood on his wrinkled fingertips from how tightly he's clutching the concrete. His arms give out the first time he tries to pull himself up, and it takes him two more tries to heave his body over the edge.

He rolls away from the strong stench of sewage water and falls onto his back. His ears ring from adrenaline, and his eyes once again suffer through readjustment to the aggressive white lights above him. Then the ringing begins to fade, just for his senses to get assaulted by an even more obnoxious sound.

Applause thunders against his eardrums as he tries to catch his breath on a dry, clean floor.

Rovis looks up and sees metal bars all around him, where other prisoners watch him with apathetic expressions. Their hands are clapping, though the movements are so mechanical that he wonders if they're androids, rather than humans. All the cells are side by side, stacking a long line of criminals and extremist revolutionaries. He recognizes a few faces from the news of their arrests, from serial killers to prominent protestors.

The trap door slams shut, and the edges disappear, as if the floor has always been continuous.

In unison, the prisoners stop clapping and return to one side of their cells. Rovis struggles onto his feet to copy them and looks out the glass viewing window beyond his cell bars. His heart stops beating once he realizes where he is.

Below him lies an expansive arena, where a robot scorpion, around the size of a six-story building, runs through a girl's chest with its sharp iron tail. It waves her body around and tosses the corpse into a pile of armored but dead gladiators.

Rovis's knees buckle and hit the ground.

His body goes cold like he's already dead. He tries to tear his eyes away from the tournament, but he can't move a single muscle. The cruel truth sucks the last ounces of hope out of him.

Rovis is in Drokklo's Playground.

And he's never going to see Rena or Tal again.

On the other side of the stadium, opposite the prisoners, sits a rowdy crowd of wealthy Purish families. Holographic numbers float next to them in various colors, shifting quickly as some bidders lose their money, while others gain millions of units.

His eyes fall shut. Memories of his past flood his mind like a tsunami. Marudas, that bastard, tore open all the wounds that Rovis had carefully sewn shut when he became the Scavenger. And now that the secret that

Rena is his sister has been thrown out to the open, he can't stop remembering all the things he's been too scared to think about.

The sound of measured footsteps turns Rovis's head. Fifteen Agents march down the hall, a trio breaking out of line to snatch a prisoner out of a cell.

When they pass by Rovis, three of them enter his cell and take out long black sticks that crackle with red electricity. He stands and meets them in the middle, though he doesn't attack them. There's no point; this arena is the most secure place on the planet. He can't get out.

Yet when one of the Agents raises their stick, Rovis leans back to avoid the swing.

He reaches for his gun out of instinct, but of course it's no longer there. They already confiscated it, along with his other weapons and forearm guards.

Fortunately, Rovis has been in more street brawls than these Agents. He can see their next moves from a light year away. When he sees the opportunity, he grabs onto an Agent's hand and twists until the wrist cracks, catching the handle of their electric stick and turning just in time to block a hit.

Taking advantage of the surprise, visible in the way that the Agents tense up, Rovis swings at their legs.

Except a searing pain rips through his brain, and he collapses onto his knees.

His face explodes as his head snaps to the side.

Rovis tastes fresh blood when he falls onto his elbow.

He spits out a tooth and glares at the drone that has lowered to his level, which he has finally put together to be a camera for the entertainment broadcast.

Whoever is in control of the mind-control program for Rovis must have entered the first command to distract him and force him to accept his beating.

His back lights on fire when another strike lands between his shoulder blades. His hand slams on the ground before he could collapse onto his stomach.

But then the hits keep coming, scattering all over his body.

I was eleven when my father married her.

Rovis thinks his shin shatters.

Rena tried to warn me, tried to warn my father. He didn't believe her, and I thought I could protect her. But when the leather belt first smacked my bare back three nights after the private wedding, I realized I was wrong.

Another blow on his back knocks his breath out.

My stepmother, Rena's birth mother, manipulated my father into working extra hours at night to pay the rent, while all she had to do was stay home and watch television. She didn't marry him for love; she was a parasite who found a host.

⸺◆⸺

The voltage numbs his arm when one of the Agents plunges their stick into his shoulder.

⸺◆⸺

One time, in the kitchen, Rena stood in front of me, facing her mother after years of keeping her head down. She might have been eight, or maybe she was seven because her birthday was late in the year. The belt landed on her face, and it immediately bloomed red. I tried to push her behind me, but her mother already took out the cleaver.

⸺◆⸺

Rovis doesn't know when the beating stopped, but the next time he opens his eyes, the Agents are dragging him down the hall.

⸺◆⸺

Rena somehow talked her mother down and flicked her fingers behind her back, signaling me to leave, but I refused. During her desperate attempt to push me out, the cleaver dug into the wooden cabinet right in front of my baby stepsister's face.

⸺◆⸺

The Agents drop Rovis onto the floor, kicking him for one last round.

——————⚬——————

"It happens all the time," Rena whispered to me later while rubbing ointment on my back, when all the lights were off and the night was silent. "If you stick with me, I can deal with it. She wouldn't kill her own daughter."

——————⚬——————

Parts of a metal armor crash into a bulky pile in front of his watery eyes, and Rovis tries to breathe through the pain blossoming all over his bruised and cut body.

——————⚬——————

"She can do other things to you," I argued. "I'm your big brother now. I can take it. If she focuses on me, she'll forget about you."

——————⚬——————

Rovis pushes himself up on his fractured arms, wincing. Four other gladiators are readying themselves for the next round of the tournament, and he knows he should hurry up. He's seen enough of the holographic livestream around the country to know that he's joining the next program of entertainment for the Purish.

——————⚬——————

Rena started crying then, because she was still a child who was hurting, but not completely beaten numb by the world.

✦

He clasps the pieces over his left forearm.

✦

"I told you not to let your father do this."

✦

Then his right forearm.

✦

"I didn't want you to be alone," he answered, closing his fingers over her tiny wrists.

✦

Weak energy shields whirs around his upper body. It'll likely only protect Rovis from one medium force blow. He can feel pus or blood oozing out of his wounds as he staggers to the weapons selection, and he can hear the audience roaring impatiently for the next fight.

✦

"I never asked for this," Rena said, hiccuping. "I'd rather you be safe. You've only known me for a year."

Does Rovis even have any fight left in him? He knows it's only a matter of time before he dies in this hellscape. Especially with all the particles running through his blood, ready to take control of his neurons and his body any minute of the future, Rovis can't find a reason to go out to the arena and waste his energy fighting giant robots, all for the amusement of people who never have to know what it's like to live in this world for someone like him.

"You're my sister," I insisted. "I choose you, regardless of our parents' relationship."

"He knew," Rovis mutters in his seat by the wall, ignoring the odd looks from the other prisoners, as they wait for the gates to open.

I begged my father to help us. After the first week of the beatings, I told him the truth. I begged him to come home earlier and make Rena's mother go to work, too. I even begged him to leave her and take Rena with us. But every time, he only looked away and said, "I'm tired, my son. You should go to sleep."

That's why Rovis bears the scars from six years of abuse. Perhaps that's why Rena holds so much bitterness towards his father. Somehow, she remembered, and Rovis didn't. For some reason, he completely forgot that his father neglected him as a child and allowed the beatings to continue. He forgot that his father knew the truth, and did nothing. He forgot that his father lived like the victim of everything that happens to him in life. He was a defeatist, who only knew to do as he's told and keep his mouth shut.

Rovis forgot.

But I remember now, he wishes he could tell his sister. *I remember everything, Rena. All this time, you were the only family I had.*

A clamor of cheers stab his ears when the gates roll open, and the white light of the stadium bore through his eyeballs.

He slams the butt of his spear on the ground as he stands again, blue electricity buzzing at the blade as his injured shins and bruised thighs protest.

No logical explanation can give him a reason to go out there and fight.

The image of Rena's tentative smile during the Moon Festival, before the Agency killed Jacek and Levi and Ayssa, fades into his mind.

Then again, love is never logical.

Rovis trudges out from the shadows of the preparation room and into the midst of roaring and booming cries.

A giant lizard stalks toward him.

He angles his spear as he lunges on aching legs.

"For you," he whispers, "little sister."

12

Code Black

When Tal and Rovis stole Wyatt Revyxon's old rickety watch for the encoded list of his family's expensive properties all that time ago, they missed something.

Holographic blueprints of spaceships and nuclear bombs hover above the crowd of rebels in the sinister bunker. Tal holds up a holographic display shining from his metal palm, comparing the serial number of one of the ships to a line of digits extracted from the edges of wheels inside Revyxon's watch. Back then, Tal thought the random numbers were just meant to fill in the blanks between addresses for luxury houses, which Rovis planned to either sell anonymously or convert into another Aconite base if it's close to Dyvris.

"The government made a deal with the richest families," the woman on the raised platform explains, her words amplified by speakers along the perimeter of the bunker.

From biometric scanning and hacking into classified databases and re-trieving lost files, Tal was not able to learn who the woman was. Only from asking people around him, like a clueless transfer student at a new school, was he able to find out that she's Raven's mother, Nova Ly, and one of the last surviving Zessroans. She doesn't exist in any database because the Zessroans don't exist. They let the Purish believe that they're extinct, never leaving a single trace of evidence that they still live. Unlike most of the Damned, who join organizations during their lifetime and have to erase themselves from the government's records, the Descendants are never reported in the first place. They inherit the secrets of their ancestors and are born into a ghostly life of fugitives.

Tal remembers the day of Levi's funeral, when Raven said goodbye to Zero and disappeared with a mysterious car that he wasn't able to trace from camera footage or satellite signals, not even from the secret sources of surveillance that he planted in Aconite territory. She must have gone back to her mother that day, rejoining the Descendants. Why she chose to leave Zero during such a vulnerable time, he'd never know. Did Zero know Raven's true identity, or was even the Ace of Crowns unaware of the Zessroans' survival? Her vacant expression as Raven's car drove away revealed no answer to his question. Tal doesn't really understand the dynamics of Zero's high school friend group, and he doesn't think he ever will.

But Tal also remembers the fluent Riyssolan words flowing out of Zero's mouth and into her phone as soon as Raven left. With everything that Tal knows now, chances are that it was a call to Enyo Zhao. He frowns, calculating. Zero and Raven must have had a plan of some sort, then. He blinks out of his thoughts, unable to fathom how they could function so soon after the death of another friend.

Tal glances at Saige, whose sharp gaze is focused on Nova. She looks fierce, despite her small frame. After she told him the truth about their parents, a new mixture of pride and admiration burns in his chest every time he looks at her. She's a survivor, just like him but in her own way. They each took their own path out of that hellhole house and made something of themselves. Well, Tal became a lowlife, but at least he's famous. Saige, however, still smiles and laughs like she never went through all that she did, all while fighting for a better future for everyone in Pureland. Between his sister, Raven, and Zero, Tal is convinced the girls of their generation secretly have some alien nucleotide in their genes.

"They know the planet is dying," Nova says to the crowd now, her voice reverberating in the shelter. "And they've made escape plans. To where, we do not know, but to make sure that none of us can follow them, the Purish are building self-destructive bombs to level the whole continent after they leave."

Angry shouts in response to the declaration assault Tal's ears, and he squeezes Saige's hand. They exchange glances, before turning their attention back to Raven's mother.

"They took my people's land," she shouts. "And they claimed it as theirs. They've drained all life out of mother nature and turned it into a high-tech wasteland, all while denying the consequences of their actions. They tried to silence us; they tried to drive us to extinction. They glorified their roles in history and dehumanized us as we were forced to hide for centuries, waiting for the time to strike back. My allies, that time is now."

More cheers and shouts echo off of the walls of the bunker. Behind her mother, Raven scans the crowd with her arms crossed. When her eyes find Tal, she takes a second to process his presence before she nods at him, a curt acknowledgment. Then when her gaze shifts to Saige, Raven freezes, shoulders tense.

"Let me guess," Tal says to his sister loudly over the clamor. "You two were friends?"

"Acquaintances," Saige corrects, waving to Raven innocently. "I think she's more surprised that I'm alive. You know, live broadcasting of my fake death and all."

"The usual," he comments, nodding.

Raven's still watching them, and Tal can see the pieces of information clicking in her head. Her stare flickers between him and Saige, no doubt noting their similarities, before glancing down at their linked hands. Raven narrows her eyes.

Chuckling at her reaction, Tal pulls Saige's hood back and scrambles her hair with his hands, winking at Raven.

Saige shoves his arms off, rolling her eyes. At Raven, she shakes her head and throws up a hand, as if saying, *My brother is annoying. What can you do?*

The corners of Raven's lips twitch, and she finally tears her gaze away.

"Wow." Tal complains, "All you children do is make fun of me. You didn't even need to say anything to each other just now, and you still managed to insult me."

"All of us?" Saige laughs.

"Well, yes. Clearly, you and Zero talked about me behind my back. What did you say? 'Haha, my brother is so lame, and he has no idea that you are feeding me information about him'?"

"Something like that." A funny smile tugs at Saige's lips.

"What?" he demands. "What else did you say?"

"Oh, you know." Saige pretends to inspect her nails. "We may or may not have ongoing bets about you and Rovis."

"*What?*"

"Don't worry about— Wait, is that Zero?"

Tal follows Saige's wide-eyed stare and sees Raven crouching down to speak to someone on the lower ground next to the substitute stage. Her face is blocking Zero's as they whisper into each other's ears, but Tal recognizes the red and black hair.

"Speak of the *devil*," Tal exclaims, aghast. "Why— How did she get here?"

"Raven probably told her to come," Saige hypothesizes, unconcerned.

A deep voice interrupts behind them. "Gierkas."

Tal turns to see Damian Narvaez breaking away from the shadows in his oversized gray coat, his silver eyes piercing even in the dark of the bunker.

"The Ace of Crowns has asked me to pass along her request for you to return to Dyvris," Narvaez says.

Tal frowns. "Why doesn't she come and tell me herself?"

He glances back at the platform, but Raven has resumed her previous position, and Zero's nowhere to be seen.

"What the fuck," he breathes.

Standing on his toes, Tal tries to find the little troublemaker.

"She's gone, Lithium. She came to me a couple hours ago, and I gave her a ride here, but she has other matters to attend to."

Tal ignores him, still trying to see where Zero disappeared off to.

"Saige," he hears Narvaez address his sister, "she wants you to convince the Faceless to bombard international media outlets for the next week with everything that the Purish government, the Purity Syndicate, and the Agency has done over the past few years. Everything."

"What?" Saige's voice goes up two octaves in pitch. "All next week? Why?"

Tal drops back on his heels and stares at Narvaez.

"You should also broadcast the procedures for someone who has been injected with the mind-control drug," he continues. "The Agency is going to be distributing the drug shortly, and there's not much we can do to stop it, so people should be prepared for the blood transfusion process. We're out of time."

Both Tal and Saige go quiet, stunned.

The revolution is really happening soon, isn't it? And it is happening way sooner than any of them expected it to.

Tal lets out a long breath, wondering how they got here. It feels like yesterday when he's just an uncaring teenager with the Aconites, thriving on money that doesn't belong to him. Now, everyone who isn't rich and Purish is heading to war against their oppressors.

Narvaez sighs at Tal's and Saige's bewildered expressions. "If you've been down here, then you haven't heard."

That catches Tal's attention, and suddenly every cell in his body is vibrating on a higher frequency. Narvaez gestures for them to follow, and he leads them back to the garage area. Tal's shoulders tense up, and his metal fingers could break tungsten from how tightly they've curled up into his palm. He's never seen Narvaez this far off his high horse; something must have gone seriously wrong.

"Rovis is…"

As soon as he hears the name, Tal's blood runs cold, and everything in the world goes silent as he waits for the next words. But Narvaez trails off, so Tal rushes forward and grips the other man's shoulders, heart pounding against his ribs. "What about Rovis?"

"He's been captured." Narvaez looks away. "They took him to Drokklo's Playground."

Tal flinches and shoves him back as though burned, seething, "You're lying."

Narvaez doesn't react to his accusation. "Once you return to the surface, you'll see them filming the arena. It's all over the place, always has been."

"No," Tal insists. "He's not in it."

"Denying it won't save him," Narvaez responds, apathetic.

"Barely anyone can survive that shit-hole for more than a few hours!" Tal's voice shakes, and something inside of him burns. "Rovis can't be there. He just can't."

Because if he is, then he's probably already dead.

And Tal never got to say goodbye. He never got to be with Rovis, in the way that he's wanted to for over *five years*. He never got to kiss Rovis or tell him about all the things he makes Tal feel. The closest thing they had was an 'almost.'

He drifts on his feet in a daze. His chest feels hollow, like he's too afraid to breathe when his lungs are sliced open.

"Tal?" He feels Saige's soft touch on his elbow, and his fingers slip off of Narvaez's expensive coat. "Did you hear what Damian just said?"

Tal blinks and shifts his blank eyes towards Narvaez, who holds his stare and repeats, "Rovis is still alive. He's a tough son of a bitch, and he's going to survive."

"For how long?" Tal presses. "What does it matter, if he's going to die in there, sooner or later? Fuck, I never should have left him."

"And you would have, what, stayed by his side every minute of the day and stopped the Agency from getting their hands on him?" Narvaez raises an unimpressed brow. "Look, we're going to break him out, and he's just going to have to hold on until then."

"Break him out?" Tal scoffs, incredulous. "Are you crazy? It's not possible. The Playground is impenetrable. There are too many Agents, and too much security. Whose bullshit idea was this?"

"Weren't you the kid who broke into President Feyrer's 'high security' artificial intelligence program and rewrote a section to make his personal mansion play a children's movie about axolotls on all the walls for a month straight?"

"You did what?" Saige steps closer with too much excitement, mischief and glee dancing in her eyes.

"It was a dare," Tal shoots back. "I was a fledgling who had to go through some weird hazing thing that the Aconite Digitals had back then."

Saige laughs. "You hacked the president's house when you were twelve? I'm offended that I missed out on this."

"The point is," Narvaez interrupts, "the security system isn't the problem. We will be outnumbered, even if I can manage what Zero asked me to do."

"Even if I can— Wait, what did she ask from you?"

Narvaez rolls his eyes and sighs, shaking his head. "Something next to impossible. I almost want to ignore her, because what would a child know? But she has trapped me in her logic, so I don't want to risk Rovis's life by not taking her seriously. We don't call her the Ace of Crowns without reason; she knows more about other organizations than any of us. She knows exactly who holds what kinds of power and where. If she's playing a bigger game and I'm a piece of it, then so be it. I will do as she asks. And you should do the same. Go back to Dyvris, now. I have no idea what she's up to, but I'm sure she has her reasons."

"Hold on." Tal flexes his metal hand, scowling. "I should be in Torch City, ripping apart the Agents standing between me and Rovis. Why the hell should I go to some depressing mountains and play mother hen in a floating house?"

"I don't care what you do," Narvaez says impatiently. "She said something about needing people loyal to Rovis as backup and guards after the main event, because he will be in terrible shape when we get him out."

Tal crosses his arms, still irked. "A text message would have done the trick."

"Like I said, I don't know what she's thinking. I personally think you'd be much more useful helping me claw through the Playground. Is that your plan? To come with me instead of going back to Dyvris?"

Tal falters. That's what he would *like* to do, because all he can think about is Rovis. He tries not to imagine the light fading from Rovis's eyes when one of the government's colossal robot pets crushes his chest. Every muscle in Tal's body screams at him to get to Rovis, keep him safe and away from the Agency, and never let go again.

But Zero is playing another one of her games, this time with more players than Tal can ever think of, and with more motivation to win than she's ever had.

She has been caught off guard before, and she isn't without her miscalculations.

So what if she's wrong this time? What if Tal's placement is what makes or breaks this plan? What happens if he goes to Torch City with Narvaez? And what happens if he goes back to Dyvris to take over the Aconites?

Tal glances at Narvaez again.

How did a seventeen-year-old girl convince the head of the Rose Skulls to go with her plan, no doubt only providing a small percentage of her thoughts?

This is the same girl who chewed out Damian Narvaez for trying to drug Rovis, scolded him like he's a child, dumped the spiked drink over his head, then passed out in Tal's arms several minutes later because she was brash enough to gulp down the drink for Rovis.

Tal's head hurts trying to decide if Zero can be trusted for this particular matter.

"Oh." Narvaez tilts his head. "She also said to remember what happened the night before you left Dyvris."

The image of blue light crackling from Rovis's stick and a furious glare slams into Tal's mind. He staggers back and clench his hands into fists, trembling and drawing blood from his left palm, as if that would erase the terrible memory already branded in his brain.

"What?" Saige demands, grabbing Tal's arm. "What happened that night?"

"I…"

"I'm heading out," Narvaez interjects. "Contact me if you want to join my people in breaking Rovis out of the Playground."

Tal nods absently, and the siblings watch the Skull boss leave before Saige turns back to her brother with a serious expression.

"Tell me."

Tal sighs, closing his eyes. "I almost hurt her."

"You did? Zero?" Saige curls her fingers on his arm. "You only said you left things on bad terms before. And I thought she led you to me. She still helped you?"

"She did. She didn't care. Actually, Rovis was angrier about it than she was."

"It's Zero," Saige says as though that's an explanation in itself. "She couldn't give less shits about it."

"Then what does she want from me?" Tal growls, glaring at the Zessroan character carved onto the column. "Does she want me to feel guilty about it still, after months have passed, after I dropped everything to track her down when the Syndicate got her? Does she want to appeal to my duties as the underboss, so that I'd go back to Dyvris and make up for the fact that I left? Does she want to mock me for running away, every single time things get hard?"

He pauses.

Then he says, voice low and shaking with fury, "Does she want me to stay away from Rovis?"

A soft chuckle pulls him out of his speculations. Saige leans against the nearest car and stares out into the distance in this dreary bunker.

"What's so funny?" Tal seethes.

"I think she just wanted to give you more reasons to fight." His sister smirks, amused. "She has clearly succeeded in doing so."

Tal narrows his eyes. "I don't understand."

"Knowing Zero, she probably has prepared for whichever choice you make. Go to Torch City, or return to Dyvris, you're not going to affect her plans too much either way. That's why she had Damian pass along the message, so that you'd know what your alternative is. She probably prefers that you go back to the Aconites, though, and I don't know for what reason."

"You got all that from one cryptic sentence?" Tal raises a brow, doubtful.

"You do remember the amount of code you had to get through to figure out where I was, don't you?"

"Okay, fine. You little teenagers have your own weird way of communicating. She could have told me all of this herself. Zero was here, and she definitely knew we were here, too, so where the fuck is she?"

Saige sighs. "Are you really going to waste time trying to understand the inner workings of Zero's mysterious psyche? The love of your life is in danger, and you're still standing here."

"I wouldn't even be saving him if I went back to Dyvris."

"If that's how you see it, then go to Torch City."

"But—"

"Stars and bloody cities, you are so whiny." Saige rolls her eyes. "Just get out of here and start driving east. Both cities are that way anyway. You'll make the right decision."

Tal frowns. "Are you not coming with me?"

"I'm staying," Saige says plainly. "I'm going to help the Faceless push through this last barrier and do what Zero suggests. What she's asking me to do makes sense to me. Besides, I'd be no use whether you choose to go to Dyvris or Torch City."

"You almost lost your life just a few months ago," Tal reminds her.

Saige gestures at the hidden door, and they can hear the thundering of all the people that showed up to this conference to rebel against the Purish.

"I'm not alone," she says. "At this point, in this depraved country, the only road left for us is to fight. I'd rather die having told the world our story, than die a coward and a bystander in denial of what's to come."

Her eyes glow faintly in the darkness of the cave. Tal can't help but reach out to tuck a strand of white hair behind her ear. Too many words rise in his throat, but none come out. Whatever he wants to say, she already knows.

How unfair, Tal thinks bitterly, *that our luck was so bad we grew up in this universe.*

"Do what you need to do, *hrienalo*," Saige says softly.

Tal cups her face and presses a kiss on her forehead. "Be careful."

She pushes him lightly toward his Shapeshifter, and he goes. When he opens the door on the driver's side, he looks back. Saige shoos him impatiently.

"Are you going back to the mansion?" someone calls from the entrance to the conference.

Raven treads towards Tal, her black boots heavy against the concrete ground. Tal considers her question, still the ultimate decision he has to make.

The memory of Zero holding out a bundle of flowers for Rovis on Tomb's Day floats across Tal's mind. That was the most normal day Tal has ever had with the two of them, and it was in a cemetery.

Whatever their differences, Rovis and Zero would burn down the entire world for each other. Tal just needs to put his trust in that truth, and hope it's enough to save Rovis.

"I am," he says.

When Raven reaches his side, she nods at Saige, who beams at her.

"We need to talk about this later," Raven says.

"We will," Saige promises, a genuine smile lighting up her face.

Raven snorts and turns to Tal. "Let's go."

"You're going back to the Aconites?" Tal asks, raising a brow. "Did Zero put you up to this, too?"

She clicks her tongue, narrowing her eyes. "Do I look like Zero's sidekick to you?"

Tal opens his mouth, affronted. How is he supposed to answer this? If he says yes, Raven might just laugh and ignore him, but she'd tell Zero, who would threaten to cut his tongue out with his own knife the next time she sees him. But if he says no, Raven would accuse him of suspecting her intentions with Zero and go into a whole other rabbit hole of putting words in his mouth, just to mess with him. He knows from experience, because Raven did that several times when Rovis first recruited her, after their high school burned down. This is why Jacek was Tal's favorite. Jacek was nice.

Putting his fists on his hips, he says, "I'm not answering that."

Raven smirks, with Saige laughing in the background. "Coward."

"Well, come on then." Tal jerks his head to the car.

He settles in the driver's seat when Raven pulls open the passenger door.

"Bye, Raven!" Saige waves.

Raven salutes her, shutting the door. When Tal drives out of the tunnel and gets back on the highway, she asks, "How is your sister alive?"

Tal snorts. "She made a deal with Damian Narvaez."

"Ah."

As if that explains everything.

Tal shakes his head and focuses on driving. The car follows the curves of the road as the sun traces from the horizon to the center of the sky. Spaced-out buildings on the right give way to ashy remains of Divako. Only a few skyscrapers remain, likely the headquarters of companies owned by more rich Purish people. All the small shops and apartments have been reduced to rubbles, an eerily similar image to Lime Gateway High School. It's physical proof that their privilege makes them immune to every disaster that strikes.

The Skulls may have escaped the fire and the explosions without any losses, but what about the tourists? What about the regular people who live there? They're the ones who not only suffer from inequality, but also try to scrape by without breaking any laws. They work themselves to death to survive. They've done nothing wrong.

Even from a distance, from the highway, Tal can see Agency cars and planes and mechanical bulldogs monitoring the remains, as if waiting out the starving monsters hiding in the wreckage. Frankly, it's a scene straight out of a post-apocalyptic movie.

For a moment, Tal wants to give up.

Just stop the car right there, in the middle of the highway, and cease to exist.

This world isn't built for people like him. All the power he has is fake. The Damned can only go so far when the shades of their skin, the random programming in their genes, the lack of choice in his heritage already decided that their worth, their place in society. His reputation means nothing when the people in power consider him undeserving of life. It won't protect him when armies of Agents come to hunt him down. It won't protect his city if they want to burn it to ash. It certainly won't protect anyone that he cares about, when the Purish escape this planet and nuke the entire continent with a single command.

Tal is still the same boy that got ambushed by Purish sadists, on an ordinary walk after school, because his fate has never been his to choose.

Is this what Zero felt, so strongly and for so long, that she stole a vial of poison from the wolfsbane garden at the Aconite mansion, to break out of this life?

The confiscated vial still sits in Tal's metal arm. It feels heavier than a block of osmium.

Lost in thought, Tal almost misses the highway exit an hour later. Muscle memory saves him from flying off to the coast, and he's relieved to see Dyvris still intact. It's still his home, even though he ran away. He drives across the desert, through the glittering city, and dips into one of the

Aconites' secret tunnels, the momentum speeding up the journey below the lake and flings the Shapeshifter up into the garage.

Raven walks behind him as they ascend to the surface level in the Poison Core. Most members must be in the dining room or taking naps this time of the day, but a few Aconites are hanging around the billiard room when he walks in. They all look towards the entrance out of habit, but Vanneza does a double take, widening her eyes.

"Tal?" She drops the cue stick in her hand onto the pool table, as if unable to believe her own eyes.

He grins and opens up his arms. "Miss me?"

"Stars, you're back," Vanneza breathes, grinning. She walks over and squeezes his shoulder. "Boss would be so happy about this."

If he were here, she doesn't say. At that, the smile slips off his face, and he feels cold again.

Avery jumps up from their stupor behind her and dashes past them, shouting, "Guys, Tal's back! Stop draining our 192 proof vodka supply, Tal came back!"

Tal doesn't even have a moment to catch them before they sprint towards the Opulent House to spread the announcement. It's so typical of them that Tal shakes his head, heart aching at how different he feels being back here, how much he's changed since leaving months ago. He thought he was going to stay with the Aconites until he died, and he never expected Saige to even want to find him. But his sister turned out to be a relentless force aiming for bigger things than he imagined. Tal can no longer live life the way he has been, complacent with his stolen wealth and relishing in every law he breaks.

No, now he's going to help his sister change the world they live in. They're going to build a place where their survival isn't wrong, illegal, forbidden.

Following Vanneza, Tal makes his way to the kitchen, where Daleyza emerges from the main entrance, her eyes searching for him. Her tough features soften when she sees Tal, and she holds out a hand when he gets close enough. Tal clasps her hand, their grips tight with unspoken words. Anyone else who passes by might think they're arm wrestling.

"Welcome back, Lithium," she says, the corners of her lips tilting up. Summer comes up behind her with her arms crossed, smirking.

"It's good to see you again." Tal nods to both of them, releasing his grip on Daleyza. "Do you know how Rovis is doing?"

Daleyza's face shutters, and she tilts her head at the news holograms.

Tal frowns, looking over. A breath escapes his chest.

A video footage of Rovis almost drowning in mucky waters plays on one projection, while another shows him stabbing a robot lizard between metal plates with his spear, killing the machine in one strike. Given the timestamps, these must be replays.

"He's managing," Daleyza says. "One night is already longer than what sixty-eight percent of the prisoners in Drokklo's Playground can last."

"That won't mean a damn thing if we don't get him out of there," Tal says darkly.

She sighs, pinching the bridge of her nose. "And how are we supposed to manage that?"

Tal opens his mouth to answer, but he freezes when the entire mansion is suddenly bathed in red neon.

Alarms start blaring throughout all four buildings, white lights flashing.

In the hallway, all Aconite members tense up, scurrying to the security centers of each building.

"Warning," N.A.D.E. announces, "The Agency of Justice has reached Dyvris. Six Aconite fronts destroyed. Arden's Sunset in critical condition. One tunnel has been discovered. Self-destruct of Passage Number 4 activated. Five Agency jets have invaded the mountain range. Drones are on shoot-to-kill. Effect on the Agency: little to none. Jets advancing. Evacuation strongly recommended."

Tal clenches his jaw and resists the urge to punch the nearest wall. He can't seem to catch a break today.

Daleyza disappears to direct various teams to prepare against the Agents. All the Reapers have already gotten on the rooftops, and Tal can see moving shadows on the top floor of the Tech Hall, where the Digitals are activating all their defenses hidden in the area.

The Aconite mansion has of course been under attack before today. But it has always been petty feuds, exchanging blows with other organizations of the Damned when they feel that their territory is being threatened. The Aconites have protocols for those situations, passed down from generations of reigning over the Eastern Desert.

But they're not prepared for this. Not against the Agency.

Tal goes through the remote operative panel in his arm, fingers flying over holographic commands. He opens up all the communications channels, connecting with every single member living in this mansion and every associate spread out through the city and suburbs.

He orders everyone to leave Dyvris.

13

The Daggers of Loveias

The blade on my neck gave me shivers.

I'd been forced on my two dislocated knees for what felt like hours. Maybe it had been, given the people I was captured by. The hooded girls around me said nothing and didn't even move a hair. The one holding the sword pointed at me didn't let it dip a single time. If it weren't for the impossible way she moved when we fought earlier, I would have thought they were all androids who only looked like humans.

When I started feeling so light-headed that I though I might pass out and accidentally off myself against the edge of the blade, the door behind me swooshed open.

"Mistress," the girl bowed her head, while the rest of them gracefully floated down to one knee. The tips of eight matching silver daggers didn't scratch the shiny floor, carefully held pointed down by each of the kneeling girls in some eccentric reverence.

"You can put away the sword," answered the candied voice, regal and dangerous.

With a silver flash, it disappeared. I immediately slumped over, depositing all my weight onto my hands, but I knew better than to relax. Shiny heels clicked against the cold floor, measured and unhurried, until they stopped before my face.

A careless hand tipped up my chin, and the feeling of cold, bare fingers made my stomach lurch. I couldn't say a thing though, only glared into calculating gray eyes.

"How old?" the woman asked.

"Fifteen," the girl I fought earlier answered.

"Hmm," the woman hummed. "Not bad."

A wave of nausea hit me, and I hissed against my better judgment, "Don't touch me."

She lifted a brow, surprised but unimpressed, while electricity zapped a stripe across my back. A gasp tore out of my chest before I swallow it.

"Watch your tongue," the girl snapped. I had to wonder just how bad my luck was, that my first field assignment from Quade and Abigail was so far beyond my level of expertise. I was an unmarked fledgling for the Heartless, a nobody, hopelessly out of my depth. Amongst the Damned, I was vulnerable, weak, and naive. I might've been smart enough to track down Rovis and find the Aconites, but I was not prepared to enter such a world of 'kill or be killed.' I was a survivor, not yet a fighter. I hadn't learned everything there was to know about the organizations or held secrets that could turn the tides across nations.

In other words, I was really fucking stupid.

"Now, now," the woman chided. "Allegra, do control yourself for a moment."

"She's after the Daggers," Allegra protested.

"Is she?" The woman tilted her head at me, a dark smile creeping up her lips. "Who do you work for, dear?"

I swallowed and pursed my lips. Throwing up in her face would have been absolutely a terrible idea. Yet, I was also afraid that if I answered, she'd bring harm to the Aconites, which meant harm to Rovis and Tal.

The woman sighed and straightened, letting go of my chin and turning away. "I will not ask a second time."

"What's it worth to you?" I dared to ask.

Allegra raised her whip again, but the woman held up a hand without turning. She didn't look at either of us, yet Allegra obeyed and stilled.

"It's worth nothing to me," the woman said. "But it might be worth a great deal to you. It doesn't take a Damned to see you have no idea what you're doing. If you give me the name of your boss, I might be able to take care of it for you, and you'll become one of my Daggers. If you're worried about someone you care for, then you should hope that they never got on my bad side, because I will bury them regardless of what you say or don't say. If you don't answer me... Well, then you're on your own."

I didn't know who she was back then. I didn't know that Loveias was a dark empire ruled by a notorious queen. That's how unqualified I was for the job. I was reckless, chasing after a ghost just because I was lonely and sad, and I had no idea what it was like to navigate the realm of crime and betrayal, to control the tides, to dominate the game. I had no idea that, amongst the Damned, that was necessary for survival.

All I knew, from looking around the room, was that this woman owned an army of girls. She was cold and clinical, but that also meant pacts and loyalty. Despite how dangerous she seemed and how little experience I had, it was a gut instinct that she would keep her word.

I licked my lips and said, "I work for Quade Bianchi."

Allegra suddenly stood over me, hand twisting in my hair. She seethed, "What did you just say?"

My mouth clamped shut.

The grip on my hair yanked harder. "What the hell are you doing with my father?"

"Don't touch me," I growled, louder that time.

"You—"

Allegra struck me across the face. Before I could recover, harsh fingers tugged on my ear, and it was so much, too much like my mother, that I reached for the one knife I had left. It was hidden within the sole of my worn-out boots when they searched my weapons, and I didn't hesitate to shove it into Allegra's calf the moment I pulled it out.

And then I vomited onto the marble floor.

"Stand down," the woman said, finally interested enough to look over her shoulder with a new glint in her stare. All the girls had closed in on me, various weapons drawn, but they didn't move against the woman's order. Not even Allegra, who snarled at me on her bleeding leg, sharpened mace in hand.

"I see no reason to spare her," Allegra said.

"Do not question me," the woman warned, and Allegra backed off, but she still clearly wanted to murder me. Of course, I didn't know back then that Quade sold his daughter to a trafficking ring when her mother died and couldn't take care of her anymore.

I didn't know that this woman, who was studying me, found Allegra but did not buy her, instead gave her a knife and an ultimatum, to kill her captors and fight her way out, or to stay a victim for the rest of her life. Nor did I know that the woman did the same for hundreds of girls trapped in trafficking, domestic abuse, and slavery.

Blood red lips curved into a sharp smile. "I'm guessing you weren't born with that touch-aversion, little one. Am I correct?"

Still coughing out bile that burned in my throat, I quite literally spat, "Maybe."

"You're a fledgling Heartless with the Aconites," she deduced, scrolling on her phone. "Zero, I presume?"

My silence was enough of an answer for her.

"Well, hello, Zero. You are quite a nuisance, trying to trick me and stabbing one of mine like that. At least you've got spine." She leaned forward, peering down at me. "My name is Enyo. I would like to offer you a deal."

⸺⸺◦◦◦⸺⸺

A cold point of a dagger pokes Zero's cheek, not hard enough to draw blood.

"Hey, baby Ace." Allegra nudges her. "Stop frowning."

Zero rolls her eyes and bats the dagger away without sparing her a glance.

"Uh oh," Allegra says, apparently unable to leave Zero alone today. "Someone's in a mood. Where'd your head go?"

Sighing irritably, Zero answers, "My first night here."

They're sitting in the upstairs lobby of the grand hotel that Enyo owns, exactly the same place where Allegra dragged Zero to get punished by Enyo two years ago. Zero has been lounging on the couch for almost an hour, waiting for an irrelevant businessman to finish his meeting with Enyo so she can go in to make deals with her to save Rovis. At least it's a really, really nice couch. The black leather shines under the dim light, the solid yet flexible material perfect for her aching joints. She could sleep here for days. Zero tilts her head back onto the comfortable leather and glances at the other Daggers standing around on their phones, too engrossed in their co-op game to pay attention to her and Allegra.

"Ah, yes." Allegra sinks back into the cushions, grinning. "You were truly a baby back then. Look how much you've grown."

"I stabbed you," Zero says blandly.

"But then you got my awful father killed, so we're more than even."

Zero hums absently. The logic of that statement has more than a few flaws, but her mind is too occupied with all the other pieces of her plan to break Rovis out of Drokklo's Playground. This memory of the Daggers is yet another secret that she needs to tell him about, even though she very much tried to bury it in the landfills of her brain.

But Zero needs to come clean about why Rovis lost his finger.

Don't you dare die before me, she tells him silently, from halfway across the country. *Otherwise I'll just take another vial of aconitine and follow you right down to Drokklo's realm.*

Another poke on her cheek has Zero snatching the knife from Allegra's fingers and throwing it across the lobby. It lodges in the wall between two paintings, drawing the attention of the other Daggers.

"Seriously, Zero, what's gotten into you?" Allegra demands after a moment of shock. "Is this what it looks like now that you've finally developed a rebellious phase on top of the regular angst of being alive on this planet?"

"Let it go, Allegra." Another Dagger, Bryn, says with a bored voice as she returns to her game. Without looking back up, she comes over and coaxes Allegra into scooting over so she could sit in between them, thumbs furiously spamming buttons on her phone to fight zombies. "Something's clearly on her mind."

Whooshing of the doors to Enyo's office opening saves Zero from the rest of this conversation. A haughty man stalks out, and Hallow, the Dagger standing on the other side of the lobby, decides in that moment to pull out Allegra's dagger and fling it back.

The blade flies so close to his face that a few strands of his hair twitch from the trailing breeze, before the handle lands neatly in Allegra's grip.

Chuckles sound around the room while the man glares indignantly at Hallow, who casually tosses her own knife. Zero stands, lips twitching to hide her amusement, as she moves to enter Enyo's meeting room.

"I'm coming with you," Allegra says.

Zero waves a hand without turning and responds unenthusiastically, "Fine."

Allegra continues, "You're too volatile today. I—"

"I'm pretty sure Enyo would slice my throat three times before I can even take out the knife in my sleeve," Zero interrupts, "but okay."

The top-ranking Dagger probably would have said something more if they weren't walking right into the room, where Enyo forbids useless bantering. Zero should adopt that policy someday. Enyo lounges on her long red couch with her legs crossed, idly swirling a glass of red wine. Gothic finger claw rings sparkle against the stem of the glass. Her jet black long hair drapes over the top of her dark gray three-piece, bringing out the silver in her eyes.

"It's been a while, baby Ace," she drawls without looking up from the mini-whirlpool in her hand. "To what do I owe the pleasure?"

"Three deals," Zero states.

That earns her a raised brow and Enyo's full attention. "Go on."

"One: Send Damian Narvaez all the files you have on Drokklo's Playground. Maps of the place, blueprints, robot designs, everything."

Enyo chuckles and takes a sip. "That will cost you a limb, at least."

"I'll pay it."

"Can you?" Enyo flicks a pointed look at Zero's leg, twinkling with prosthetics between the slit of her black dress. It's the reason why she isn't able to bow properly today, in contrast to Allegra's knelt form behind her. Zero isn't that nimble with the nano-skeleton at the moment. Fighting may have the boost of adrenaline, which she has learned to use to her advantage with her new condition, but staying in one position for an indefinite time is another matter. Even walking or standing isn't the same anymore.

"I heard about Ferrisque," Enyo continues. "What were you doing there, all alone?"

She either got her information from her astounding network of spies, or Alexei followed Zero's advice to come to Loveias and told on her. Zero doesn't have enough context to find a way to distract Enyo, so she only repeats, "I'll pay whatever price you name."

"I know you will. But I asked you a question, Ace."

Zero internally sighs. "Vacation."

"Vacation," Enyo echoes, not at all buying Zero's lie. She scoffs and takes another sip. "Sure. Next time you go on vacation, at least go somewhere a Dagger is stationed at. Or any of your contacts. What's the point of knowing people in a dozen organizations if you're not going to reach out for help? You're lucky the Starcatchers were there that night."

The point was so they wouldn't help, Zero thinks but doesn't dare say out loud. The truth is irrelevant now, washed away by the trauma of almost losing her leg, getting mind-controlled, and finding out Rovis landed in Drokklo's Playground. She has a promise to keep, and she can't do that by wallowing in self-loathing.

"Alas, it's in the past," Enyo waves off Zero's silence. "What's your second request?"

"Order all the Daggers you have inside the Agency to tear it down. Blow up all the labs and drug manufacturing plants."

"Oh, is she a revolutionary now?" Enyo laughs, a sharp sound from her throat. "Fortunately for you, I already did. As of this morning, all Daggers within Agency centers across the country are to kill all the Agents at their station and destroy all of their work. I told you about their exoplanets research even though I let you spy on the drug experiments, remember? You saw what Nova Ly was talking about. Darling, did you really think I'd live in a world where my girls can be once again controlled by men and the self-righteous Purish?"

Zero keeps her mouth shut, recalculating.

If the Agency is toppling down all over the country, then maybe the Agents stationed in the Playground might be distracted. They might even be sent over to the labs, which means Damian might have a chance to actually brute force into the arena and get Rovis out.

"It's not a deal if I'm not doing it for you," Enyo says. "Finish speaking."

Zero swallows. "Also have the Daggers inside Drokklo's Playground fight their way out in a couple days. I have people going in."

"By 'people' you mean the Rose Skulls." Enyo narrows her eyes. "That's why you want me to give the information to Damian Narvaez. And you want my people to meet yours in the middle. Tell me, what is this fixation on the Playground? I saw your Aconite boss on the livestream. Is he the one you want?"

Zero's jaw clenches.

Enyo laughs, this time incredulous. "This is more than loyalty. Who is he to you?"

"I do not ask for your reasons when you make your requests, Enyo," Zero hears herself grit out. "Do not pry into mine."

She hears a hitch in Allegra's breathing behind her, and before her Enyo's gaze has fallen cold.

Slowly, Enyo uncrosses her legs and sets her second heel on the floor. She rises. Chills run across Zero's skin, and suddenly Zero wants to hide in a coffin. When Enyo takes a step forward, she hurries two steps back and slides onto her bad knee next to Allegra, dropping her eyes as she bites back a grunt from the pain. Her own silver dagger slips out from her sleeve, tip pointing down toward the marble.

"My sincere apologies, Mistress." Zero says to the floor. "I mean no disrespect."

The clicks of heels don't stop, and for a second she thinks she might have time-traveled back to that night when she was fifteen. Except, this time,

Enyo brushes Zero's chin with cold, dull tips of her long finger claws, rather than the skin of her own fingers.

"Oh, child." Enyo gently tilts Zero's head back so that their eyes meet. Her gray eyes have a frosty warmth to it, like the shining moon on a winter night. She whispers, "Get up."

Gritting her teeth, Zero heaves herself up on her right leg and drags her left one up to standing. Enyo watches her with one arm across her chest, holding the elbow of the other that's holding her wine glass still.

"I suppose I have my answer anyway," she says. "That's why you sent Alexei to me, isn't it? It appears that I've had quite a few misunderstandings with my sibling, but we've begun resolving them, thanks to you. Perhaps I owe you one favor, out of your two requests."

"That's not..." Zero trails off, a bit lost, then restarts, "I didn't do it for that."

The icy finger claws brush through Zero's hair. "Baby Ace. I know that. In exchange for Alexei, I'll have my people ensure that Rovis Bozyd-Wei makes it out of the Playground alive. And for the information I will send to the Skull King, I demand a truth from you. Who gave you the touch-aversion?"

Zero stares at Enyo, shocked. She doesn't see how this is a square deal, when Enyo is giving Narvaez decades of research upon Zero's request, and all she's asking for is Zero to tell her who broke her. What would she even do with this information? It can't be used against Zero, unless someone has successfully invented necromancy. Enyo already knows everything she wants to know about her people. Perhaps it's a test, to see if Zero has truly moved on and gotten stronger, if she's fit to be a Dagger. Or perhaps Enyo Zhao is letting Zero off easy, for some mysterious reason. But then again, this might not be as simple of a question for the other Daggers to answer, knowing the things they've been through.

Enyo only raises a brow when Zero hesitates.

The question is, to Zero's own surprise, less suffocating than the previous one about Rovis. Zero has long come to terms with the memories of broken glass and flying cleavers in her childhood home. The Ace of Crowns is born from nightmares, because Zero was raised in a nightmare. No one can use it against her mind as much as herself.

"My mother."

And it comes out just like that. It's a pebble that falls onto the ground and doesn't bounce or echo. It's a drop of rain that makes no ripples when it meets the surface of an ocean. It's a photon that flies past the event horizon and gets lost in the rupture of spacetime.

It's simply meaningless.

"Is she dead?" Enyo asks, disinterested.

"Yes."

She gazes at Zero with a slight tilt to her head. Her silence makes Zero twitch, but she stays quiet and waits.

"You will not kneel for me again."

Zero freezes. The words suck the air out of her lungs, and her heart pounds loudly in her chest.

At her expression, Enyo huffs. "I'm not banishing you, dear. You were never my subordinate, only a wild card. Did you forget? You were an Aconite first."

"You made me who I am," Zero says, uncomprehending.

Enyo clicks her tongue. "That was mostly because I owed your cousin a debt. But you did not disappoint."

"You do know Dziye," Zero deduces, mildly stunned.

Enyo only raises a brow, as a non-answer. She repeats, "You will not kneel for me again. Understand?"

Zero hesitates, but then bows her head. "Yes, Enyo."

Enyo nods and walks away. She gestures for Allegra to stand. "I accept your deals, Ace of Crowns. You are both dismissed."

As soon as they make it out the door, Allegra asks, "Is your leg okay?"

Zero forgets to answer, as her thoughts spin from that interaction and her brain tries to work out the next steps. Damian's and Enyo's forces combined should be enough to tear apart the Playground. But as always, her backup plans need to have backups.

Then a familiar redhead catches Zero's eyes when they reach the ground floor.

"What's Didier Whiston doing here?" She turns to Allegra with a suspicious look. "Enyo should know that he has WVM-67 and not to have anyone near him."

"Relax. We're going to poison him."

"Oh." Zero lets out a breath of relief, though she doesn't know how she has the mental capacity to worry about a brainless and irrelevant Purish boy right now.

Unfortunately, Whiston sees her.

Even more tragically, he has the audacity to approach her.

"Would I be ruining any plans if I kill him before you get to poison him?" she mutters to Allegra under her breath.

Allegra scoffs. "You? Killing someone? I'd like to see that. But yes, you would. We have to deal with something first."

"Damn it." Zero plasters on a smile as Whiston comes to a stop in front of them, right outside the bar. "Hello, Didier."

"Genesis," he says the fake name she gave him before, then nods at Allegra. He smiles at Zero. "Fancy seeing you here."

"Oh, I'm just visiting family. What are you doing here?"

"I see. I'm here on business, as usual." Whiston offers an arm. "Would you like to take a walk with me?"

"Of course," she says, hooking her arm through his.

As he guides her away, she waves goodbye over her shoulder to Allegra, with a smile that says, *I'll try my best not to murder him.* Allegra narrows her eyes and flicks a warning glance toward Whiston's other arm, tucked in his pocket. Zero understands immediately and nods, sharpening the edges of her grin.

When Whiston takes her to the outdoor pool, she anticipates the moment he draws the switchblade. With reflexes she gained from training sessions with Daleyza, Zero grabs his hand, twists his wrist, and catches the blade falling from his grip. With a precise kick behind his knee, Zero lets him fall to the ground and turns away. Gathering up potential, she runs several steps up the side a column of the cabana, and pushes off of it with enough force to spin sideways in the air once, before she crashes into Whiston.

The moment she lands, the impact of her left foot slamming into the ground sends out a blast that quakes everything around them within a thirty-two-meter radius.

The energy in the prosthetic and her boots, stored from all her moves since leaving Dyvris, was enough to fracture all the bones in Whiston's body. She hears the satisfying sound of heads crashing against the wall around them.

"Two watchers, one getaway car," Zero counts, pressing the blade against Whiston's neck. "Either you're really good at hiding the rest of your backup, or you really, really underestimated me."

Whiston cries out in pain beneath her, and Zero rolls her eyes.

"No killing!" she hears Allegra yell behind her.

Zero growls and sends five of her larger and more expensive spider-bots down her sleeve, recently enhanced to accelerate bone healing. Whiston doesn't stop groaning while the bots fix him up, and Zero doesn't stop rolling her eyes at the amount of noise he's making from such minor and short-lived injuries.

A shadow falls over her.

Zero looks up to see Hallow standing on an antigravity disk, watching with her arms crossed. Despite her posture, she looks amused.

"You can put the knife away, you know," she says.

Sighing with disappointment, Zero stands and slips the switchblade into one of the inside pockets of her coat. Allegra appears next to her, throwing two unconscious Purish men onto the ground, and Bryn joins the chaos by flying in on another antigravity disk. When the spiders finish their work and crawl up Zero's leg, Whiston is still gasping on his back.

Pathetic.

"This is such a waste of my time," Zero says, turning to leave.

"Wait," Whiston has the nerve to call out.

"No killing," Allegra repeats without moving.

Slowly, Zero turns her head and slants Whiston an unimpressed look. He's on his knees now, gingerly standing up.

"That really, really hurt," he says, chuckling. "But that was sexy."

What the fuck, is all Zero thinks before she throws her right hand out. The three sharp cracks of metal snapping into place could cut falling leaves in the air.

Whiston flinches back with wide eyes when his face is suddenly bathed in red light from the crackling electricity of Zero's extra-long shock stun baton, the weapon swinging towards him.

But the blow doesn't land when Allegra catches Zero's arm.

"What, I can't even slap him around a bit?" Zero scowls at her.

"The Mistress is getting impatient," Allegra says, voice low.

"Hey, now." Whiston holds up his hands, grinning easily, as though unthreatened by the women surrounding him. "My father's orders were to kill you. I simply want to offer you a deal. That is how the Damned operate, isn't it?"

"The Damned make deals and follow through with them," Zero sneers. "The same cannot be said about people like you."

"Is this about the virus? I must say, that wasn't anything personal. I've given it to— Oh, I don't know, thirteen girls now?"

She laughs darkly. "Don't worry, I already knew that. I don't want anything to do with you, so hurry back to your hotel room before I cut your tongue out."

"And what will you do after that? Die along with the rest of the roach population? I'm here to offer an alliance. After our time together, I realized that not all of the Damned are worthless. You've got a brain behind that pretty face. I'll keep you from a pathetic death, if you'll give me the names of all the mindless rebels tearing my country apart."

Zero tilts her head, slowly, and narrows her eyes. "Is that really the best you can do?"

Whiston falters. His throat shifts as he gulps. Zero almost rolls her eyes. Such a terrible deal, and an even worse delivery.

"Look, Genesis, if that's even your real name—"

"Your father didn't tell you my real name?" Zero asks, sharp with derision.

"He never tells me anything," Whiston shoots back. "He always orders me around, but he won't ever give me more than that. I'm going to do things my way now, starting with you. If you work with me, I can get us a safe life, in a safe house, away from all the disasters that are mysteriously hitting the country."

Mysteriously, she mocks in her head. The Purish really don't believe in consequences, do they? They think nature just randomly started acting up and self-destructing, rather than taking responsibility for all the ways they're hurting the planet. Stars, where did all the people with a nonzero intelligence quotient go?

"You're one of the best spies in the world," Whiston continues, "and I have money and power. If we have each other, nothing can stop us. You can even marry me."

And that. That is a sentence Zero wishes to never hear from a man.

Disgusted by and incredulous of his general existence, she curls her lips and kicks Whiston into the pool.

Did he really think he could bribe her, just like that? With no insurance or blackmail or any sign that he did any research on her at all? He must be truly arrogant to think that a Damned would take his shitty deal. And truly desperate, if he wants the Ace of Crowns.

Zero shudders at the thought. She wants to tear her skin off from hearing his last sentence. Never has she ever felt so repulsed. As revenge, she takes a powder bomb and tosses it into the pool, where Whiston splashes around, trying to get back to the edge. He yelped when the powder bomb explodes in the water.

"What is this?" he demands.

"You'll see," Zero says, voice flat.

As though on cue, he starts scratching his neck, red lines blooming on his pale skin. Then his nails dig into his face, the clawing movements becoming more and more erratic. Whiston's eyes widen, indignant.

"How dare you!"

Laughing, Hallow waves her hand and says, "We'll take it from here, Zero."

After one last glare of disdain, Zero strides out to find her motorbike and swing her leg over the seat, her long coat swishing with the motion.

Back in the abandoned bunker, Zero set in motion four different parts of her scheme, but then had to make a detour to Loveias to appeal to Enyo, before going back to downtown Aurodus for Jordan Faal. That's just the order she had to go with, to optimize her eighteen-step plan. Now her bike flies through glittering streets and dusty rubbles alike, forever beneath the ominous sky in its various shades of fire. Cities crumble and fall one by one, and Zero is at war with time, placing her bets on all of her last cards.

When she finds the restaurant front where Damian said Jordan would be, she doesn't bother looking around the bustling tables. Zero stalks over to the nook by the kitchen without even glancing at the members of the Crystal Ring who are standing and yelling at her to stop. All she has to do is hold up her Ace of Crowns signature card to the ones guarding the 'Staff Only' door to a hidden stairway, because Damian already called ahead to say that Zero's coming.

Besides, none of the organizations can care much about lines and feuds when the government is burning them to the ground, until they're nothing but cinder and ash.

She follows one of the guards up the stairs, dimly lit with blue and purple hues. He knocks on the door to Jordan's office when they get to the top. The top floor looks a lot like the Tech Hall, with too many monitors and people crowding around incomprehensible lines of code. The Crystal Ring is indeed the central hub of the dark web and illicit information flow.

"What business?" a faint voice calls behind the door.

The guard cracks open the door and pokes his head into the office.

"The Ace of Crowns is here, Boss."

"Let her in."

He widens the door and steps back, gesturing for Zero to go in. She gives him a curt nod before focusing on the scene in the office.

Jordan looks up from xyr work on the desk, surrounded by other Rings and holographic maps, likely planning for the best escape when the Agency inevitably comes for them next.

It takes Jordan a moment, but Zero sees the second xe recognizes her.

Xyr eyes brighten, lips parting with wonder.

"You," xe breathes.

Zero allows herself to smile, an echo of her past. Gentle hands of a high school volunteer once taught her how to solder, in the crowded middle school robotics room, when she was addicted to gambling and winning while Jacek, Raven, and Lila did all the actual work for competitions. Back then, Jacek was in charge of software, Raven hardware, and Lila logistics. Zero was only there to fill the fourth spot needed to compete, but Jordan always made her learn.

"Everyone out," Jordan orders.

"Boss," the guard protests behind Zero.

"I trust her," Jordan says firmly. "Everyone out."

Confused glances are thrown around the room, but the Ring members shuffle out without another word against their boss. Once the door shuts, Jordan stands, studying her.

"You've gotten taller now."

"I would hope so," Zero says, sarcastic but not scathing. "Last time you saw me, I was thirteen. It's good to see you again, Jordan."

Emotions flit over xyr face at the sound of her voice.

"Will you finally tell me your name now?" xe asks softly.

Zero never did tell xem. Xe was only a volunteer who didn't have access to registration sheets, and she didn't care to connect with anyone other than her existing friends. Jordan didn't know who she was to Rovis, nor did xe know that she disappeared during high school to join him in the Aconites.

Years later, Jordan once again requested to know her identity when she sent xem Griffin's file during her time in the Agency anonymously, no face, no name. But she ghosted xem then, too.

Today's different.

For once, for Rovis, she tells Jordan the truth. Zero's lips shift into a minuscule smile.

"My name is Sirena Wei, and Rovis Bozyd-Wei is my brother."

14

Sweet Dreams

H e doesn't know how much longer he can last.

Rovis leans his elbows heavily against his knees on the bench in the preparation room, clutching the spear in one hand, head bowed as he tries to breathe through the pain.

After the robot bear tore his shirt, Rovis ripped up the remains to wrap up his cuts. So all the scars and tattoos written over his torso have been exposed to the world by the hovering drones. And permanently on the internet for anyone to search up for entertainment. He has never hated technology more. Tal might be a little offended by that sentiment, but he isn't here.

Rovis struggles to straighten, head spinning. He has no idea how many days it's been since he ended up here. It feels like it's been years, but it's probably not even a week. And because the Agents keep throwing him back into the arena with few meals and very little time to sleep, Rovis feels as though every single cell in his body is rotting from the inside out. It takes all his energy to not walk into a wall when he's on his feet. He swears that he's been on the field more than any of the other prisoners, but he can't be sure, with his barely lucid state.

His brain feels like expired mashed potatoes mixed with spoiled milk.

Marudas played with his mind several times while he was out fighting, but not enough to give him a fatal wound.

Rovis almost wishes that he'd finish the job and make the kill.

But then he'd be a hypocrite, wouldn't he? After all the shit he gave Rena — and all the ugly thoughts he couldn't say out loud, that he stormed out and kept them inside his head instead — how could he give up? He can't, because he's survived the Purish for way too long to die now. Yet he can't see a way out, and everyone knows there isn't one in Drokklo's Playground. So what's the point?

A flurry of Agents rush across the hall outside the bulletproof glass walls surrounding the Playground's next victims. Rovis frowns, watching them through bleary eyes, vision swimming like a kaleidoscope.

The world must be in chaos above ground, if they've been running around nonstop since Rovis's second round in the arena. One time he even hallucinated some Agents talking about being sent away to protect spaceships. Spaceships. As in, vehicles that carry passengers into space. That might have been the most bizarre thing his brain has ever come up with.

More plausibly, he's overheard that the Daggers of Loveias have been destroying Agency centers and labs all across the country. Even if he has to die here, alone and humiliated on national television, he feels a bit of satisfaction that the Damned are fighting back above ground, against the people who forced them to become monsters. He's been seeing the same two guards lately, judging by height and voice, which means the Agency is suffering a staff shortage at the Playground. Perhaps they're sending Agents to recover the drugs that the Daggers are demolishing. He'd guess that the government prioritizes controlling the larger population more than entertaining the rich.

Rovis digs his knuckles into his forehead, brows knitted. What use is it, to try to figure out what the Purish are doing? He sighs, his shoulders sagging as his chest caves in.

"Just hold on a little bit longer, Rozzie," Rena says, soft yet adamant.

Rovis jerks his head up, heart pounding and eyes flitting over the room. But of course the only other people in here are Agents and gladiator-prisoners.

Great. He's imagining the sound of his sister's voice now.

Stars, he misses her.

The gates crank open once again. Rovis has to look away with the amount of light coming from the arena. His fingers curl into fists as he forces himself to get on his feet and go through another round of this torture.

A surge of suffocating and poisonous animosity swells in his chest at the simulated sky. Every prisoner here knows they're trapped underground in this twisted game until they die; the decorative projection only mocks them.

Mechanical snarling grounds Rovis back into the present, just in time to roll beneath the shadow of a leaping, gigantic, metal wolf.

His joints creak with effort, but he grits his teeth and gets back on his feet, squinting his eyes through the dust left flying behind the wolf's clumsy landing. When the house-sized robot lumbers around, its spiky tail swishes and impales through one of the other gladiators, too occupied with the copper hippo to watch their back.

Disappointed by the kill stolen from it, the hippo turns to growl at Rovis.

"Okay," he mutters. "One of you has to go."

The wolf is faster, so Rovis waits for it to come. Its red eyes gleam when it runs toward Rovis again. With the energy boost from Tal's design of the boots, he manages to flip onto the wolf's head, but he scrambles to stay on with the excessive momentum and lack of grip. His fingers catch onto the plate at the neck where there has to be a socket for the metal head to rotate, and he digs his feet into the sides.

He thrusts the spear into the crack, hoping that the useless thing doesn't snap as the wolf shakes its head violently in an attempt to get rid of Rovis. The jerky movement throws the body on its tail outward, which miraculously hits the hippo's bulky face, blocking the sensors for just a moment. Rovis only spares a single, quick glance at the hippo to make sure no deadly teeth are anywhere near his body. With a grunt, he forces the spear even deeper with aching arms and pulls the handle.

The wolf's head pops off, wires ripping apart.

Either Rovis is stronger than he realizes, particularly in desperate situations, or the spear is more durable than he thought.

Rovis hops down and rolls away before the rest of the wolf collapses into a heap of metal that Tal would delightfully scavenge through for parts if he could get his hands on it. The hippo clambers over faster now, and Rovis hurries to pull out the wolf's tail with force he didn't think he'd have left. Sparks of electricity burn his eyes as more wires snap.

He turns just in time to fling the spiky tail into the hippo's wide open mouth waiting to crush him before it bites down.

The massive tail is larger than a party bus, so Rovis drops it as soon as it penetrates the hippo's brain, and the monster shuts down, mechanical eyes dimming. The three other gladiators are still busy with their own robots, so Rovis dares to dart his eyes over to the roaring crowd.

Instead of obnoxious cheers, the cacophony seems to come from fights breaking out among families in the stands, with some dots of red and brown uniformed Agents trying to keep things civil. Rovis thinks his mind is breaking, trying to understand what's happening.

"Rovis, *get down.*"

He instinctively listens, sliding into a lunge to avoid getting bowled over by a tiger.

A shadow falls over him before the tiger could come back for Rovis. He looks over his shoulder to see a familiar man in a gray coat shooting the robot with a freezing blaster, and he's all too certain that this is just a dream. The voice he heard belonged to Rena, not this man.

"Damian?"

Rovis quickly glances around to note that the other three gladiators are somehow now dead, either because the game masters decided to paralyze them, or because they lost control of their fights in the two seconds that Rovis looked away.

His reaction time is getting worse, he realizes as he jerks back from a pair of red, glaring headlights. A scorpion tail is about to slice open his skull when a violet energy shield appears over him like a magical sanctuary.

Rena's feet slide backwards in the sand when the tail hits the shield coming out of her forearm guard, stopping just before his own pathetic, curled-up form. The red ends of her hair swing behind her lean shoulders even as Rovis blinks several times to will away the hallucination.

"This has got to be the cruelest dream ever," Rovis mutters, staring up at her.

"Are you calling me fake?" He hears her snap, both in front of him and in his ear, and he realizes that there's a comms device in his ear. Rena goes on to say, "You know I'm quite sensitive about that."

Rovis freezes, his thoughts exploding in chaos. Theories formulate in his head to explain what he's seeing and hearing, but he has no idea how any of this is possible. To challenge his sanity even more, his two Agent guards are flying out on antigravity disks and attacking the very last robot, a hybrid of a bat and an elephant. The rest of Agents are fighting against themselves, and Rovis is even more confused to see Lasans in the mix, branded with marks of organizations from all over the country, as he vaguely remembers from the Aconite database.

Suddenly, a piercing headache tears a howl of pain out of his chest. His fingers are pulling his hair out, but all he can feel is an overwhelming urge to stand up. Even though his body is saying *absolutely not,* his limbs stubbornly push beneath his body on burnt knees, scraped arms, broken wrists. He stumbles on his feet, and voices shout at him, but he can't understand the words.

His vision starts to dim. Rovis thinks the last three robots explode into tiny bits, raining down on him, debris catching in his hair, before all he can see are shadows of different shades. The loss of sight causes him to lose his balance, and his right wrist breaks even more, possibly jamming into his radius or ulna bones when his head spins and the ground tilts.

Someone grabs his shoulder, but another jolt of pain forces him to lash out. With no control over his muscles, he's fighting, and he doesn't know who it is, only faintly aware that the dark shadow in front of him is taller than him. When his body starts slowing down, fatigued, the headache intensifies again until Rovis forces himself to land more hits.

He winds back for another punch when warmth closes over his wrist. Rovis kicks away the tall shadow in front of him with a growl and tries to bat away the one standing too close to him, but this shadow is smaller and slippery and leading him away. It's almost like how his paint brushes swirl through watercolor, the way that the shadow takes up every possible negative space to avoid his hits.

But everyone has a pattern. The small shadow favors its right side. And Rovis identifies his attacker's pattern quickly, urged on by the pounding inside his skull, and catches their neck swiftly, before he slams them to the ground.

He feels more than sees the shadow struggle. Nails claw at his fingers, yet the jerky movements are nothing compared to his strength. An unwelcome and unexpected surge of joy blooms in his chest, and he doesn't understand what it means, but he tightens his grip.

Then something hard smashes the back of his head.

It hurts a hundred times more than the throbbing from before, so much that Rovis's vision completely blacks out, and all the last bits of his energy drain out of limbs like a vacuum is sucking the life out of him.

Suddenly, he's falling into true darkness, nothing like the sleepless nights in the cities. There's no warning written in the red sky, no flashing buildings infested with parties. There's nothing, and he is nothing.

"It's almost over, Rov," a soft voice caresses him like ocean water lapping at the sand of a beach. The words echo like he's in an empty cave, expansive like the depth of space.

Violet crystals blink back at him when he cracks open his eyes. A flying pod shoots across the glittering mountains of amethysts, faster than anything he's ever witnessed. That's saying a lot, he thinks absently, because he works with Tal. Grimacing, Rovis turns his head slowly, though none of the pain he expects throughout his body comes.

A sharp pinch to his heart steals his breath instead.

The dark curls, the silver nose ring, the soft eyes. Rovis feels as though he's been taken out of time and space, for this moment cannot possibly exist in his cruel reality.

Griffin Faal smiles down at him.

"This is where your mother comes from, remember?" he says.

Rovis tries to answer, but the darkness seems to have taken away his voice. A lump burns in his throat, fire dripping down into his lungs.

"I hope you find this place someday," Griffin continues, looking up at all the magnificence of the Amethyst Cascades. "Even if you want to stay in Pureland, it wouldn't hurt to visit. I'm glad you know the truth about my death, but now it's time for you to find peace among the living."

Rovis grabs Griffin's hand, silently begging him to forgive him.

"I'm dead, Rovis," he answers gently, as if he can hear Rovis's thoughts. "You're the one who needs to forgive yourself. Deep down, you know that we would've talked things out, and we would've been okay, if I hadn't run into the Agency that day. Remember the world you live in. Some of us are meant to die young. None of us ever stood a chance. Hold on to your life and your love, Rov. Cherish every moment of it, before it gets taken away from you, too."

The scene starts to darken and blur. Panic rises in Rovis's chest, and he clutches Griffin with a death grip, because he doesn't want him to slip away again. He doesn't think he can take it, having his heart ripped out one more time.

"Shh," Griffin brushes back Rovis's hair to kiss his forehead. "You know I love you, from the next life and every alternate universe."

Don't leave, he wants to say. *Don't leave me alone with my grief.*

But the darkness takes him anyway. It always does.

Awareness returns to his body, and the pain of his injuries has faded to soreness. Rovis feels as though someone pulled the skeleton out of him, drained the blood, dried the skin like raisins, and stuffed the bones back in. His back has fused with the damp bed sheets beneath him. His face drips with cold sweat and tears streaming out of his glued-shut eyes, and his tongue feels scorched.

A faint beeping brushes his ears.

With all the will he has left, Rovis peels open his heavy eyelids. He stares at the blank ceiling before he shifts his head just slightly, eyes searching. His heart nearly stops when he sees who's sitting next to him.

"Griffin?"

A dream within a dream. Rovis's subconscious has reached a new low. Griffin looks much older, and a thousand times tougher. Silver piercings dot his left brow, his nose, his lips, and his ears. With a soft gaze on Rovis, he just smiles sadly.

"Close, but not exactly."

The three remaining brain cells in Rovis's head trudge slowly through the haze, processing those four words until it clicks like chains pulling taut on interlocking gears. More tears slip out, and his face contorts.

"Jordan," Rovis whispers.

"Yeah," xe answers, placing a hand on Rovis's cheek, wiping away his tears with xyr thumb. "It's okay. It's over now. You're out. You're surrounded by friends."

"I'm sorry," Rovis says, and the tears keep falling, because there's no end to the torment of losing Griffin again, even if he was an illusion. His lungs are bleeding, and his heart is shriveling up like leaves in winter. "I'm so, so sorry."

"It's *okay*."

A scoff drags his attention to the door, where Damian leans against the frame with crossed arms with his usual look of murder. Rovis belatedly realizes he's in an unfamiliar bedroom, with no markings of any personalization. Other than the bed he lies in, the small sofa that Jordan sits in, and the nightstand next to them, there's nothing. No shelves or dressers, not even a closet or window.

"Your sister and Damian dragged you out of the Playground," Jordan explains, ignoring xyr partner.

"My sister," Rovis repeats, before his brain catches up.

His heart starts to race, and he tries to get up, but his arms are too weak. Standing, Jordan helps him lean against the wall with a gentle but solid grip on his shoulders.

"Where's my sister?" he demands, voice weak but urgent.

"I'm right here."

Rena appears at the door and moves toward him, but Damian blocks her with an arm without looking, still glaring at Rovis. She rolls her eyes, shoves Damian's arm out of her way, and closes the distance between them.

As soon as she's close enough, Rovis pulls her into a tight hug, sobbing into her scarf.

At first, he's crying out of relief, because he thought that he was never going to see her again. With everything that's going on in the world, it's a miracle that both of them are still alive, and impossible that they've found each other.

But once he's started, he can't stop. Like water rushing out of a faucet at maximum velocity, when the handle breaks, he can't turn it back off. All the terrors from the Playground are hitting him full force, tearing his chest open, and pouring out into Rena's shoulder. Every time his hand slipped on his spear in the arena, he thought it could be the last moment of his life. He was a caged animal, alone and ridiculed, worlds away from his family. The only end to his torment was to let the Agency win, and he was clinging onto the last shreds of his dignity so he wouldn't succumb to that. Never did he dare to imagine holding his sister in his arms again.

Rena rubs circles into his back, and Rovis is convinced all of this is too good to be real.

"I must be dreaming," he chokes out when his lungs pull in enough air.

"Then keep dreaming," Rena says, resting her fingers on the back of his head. "I'm not going anywhere."

She shifts, turning her head to speak to Jordan and Damian. "We need to go. I just got word that Dyvris has been destroyed. I'm taking him to one of the houses we commandeered from a dead Purish family. Regardless of what you decide to do with yourselves, I'm going to need help getting him on the truck."

"Wait." Rovis sniffs, rubbing his eyes with numb knuckles. The back of his hand slides against his face from the wet tears. "What happened to Dyvris?"

"Don't worry about it," Rena answers quietly, fidgeting with his hair.

Rovis doesn't relent. "Don't coddle me. I'm not a child."

She sighs. "The Agency happened, of course. What else could have happened?"

The Agency. Always the Agency. Of course, now he believes this isn't a dream. Rovis feels his wrath resurfacing and reenergizing his limbs, thinking back to everything they've done to him, everything Marudas did to him in that dark room beneath the stadium.

With a gasp of realization, Rovis shoves Rena back. "They put the drug in me."

"Yeah, we noticed," Damian interjects dryly. "Obviously we got it out of you before we let you wake up."

Jordan looks affronted and scolds, "Damian."

Rena shoots Damian a dark look that Rovis doesn't miss, so he demands, "What did I do? Did I hurt anyone?"

Damian snorts. "What do you th—"

"We need to go," Rena cuts him off. "You can fucking catch up later, but we're only borrowing this Starcatcher front."

Starcatcher?

Rovis starts, "Hold on—"

"*Later,*" Rena growls, and he clamps his mouth shut. Her tone temporarily shocks him and halts his breakdown. Rovis exchanges looks with Jordan, then with Damian. Both of them shake their heads at him, as if they've decided that Zero's not one to be messed with, despite being much older, larger, and stronger. Sighing, Rovis allows Jordan to help him to his feet, while Rena pulls Damian roughly by the arm out of the room before Rovis could even take a single step.

Now alone, Rovis sneaks a glance at Jordan, who still looks too much like xyr twin, even after all these years, even when Rovis is awake enough to tell that xe isn't Griffin. The arches of Jordan's brows are softer than Griffin's, xyr eyes equally sharp but deeper. And while Griffin had defined cheekbones, Jordan's features have always been rounder with less edges.

"So," Rovis says as casually as possible, "you and Damian."

Jordan coughs, and xyr hold on Rovis slackens.

"Stars, you haven't changed a bit," xe mutters, though the corner of xyr lips twitches. Xe leads Rovis down the stairs, weaving through narrow hallways. Rovis thinks he might have seen Katina Golubeva while passing the kitchen, but it was too brief to be sure. Jordan takes him through a door and helps Rovis around to the back of a cargo truck in a packed but oddly tall garage. Rovis takes one glance inside and sends Rena an exasperated look.

"You've been busy."

She rolls her eyes again, and at this point Rovis thinks it's just her signature guise and default reaction to everything a man can possibly say or do. Jordan pulls him along to rest on what's practically an actual bed, with the amount of pillows and blankets piled on the floor of the truck, just without a frame and mattress. Not to mention the amount of food and water stocked to the side, plus plastic containers of what's obviously freshly cooked Avyrian dishes.

"What did you do, rob a whole town?" Rovis asks when Rena climbs into the truck, while Jordan sets him down with his back comfortably against a wall of pillows.

"Is that judgment I hear from a Sleightist?" she retorts, scarf billowing with her movements. Brain finally catching onto that detail, Rovis narrows his eyes at the piece of decorative fabric, because he feels as though his bones are boiling from the heating inside this safe house. Rena doesn't pay him any mind, throwing a blanket over his legs.

Damian raps his knuckles on the floor of the truck, snatching their attention.

"Zeke will drive you, so your sister can watch you in the back," he says to Rovis. "I'm lending you my second until yours makes his way to you. Jordan and I have our own people to look after, so this is where we send you off. With everything that's going on, the Agency is too busy to hunt you down. Just be careful."

He disappears, and Rovis is stunned into silence.

The Agency, too *busy*?

Jordan shakes xyr head and passes over a black bag from the side of the truck. Rovis looks in and is even more stunned to find all the weapons the Agency stripped from him while he was unconscious at the Playground.

"How?" he asks.

"Rena can apparently be the most social person alive if she tries," xe answers cryptically.

Rovis glances up at Rena, nonplussed.

Unsurprisingly, she rolls her eyes. "Remember how Jordan volunteered to help our robotics team prepare for tournaments? You should, because you talked my ear off about not telling xem who I was. Anyway, xe's still grumpy about me not participating during practices even though I absolutely did not need to do anything."

"Then what were you doing there?" Jordan asks, exasperated.

"To make money from dumb high school kids and to be the fourth person Lila needed to enter the competition," Rena answers seriously.

"Literally none of that answers my question," Rovis mutters.

"Your sly little fox of a sister somehow got Enyo Zhao of Loveias to have her Daggers stationed at the Playground to get everything for you and make sure you leave that hellscape safely," Jordan says, crossing xyr arms.

"Jordan," Damian calls, appearing outside the truck again with a scowl. "They need to leave, and so do we."

"Yeah, yeah." Jordan clasps arms with Rovis. "That was enough stupidity from you for the rest of my life. Don't do it again."

"I'll try not to. Getting tortured in Drokklo's Playground was not exactly on my bucket list," Rovis retorts.

Jordan punches him lightly on the shoulder. "Seriously, be careful. You and I both know that we need to talk, so I expect you to be alive and not on the brink of death for that."

Rovis sighs. "Yes, your majesty. You be careful, too."

Xe chuckles and hops out of the truck, shutting the door, and Rena moves to lock it. She returns, sits down with her legs crossed by his side, and hands him the warm plastic containers. Zeke Reyyez knocks the divider twice as a warning before he starts driving.

"Eat," she says softly, hair swaying with the truck's movements. "I made these while you were sleeping."

Gratefully, Rovis digs in, shamelessly inhaling food and water after however much time of starvation and dehydration.

"You were in there for four days," Rena says, as though she knows what he's wondering. "It took us a day to get you fixed up, then you slept for two days."

So it's been a week since Rovis stormed out on her.

"Finish the food," she nudges before he can say anything. "Then we'll talk. Promise."

He doesn't need any more encouragement. Within a few minutes, Rovis plows through five meals' worth of food. Feeling more like himself, Rovis sighs and wipes his mouth. He starts with the question that's been burning in his throat for months.

"Enyo Zhao."

Rena takes his hand with both of hers. "I'm getting to it."

He waits, and she takes a deep breath.

"I'm sorry for all the times I've hurt you."

Rovis blinks at her, the gears in his brain turning too slowly to understand her path of logic. "What? I wanted to know—"

She taps Rovis's metal finger, miraculously still intact after all his matches in the arena.

"This is my fault," Rena says. Then she brushes her fingers up over his forearm, over the self-inflicted scars. "And so is this."

Rovis frowns, puzzled. "No, it's not."

"Rovis, I'm a Dagger." Rena gazes at him steadily, unflinching as the truth flows out of her. "Quade convinced Abigail to send me to gather information on his daughter as my first job, and she turned out to be a Dagger. I didn't have all the information, and I didn't stand a chance against her. She took me to Enyo, and Enyo made me a deal, offered me protection, a dangerous reputation, another family, in exchange for getting Quade killed and for working as a Dagger alongside being an Aconite. She knew I'd be a good double agent. I didn't just go to the Agency to figure out what happened to my father. Enyo wanted me to find out some other things, too."

Gaping, Rovis says slowly, "But I killed Quade. Tal and a few others helped me. It was a whole year after you were sent off, too, I think."

"Yes." She looks down. "I had to plan it out. You killed Quade because you had to. Because Quade found out we were siblings."

"Well, yes, but—" His eyes widen at her implication. "*You* told him?"

"Anonymously, from the safety of Torch City," she says bitterly. "I used you. And you paid for it."

Rovis stares at her, struggling to take in the information. Then he shakes his head.

"There's no way," he says. "You can't be a Dagger. Enyo Zhao does not keep double agents."

Rena sighs and pulls her hands away. A small flashlight appears between her fingers, as she pulls her hair back from her left ear with her other hand. She flips on the UV light and shines it onto the stretch of skin between her ear and her hairline.

An ornate dagger design glows blue under the light, a purple outline of a sun circles the blade with solar flares flowing out, and a bright, white crescent moon cuts through the center of the sun.

Words die on Rovis's tongue. He can only stare at the Dagger mark that's been hidden on Rena's skin for years.

"And that is why," she drops her hands, turning off the light, and says softly, "I needed to get you out of there so badly. Because I needed you to know the truth. And it's why I cannot allow myself to cheat out of the white vein disease."

"Don't say that," Rovis rejects, voice rough. "That is not the real reason why you broke me out. It's not the only reason. And I do not want you to punish yourself for decisions you made under the shitty rule of Quade Bianchi. Not to mention running into the Daggers unprepared. With the way things were going, I was going to kill him sooner or later."

"I could have used someone else."

"Like who? Tal? I don't think—"

"No," she interrupts. "It's too late to think of a different plan now. But using you was the worst thing I could have done, and it was the only plan I had in mind."

Rovis purses his lips. Cautiously, he reaches out one hand. When she doesn't move away, he ruffles Rena's hair and gingerly cups her face with light fingers.

"Let the past die," he says, gentle yet firm.

Rena nods, still not meeting his eyes.

"And the self-harm relapse might have been partially because of what you said," Rovis adds, "but there's no use blaming yourself. I'm guessing you remember what happened during your fever."

"When breaking you out of the Playground was the only thing on my mind, all kinds of memories resurface." She covers his hand with her own. "I can't believe you still took care of me while I was sick, even after everything I said."

"Of course I did. I'm your brother," he says simply. "And you weren't wrong. About my dad. I remember everything now. And I'm sorry I forgot. I'm sorry I let it slide, his ignorance and his inaction."

"You trauma-blocked it," she answers. "It happens."

Rovis sighs and shakes his head. "My brain is so unreliable. I hallucinated your voice in the Playground, on the last day."

Rena tries to smile. "You did. It was me. I'm sorry I was late, but I managed to get two of the Daggers to swap out your guards, and they put in an earpiece while you were unconscious so I could talk to you in case no one could get to you fast enough."

Rovis frowns. "How many people did you get involved with my escape?"

Rena blinks, face deceptively blank. "Yes."

"What?"

"You'll see. It's not quite over yet. No, don't ask."

Rovis sighs, too tired to pursue it. "Fine."

His eyes catch on her scarf again, and he reaches out tug at it. She doesn't stop him. Rovis is afraid he might already know why she's wearing it.

"It's snowing outside," Rena tries with minimal effort, while Rovis is halfway through unwrapping it.

He forgets how to breathe when he sees the bruise.

"Like you said," she says firmly through his silence, "there's no use blaming yourself."

"I can't believe I did this to you," he says, feeling faint.

Rena huffs. "It's hardly anything compared to what I've done to you."

His fingers twist the fabric of the scarf. "That does not mean you deserve it. I don't believe that, and neither should you."

"Sure," she says, not at all taking his words to heart.

Rovis releases his grip on her scarf, deciding to leave this conversation for another day. Then another thought occurs to him.

"Did..." Rovis swallows. "Did you give me blood, too?"

At that, Rena snorts, rolling her eyes. "No, actually. I was going to, but then Damian said I was the 'human equivalent of a tube of travel toothpaste' and would drain myself dry before the drug is even halfway out of you. So he shoved me aside and gave you his blood instead."

"Damian's the one who gave me blood?" Rovis asks, incredulous.

"He doesn't actually hate you, you know. We've all got issues, including him. But he really needs to correct his behavior. I tried to beat some sense into him, but the rest is up to himself and some bribing from Jordan. Don't worry about him." The truck comes to a stop, and Rena checks her watch. "We're here."

She opens up the door, and Zeke helps her down. Once they've moved Rovis to the master bedroom and stocked up the kitchen, Rovis hears them speak softly in the living room before Zeke goes upstairs, and Rena comes into the bedroom.

"Can I?" she asks, tapping the bed.

"You never need to ask," Rovis answers, shifting to the side to make room for her, but she surprises him by curling up right next to him, her head on his shoulder and her knees against his hip.

It takes him back five years, before he left her for the Aconites. He used to hold her every time she got scared when there was a shooting in their building or when the power went out. Rovis has almost forgotten this version of her existed, after meeting her again in Dyvris but as a completely different person, as 'Zero.'

Rena's fingers curl into a fist over his heart, clutching the fabric of his sweater.

That's when Rovis realizes how terrified she must have been. She'll never tell him the things she went through during his capture, and he probably won't tell her about the horrors on the Playground, live streamed or not. Knowing her, he'd guess that she barely slept and ran around with her emotions turned off until this moment.

"I'm okay now," he tells her quietly, in the darkness of the room.

"You better be," Rena answers, likely meaning to grumble, but it comes out soft and fragile and uncertain, everything she buries beneath the armor of the Ace of Crowns.

Sighing and closing his eyes, Rovis wraps his arm around her shoulders.

He focuses on the warmth of her small body, the shifting of her breathing, the solidity of her presence, before he drifts off into the darkness once again.

15

Lithium

Tal could vaporize the Agency car with his glare alone through the window.

They are worse than cockroaches, he swears. He's been on the run before, on longer jobs, but it has never been this tedious. And after everything the Purish put him through this past week, he has half the mind to crush the car into a lump of metal with the Agents still in it. Unfortunately, he does not have a large hydraulic compactor at the moment.

He'll simply have to think of another creative way to torment then kill them, for all the Aconite lives they've taken.

During the invasion of Dyvris, the Aconite drones were able to shoot down three of the five jets sent by the Agency before they could break through the mountains, but the remaining two made it to the mansion. Only half of the Aconites had escaped by then, since the tunnels were blocked, and the antigravity vehicles weren't the easiest to maneuver around mudslides at a low altitude. Tal stood there on the ground, surrounded by flurries of Aconites and gunshots, momentarily paralyzed.

He'd always known that a massacre was possible, ever since the Agency was exposed by the Faceless.

But watching this violent yet clinical demise fall upon the Aconites with his own eyes was another thing entirely.

From the jets, Agents shot at the mansion with standard blasters at first, and the Reapers sniped back with nuclear rifles from the ground and the sky. Tal got himself moving again, powering up the weapons in his arm to aim alongside them, while directing the rest of the Aconites to get out through the comms. His mini missiles flew with the Reapers' shots, piercing through the air. A few Agents fell from the sky, but the pilots were uncharacteristically competent, dodging the explosions with precision and speed.

"These fuckers," Daleyza swore and dragged out a machine gun from beneath the courtyard.

"Tal." A bruising grip on his arm had him flinching and staring at Summer blankly. She tugged at him and said, "Go."

"Hell no," he hissed just as Daleyza fired a round at the Agents. Energy shields closed in around the jets, blocking her attack.

Then the roles swapped, with the jets raining bullets on the mansion, and all the Reapers had no choice but to hide behind their own shields.

A car drove up behind Tal and beeped while he was stuck in the midst of the attack. He glanced back to see Raven in a Shapeshifter, gesturing for him to get on, with a couple fledglings sitting in the back.

"Go," Summer repeated. "We can't fight them from the ground."

"N.A.D.E., did everyone get out?" Tal demanded.

"All members have exited the premises. However, fifty-two percent have yet to escape the Dyvrian mountains."

"Alright," Tal shifted, preparing to run into the Shapeshifter. "But you and Daleyza get out, too. That's an order."

"Don't worry." She jerked her head at a two-seater pod parked by the Core. "We've never disobeyed you, have we?"

Tal nodded and got in the passenger seat. Raven took off as soon as he shut the door, and he wasted no time using all the weapons on the Shapeshifter to fight the Agency jets, running every combination of attack from muscle memory. All the Reapers in the sky did the same, so that the other members had the chance to flee.

Tal knew it wasn't enough to save everyone. He just refused to believe it.

Then panels of the Agency's jets opened up to reveal massive antimatter cannons.

Raven tried to dodge, but the radius of a single hit was too large.

The energy shield around their Shapeshifter disintegrated, and the vehicle plummeted in altitude before Raven got control of it again. The fledglings in the back yelped but immediately quieted. Tal didn't have chance to check on them when another cannon blast flew at them. Raven floored the accelerator this time and narrowly avoided total annihilation.

"Shit," she growled. "Tal—"

"Let's leave," he ordered quietly, clawing the edge of his seat.

Tal wouldn't have prepared the Aconites for these cannons even if he had been in the city for the past several months. When and how the Agency figured out the secrets to produce antimatter at such large quantity, he did not know.

Of course he wanted to stay and fight and drag the Agents to hell with him. Of course he should have been the last line of defense with the rest of the Reapers. But he wasn't alone in that Shapeshifter, and he was responsible for four other lives.

Aconites dropped like flies all around them as Raven zigzagged through the mountains, dodging heavy boulders and blasts from the Agents. The mansion exploded behind him, magnificent and bittersweet like a supernova, and rained down burning debris all over the lake. A familiar black piece of gothic architecture that must have been part of the Wraith Tower crashed into one of the two remaining Agency jets, setting it on fire in a spectacular paradox.

Tal tried not to flinch when he watched three of the Aconite pods coordinate a sacrificial attack in the rearview mirror, so detached that he could have been watching a disaster film and not real life. With full speed, the three pods crashed right into the remaining jet from different directions and blew up their engines.

It was the only way the rest of them could have gotten away, knowing that the Agency would send more to clean up, just like they did Divako.

His heart chilled as he wondered if one of the pods was Daleyza and Summer.

Now, almost a week later, Tal still hasn't had the time to do a headcount and figure out who they've lost and who took out the jet. He's currently too busy running around the borders of Pureland, at the edge of Water Lord territories where the Avyrian mafia look the other way and let them hide, but then disappear instead of fighting Agency squadrons to help out. It's understandable, really, because the Lords don't need small organizations like the Aconites. They needn't waste their resources to save them when they're working with the Starcatchers to go up against the Agency together.

If Zero were here, she'd probably have a friend to make a deal with or charm her way into a base to lay low. If Rovis were here, he'd probably reprimand the wits out of every person they pass by and melt them with his stare to ensure that the Agency can't find them.

And it probably would have helped that both Zero and Rovis are Avyrian.

Tal is unfortunately neither of them, and his Lithium brand of manic serial killer apparently doesn't work quite as well as the Scavenger's reputation.

Clearly the Lords don't care much for savages like Tal. He has a feeling it has to do with their history with Enyo Zhao.

So here he stands, in a shabby motel on the southern beaches off the highway in Myroxia, glowering at the singular Agency car parked out front, waiting patiently for Tal to make a move as the sun rises slowly. On the bright side, the number of Agents coming after them has significantly decreased. And after hearing the news about the spaceships and the lab explosions, Tal is certain that the Agents are only chasing after the Aconite stragglers because their original orders were to make sure no one makes it out of Dyvris, but now they're spread too thin to carry it out. The Agency is losing their grip, and everyone knows it. Soon, the Damned are going to hit back a thousand times harder.

Tal's stare hardens, a promise of vengeance glinting in his eyes. He lets the curtain drop and turns. The fledglings cower back, still imitated by his reputation despite his saving them, while Raven doesn't even flinch, arms crossed. Her black tank top reveals the contours of her biceps, muscles toned from her work as a Mech. The girl is full of surprises, with a lot more grit than he expected when he brought her in along with Jacek after the fire. Tal's been too careless, to have only recently noticed Raven's quiet yet steady strength. He's always known that she's smart and diligent, but he never fully grasped her sense of loyalty and adaptability until her return.

If it weren't for the recent reveal of her Zessroan heritage, Tal would probably think that she and Zero are secretly fraternal twins.

"How bad?" Raven asks when he doesn't speak.

"Not a serious concern. There's only one car, and I set down the dragée cameras around the perimeter last night, so I'm sure that it's the only one."

Dragée cameras, named after the decorative sugar on cakes, are smaller than an eighth of a fingernail, and they look like tiny silver balls that stick to any material. Unless an Agent is purposefully looking for it, which they aren't smart enough to do, they wouldn't find it. They may be trained to enforce the Purish rule and exterminate the Damned, but they have no idea what it's like to survive the world of the Damned. They don't have the paranoid instincts or hard-learned lessons from near-death experiences on the streets. Tal doubts they've ever even seen half the technology the lowlifes of society have invented to help themselves stay alive.

"The Shapeshifter isn't in any condition for another high speed chase," Raven says.

Tal snaps his fingers and points at her. "Yes, you are correct. That's why I'm going to pretend I'm leaving to buy breakfast and take it out while you grab the children and drive."

She narrows her eyes. "You really think they're going to buy that?"

Tal scoffs. "You think they're smart?"

Raven considers that with a raised brow, then nods. "How long will it take you?"

"Fifteen minutes, max."

She picks up her army green bomber jacket and throws it on in one smooth motion. "Alright. Don't take your time."

"Thanks," Tal says, sarcastic, then opens the door. He tosses a few coins in one hand. "Keep your comms activated."

The sky is a hazy shade of dark orange as Tal prances down the stairs, whistling inside his helmet. The Agent rolls down their window, acting casual, and aims a sniper rifle with no subtlety whatsoever. He wonders if the government's top notch secret sector even has any proper espionage training. A Heartless from any criminal organization can do better than this.

Tal's gas mask lenses zoom in on the trigger as he continues strutting through the parking lot. He doesn't get quite close enough when the finger flexes to pull, but he flicks one of the coins into the Agent's eye over the ugly mask. His shield appears and closes over his entire body like a bubble, right when the bullet flies. His gun slides into his hand, glowing red with gathering energy. Tal's metal fingers twitch as his jet boots activate and push him into the air. The gunshots follow him, and he pitches his body forward, barely catching himself from falling onto his face with the opposing force of the blast exploding out of his metal palm. He soars toward the highway, away from Raven and the fledglings.

The Agents follow Tal onto the right lane, firing from their car, like the gullible creatures they are.

The jet boots start sputtering when he hovers over the streaks of neon from other cars flying on the highway. Tal drops down on top of the Agency car, chuckling when his heavy boots dent the roof. He winds back his metal arm and punches through the top, jerking back his head only when bullet shots threaten to break the lenses of his mask. Changing his tactic, Tal's claws dig around the torn metal. The outermost layer of his arm's nanoparticles crawl down to cover his torso as a thin armor.

He flips over to the hood and sprays the window with a liquid nitrogen blaster.

A white crystal-like sheet replaces the windscreen.

All it takes is one bullet, which Tal doesn't hesitate to fire. Fractures of glass shower into the Agents' faces. The car swerves, slamming against the side of a passerby vehicle. He uses two more bullets for each Agent's head.

The car spins out of control when the corpse's grip on the steering wheel slackens. Tal pushes it toward the shoulder as he leaps off, before streaks of pink, purple, and blue demolish it into a metal heap, the fast cars not even faltering from the impact. The moment opposing the Agency's car flings him out onto the fast lane. He lands on the roof of a sports car, crouched low. After he passes the wreckage of his masterful creation, Tal springs over to the shoulder, landing with an overwhelming drop in speed. The neon lights lining his boots light up as it absorbs the impact to protect his joints. Tal stabs his claws in the gravel as his boots slide back, leaving behind five slashes in the ground when he finally stops moving.

He takes a moment to pant in his lunge, out of breath.

The Shapeshifter pulls up in front of him.

"Hey," Raven calls. "Stop posing. Boss isn't here to see you. Get in the car."

Tal scoffs, mildly offended by the lack of appreciation for his hard work. Wiping the dust off his hands, he flings open the passenger's door and hops in. Raven speeds off before he gets to lean back in his seat, flying towards Gezrya, where Zero told her that Rovis would be. Apparently, one of the Revyxon houses he and Rovis got access to is in Zero's cousin Dziye Hong's territory. Not only would the Agency steer clear of Purish properties, they'd absolutely avoid the Water Lords.

And if Tal is slightly annoyed that Zero hasn't been sending him any direct messages, then he keeps that sentiment to himself.

His limbs remain tense with his worries about Rovis, even though the man's free from the Playground now. While Tal has been on the run with Raven and the fledglings, halfway across the country from Torch City, he did catch some footage of the first moment when all hell broke loose in the arena. He got to see Narvaez shield Rovis from a robot tiger before the livestream cut off, the government trying to bury the chaos from the public. It was too late though, with the Purish families in the stadium practically killing each other about an extensive web of blackmailed information.

Drokklo's Playground is gone.

But that's all Tal has seen of Rovis, which is not at all promising. He looked like he was hanging onto the last threads of his life in the footage. Zero's text to Raven a few days later was the only sign that Rovis made it out alright, but Tal still needs to *see* him. He needs to see that he's alive and well, all his wounds stitched together and not infected, his dark eyes still shining with calculation, his bulky arms and legs rested and strong. He needs to know that those ruthless hands that have been non-stop punching through colossal robots can still paint and draw and cook, because beneath the Scavenger's armor, Rovis is just a selfless man who makes the mundane parts of life colorful.

Tal wants to hold onto him and never let him go ever again.

All this distance forced by the Agency has Tal trembling in the passenger seat with fury. They've had to trace the edges of the continent to avoid all the chaos inland, carving out the longest possible path to get to Rovis. If the end of the world were a live performance, he'd reserve the entire front row to watch the Agency burn.

Tal drags in a ragged breath, trying to rein in his wrath. He almost hates Zero for sending him to Dyvris, when he should have been by Rovis's side this whole time.

Yet it made all too much sense for him to get all the Aconites and residents out of the city, because he's the highest ranking member with Rovis trapped under the capital. With his reputation as Lithium, no one in Dyvris would dare to question him. Most members of the organization are still too wary of the Heartless, especially the Ace of Crowns. While it wouldn't have torn apart the Aconites for the message to come from Zero, it would've faced hesitation and lost more lives. It doesn't help that Zero resigned her position and gave it to Rivka without a power struggle at all. Even though Tal recently found out she did so because of her illness, everyone outside the inner circle has no idea and still sees her as a wild card. So the evacuation needed Tal to be there, in his city and in the Aconites' home base.

Sometimes, Tal despises logic. Even though he's an engineer and software analyst.

Raven races across the highway without another hitch, though Tal keeps on checking if they're being followed again. Maybe he's right that the Agency no longer has the resources to hunt down individual criminals. That would ensure Rovis's safety, too.

By nightfall, they finally reach the outer ring of Gezrya in the midst of a snowstorm that came out of nowhere. Raven pulls up in front of the fancy gates of a mansion about the size of the Poison Core, snow crunching beneath the tires. She digs out her phone and shoots Zero a text, then they wait in silence.

Zeke Reyyez comes out from the side and greets them with a knock on the passenger side window. Tal rolls it down and rests his arm on top, then says, "I thought you and Zero didn't get along."

"We've come to an understanding," Reyyez says shortly. "Are these all Aconites?"

"Yes, these are my people."

Reyyez waves a hand. The gates roll open, and Raven drives through to park inside the garage among seven other vehicles. The two Shapeshifters look promising for Aconite survivors, and the tightness in his chest loosens just slightly. Tal doesn't expect all of the survivors to end up in this safe house, since they have several scattered across the country, but he did pass on the word to the inner circle to come and protect Rovis.

Not that Rovis needs much protection, if he can survive four days of Drokklo's Playground.

Followed by Raven and the fledglings, Tal walks into a lounge with a glass ceiling, covered by snow, where a few Skulls and a couple Rings are drinking beer and playing a card game. They glance up at their arrival but proceed after exchanging curt nods. The news plays on the screen next to them, announcing that Toullifuka has reinstated Lasantirk's independence and signed a treaty with Riyssolx. Tal stares, wondering what this means for Pureland.

"Tal." Daleyza's voice turns him to another entrance.

A flood of relief makes Tal sag. "Daleyza."

She hovers by an ornate door, her familiar blue jewelry glowing against the dark designs. Thousands of emotions flit across her face, fatigue heavy beneath her eyes. Tal stumbles over to her and crushes her in a hug without thinking. Daleyza freezes for a moment, evidently surprised, before gripping his shoulders in return.

"Wait." Tal pulls back. "Where's Summer?"

"She's alive," she assures him with a tired voice. "Broke two ribs on our way out, so she's resting right now."

Tal sighs in relief, thanking all the stars for every life that was spared during the attack on Dyvris. Daleyza gives him a small smile and jerks her head down the hall. Tal, Raven, and the fledglings follow her to the dining room, where a few Aconite members are gathered at a long table that could host a feast.

Daleyza says to Tal, "The rest of us have been worried. What took you so long?"

"We were forced east because two of the Agency's jets got through. Then we had to stay near the coast," Tal complains. "They kept sending Agents after us."

Raven nudges the fledglings to sit at the table, where freshly cooked dishes lure at him, at all of them, after the exhausting journey.

"As soon as we got out, we went north," Avery says, sipping on their mug. "It was faster through Starcatcher territory because they're more inland, and the Agency can't touch them. Plus, no one wants to stop in Hilobis."

"Smart," Tal mutters, though he doesn't miss the vacant look in their eyes and Kagiso's notable absence.

"But you left before the Agents broke through. Our choices were much more limited once they got past the mountains," Daleyza points out, putting a hand on Tal's shoulder. Quietly, she adds, "He's in the kitchen."

His heart skips a beat. He must have a ridiculous expression on his face, because she smirks and pushes him toward the sound of sautéing. Tal's stumbles through the door. His feet are rooted to the floor when his eyes catch onto what he's been searching for.

Rovis is shoveling around beef and vegetables in a pan, the sleeves of a comfortable-looking sweater rolled up to his elbows.

A lump forms in Tal's throat.

Eventually, Rovis looks up. And he almost drops the spatula. His reflexes are fast enough to catch it before it burns his feet, and he turns off the stove, setting the pan on a back burner. With restrained steps, he pads over to Tal, until they're standing almost chest-to-chest.

"Should you be up right now?" Tal asks, so softly that he can barely hear himself.

Rovis quirks his lips. "Slept all day. Had to cook for all my friends who rushed here for me, didn't I?"

"Sure." Tal swallows, and Rovis's eyes dart down to his throat.

Their gazes meet again when Rovis brushes his knuckles against Tal's cheek.

"You look tired."

"Look who's talking," Tal chides without heat. "Which one of us was trapped in Drokklo's Playground?"

"Yeah," Rovis whispers. Haunted ghosts float through his eyes before they disappear. "But I'm out now."

"A miracle, really."

Tal dares to put his hand on Rovis's chest, feeling the gentle beats of his heart. He feels Rovis tense, his hand freezing on Tal's jaw. The rhythm beneath Tal's fingers grows erratic, and he feels his own heart speeding faster than it ever did while he was on the run.

But he's not running now. Not from Rovis, never again.

Tal closes his eyes, his fingers curling on the soft material of Rovis's sweater. Moments later, he realizes they've synced their breathing, as if they'd always end up on the same tracks, no matter how far the chaotic universe drives them apart. Despite all odds, Rovis survived. He crawled out of the twisted hellscape designed to exterminate people like them, once again proving to the world that he is the king of all demons on this planet. He tore apart Quade Bianchi's old business and made Dyvris a shelter for those who have nowhere else to go. He endured years of physical abuse, the proof written on his back, as revealed by the merciless broadcasting of the Playground. Even if he chooses to never speak of it, Tal will carry it silently, because the man he loves is a survivor.

When Tal flutters his eyes open, his vision is blurry.

Rovis gazes back at him, and his face has crumbled with too many emotions that Tal can't name. The world might have made Rovis into a monster, but he's never been one to Tal. He protects his people like they're his own family, watches over Zero like she's his lifeline, and trades truths with Tal like he's never been hurt or betrayed before.

He's insane, Tal thinks, for keeping his heart so big, when the world is giving him every reason to shut it down. He's a deadly criminal with blood on his hands, but he's a force of nature beyond humans.

Rovis Bozyd-Wei is the Scavenger, a monster and a savior.

"My angelic demon," Tal whispers, eyes burning with overwhelming admiration and relief.

The hand on his jaw wraps around the back of his neck and tugs him forward, and Rovis is kissing him. He's closed the distance between them that Tal has been too scared to cross. He presses their lips together, like he's worshiping this second chance, like a man who returned from the dead and decided to live a hundred times more fully.

Remembering himself, Tal cups Rovis's neck with his hands and deepens the kiss, a hot tear slipping down his face. Because this is what he's wanted since the first time he saw Rovis. It's what he didn't allow himself to have when he decided that he needed to get clean and throw away all the bottles first. It's what he couldn't have when he realized he still had a sister to find and look after. It's what he can't control himself from taking now, after almost losing Rovis. He refuses to walk away with regrets this time.

Rovis lets go first, leaning his head against Tal's, panting.

"I'm sorry," he whispers, and Tal doesn't know why he's apologizing, but Rovis goes on to say, "I had to do that. At least once."

A thumb brushes away the tears on Tal's face. He notices the glistening in Rovis's lashes, hiding away glossy eyes.

"Were you scared?" Tal asks quietly into the space between them. "In Torch City?"

"No. Just..." A soft sigh caresses Tal's face. "A bit hopeless. I thought I was never going to see you again."

"Me, too." Tal brushes his thumb over Rovis's skin. "And you have nothing to be sorry for. If I were any braver, I would have done it first. What we agreed to last time... I think we're ready now. I'm ready."

"Is your sister doing okay?"

"Yeah," he answers. Saige told Tal that she'd be joining him soon, since the work with the Faceless is done, now that protestors have completely taken over the streets. "Zero?"

"Fine." Rovis laughs softly. He drops his hand and straightens. Tal immediately misses the warmth, but he finds solace in those warm eyes again.

I'm home.

Tal smiles, and Rovis smiles back. For a few moments, it doesn't matter that the world is in chaos outside. It doesn't matter that he was on the run for a week, because he's here now. It doesn't matter that the revolution outside has reached the point of no return in Pureland, or that it needs to pull through in order to end the Agency for good, or that they need a new, stable government soon, otherwise the foreign countries will be splitting it apart like red velvet cake. None of it matters, when Rovis stands before him, solid and real.

Tal's stomach growls.

Rovis snorts at that and goes back to cooking the dish that's surely cold by now. "You've been on the run. I assume you haven't eaten much. Go sit with the others, I'll be right out."

"Yes, sir." Tal turns but hesitates. "Where *is* Zero, by the way? We need to have words."

Rovis looks at him again, frowning.

"I just want to talk," he explains. "She's been avoiding me."

The frown deepens. "Are you sure? I haven't noticed."

"That's because you've been busy being half-dead in a modern dystopian gladiator arena under the ugly labyrinth that the Purish society calls their capital," Tal snipes. "And I had to get fifth-hand updates on you through other people around me because *someone* refused to directly message me, for whatever reason."

"Oh, wow." Rovis scoffs. "Tone down the sass, will you? Rena's in the bedroom down the hall. She should be awake now. She can't stay asleep if I'm gone for too long."

Tal blinks. "Rena?"

"Right." Rovis sprinkles in salt. "I don't think she'd mind if you know. That's her real name."

"Okay," Tal says, feeling dumb. He follows the directions and pushes open the cracked door to the master bedroom. Zero is indeed awake, reading in bed, wearing a soft turtleneck.

She only glances up at Tal for a brief moment before looking right back down to her book, and says, "Rovis is in the kitchen."

"I know," he answers. "I'm looking for you."

The movement's slight, but Tal notices the way her bare fingers tighten around the spine, and her eyes flick over to the window then to the bathroom without lifting her head. She's mentally noting her exits, and the observation hits Tal like a punch to his gut.

"I'm reading," Zero says.

Tal approaches the bed carefully and holds out a hand when he's close enough.

He's not surprised that he gets a flat, "No."

"I know I hurt you," he says softly. "I'm sorry."

"Do you even know what you're talking about? Because I don't."

"You told Damian to tell me, 'Remember what happened the night before you left Dyvris.' And I remember, Zero. I never should have turned against you. I'm sorry."

Zero shuts her book and rolls her eyes at the ceiling, annoyed. "Don't be. Your reaction was expected and even welcomed."

"That doesn't make it hurt any less. Though you didn't seem this bothered by it when I came to get you in Ferrisque," Tal comments.

"I was desperate," she says, voice clipped.

"Desperate," he repeats. With a heavy sigh, he puts one knee down on the carpet so he can lean his elbows on top of the bed, looking up at her. She still won't look at him. He prods quietly, "Rovis said your name is Rena."

Zero twists the ring on her finger, white veins glowing faintly. She must have told Rovis the truth about her illness, if she's leaving her arms this exposed.

"It's Sirena." Her gaze is far away. "Rovis gave me a less menacing nickname when our parents got married. A loveless marriage for tax benefits, but at least I got some family out of it."

Tal stares at her, jaw slack. "You're step-siblings."

Finally, Zero slants a look at him. "You didn't figure it out?"

They've been quite obvious in front of Tal, come to think of it.

"I guess not." He tilts his head, still watching her. "Was sending me to Dyvris your way of keeping me away from your precious brother?"

Her brows twitch in confusion. "No. I did have a selfish reason for it, but it wasn't that. How many people did we lose?"

"About a third of the organization," he says, heart heavy. "What was the other reason?"

"It would have been more if you weren't there."

"I see that now. Answer me, what was the other reason?"

She sets the book down on the mattress next to her and says, "You would have been safer there."

"Safe?" Tal laughs, incredulous. "The Agency blew up the damn place as soon as I got there. I didn't even have enough time for a light snack."

"Safe from yourself, Tal. If things went sideways in Torch City, and I failed the one thing I was supposed to do, you would be drowning in alcohol right now."

Tal leans back, speechless.

"Yes, if I'd lost Rovis, you would have found out eventually," Zero continues. "But hearing about his death and watching it are two completely different things, and you absolutely could not have handled seeing it happen after Levi."

"And your sudden aversion to speaking to me?" Tal snaps, woken by the last jab. "Why did I have to hear from Narvaez that Rovis was in danger and that you had a plan? Why did I have to hear from Raven that you got him out safely and found a place to lay low? Why didn't I hear any of that from you?"

"We were coworkers. When you left, that was no longer the case. I'm not your real sister, Talon, so leave me alone. I want to read my book."

"Is that what this is about?" He can't help his rising volume. "You thought I was just using you to project my issues with Saige?"

"You know what?" Zero throws the blanket off of her and hops out of the bed, eyes on the floor. "I know you and Rovis just made out, so if your next step was to sleep together and you needed the room, you could have just told me. You didn't need to get on all seven trillion of my nerves."

"What the fuck—"

"Nope." She grabs her book and walks away. "I'm a dying woman, leave me alone."

Without thinking, Tal throws a knife at the door, forcing it shut with a loud bang that surely gets the attention of everyone in the house. And predictably, when Zero yanks the knife out, throws it to the ground with a few clanks as it rebounds, and rips open the door, Rovis is standing over her with a blank face. His eyes dart between Zero and Tal, while Zero falters, taking a step back. The tension bleeds out of her shoulders.

"You," Rovis looks at Tal first. "Don't throw a knife at her again."

"Sorry," Tal says, quiet but genuine, albeit a bit puzzled.

Rovis flicks his stare toward Zero pointedly, signaling to Tal that he'll explain later. Tal nods, and Rovis turns his attention back to Zero.

"You're doing it again," he says to her quietly. "Five years left, and you want to make the same mistake twice?"

"This is different," she bites out.

"Is it?" He looks over both of them again and says, "Food's ready."

Then he disappears, but Zero doesn't follow. She grudgingly returns to the bed, where Tal is still frozen on one knee, and she curls up under the blanket. Even though she's not looking at him, he knows she's listening.

"You did remind me of Saige," Tal admits. "But you are important to me as yourself, too. I know you felt vulnerable at Ferrisque, and you're afraid of letting your guard down again, but I'm trying to do better. All of us are just trying to be better people to those we care about. You, me, Rovis, even Saige. You don't want to hear it, but this is me apologizing. You are young, and too many people have already hurt you. I'm sorry that I made it onto that list."

"Stop," she says quietly.

"You don't need to be so strong around me," he continues, relentless. "You are allowed to feel pain. You are allowed to be angry at people."

"No, I'm not," Zero says, words flat and deliberate.

Tal's brows crease, taken aback. "You're young—"

"Stop glazing over the things I've done, Tal. I know I'm a lost cause. I warned you."

"You're not," he insists. "And definitely not to me. Why can't you see that? In Ferrisque—"

"That was fucking embarrassing," she grumbles.

"Literally none of that was your fault," Tal says, bemused. "You can't tell me you deserved any of that."

"Well—"

"Okay, no," he interjects. "I don't want to know your answer to that. Have you talked to your therapist about this?"

Zero's hands twitch beneath the fuzzy covers. Her silence is answer enough.

"Then talk to me," Tal says, unyielding. "Rovis may legally be your brother, but since when did we care about the legality of anything? I choose you just as much as he did. I don't have your past, but that doesn't mean I care any less. If your thoughts are spiraling, tell me, so I can prove to you that they're not true. You dragged me out of my relapse when Levi died, remember? It's my turn to help you."

Zero sighs, a long breath of heaviness. "Fine. Okay. Do whatever you want. Now go eat. You've lost weight."

"Are we going to be okay?"

"Yes. I'm just too tired tonight."

Tal squeezes her fingers over the blanket before he pushes down on the mattress, standing. When he gets to the dining room, however, he starts sprinting at the sight of Saige's beaming face, immediately shedding the heaviness of the conversation he just had with Zero.

"Ow, ow, you're crushing me," Saige whines.

In retaliation, Tal hugs her even harder, and Saige feigns choking noises. Laughing, he lets go and messes up her hair. When he sees Rovis staring at them with a small smile, Tal involuntarily grins at him, too.

But of course Saige catches that and groans, "Damn it, I lost the bet."

Tal smacks the back of her head lightly. Despite the gloomy state of the world, they all have a nice dinner together, even when Rovis leaves halfway through to coax Zero into eating. Tal helps Daleyza do the dishes afterwards, and Saige drags him to the top floor to have hot chocolate with marshmallows together.

"What's with the frowny face?" Saige pokes his cheek, and he bats her hand away.

"I'm not frowning."

"But your whole aura is frowny."

"That doesn't even make any sense."

"Just go with it."

Tal chuckles, shaking his head. But the itch in his chest doesn't go away, so he lets out a sigh and says, "The government almost executed you."

Saige lifts a brow. "Yes, I remember that."

"I can't help but…" Tal stares out the window, gentle flakes falling. "Zero broke Rovis out of a place that was impossible to penetrate."

"She does have a habit of challenging the impossible, yes."

"Yet I couldn't even get you out of a moving vehicle."

Saige wraps her skinny fingers around Tal's wrist. "That's because I already had a plan. It's a good thing you didn't, because that really would have messed things up. And I'm sure you could have saved me, if I didn't have a plan."

"How can you be so sure? What if you didn't have Narvaez?"

"You're such a big fan of 'what if's," she remarks. "I'm sure because no matter what happened that made you leave, no matter how long we led our own lives separately from each other, you are my brother. Even when I was a stupid toddler being mean to you, you took care of me. You've always been the best brother I could have asked for, and I know that you would have gone to hell and back and tore down the heavens to save me."

Lips twitching, Tal shifts to wrap his arm around Saige, her head against his shoulder, and his head on top of hers, steaming mugs warming their hands.

"I'm glad you know that," he says. "Even though you don't need saving."

Saige smiles but doesn't say anything else. Tal watches the snowflakes dance outside, beautiful and free from the complications and heartaches of the human world. He wonders if, perhaps, he'd find a life like that on the other side of this revolution. He'd give up the luxury and the riches for small simple joys, if he gets to keep his people by his side.

He can only hope that they all survive long enough to find out.

16

Malware in Gezrya

Zero claims a different bedroom on the third floor the next morning.

As nice as it is to steal her brother's warmth while dozing off, she knows when she's supposed to hightail it out of the master bedroom now that his boyfriend's here. Besides, Zero has more or less calmed down, with Rovis being protected by three organizations' worth of criminals in a comfortable house, while the Daggers are out there demolishing every last bit of the Agency.

She is not twelve anymore, and she doesn't need comfort.

Her new room has a better view of the snow outside anyway.

Wandering the halls, Zero searches for a green bomber jacket. She means to catch up with Raven, but that girl seems to have disappeared again. After trekking through the entire safe house twice, she gives up and returns to the small but cozy bedroom she picked out for herself. Plopping onto the bed with a sigh, Zero scrolls through her contacts on her watch.

As soon as her first call goes through, Zero asks, "Did you do it?"

She can hear her cousin taking a drag of nicotine through the phone. "I did my best. It's out of my hands now."

"How many Lords listened to you?"

"Most, if not all," Dziye says, apathetic.

"That... is better than I expected," Zero admits.

Dziye snorts, though he takes no offense. "Avyrians only coexisted with the Purish because they had to. Some even wanted to fit in with them. But none actually liked them, you know, with the whole trade balance garbage."

"Trade balance?"

Zero might keep herself informed about her contacts, people in relevant areas, organizational feuds, and even world politics, resentfully, but economics is just too far out of her interests. All this scrambling for money that only exists because some random person came up with a weird system millennia ago bores her. It can be 'important' to her because it's a weakness for many of her past targets, but it's dreadfully tedious.

"Do you not know your history, my little cousin?" Dziye teases. "See, the islands had a huge abundance of resources that Pureland didn't have, so the Purish monetary unit started to lose its value because they were importing more from Avyria than they were exporting. Of course the Purish couldn't have that, so they forced hallucinogenic drugs into the island ports to balance it out, even though Avyria didn't want it."

"Wait," Zero interrupts. "Same hallucinogens as the ones Enyo Zhao trades?"

"Ironically, yes."

"Well, that's awkward."

She doesn't know if that was also a reason the Lords banished Enyo, or if Enyo started trading in Loveias out of spite after her banishment, a result of lingering bitterness towards the Avyrian mafia. But that certainly contributes to the irreversible damage on her relationship with the Avyrian communities in Pureland.

"Indeed. Anyway, it's easy to persuade the Lords and the Avyrian government to go against the Purish government as long as they get a new trade deal with whoever else is coming out on top post-revolution."

"So they agreed to help?"

"No," Dziye answers grimly. "The mainland Avyrians can also easily not care about what happens here. Worst case scenario, they lose all the unfaithful descendants that wanted to leave the islands and move to Pureland in the first place. They don't have to deal with the Purish anymore because on this day Riyssolx and Toullifuka are clearly going to take out the corrupt government anyway. Even if Avyria joins in on the power struggle, they could be on the other side fighting for a portion of Pureland. Well, that's assuming Riyssolx and Toullifuka accept the alliance with Avyria. A decade ago, they'd probably have to. But now they're powerful enough to not need Avyria at all, so the alliance would only mean less rewards for them at the end of the war. We as the Avyrians living in Pureland would need to give the islands as reason to stand on our side."

"Essentially we're counting on someone in the Lords to have a significant relationship with someone who has power over there on the islands, then," Zero deduces.

"Yes." Dziye pauses, probably to dispose of his cigarette. "How's Rovis?"

"Oh, he's doing great," she says dryly, thinking about that ridiculous glow around him when he went to bed last night. "Yeah, you wouldn't be able to tell that he was tortured, drugged out of his mind, and forced to fight giant robots just a few days ago."

"I sincerely cannot tell if you're being sarcastic or not."

"I'm not."

"Then why the sharp tone?"

Zero scoffs. "Because now that he's fully recovered, I have plenty to tease and complain about him."

"You were basically hauling planets and moons around the universe to save him a week ago," Dziye points out, nonplussed. "Stars, I'll never understand siblings."

"Oh, so now you claim to be an only child. One day you call me your baby sister, and the next day I'm a stranger, apparently."

"Don't be so sensitive, dear cousin. You know you're my favorite."

"Yeah, yeah." Zero checks her watch. "I'll catch up with you later. I have another call to make."

"The winter solstice is coming up," Dziye says before she can hang up. "Any plans for your birthday?"

She rolls her eyes. The 'winter solstice' isn't even the winter solstice anymore, with the erratic weather caused by the planet's warming. But Dziye and Rovis still refer to it because it's easier to mark her birthday.

"Only to not get killed by some stupid Agent," she answers. "If we all survive this, and everything goes the way we think it might, then we can just combine my birthday with the Passing Reset and call it a year."

"Always the pragmatist," Dziye says, unimpressed.

"Whatever," she grumbles. Zero swears her cousin and her brother care more about the stupid day than she does. "Stay alive."

"You, too."

Zero disconnects and flops back into the soft pillows, pushing the heels of her palms into her eyes. Everyone else thinks it's over, but for her it really isn't. Yes, most of the Aconites survived, the Agency is almost gone for good, Rovis is out of the Playground, Tal has returned to his side, and Saige got the Faceless to successfully rallied people on the streets. But is any of this permanent? Does no one else see how quickly it could all go to shit if one small thing goes wrong? What if the government has more secrets that none of the Damned discovered? What if Ezclovia decides to make a second attempt on this land? What if the new government is worse than the Purish? What if Riyssolx and Toullifuka take over and split Pureland in half? The dynamics of world politics would change drastically. It might even make all the remaining countries even more volatile and prone to war, given the new geographical claims.

A knock on the door jerks her out of her spinning head. She assumes it's one of the Aconites, so she says, "Come in."

But she does not expect this particular Aconite to reveal himself behind the door, since his group of fugitives clearly did not come to Gezrya as soon as they escaped Dyvris.

"Hey, Zero," Kagiso says, cautiously entering the room she's claimed.

Zero stares at him. "You."

"Look—"

She slowly rises from her bed and glowers at him. "We had a deal."

Kagiso flicks his gaze down to her hand, where the dragon ring she tried to trade for his silence rests on her finger. "I renounced it."

"You don't *do* that."

"For regular deals, no. I love my collections. But the deal was null to begin with." He steps closer, and Zero whips out her Dagger knife to keep him from advancing even more. Kagiso holds up his hands in surrender. "You must truly think so little of me, to think that I'd look the other way when your life is in danger. Yes, I am a monster, but not to my own. No fancy weaponized ring could bribe me into letting you do that to yourself. How did the gin taste?"

Zero blinks, about a thousand insults melting on her tongue. "What gin?"

"The gin I swapped out the poison with." Kagiso tilts his head, narrowing his eyes. "You didn't drink it."

"No, you wrinkled teaspoon, I couldn't go through with it," she snaps. "My issue is that you told Rovis before I could get the chance to."

"Were you really going to tell him?" he shoots back. "He spent a couple days with you when he went looking for Tal, did he not? And you were calling him everyday after he came back, weren't you? You had all those chances to tell him, yet he still had no idea when I accidentally spilled it to him."

"You *don't care*," Zero reminds him, with more aggression than necessary. Because he's all too correct that she never actually planned on telling Rovis about her almost-attempt. Especially not after she had to tell him the truth about the white vein disease.

"I lied," Kagiso seethes, stepping forward until the point of her knife is touching his chest, and he wraps his fingers around the blade. Zero stays perfectly still, lest he cuts himself. "Stars, you are the queen of reading other people, but you've always been oblivious when it comes to yourself."

Zero stares, bewildered, then blinks five times in five seconds, like something got in her eye.

"I mean," she says slowly, still trying to process the implications of his words. "I'd help you out, but I've got the white vein virus now—"

"*No*." He tightens his fingers, and the blade turns dark beneath his skin. Blood seeps out over the shiny silver and paints his thumb. Kagiso pays it no mind, saying, "It was like that at first, but then it wasn't."

"Kagiso, let go," Zero says, voice clipped.

"Listen to me—"

Out of patience, she raises her voice, "I will if you let go, dumbass."

Kagiso drops his hand, dripping blood onto the carpet. Zero tosses her knife to the side and grabs his fingers, inspecting the damage while a stitching spider crawls out of her sleeve to heal the cut. Then, as if unable to contain her annoyance at the boy, she slaps him in the face. His head snaps to the side, cheek blooming red. He doesn't move, doesn't fight back, doesn't look at her.

"I hate you," he only says quietly.

"I hate you, too," Zero snaps. "What were you thinking?"

"I wasn't. I can't, when you're around."

Zero sighs, running a hand down her face. What does that even mean? How and when did this happen? Hearing these words coming out of his mouth, her heart drops and then cracks, and the back of her neck burns. This absolutely should not be allowed, because the last person Zero worried about hurting was Kagiso Ihejirika.

"You are a Sleightist," she says. "You are the head of the Opulent House. Before it got blown up, anyway. You have a reputation."

"Well, are you anything like your reputation?" he asks softly. "I'd say the only rumor about you that has turned out to be true is that you disprove the impossible. Because in the eighteen years that I've been alive, you are the only one who made me feel these things."

"I'm a Heartless," Zero says. "Or I was. I can't..."

Kagiso gives her a small smile when she fails to finish the sentence. He says, "It's okay. I know. It's why I never said anything. I know you have people, and that I'm not even five percent of the kind of people that they are. I'm not Raven or Jacek, Tal or Boss, or whoever else you've got in your support system. But I just wanted you to know the truth. None of us know how much time we have left. You, especially, don't have a lot, if you still refuse to take the antiretroviral. I just hope someday we can be friends."

Zero sighs again, a heavy feeling in her chest. "Sure."

"Then that's already more than what I expect from you." Kagiso pats her shoulder and steps back. "Vanneza and I, plus a few others, we just got in. We had to take a detour when they blocked off Aurodus, so I'm going to go rest for a bit."

She nods. "You should. Avery's been worried about you."

"I know," he says, expression softening. "I talked to them as soon as I got here."

"Good."

Zero watches him leave and shut the door gently behind him.

"What just happened?" she says to the empty room.

She sinks onto her bed, clutching the bedsheets with weak fingers. Being aromantic and asexual has never bothered her before, because she never cared to understand other people's desires for non-platonic intimacy. It's a part of her identity that she learned to weaponize when she became a Heartless. But she never considered those kinds of relationships to ever become real in her life. Not in the possibility of her falling for someone, nor the possibility of someone falling for her. Frankly, it seems like too much work and too much drama.

Kagiso has always been more like a low-commitment frenemy to her, a nuisance that she doesn't really want to get rid of, so replaying his confession in her head makes her scalp prickle with unease. It has somewhat broken her perception of reality.

Kagiso? Really?

"Stop," she scolds herself, pulling at her hair.

The sting grounds her, and she just focuses on breathing, minutes stretching to an hour. Finally, she steels herself and taps her watch to call Enyo.

"Your timing is impeccable," Enyo says as soon as she picks up. "The Agency is gone. I don't know what you did with Jordan Faal's Crystal Ring, but they blackmailed and threatened anyone who's not dead to back off. With the chaos they incited among the Purish families that keep the Playground running, combined with the Lasan forces and my Daggers, the capital is in complete disarray now. All the labs are nothing but cinder and ash. *And* the Riyssolans nuked all the spaceship camps when the locations were leaked online. The Purish have nothing left, no escape from this planet that they've destroyed. You are quite thorough, my little Ace of Crowns."

Zero frowns at the uncharacteristic rambling. "But?"

"We still need to get rid of all the symbolic figures of the country, if we want to avoid getting sliced apart by international invasions. We need to get Emery Marudas, his son Didier Whiston, even our puppet president Patrikk Feyrer."

"I thought you took care of Whiston," she says, thinking back to her conversation with Allegra.

"Mithridatism."

"Damn it," Zero swears under her breath. Then she thinks about it again. "Wait, really? I did not expect that snowflake to have a spine."

"It actually works out." Enyo clears her throat, clearly unused to speaking this much. Even as Zero grew closer to the woman over the years, she's never heard this many words from her at once. "The Dawn Council wants them alive anyway."

Zero frowns and narrows her eyes, staring intensely into empty space as she tries to piece together what the hell the Dawn Council is and where it came from. Maybe this is what Raven left Dyvris to do after Jacek's death, to prepare for the next government that would usurp the rule of the current Purish president. And possibly a reformation of the Faceless. Zero guesses that it's a multiracial council, with the Zessroans back in power as the true rulers of this land.

"It's led by Nova Ly," Enyo explains when Zero doesn't respond. "Apparently the Zessroans aren't extinct. They've been calling themselves the Descendants of the Originals to preserve what's left of their race over the last few centuries."

"Yes, I'm aware," Zero says absently.

Enyo scoffs. "Of course you are."

The queen of Loveias may have more reach across the country with her drug empire and her personal army of assassins, but Zero's best friend happens to be one of said Descendants and the daughter of the Council head.

Enyo continues, "I'm sure you know or have guessed that the Dawn Council is a committee of revolutionaries formed by the most prominent rebel leaders of each racial group. They want help from the Damned to capture Purish leaders, as part of a deal to take into account our contribution to them when the new government forms. In other words, they're bribing us with postwar amnesty, because the things we do now will still be illegal once they're in power. Currently, Marudas and Whiston are fleeing to the west coast. Where you are, actually."

Zero stands. "I understand."

"Be careful. Don't do anything stupid before my Dagger in the area gets to you, baby Ace."

Zero's already halfway out the door by the time she hangs up, hurrying downstairs to tell Vanneza to track down everyone's least favorite father-son pair. The Aconites lost their supercomputer when the mansion exploded, so Vanneza has to split the work among all the Digitals in the house. Cards and board games are abandoned, and holographic lines of code glow in the air instead. Zero slips out from the dining room full of criminals who just had their breakfast ruined by reality, very much lacking in enthusiasm to play bounty hunter for rebel leaders after days of lounging around and drinking.

When Zero passes by a window, she almost jumps when she sees a few of the robot monster models have made it out of the Playground and are stomping around Gezrya. Marudas must have sent them over to distract everyone while he and his son escape out the harbor. Her mind flashes back to Rovis's time fighting against these giant machines of doom, and her lungs struggle to keep her breathing even. She can feel her veins burning, and it's not just because of the virus.

"That's it," she mutters to herself. "We need to put an end to this freak show."

When Zero strides down the hall leading to the master bedroom to find Rovis, her steps begin to slow as she starts to get a sinking feeling of discomfort. The door is shut, and she can gather from the crack beneath it that the lights are off. Her lips twist into a grimace.

"Stars and bloody cities," she grumbles, already knowing what she's going to find.

The door is surprisingly unlocked, when she slowly tries the knob. But surely enough, something heavy is blocking the other side, so she can't push it open. Sighing, she charges up the energy in her prosthetic leg skeleton, the electricity whirring louder, and practically blasts it open with an aggressive kick.

Four guns are pointing at her when the door disappears from view. Zero only rolls her eyes at Rovis's and Tal's disheveled states. Rovis's hair is completely messed up, and Tal's bottom lip is swollen. Both of their shirts are completely undone, a gun in each ungloved hand. Tal stands just slightly in front of Rovis, probably the one pushed up against the door.

Zero stops herself from making more deductions out of habit. She does not need to know anything. She suddenly regrets everything she's learned from being a Heartless.

Sometimes, it's better to leave the puzzle pieces scattered around and to never find out what picture they make when put together.

Instead of trying to create drugs to control people's minds, the government should have tried making some that can erase select memories. It has a very high potential for disaster, but at this moment, Zero has decided that she would absolutely buy that.

"I'm not going to lie," Zero says. "Part of me thought I was going to die before I ran into this problem."

"That's *not* funny," Rovis snaps at the same time that Tal growls, "Fuck off."

Zero rolls her eyes again and sighs. "Fix yourselves, will you? We have one last fight to deal with, then you can have all the alone time you want in the world."

"You could have knocked," Tal bristles, completely missing the point.

"We're kind of in a time crunch here," Zero says impatiently.

"Wait, what's happened?" Rovis asks.

"The rebel council looking to become the new government wants us to take in Marudas and Whiston. Alive, unfortunately. At least it's paid revenge. They're headed our way, so we need to be at the front line, but I'm sure we'll have backup soon." Zero claps her hands, trying to disperse the frustration radiating from the two men. "Vanneza is tracking them down right now, so you have until then to... get yourselves situated. Five to fifteen minutes. Rovis, don't go outside. Just help through the comms."

"What?" He stares at her, brow twitching. "Why?"

"Because the Playground bots are here. Do as I say."

Tal's expression darkens, and he looks to Rovis. "Listen to Zero. Stay here."

"I'm not a child," Rovis protests with narrowed eyes. "You cannot expect me to hide while both of you are out fighting."

"Yes, I do," Tal shoots back. "I am not letting those things hurt you again."

"And surely you've had enough of them," Zero adds.

Rovis scoffs, defensive. "I was injured, starved, and tortured on that field. And the weapons they gave me sucked. Trust me, I can easily fight those bots now that I'm in better conditions."

"Proud of you," Zero deadpans. "Didn't ask."

She stalks away without waiting for his retort. The lovebirds can fight it out. Zero has had enough of third wheeling and wishes to never repeat that experience again. If Rovis really wants to get out and fight, not even she or Tal could stop him anyways.

Maybe the five-year limit is actually a blessing in disguise. While she's been optimistic about it to Rovis, in truth she's been mildly terrified of the idea of fading away into nothing. Wanting to take her own life and having her life taken from her are two different matters. She's seen what happens in the end, when the virus takes over the all the veins and burns the body from the inside out. But Zero can start to see the appeal of dying young.

Walking in on, or in this case, forcibly breaking apart Rovis and Tal just made it to her 'Reasons why dying is a good thing' list.

"You look disturbed," Zeke remarks when Zero's feet carry her into the kitchen. He's leaning against the island with a bottle of beer, a smirk on his face. Now that he isn't slamming her head against a wall every time he sees her, he's actually grown on her quite a bit.

Zero yanks open the refrigerator with too much force, accidentally slamming its door against the wall, which leads to a violent rebound that she has to catch before it falls shut. Eyeing the bottles of chilled vodka, she snatches one and chugs down half of its content. The alcohol plasters a false sense of calm over her jumpy nerves. Zero wipes her mouth and asks, "Did you ever have to interrupt Damian and Jordan?"

"Oh," Zeke laughs when he understands, doubling over. "Oh, you are in for so much fun ahead of you. I walked in on them at least once a week, when they were running organizations in different cities. You, however, have to deal with two formerly emotionally repressed men who live together."

"Comforting," she says, the word sharp with sarcasm. Softer, she mumbles to herself with a sigh, "Just less than five years left."

But of course Zeke catches that, and the humor slips from his face. "You still seem set on not taking the medication."

"Why would I change my mind?" she retorts indifferently, rummaging through the fridge to find something to give her an energy boost before the fight. Her hands are starting to tingle from anxiety, so much that the pins and needles in her fingers hurt to even pick up a blueberry.

"Well, your brother is happy, now that Lithium has returned to him."

"Exactly." Zero dumps a bunch of fruit and protein powder in the blender, and the loud grinding drowns out whatever arguments Zeke is about to make. He shoots her an unimpressed look, and she only shrugs in return, trying to ignore the erratic tapping of her foot against the floor. The more her leg bounces, the faster the muscles want to move.

Now that Zero has fixed things with Rovis, he's free to explore his relationship with Tal, who has reunited with Saige. Everyone's good to go, so Zero's work is done. No more deep, dark secrets to come clean about. No more scheming to fix miscommunications. No more games as the Ace of Crowns. If they all survive this last bit of the revolution, then she'll just live out the last of her days doing absolutely nothing except for reading books.

She ignores Zeke's pensive stare as she grabs her smoothie to sip on while she enters the dining room full of people glaring at flashing holograms displaying a stream of updates on the tracking programs. Zero's body becomes more restless, and the tapping of her feet doubles in frequency where she stands in place. She can feel the subtle vibrations of the liquid metal in her leg as she lingers by the door, watching. Everything's about to change, yet it can't seem to morph into a new reality soon enough.

Rovis and Tal have just entered the room when Vanneza abruptly stands and bursts out, "Found Didier Whiston!"

Zero drains the rest of her smoothie and slams it on the table, running out the back door and into the snow as Vanneza explains that Whiston isn't with his father, but he's in downtown Gezrya. She doesn't know why he'd be there, strolling through a lovely beach town as if on vacation, when he's supposed to be leaving the country. Some people are calling after Zero, but she just wants to get out and get this over with. She's itching to throw herself into the violence until the world around her is no longer ruled by the Purish. Plus, she has a personal grudge against Whiston. Her boots and her leg prosthetics charge with energy as she jogs, while she tucks her ring away and pulls on her gloves.

A shadow falls over her, and Zero swerves to the side.

She narrowly dodges getting stomped on by a robot elephant.

People are screaming all around her, while flesh and bones and snow crunch beneath the massive foot, red spreading through the white beneath her feet. The irrelevant thought that the elephant would be much more useful in a smoothie factory than for the Playground only crosses her mind for a millisecond. Her gloved fingers dig into the snow when she ducks to avoid its swinging trunk.

Zero debates her choices between taking out the colossal elephant to save some people and searching for Whiston to wrap up the revolution quicker. Every second she spends standing here is a second she could be using to find that troublesome boy.

But then a Water Lord makes the decision for her.

A projectile breaks through the surface of the ocean near the half-drowned city off the current coastline, and a rocket weapon lodges into the flank of the robot. It must have some multiplication mechanism built in it, because the metal starts fracturing like broken glass, and the whole thing explodes. Zero puts up an umbrella shield and sprints through the falling ashes to get farther into the town of Gezrya.

She zooms in through her contact lenses on every pedestrian with a hood.

In the end, it turns out she doesn't need to, because Whiston is waiting for her in an alley where graffiti covers all the brick walls, ginger curls dull compared to the endless painting in the sky. He's studying the section that displays a large version of her signature card, a violet backdrop with a green crown that has a specific pattern to indicate the Ace of Crowns. Within Water Lord territory, she isn't too surprised to find that she has a fan.

"I always knew it would end with us," Whiston says when he catches her approaching him. "I knew, wherever my father was taking me, you'd find me."

Zero grimaces at his words, vaguely wondering if he's been studying for the role of a poorly written villain in a children's theater production.

"That is so random," she mutters, unable to hide her distaste for Whiston. "I don't even know who you are."

This boy has the audacity to look offended. "Of course you do. We shared such an exciting night together."

Zero snorts, rolling her eyes. "Did we? I can't remember."

His ears turn red. "You do. You obviously do. Why else would you come for me?"

With an impatient sigh, Zero draws a knife.

Whiston widens his eyes over his bulky black mask and holds up his hands. "My offer still stands. Join me, and I'll make sure you live a good life."

"Backed into a corner and still so arrogant," she spits out in Avyrian. "Someone truly thinks he's the main character of this story."

"What?" he almost shouts, as if switching languages has made her more unintelligent. "I didn't catch what you just said. Speak Purish."

The knife slices his shoulder.

Zero grins at his yelp.

Bullets start flying at her from the roof, defacing the art on the walls. She throws up a shield, but not before a shot catches her side. A grunt tumbles out of her mouth as she staggers back one step.

Whiston is clutching his shoulder, hissing. The two stare each other down.

"See," he grits out, "I was smarter this time."

Footsteps pound behind Zero, and she spares a single glance to see that five hooded figures are joining them in the alley. She did guess that Whiston had an entourage this time, even correctly guessing the numbers on the ground, but she didn't account for the roof.

She can almost hear her cousin clicking his tongue and saying, "You're getting sloppy, Rena."

Growling, Zero curls her left hand into a fist and shoots Whiston with a taser blast from a device wrapped around her wrist. He falls onto the ground, convulsing, eyes rolling back. Zero spins around and traps two of the hooded figures in ice sculptures with her freezing blaster. Sometimes, she loves winter. The other three assailants quickly adjust to her speed, and the four of them clash in a flurry of flashing electric whips and lightning sticks and swords composed of pure energy. They're too close for the shooter on the roof to try to shoot Zero, especially when her head is protected by her helmet. She carries her momentum with every dodge, never needing to change directions abruptly, and when she sees a window of opportunity, she doesn't hesitate to shove her the spikes of her war fan into an attacker's gut.

A shower of bullets comes from the same direction again, and she jumps back into the space of the other two assailants to avoid it. One of them catches her neck with a wire, and her fingers immediately grab onto it, uncaring of the metal digging into her skin. She crouches slightly, shifting closer to her assailant, and uses the weight imbalance to flip them over their shoulder. Quick like lighting, she flips out her knife and buries the blade into their calf. Once released, she rolls away and reactivates the shield to hide from the bullets, but she can feel herself losing energy with the piece of lead in her side and squeezing out blood every time she moves. The last standing attacker waves their whip, and Zero spins out from behind her shield to catch it with her gloved hand, collecting the electrons for her charging forearm guard.

Without a warning, her prosthetic leg gives out.

She falls onto her knee with a grunt, the cold spreading up her leg, and all she can think is, *Impossible. Starcatcher technology never fails.*

Zero stares at her open palm, then realizes that the electric whip has disappeared, too.

She looks up to see that all the buildings have gone dark, the streets dull and gloomy in the winter storm without the neon lights. The entire city of Gezrya has blacked out.

Zero hears the blow before she sees it on her night vision screen. She jerks back and spins on her knee, twisting the snow, before she slices her knife through the assailant's patellar tendons. Then she tries to roll away, but her paralyzed leg slows the movement. The moment her hands hit the ground again, she pushes herself up onto her good leg.

The whistle of a circular saw blade cuts through the darkness.

A loud clang rings louder when something else stops it, the sound reverberating against the walls.

Zero clutches her tungsten baton as her arm buzzes from the impact, and she loses her balance when the baton ricochets off the saw blade with high velocity, the weapon pulling her back just as aggressively as she just swung it at the saw blade.

Lean yet strong arms catch her before she hits the ground.

Zero blinks up at Raven's swept back hair, her entire face covered by a black mask. A shadow darts out from behind her. In quick succession, five loud cracks of bone crunching resound in the alley as the Zessroan snaps the neck of all the hooded people. Raven sets Zero down on the ground and blocks a feeble punch from Whiston, who must have gotten up when the taser blast expired, before kicking him in the face and knocking him out cold.

"You okay?" Raven's muffled voice asks.

Zero blows out a breath. "Were you always this badass and only watched me pretend to be a cool, mysterious demoness for your entertainment, or did you recently have a crash course on hand-to-hand combat with the Descendants?"

Raven huffs softly, before she pulls Zero into a crushing hug. Zero clutches at Raven's shoulders, swallowing down the rest of her questions. The familiar warmth drains all the tension out of Zero's body, and her bullet wound starts throbbing. Her muscles slacken as she allows herself a small break, holding onto Raven.

Small flakes of snow land on her arm and immediately melt.

Zero closes her eyes. It'll all be over very, very soon. The bullet burns in her side, but she doesn't let go of her friend. At this moment, all she wants to do is hear their heartbeats pounding steadily in their chests.

17

Deactivating...

Rovis is in the middle of wrestling an oversized platinum **tortoise when** the city powers down.

The robot falls limp right as he shoves his energy sword through its belly. But since the sword isn't actually made of any physical material, he ends up punching the metal with his fist with improper form.

"*Fuck,*" Rovis growls. He leaves a dent in the robot, but the impact sends a painful shock through his bones. Scowling, he drops the tortoise and rips the head off, sparks flying from the torn wires.

His eyes are a thousand times sharper than when he was in the Playground while he scans the childish scuffle around him. His head is clearer than crystal, and he's never appreciated a lucid mental state more. Tearing through these bots now is easier than tearing apart cotton candy.

A gunshot turns his attention to the shore.

Marudas breaks out of a Skull's hold and tries to make a run for the docks. With a expert fling, Jordan throws a knife at Marudas, who falls on his face when it lodges in his thigh. Rovis moves to detain him, but one of Marudas's minions distracts him with a swinging fist. Annoyed, Rovis blocks the amateur hook and returns with a double jab into a rear uppercut that knocks them out.

The former director of the Agency still manages to have a couple hundred Agents loyal to him, even after his entire life's work has shriveled into dust in the span of one week. Rovis doesn't understand what his lackeys think they're fighting for. Are they sacrificing themselves so that Marudas can get away then come back even stronger? Like a savior rising from the ashes?

Oh, spare me, Rovis thinks with derision when another Agent gets in his face like a brainless fly. *Marudas wouldn't survive a single day outside this country.*

He dodges a spiky mace and rounds to the back of his assailant, his brisk steps practiced and precise. He snaps their neck with his bare hands.

Out of the corner of his eyes, he sees Damian slam the heads of two Agents together and throw their unconscious bodies to the side, before he sweeps the legs from underneath the third one coming at him.

Earlier, Damian and Jordan appeared by his side while he was taunting a steel hyena, after he lost Tal in the chaos. Rovis doesn't know when they evacuated to the west coast to join him in Gezrya, but they must have been on their way to join Rovis as soon as they got here. He can only guess that they left when Aurodus was scorched by the last of the Agents in the area. The news set off all the Skulls and Rings at the safe house, especially because those Agents were just a small group that couldn't have been more than forty people. The Daggers killed all of them soon after, just moments too late to spare Aurodus. But Rovis is just glad to see that his two oldest friends have made it out alive.

The three of them have lost their stronger weapons with the inexplicable blackout, but so have the Agents. The battle isn't looking good for Marudas's minions, when their enemies are crime bosses who used to win wrestling championships every year since middle school.

Rovis twists his body to catch the handle of a flying knife, holding up his forearm guard to block bullets targeting his face. Then he dislocates an Agent's shoulder, shatters a kneecap, and breaks a wrist. The free knife he got is nicely sharpened, so he cuts through tendons and slices through between ribs of any Agent who tries to stand between him and Marudas.

Every time they attempt to clear out a path for Marudas to escape to the docks, either Jordan or Damian throws something at him to slow him down, while Rovis focuses on reducing their distance to him.

"I'm going to kill you," Marudas seethes when he trips over a fishing net.

"You can try," Rovis mutters under his breath as he pulls his bloody knife out of another ruptured heart.

He turns just in time to see an Agent helping Marudas onto his feet, and he can't help but scoff, incredulous.

A poor man who has never had to do anything by himself, Marudas can't even get up off the ground without his minions. He only knows how to create the most twisted ideas for the Agency to carry out, without ever having to lift a finger. Now, with his organization torn apart, he has nothing to hide behind.

Jordan and Damian have whipped out their stunning blasters, both shooting at Marudas's feet. He falls into the snow every time they hit him, yowling as if he's never encountered pain before.

And Marudas had the audacity to mock Rovis, in that dark cell beneath Drokklo's Playground.

A girl with a hooded cloak materializes next to Rovis and moves through the Agents like the wind of a snow storm, looping around in spirals and never ceasing. She's much taller than Rena, but the way she fights can almost fool Rovis into thinking it's his sister. It isn't until now, after Rena showed him the Dagger mark behind her ear, that he realizes her fighting style is a mix between the Loveias assassins and desert Aconites. The cloaked girl must be the only Dagger Enyo dared to plant in this part of Lord territory, due to her banishment.

When Rovis finally reaches Emery Marudas, the fallen man springs up and swings a punch at him. Without blinking, Rovis catches the fist and twists. A groan of pain accompanies Marudas collapsing down on one knee.

"Get your filthy hands off of me," he snarls. "You have no right to be so disrespectful. My family has been the backbone of the country for—"

His sentence turns into a grunt when Rovis shoves his face into the snow.

"You were right, you know," Rovis says with a sneer, just loud enough for Marudas alone to hear. "You dug up my past and turned my head inside out. Played with my memories like a music box. So I've been thinking a lot lately, after I broke out of your family's favorite circus. You were right about everything except for one thing."

He tosses the knife into the snow. Marudas yells when it embeds itself right in front his eyes, blade stained with blood, a casual warning.

"I don't give a shit about you. You're nothing but an animal," Marudas spits out.

Rovis twists his lips into a dark and sinful smirk. "Is that so?"

Black metal glints as he draws out a mechanical gun and presses the barrel into Marudas's temple, slow and deliberate. The thick heel of a heavy boot bears down on the back of his neck. Rovis leans his elbow on his knee, humming.

"I seem to recall a monologue about how much I drew your attention for killing Quade Bianchi. You were even obsessed with me. Which one is it, Marudas?"

"Fuck you," Marudas hisses.

"No, thanks," Rovis shoots back, nose twitching with revulsion. "Tell me, did you ever count how many people I've killed when you dedicated a whole team at the Agency to thoroughly research me?"

At that, Marudas stops struggling and widens his eyes.

Rovis chuckles, a crisp sound colder than the air. "That's right. One hundred and forty-one, not counting today."

"Don't," Marudas begs. "Don't kill me. Please. I have a son."

"A son that you beat up every time you drink too much? Color me unconvinced by your reason for me to spare you."

"I chose not to kill you," he tries with a trembling voice. "You have a chance to prove to the world that you are not a savage, by returning the favor."

"Oh, I'm returning a favor alright," Rovis says, remembering the syringe tucked away inside his jacket. He pulls it out without moving the gun away, then flicks off the cap with his thumb. The needle gleams, simple yet ominous.

Marudas recognizes it immediately and starts thrashing beneath Rovis's foot.

"No. *No.* Don't you dare."

"It's only fair," Rovis drawls. "I'm just returning a favor."

Before Marudas can get another word in, he injects the Agency's perfected mind-control drug into the bottom of Marudas's skull.

"That's for my sister," Rovis says when Marudas stops struggling and accepts his defeat. "For testing the drug on her first, and for controlling me with it, which caused me to hurt her."

Marudas's face contorts. "Ace of Crowns…"

"Yes, her." Rovis leans down further, putting more weight on the foot keeping Marudas down. "Here's the one thing you got wrong. I've killed over a hundred and forty-one people, and every single kill was for her. In no universe would she be one of those kills."

"What—"

Rovis flips the gun in his hand and knocks Marudas out with a satisfying crack.

He lets the body drop into an ungraceful position, blood staining the snow, and walks away.

No, he doesn't feel quite satisfied. What would have been pleasing was listening to the man scream, hearing him beg, watching him sob, for hours, days, weeks. Trapping Marudas with Tal, with *Lithium*, would have been the payment needed for everything he did to Rena, her friends and family, to Griffin, to Rovis himself. He might be thriving on hatred and vengeance at the moment, but once he processes what he went through in Drokklo's Playground, he's afraid he won't be this resilient. Rovis would have enjoyed tormenting Marudas, but he hopes that Drokklo is doing that for him down in hell.

Because as much as Rovis wants all that, he wants even more to focus on his friends, his sister, his Tal. Rovis glances around, watching the battles come to an end, as the Dagger tears through the last fifty Agents by herself, leaving nothing for Damian and Jordan. The two crime bosses have just settled for standing and watching her work. Damian's holding a bag of dried fruits that must have spawned out of thin air to share with his partner. And somewhere between the docks and the house, Tal is no doubt chasing down every last robot from the Playground. Rovis is sure he's holding his own, but he can't help but worry just a little bit, especially with the bl ackout.

"I thought you were supposed to take him alive," Jordan says when xe walks over to Rovis with Damian.

Rovis blinks, then looks down at Marudas. "He is. He's just unconscious. Dziye came by earlier to give me a dose of the Agency's mind-control drug in case I wanted to use it for revenge, which is exactly what I did."

"Your cousin?" Damian asks, voice rough and brows furrowed. "How'd he get his hands on it?"

"The Daggers blew up the labs, so I assume they took some of the drugs."

"And you think a Dagger, working under the only person the Water Lords have ever exiled from all of their territories, gave it to a Marquess of the Lords."

Rovis opens his mouth to explain, but a group of people he doesn't recognize emerges from behind buildings all around them, wrapped up in earth tones, spears in hand. They've clearly been in fights, too, judging by the wounds and blood stains. Rovis readjusts his grip on his gun, wary.

"Hello, Scavenger," the woman in front says, and something about her voice seems familiar. "I thank you for your help in capturing Emery Marudas."

"You're the head of the Dawn Council?"

She inclines her head, shiny mask glinting. "Yes. My name is Nova Ly, and I believe you once saved my daughter's life."

As if on cue, a livestock trailer pulls up on the road next to them, where two people are riding on the roof. A lean arm with a familiar, rolled-up green sleeve sticks out the driver's window. With an impatient tilt of her head, Raven knocks on the rusty door.

"Mom," she calls. "We've got Whiston and all the project managers of the Agency."

Nova raises a hand and flicks her fingers. Her people immediately move to grab Marudas by the arms and drag him into the trailer. Meanwhile, Raven catches Rovis's eye and salutes him with two fingers. He nods in return. Then he digs out a small device, shaped like a bat, that was paired with the syringe.

He holds it out to Nova. "This can control Marudas, if you want it."

Nova doesn't move. "You don't want to keep it for yourself? I can arrange something with the Council if you'd like some revenge. The whole country has seen what he did to you."

Rovis shakes his head. "I want to move on. You may choose to use it or sentence him to death. It's all up to the Council now."

"Very well." She takes the device with a nod. Then she gets in the passenger seat of the livestock trailer, next to her daughter. Her people follow, climbing onto the top. Rovis watches Raven drive off, though no emotions stir up in his chest. His legs are solid beneath him, and his hands remain relaxed by his side. He doesn't feel a sense of closure or peace, nor does he feel a loss or an unfulfilled vengeance.

Although, he can't ignore the inquiring stares burning into the side of his face. Rovis tilts his head at Damian. "I heard you're the one who gave me blood."

"Well, I was not about to let your brainless sister do it," he says aggressively, scoffing. "I had to stop you from strangling her to death, you stupid fuck. At least I got to hit you really hard on the head. It's not like you'd have any brain cells to lose from the damage."

"Damian," Jordan scolds, exasperated.

"It's fine, Jord." Rovis chuckles, shaking his head. He pats Damian on the shoulder, who leans back, looking royally offended. Rovis adds, "Thank you
."

"Fuck off," Damian grumbles. "What are you thanking me for?"

"Seriously," Jordan interrupts, throwing xyr hands up. "I thought I taught you manners. Why are you still such a wet cat around Rovis?"

"I am *not*—"

"At the very least," Jordan ignores Damian, "listen to Rena if you don't want to listen to me. Would you like to endure another one of her roasting sessions?"

Damian looks away, shoulders hunched, and mutters "No."

"Thank you," Rovis repeats, looking at Damian earnestly. "For giving me blood, for breaking me out of the Playground, and for having my sister's back."

"We've been friends for ages." Damian glares at him. "There's no need to thank me."

That's about the best that Rovis can get from Damian Narvaez, so he laughs and slings an arm around Jordan's shoulders. They start trekking through the snow accumulating on the streets of what's now a ghost town. Dots of blood cover their shirts, on Rovis's front, Damian's sleeves, Jordan's collar.

"And you," Rovis says to Jordan in Toullish. "Thank you for everything."

"I'm going to have to second Damian on this one," Jordan responds, eyes gleaming with amusement.

"I heard my name," Damian calls from behind the pair.

"You're imagining things," Jordan shoots back without missing a beat.

Rovis rolls his eyes. "What do you two want for lunch?"

"Oh." Damian catches up to walk beside them, perking up. "Do you still know how to make that spicy beef slices thing?"

"Sure."

The sun shines distantly above them when they make it back to the house, shielded by the polluted clouds and tainted snowflakes. Most of the people who made it back early are already regrouping in the lounge, the dining room, and the living room. Rovis finds his jacket and puts it on when a soft bump on his leg drags his attention down.

"Who managed to save the cat?" Rovis exclaims, picking up Starlight, petting the black fur. He honestly forgot about zir, but he would have assumed that ze died along with the Aconite mansion.

Both Avery and Vanneza point to the corner by the gigantic flatscreen, where Kagiso smirks and lifts his drink. How he manages to still look so sly and devilish when Ofir is hovering over the large gash in his arm, where a mending spider is stitching his flesh back together, Rovis will never know.

"But to be completely honest with you," Kagiso says, "it wasn't me. Did you know this cat is two hundred years old?"

Rovis stares. When he realizes Kagiso isn't joking, his eyes widen. "Starlight is a mutant?"

"Yep. Best kept secret of the Aconite Heartless. Starlight actually saved a dozen fledgelings."

At that, Starlight meows in Rovis's arms. Upon a closer look, Rovis notices zir teeth aren't covered in enamel; they actually look like platinum.

"What the hell," he says.

The cat meows again before jumping out of his arms and disappearing under a couch. Rovis doesn't move until Avery's waving their hands in front of his eyes.

"Hi, Boss," they say.

"Hi," Rovis says. Then he turns to continue his search for Rena and Tal.

When he doesn't find either of them on the ground floor, he climbs up the stairs, heart beginning to speed up. Dread sinks in his chest, slow and thick, like tar trickling down the gaps between permeable rocks. The second floor is filled with Damian's people and a few of Jordan's, but still no sight of who Rovis is looking for.

He tries the doors of the third floor, most of them empty.

Until he sees Tal's bloody face, sitting on a bed, with his metal arm laid in his lap.

"Tal," Rovis breathes, rushing to cup Tal's neck and inspect the damage. His left eye is swollen shut, and a shallow cut is oozing with blood below on his cheek.

"Hey," Tal whispers, smiling weakly. "It looks worse than it feels, I promise. I'm just taking a break before I fix it."

"I'll do it," Rovis murmurs. He finds a towel in the bathroom and rinses it with hot water before returning to clean the blood off, before his spider crawls up his hand to heal the cut on Tal's face. He pulls out an instant ice pack from his jacket and presses it underneath Tal's eye.

"I hope you ripped apart whoever did this," he says, a soft growl low in his chest.

Gentle fingers wrap around his wrist. Tal takes the ice pack and puts it against his brow. With a ghost of a smirk, he retorts, "What do you take me for, Rov?"

Amused, Rovis huffs and strokes the uninjured side of Tal's face with a gentle thumb. His gaze flicks down to Tal's lips before he could stop it. Tal catches it, drops his hand to the side, and lifts his chin, a silent permission. Gingerly, Rovis leans in and brushes their lips together in a chaste kiss, brief but achingly sweet.

Before Tal gets greedy, Rovis pulls away and glances down at the arm. "What happened?"

"The blackout." Tal snorts. "It was deadweight, so I took it off and started batting it at the Agents. Not my best fighting technique, I dare say."

Rovis laughs, too, but he traces his fingertips at the edge of Tal's shoulder where he had to amputate his arm. "Did it hurt?"

"No, just..." Tal considers. "Odd. It altered my balance, you know. I got used to having this extension of myself, and it was just gone."

Nodding, Rovis picks up the arm and sits down next to Tal to put it back on. They've been here countless times, when Tal was obsessed with upgrading his arm, and Rovis was the only person patient enough to sit through all-nighters with him. He remembers Levi's delighted grin when he manipulated Rovis into it, so that he himself could finally get proper sleep. Tal would always say that the Purish viewed him as a weakling and tried to make him weaker, but he'd turn it against them. He truly delivered upon that.

"Where's Zero?" Tal asks quietly, staring vacantly at the line where the wall meets the floor. "Or... Rena. She ran out earlier. Is she back yet?"

Rovis frowns, fidgeting with the latches. "I don't know. I'm sure she's fine."

Rena has been running around not telling Rovis anything for years now. He had to get used to not knowing at some point. It doesn't mean he likes it, but there's only so much he can do without driving himself insane.

The window clicks.

Tal and Rovis exchange glances.

Rovis sets the arm down on the bed and stands, gun in hand. Tal also takes out one of his knives, though he stays sitting. Behind the curtains, the window slides up once, twice, then all the way on the third time. A shadow crawls through and extends to the floor, before rolling out from between the curtains.

Rena clutches her side on the floor, face pale.

Rovis stares, dumbfounded. Tal reaches forward and puts a hand on Rovis's gun, which is still pointed at Rena's face, then pushes it down slowly. To his horror, Rena takes out a knife and stabs herself, face twisting with pain. In two large steps, Rovis strides over to the window and stumbles onto his knee, grabbing her wrist.

"What the fuck are you doing?" he hisses.

She blinks at him with unfocused eyes. When the haze clears, she says, "Oh, hey."

Then she tries to stab herself again.

"Rena," Rovis snaps.

"What? I'm trying to get this bullet out."

Tal makes an incredulous noise and exclaims, "With a steak knife?"

"It's fine," she says, apathetic, and attempts to move her arm again. Rovis doesn't budge, only using his other hand to move her jacket out of the way to see dark red staining her gray sweater on her side. At least the bullet didn't get anything vital.

"Shit," he breathes. "Are you stupid? You don't just carve it out with a knife you probably used to stab somebody just now, not to mention the wrong type of knife. Here, let me. I think I have a scalpel."

"No, just give me the knife and tell me what to do."

Rovis scowls. "Now is not the time to be stubborn. You can't do this by yourself."

"I have to." Rena lets go of the dirty steak knife and squeezes her eyes shut, steadying her breathing. "I'm going to throw up."

"Then just clean the wound and leave the bullet in. Your body will heal around it."

Rena shakes her head. "I want it out."

"It won't hurt," he promises. "The bullet will be in your body, but it won't affect anything. Trust me, I have a couple, too. And your tolerance is much higher than mine."

"I'm going to die with my veins burning me from the inside out," she says, over-articulating her words as though he's stupid. "It will be much, much worse with a bullet inside of me."

Rovis flinches back at the reminder of her disease. Then he lets out a frustrated sigh when he processes her words. She's right, of course. And Rovis doesn't want her to be in any pain for the rest of her life, but her decisions make it extremely difficult to help her.

Tal nudges him, dragging his attention away from Rena. Tal's holding up his watch, his arm reattached, and Ofir's contact profile hovers in the air. Understanding, Rovis nods. Without a missing a beat, Tal hits the call button. Rovis turns his attention back to Rena as Tal explains the situation over the phone. Rena, on the other hand, blinks bleary eyes at Tal, brows furrowed. Rovis then glances back and forth between the two of them, nonplussed.

When Tal hangs up, she points at his face with her free hand and squints. "Who."

Tal crosses his arms, unimpressed. "I can't believe I never realized you two are related; you're practically the same person."

"Hey," both Rovis and Rena protest.

"They're dead," Tal answers Rena's vague and incomplete non-question.

"Oh," she says, almost seeming disappointed. She nods and sways on the floor, and Rovis catches her by the shoulders before she topples over.

With a knock on the door, Ofir comes in and throws the blanket onto the floor, gesturing for Rena to lie down on the clean sheets on the bed. Rovis helps her, while Tal stays back and ices his black eye.

Rena reaches into Rovis's jacket when he slowly sets her down, and he startles but doesn't stop her. She pulls out his vial of chamomile and lavender, twisting the top off. Rovis smiles softly and takes it from her, holding it under her nose with one hand, while grasping her hand with the other.

She closes her eyes when Ofir cleans up the wound. Her breathing grows harsh when they start the process of removing the bullet. Rovis smooths her hair back while Ofir works. It only takes fifteen minutes for them to pull it out with forceps. When Ofir brings out a spider-bot to stitch her up, Rena settles down once again, still looking pale. After the spider crawls off her body, she asks in Avyrian, "Done?"

Rovis looks at the revealed skin, where not even a scar lingers. "Done."

Rena springs out of the bed to throw up in the bathroom.

He glances at Tal, who grimaces in sympathy.

"Make sure she drinks enough water," Ofir orders before disappearing out the door, where Saige is leaning against the door. Both Rovis and Tal jump when they see her, having been completely unaware of her presence.

"Looks like it's time for lunch," she says, ignoring their shock. "There are two childish mob bosses downstairs whining for you to cook, brother-in-law. Brother-out-of-law? Brother-in-anarchy? Brother—"

"Where have you been?" Tal interrupts, bewildered. Rovis simply doesn't know how to react at this point.

"Oh, just Faceless things." Saige waves a dismissive hand. "Seriously, I can't stand Damian and Jordan anymore. They have not stopped gushing about your cooking skills, and now everyone downstairs is starving and grumpy. Rena definitely needs food, too, if that helps motivating you."

"Yeah, Rovis," Tal turns and snarks. "Why haven't you cooked for everyone yet?"

Rolling his eyes, Rovis shoots back with, "Well, why did both you and Rena come back with so many injuries? I made it back just fine, but I still had to deal with you two."

That's when Rena trudges out of the bathroom, glaring at him with murderous intent despite her sagging posture. She flicks her eyes pointedly at her leg and then at Tal's arm before quadrupling the death stare aimed at Rovis.

He holds up his hands in surrender.

Tal clicks his tongue. "But why did you climb through the window? This is the third floor, and it could've been anyone in here."

"I claimed this room this morning," Rena growls. "Raven helped me get to the edge of the city until my leg wasn't fucking *useless* anymore, before she had to report to her mom. And then I had to limp all the way back here, so I was really not in the mood to be perceived."

"You climbed up two stories outside the house to crawl through a window, with a bullet in your psoas, just so you can avoid people?" Tal raises a brow. Then he tilts his head in a sideways nod. "Sounds about right, actually."

"Raven was there?" Saige asks Rena.

"Yes, and she's a better fighter than me. Can you believe it?" Rena snaps her fingers at Rovis and points vaguely in the direction of the kitchen. "Food."

"Alright, alright." Rovis squeezes past Saige, who covers her mouth trying to hide her laughter, and stomps down the stairs. Daleyza, a real life goddess, is already in the kitchen cooking up some vegetables. Tal trails in after him to grab wine from the fridge, evidently not helping. Rovis says, "Tal, I'm making Daleyza my new second."

"Don't drag me into this," Daleyza retorts.

Tal widens his eyes — or tries to, with his injury — and freezes, spilling wine onto the island counter. His stare darts between Daleyza and Rovis before realization clicks, and he grudgingly makes his way back around to watch Rovis pick out all the seasoning.

"What do you want me to do?"

Rovis tosses him a jar of peanuts. "Cook in a pan with oil until it turns gold."

Tal obeys, joining Daleyza on the stove. It's nice, Rovis thinks, that the inner circle is cooking together. Rovis and Tal haven't made their own food in a really long time, since the Clockworks did everything. But the organization has more or less fallen apart, and all the rankings were stupid anyway. With a new government rising, they probably won't keep getting away with how they used to make money, and Rovis is sure the Dawn Council would be working to redistribute wealth.

Rummaging through the cabinets, Rovis finds the red oil that Rena must have made while he was unconscious. She has a habit of stress-cooking. He was going to improvise with some chilis, but their secret Wei family recipe from Rovis's father works better with this one, which takes days of preparation.

He grabs a pot and dumps the beef in water with the seasoning. When his hand brushes against Tal's to put it on a back burner, he slows down.

Their eyes meet.

Daleyza very coincidentally finishes her dish and piles it in a large tray, smartly leaving the kitchen as quickly as possible.

Rovis smiles, and Tal's lips twitch in response. For a man whose facade involves a terrifying and dangerous grin, Tal doesn't give out his real smiles often. Rovis's chest warms at the thought that he gets to see it.

A loud pop of oil splattering breaks the moment.

Tal restarts his shoveling, and Rovis goes back to the island to pour out the red oil in a bowl, but not before giving Tal a quick peck on the neck.

"Tease," he grumbles.

Rovis huffs, sprinkling in salt. It only takes Tal a few more minutes to finish with the peanuts, pouring it onto a plate. While they wait for the beef to get fully cooked, Rovis directs Tal to help him with a couple easier dishes so that the hungry people outside don't get too grouchy. When they finally wrap up all of them, Rovis balances three trays of food out to the dining hall, where everyone starts cheering, clapping, and yelling phrases of gratitude.

Damian bangs on the table in excitement, as if he's still twelve. Jordan shoves him, and they start bickering again. For a moment, Rovis is transported back to middle school, and he suddenly feels the full weight of the cruel reminder that Griffin isn't with them anymore. Distracted, he stumbles into the table and almost drops a dish, but thankfully Avery's quick to catch it and set it down.

From his other side, Rena touches his wrist while they wait for people to rearrange the table, a hint of concern in her eyes. The shadows of the chandelier accentuate her dark circles. His heart aches at the sight, but Rovis only nods to tell her that he's fine. He's been living with this grief for a while now. It'll never go away, just as his love for Griffin will never fade.

Rena and Saige have saved two seats between them, so Rovis sets down the trays and slips in next to his sister. Beneath the table, she holds her palm up. He takes it, intertwining their fingers.

Next to Rovis, Tal settles down and glances at Rovis's tight grip on Rena's hand, then shoots him a questioning look. Rovis shakes his head.

"Wait." Saige's arm flies out toward the middle of the table as she stands, hand flapping to get everyone's attention. She stares at her watch with tense shoulders. "Someone turn on the screen."

Frowning, Zeke turns and presses some buttons by the door, and the entire wall opposite the entryway to the kitchen fades into a broadcast with the Faceless logo.

Familiar silhouettes line up across the screen, and gradually the lighting shines on their faces to reveal what Rovis assumes is the Dawn Council.

"The Purish government has fallen," the woman in the middle speaks.

Some people start banging on the table again.

"The Zessroans are here to take back our country," Raven's mother continues. "Yes, we still exist. We have always been here, living like ghosts until today. We are willing to exist alongside all immigrant groups as long as our culture is respected. This moment marks the end of the Purish rule. We ask that all five countries recognize us as a new nation, with a new name and new leaders."

The scene changes to Patrikk Feyrer and Didier Whiston in prison, with Emery Marudas's limp body slumped against the front of their cells, his eyes glazed over.

"We are aware that Toullifuka and Riyssolx have come to an agreement," her voice cuts in before the screen shows the council again. "I, the head of the Dawn Council, propose a global peace treaty."

She goes on into paragraphs about reforming the country and offering better trade deals, but barely anyone in the room is still paying attention. Everyone mutters about their future, reminding Rovis of his own concerns about what comes next. All his plans drift through his head, and his mind latches onto the image of amethyst caves powering technology he has yet to see with his own eyes. No one notices when the broadcast ends, and the screen changes back to the large art piece. Absently, Rovis scoops up a spoonful of cottage pie.

He turns his head to see that Tal's already staring at him. The two of them exchange a long look, calculating, but they both know that all of this is out of their hands. They used to be unlucky kids who had to resort to crime, then thrived as criminals, before they inadvertently became rebel fighters. What's comforting now, is that he knows that he'll get to figure it out *with* Tal. It's no longer a choice between him and Rena.

If they have to run, they all will.

Tal breaks their eye contact, looking past Rovis. He follows his gaze to see Rena's spaced out expression, her left hand trembling with the fork. She still hasn't touched anything, whereas everyone else has at least gobbled down Daleyza's dish. Rovis tugs at her hand underneath the table, and she jerks her stare toward him.

"What's wrong?" Rovis asks in Avyrian.

She only shakes her head and half-heartedly puts some of the spicy beef slices into her plate. The frown stays throughout lunch, but Rovis supposes he knows more or less of what's causing her dispirited mood, so he doesn't push her to talk today. Everyone's suffering some degree of fear during this period of uncertainty; they can only hope that it doesn't last too long, and that it doesn't end badly.

After putting away their plates, Rovis follows her back to the room she supposedly claimed on the third floor, where the bed is just large enough for two people. He leans against the headboard while Rena lies down flat on her back, staring at the ceiling. Her body's worn out from the fight and the surgery that followed, but her mind's still racing, he can tell.

"Rest," he says softly. "I'm here."

"I know."

She doesn't fall asleep right away, but eventually she dozes off with his hand resting against the top of her head.

18

Pureland: Terminated

Saige sips on her tea, far too drawn into some ridiculous book about magical pirates while leaning against Tal, who idly sharpens his knives, bored out of his mind.

It's been days since the Dawn Council's announcement, and the Digitals were able to unearth the information that world leaders have been on a secure digital conference call this whole time. Of course, Tal can hack into it if he wants, but he logs out of the terminal before the job's finished, every time he gets anxious enough to try. His indecision makes him want to tear down a building with his bare hands. He's dying to know how the conference is going, but he doesn't know if he can handle finding out. For once, he would rather wait with everyone else.

Perhaps it would have been smart to run, as soon as they finished Marudas. Leave the country and disappear, become someone else entirely. Or perhaps it would have been unwise, since no country would allow anyone from Pureland to cross their borders in this day and age. And pirates do exist, even if they're not magical.

A black mug is shoved in his face.

Tal looks up at Zero's blank expression. Despite the progress she's made with Rovis, she seems to have reverted back to her apathy over the past few days. She's still quiet around Tal, but at least she's talking to her brother and not actively avoiding Tal, once she let out her bitterness and insecurities about her relationship with him. Rovis says she's willing to talk to her therapist again, once she processes everything that's happened since Ferrisque.

He hopes she talks about why she went there in the first place. Wordlessly, Tal takes the cup and breathes in the leafy steam.

"He's in the master bedroom," Zero says, having absolutely no tact in pushing Tal towards Rovis at this point, like he's a child crying for chocolate in the grocery store, and the problem is simply solved by dumping him in candy land. Or he's a kid tearing up all the threads in a carpet, and she doesn't want to deal with it, so she merely puts on a movie so he'd leave the carpet alone.

Okay, the comparisons aren't the best, but either way, he feels brushed aside, and that just won't do. If Zero had as long to live as the rest of them, he'd tolerate the cold shoulder and give her space. But she doesn't.

He holds out his unoccupied hand, bare skin and free of leather, and waits.

Zero stares down at it, probably thinking it's pointless and random, judging by that unimpressed frown. But she takes his hand anyway, to entertain Tal. She's generous like that.

"What's up with you?" he asks in Lasan. Saige looks up briefly at the language switch, but resumes reading so that Zero doesn't feel interrogated.

"Just tired," Zero answers, matter of fact, removing her hand from Tal's grip. "I didn't sleep while I was working to get Rovis out, and now it's catching up to me."

Tal studies her. It's not a lie, but it's also not the whole truth.

"Something else is bothering you," he remarks. "Are you worried about how we're going to survive after this?"

"Maybe."

"We'll figure it out. I won't leave you again."

"You've promised that before," she says, frost creeping into her false indifference.

"And I'm sorry—"

"I know," she interrupts, voice perfectly bland again. "I'm not angry. I just don't trust you as much as I did before."

Tal's breathing hitches. A chill runs over his skin, as if he were standing outside in the cold without his jacket, rather than sitting inside in the cozy warmth. Of course it stings, but he also can't blame her, can't lash out for something that isn't really anyone's fault other than the world they live in. They were cruel to each other, yes, but how did they get here?

The government's impossible laws and the Agency's depravity drove Zero and Rovis apart. The cruelty of Purish supremacists took Tal away from Saige. And unfortunate circumstances caused by all of that have put a rift between Zero and Tal.

Tal could forgive Zero because he knew it was in her nature to get caught up in a web of secrets, and because everything turned out okay with Saige. She may be a liar with a whole iceberg worth of trust issues, but Tal has known that since the beginning of her time with the Aconites and chose her anyway. He's the one who went back on his word. And in the world of the Damned, they are all monsters who know too many ways to hurt and too few ways to heal. Given how much time Zero threw away with Rovis, when she was still young and lost, Tal knows it won't be as easy for her to do it all over again with him. He threatened her when she was sick and vulnerable, then left while she was dying. Of course she's detaching herself and hiding away.

If only Tal could invent a time machine.

"I'm not punishing you," she says quietly when he fails to answer. "It's just my truth. Nothing is the same as it was before; nothing can be. Maybe it'll get better, maybe it won't. We'll be fine either way, Tal."

Yet is 'fine' good enough for him?

He sighs, fingers twitching. It'd be easier to run from this, to turn away and forget any of this ever happened, starting from the day she walked up to him in that coffee shop. It'd be easier to erase her from memory and pretend she never left an imprint on his heart. It's always easier to avoid and forget, to drink himself into oblivion or throw himself into his work. At least for a while, but never long enough to matter. None of it can ever wash away all the ugly feelings he doesn't want to feel. Tal knows better now.

"It will take time," he says slowly, "but I'll work to earn your trust back."

Zero shrugs, though Tal doesn't miss the way her eyes twitch. "Do whatever you want."

"One more question," he adds before she can turn to leave.

"What." The prompt comes out flatter than a piece of paper, sharp with annoyance. Zero looks more bored at the moment than when she's reading an economics textbook. Tal tries not to take that as a personal offense.

He tilts his head, index finger tapping the arm of the couch. "The day we found Rovis at his mother's grave, you gave me flowers to give to him, but I saw Daleyza and gave most of it to her. Why did you and Rovis freeze when I handed him the last one?"

Zero raises a brow. "I don't remember this. That was ages ago."

"Eidetic memory," he reminds her. "It was an orchid."

"Oh." Something glints in her eyes, and the corners of her lips twitch. "I remember now. That made my day."

Tal stares at her. "What? Why?"

Saige chooses this moment to stop pretending that she isn't eavesdropping. She shuts her book, sitting up straight. Her expression mirrors Zero's, an inexplicable gleam in her stare, and Tal doesn't like it a single bit.

"An orchid?" Saige asks with an unsettling grin. "What color?"

Zero smirks. "Red."

Saige immediately starts cackling, doubling over from the force of her laughter, while Tal looks back and forth between them, bewildered. He can even feel waves of smugness rolling off of Zero, even though her face hasn't shifted a single bit.

"Yes, and it was apparently supposed to be pink," he says, exasperated.

"Of course it was," Saige says, still cackling like an evil witch. "Pink orchids are often used at funerals because they mean, 'I will always love you.'"

"Okay? That makes sense. What do red orchids mean?"

Instead of answering, Saige curls up and laughs even harder, slapping the couch cushions three times. Zero watches her with raised brows, clearly amused.

"This must have been bothering you for a while, Tal," Zero remarks.

He scowls. "Answer the stars-damned question. What do red orchids mean?"

Zero looks away for a second, crossing her arms and clearing her throat, as if needing to calm down and get ready for a presentation. Then she looks Tal dead in the eyes.

"Desire, passion, and love," she says with a straight face.

"Often used to express deep affection," Saige adds, practically glowing with glee.

Tal's jaw drops, eyes wide. His face burns. Invisible needles of utter mortification prick the back of his neck. His mind races back to that day in the cemetery and every interaction with Rovis that came after. Tal can't pinpoint when exactly Rovis figured out that Tal had feelings for him, but the stupid orchid incident definitely did not help. Or it did help, considering that things worked out between the two of them. But Tal would like to think that he was in control of everything on his end during their relationship development.

He points an accusatory finger at Zero. "You did that on purpose."

She scoffs. "I'm not that bored."

"You used to play with people's feelings for a living!"

"Tal, how was I supposed to guess that you were going to give Daleyza all the flowers except for one specific orchid?"

"I don't know." He glowers. "Everyone's aware that I had a history with Dakota, so maybe you guessed that I'd try to pay her back by going up to Daleyza. And maybe there's some subconscious 'pick the one that doesn't belong' game going on in my head when I was giving her the flowers, and you took advantage of that."

"Wow," Zero says, lips twitching with mirth. "People really think highly of my skills."

"And lowly of your intentions," Tal grumbles.

Saige pats his head, not at all sympathetic. With narrowed eyes, he jerks away and bats at her arm. Zero shakes her head and settles down on the couch on the other side of Saige.

"What part are you on?" she asks, looking at the book.

Saige tosses around her blanket so that it covers Zero. "Sea dragon just made an appearance."

"Ah." Zero snuggles in so that the two of them are huddling over the book in Saige's hand, pages flipped open again. "My favorite."

The sight is quite endearing, except Tal suddenly feels like the third wheel.

"Is this revenge for me getting together with Rovis?" he demands, still thinking about that red orchid. He wonders what Rovis must have been thinking when Tal gave it to him, but he's too afraid to ask.

Saige snorts. "You wish. Not everything's about you. If we wanted revenge, I'd be making out with Rena all over the place. Unfortunately this girl does not swing and does not date."

"Well," Zero says dryly, "why didn't you say so, Saige? You should know I'm only sometimes sex-repulsed."

"Right. In that case..." Saige grabs Zero's face, and Tal springs off of the couch and hurries out the lounge, scowling at the trail of laughter behind him. He decides to take refuge in the master's bedroom, where Rovis has found some paper and pencil to draw sketches of random things: cities that fell, the people currently staying at this house, and *lots* of Starlight the cat.

"Our sisters are bullying me," Tal complains, flopping down on the bed next to Rovis. Absent fingers find his hair and gently play with it while the sound of lead scratching on paper continues.

"How, exactly, are they doing that?"

"You don't want to know." He heaves a dramatic sigh and turns on his body to stare at Rovis's concentrated but relaxed expression. Tal would trace his features with his fingers and lips, but he doesn't want to disturb the peace at the moment. For the past couple of nights, Rovis has been waking up with nightmares, even though he wouldn't admit it to anyone who isn't Tal. Not even Zero, but neither of them would be surprised if she knows.

She probably does, if the chamomile tea deliveries before bed mean anything.

Tal just wishes he could help, like crawl into Rovis's dreams and slay the monsters. Or descend to hell and personally advise Drokklo's punishments for Emery Marudas. Or give everything Rovis has ever wanted in life so that the terrors of his past, of the Agency would fade away into dust.

But Tal is only human, a broken man with his own demons and shards of glass in his bleeding hands. All he can do is hold Rovis until he remembers how to breathe, until he regains strength to start another day.

———◦———

"You like him?" Levi asked, smoke expanding into the air from his mouth.

We were sitting on the roof of the Tech Hall, watching the sun sink down behind the mountains. He was sitting with one leg hanging off the edge and the other leg folded up so he could rest his arm on his knee between drags. I was leaning all the way back on my elbows, counting the faint stars as they show themselves with the approaching night. Levi was looking down at the entrance of the Poison Core, where Daleyza was speaking to Rovis, probably about their next Reaper job. It was the day after the first time Rovis came into my lab.

"No," I lied.

Levi huffed, clearly not fooled. "You should go for it."

I took a drag on my own cigarette, then blew it out. "Why would I? I don't know him. He doesn't know me."

"There's this ground-breaking phenomenon called dating," he said dryly. "Don't know if you've heard of it."

"I don't date."

"No, you just mess around with your best friend and ignore all your feelings."

"Fuck off," I said without heat. "You weren't complaining this morning."

"It's different, and you know it," Levi returned calmly.

"Well, why do you care? These are my decisions."

"I care because I want you to be happy, dumbass." He looked over at me, both amused and serious. "Just because I turned down being a Heartless, doesn't mean I'm blind."

"I'm not getting together with him," I grumbled, just to spite him. "You're stuck with me, forever and ever."

Levi laughed then, and I watched him tilt his head back to stare at the sky.

"Liar," he said.

A sharp tug at his hair makes Tal blink.

"You're thinking too loud." Rovis puts his pencil down, gazing at Tal curiously. "Where'd your head go?"

Tal's lips curl into a small smile.

He gets to hold Rovis now. Months ago, he yearned for this and didn't think it possible to have. Weeks ago, he thought he might have lost the chance forever. He's dreamt up thousands of different universes where this would work out, and he'd never believed that this universe would be among all those possibilities.

He's lucky, he knows now. And even though he's not an emissary of hell or a dreamscaper, he'll do whatever he can to put Rovis on the path to happiness.

"You," Tal whispers. "Always you."

Rovis stares, taken aback. His deep eyes search Tal's half-lidded ones. If Rovis's eyes were a black hole, he'd gladly step across the event horizon. Slowly, a dangerous look crosses Rovis's face, as a small but deadly smile tugs at his lips.

Tal's heart begins to race at the unexpected shift in mood. His face starts to burn, with Rovis looking at him like that.

Rovis leans down, brushing Tal's hair back, their faces inching closer in the sultry red glow of the sun filtered by the window. They watch each other, like the beginning of a sparring match or during the most dangerous part of a job. It's all too familiar, this synchrony. They've been here hundreds of times, as friends and partners. Tal closes his eyes and basks in the growing heat—

Someone bangs on their door repeatedly. Tal leaps out of bed, claws flexed and knife drawn in a low lunge halfway to the door.

"All six countries signed the treaty!" Saige's excited shout is muffled by the door, and Tal yanks it open to have her yell the same thing, obnoxiously, in his face. "All six countries signed the treaty!"

A presence hovers behind Tal's shoulder. He flicks the knife back into his sleeve and stretches his fingers. He feels Rovis thread their hands together, though he doesn't turn to face him yet, too shocked by the news.

"Do you get it?" Saige is practically bouncing off the walls. "We're okay! Not only are we safe, but the other five countries have acknowledged our new government as legitimate. Pureland is gone, for good."

"How?" Rovis demands, clearly unable to grasp how surreal this is any more than Tal can. "How is this possible?"

"Your cousin—"

"*I* didn't do anything," a large, bulky Avyrian man drawls with a cigarette hanging out of his lips, sauntering up behind Saige. Zero and Raven trail after him, matching postures with crossed arms. Evidently the Zessroan girl has finished her business with the Council and decided to come back for Zero. Dziye plucks out the cig and exhales, smoke dancing in the air like ghosts. "Avyria simply realized they'd benefit more to trade with new Pureland as a country, rather than trying to scramble for scraps when the big wolves of Riyssolx, Toullifuka, and inevitably Ezclovia tear it apart for themselves. If that happens, all those countries would be closer to the islands, and that'd make it easier for them to take Avyria, too."

"Yes, they just magically came to that conclusion themselves," Zero comments, dry as ever, and rolls her eyes. "Dziye has been working the Lords to the bones trying to convince Avyria to come to our support."

Dziye swipes at Zero's head, and pieces of hair fall over her face. She doesn't react, only deflates like a tired old lady surrounded by screaming toddlers.

"Because you told me to," Dziye says to her. "Why aren't you on the Council, baby cousin?"

Raven snorts. "Her? Becoming a politician?"

"I'm seventeen," Zero says flatly. "The adults living on this cursed continent have been incompetent for long enough; it's time for them to do their jobs. I don't want to run a country, and I never wanted to. I just want everyone to leave me and my family alone."

"Stars, I was just asking." Dziye raises his hands. "Kids these days. So temperamental."

"Where did you find the time to plan out this part?" Tal asks, incredulous. "You said yourself that you didn't even sleep when Rovis was in Drokklo's Playground."

"It was the first thing I did when I heard he got caught," Zero states, and then does not elaborate whatsoever. They all stare at her, puzzled, except for Raven. Kagiso strolls down the hall to join them, watching the group while sipping on champagne.

"What's going on here?" he asks, that sly smirk etched on his face, an eerie contradiction to everyone else's expression.

Rovis shakes his head and asks Zero, "Why?"

She blinks at him, then tilts her head at Dziye. "I told you I played it how I play any other game, didn't I?"

"Save all the big cards and deadly combinations for last," Dziye dutifully lays it out, "and hit them with everything when your enemies lose steam."

"That only works sometimes," Rovis points out, a hint of smugness coloring his voice. "As I've shown you, little sister."

Zero rolls her eyes again, and Tal is surprised they haven't fallen out of her skull from the number of times she does that.

"Breaking anyone out from beneath the capital *takes* a revolution," she says. "We happened to have one, brewing for centuries. So I sped it up a bit before Rovis ran out of time, brought hell to the ground surface, and decided to go all out. I was going to pull the rug from under the Agency and incite as much chaos as possible anyway, so I might as well have made sure that everything goes through to the end properly. If the foreign countries divided Pureland, it would be all too easy for the Purish to come back again, rebelling like they did against Ezclovia, and this would have been for nothing."

"So you just casually convinced the Avyrian mafia to beg for help from the country they escaped from," Tal deadpans.

Zero shrugs. "Technically my cousin did. But desperate times."

"Speaking of games," Kagiso chimes in, "Everyone's getting ready to play Keepers and Thieves until we black out from excessive alcohol, who's in?"

Despite her aversion to social activities outside of Heartless business, Zero turns on her heel, with Saige practically skipping to hook her arm through Raven's. Dziye scoffs and takes another drag before following the girls. Kagiso wags his brows at Tal and Rovis, who glance at each other. Rovis shrugs and drags Tal over to the living room.

When Rovis moves to sit next to Zero, however, all the Aconites start shouting.

"Absolutely not," Daleyza's distinct voice snaps. Summer's finally up and about now, leaning an elbow on Daleyza's shoulder and watching the scene with lifted brows.

"Woah, woah, woah," Zeke Reyyez interrupts, waving for the Aconites to shut up. "Do you guys ban your Scavenger from playing with you all the time, or is this a post-revolution development?"

"We're banning him from playing at the same table as Zero," Avery corrects him, crossing their arms. "There's enough of us to play two separate games; those two cannot play the same one."

Tal's stare darts around between the Aconites, the Skulls and the Ring, and Rovis and Zero. The Aconites have all apparently grown a spine and decidedly lost their wits. Jordan and Damian look as confused as everyone else. Rovis has a brow raised, amused, and Zero has a similar air of frivolity in the slight tilt to her lips.

"Last time they sat on the same table," Kagiso drawls, glass hovering by his lips, "the rest of the players barely got to even look at their cards."

"How does that even happen?" Damian asks, derisive and unconvinced. "It's a team game."

"Oh, come on, people," Tal interjects. "It wasn't that bad. I'd say it was quite entertaining, don't you think?"

The shouts surge up again, and Tal holds up his hands, taken aback.

"Of course *you* enjoyed it," Vanneza accuses. "You like everything involving Boss. But some of us would actually like to make some plays."

"I—"

"They can't possibly hog the game," a Ring Tal doesn't recognize says incredulously. "They'd have to have *all* the Chosen cards, and that's statistically unlikely. Maybe that happens once in a while, for just one round, but you're making it sound like they took over a whole *entire* game."

"Because they did!" Raven yells over the clamor, laughing and gesturing at the odd sibling pair with her beer bottle. "A whole afternoon and dinner!"

"Okay, that's just crazy," Jordan states. "You'd have to be extremely experienced to hog over the game for so long. Rovis did competitive wrestling, and Rena speaks at least six languages. Both of those things should take up all your free time. And then you both joined the Damned. Where could you two have possibly found the time to get that good?"

"Gambling in high school," Zero states blandly.

"Keeping her ego in check," Rovis adds nonchalantly.

"I still beat you."

"Well—"

More protests from the Aconites drown out their petty argument. Alcohol has loosened everyone's tongue, so even though the Lasans and Toullish have barely just met the Aconites, they join in on the rowdiness.

Zero raises her voice, "I'm bored. You fossils stay here. Fun, competent, aesthetically pleasing me come with me to the dining room."

The room explodes with indignant objections from the older members of each organization and bursts of laughter from the teenagers. They get up to follow Zero, too drunk to care about who they're taking orders from. Zero slings an arm over Raven's shoulders and whispers in her ear, a slight mischievous glint in her eyes. At the tail end, Zeke and Kagiso are sniggering to each other and clinking glasses together.

"She never stops, does she?" Tal remarks with a sigh, then chugs half a bottle of rice wine.

"Stop what?" Rovis asks, sitting down where he meant to before the Aconites verbally assaulted him.

"'Incite as much chaos as possible,'" Tal quotes her words from earlier, pulling a chair next to Rovis.

"Well, she is named after a creature of destruction."

"Sirena," Tal mutters. "Do you think she'd let me call her Rena?"

"Ask her," Rovis says simply, when it's not at all simple.

Damian feels around the table for the card distribution button, and when he hits it, holograms appear next to each player with starting levels and points. The center panel opens up and slides new sets to everyone. Rovis and Tal pick up their cards at the same time.

"Here we go," Rovis sings, smirking and pouring himself five shots of whiskey.

Tal shakes his head, but the grin on his face betrays his amusement. He slams down an Ace of Anchor as the first bid in the free market period, and the game begins.

They play for the rest of the day, taking one-hour breaks for lunch and dinner that the teenagers miraculously cook up. They pause their games in the other room earlier to clamor about in the kitchen, arguing about what dishes to make and probably setting something on fire twice. But they get the job done, serving up the fruits of their labor like happy little elves. Usually people think that kids hate doing chores just for the sake of hating, but Tal can see it in their loose postures and careless grins that the weight of the world is off their shoulders, if only for a moment.

"It's good," Tal comments when he tastes Saige's quesadillas at dinner.

"Yay." She grins at him, and he can't help but pat her head.

After dinner, the adults' game lasts until midnight, and of course Rovis wins without even trying. Tal could tell that he wasn't counting all the cards and calculating who might have what during each round, because Rovis kept staring at Tal.

"You definitely cheated," Damian accuses, standing up to stretch.

Jordan buries xyr face in xyr hands, pretending that xe is not associated with Damian.

"We weren't betting," Rovis points out. "Why would I cheat?"

"You were ogling Gierkas the whole entire time! There's no way you didn't tip the odds; you are a Sleightist."

Tal opens his mouth to protest, but the lights suddenly go out.

Darkness washes over them, snuffing out every conversation and petty remark.

Tal creeps over to the wall closest to the back door, claws unsheathed. He can hear the sound of weapons drawing all around him. Knives, blasters, guns, brass knuckles. A few people pull out electric whips and sticks, energy shields and swords, the faint neon glows painting their suddenly serious faces despite the light mood mere moments ago.

Tension grows among them as they spread out to inspect the possible intrusion.

Strong beats of music suddenly vibrate the entire house, and strobe party lights flash aggressively from the ceiling.

Obnoxious laughter and cheers erupt from the dining room.

"You've got to be kidding me," Tal mutters, and similar sentiments sound faintly behind him between the booming beats as he follows Rovis to the raucous of the youth.

Kagiso is kneeling on the table and chugging down a tall shot of tequila, with Zeke lying flat on his back between his legs. Kagiso then plants a hand next to Zeke's head and pulls out the lemon in Zeke's mouth with his own teeth. The children start whooping and shouting again, walls and furniture on the verge of breaking from all their banging. Even Zero's laughing between Saige and Raven, so hard that her dimples are showing on her flushed face, a bottle of sorghum liquor almost empty in her hand.

Throwing the lemon to the side, Kagiso lets Zeke sit up. He pulls the front of Zeke's shirt and crashes their lips into a bruising kiss.

"Does anyone have bleach for my eyes?" Tal hears Damian shout over the music.

Vocals enter over the electronic beats, and horrible singing adds to the cacophony that is the tragic existence of teenagers. Rovis drags a hand down his face when Saige and Raven pull Zero up on the table. Half of the girls across the three organizations push Kagiso and Zeke off so they can start dancing on it, with no room for decency between their packed, writhing bodies.

Eventually, they sway too much for the poor table, so they bound to the living room and grab all the awkward adults to join them in the dancing. The house becomes a rave, like the ones all the organizations invested in back when they were thriving in their own cities. But all of that is gone, so why not enjoy this?

Grinning, Tal pulls Rovis into the middle of the bouncing crowd and hooks his arm around the back of his neck.

"Not you, too," Rovis grumbles, but he's smiling, hands resting on Tal's hips.

"It was supposed to be like this," Tal beams. He doesn't know if it makes sense because he's a little drunk, but not too much because he knows Rovis is always watching out for him. It probably doesn't make sense, but he says it again anyways: "It was always supposed to be like this."

Rovis's eyes shine, fingers gripping Tal tighter.

"Do you know what I mean?" Tal asks him loudly over the music. "If we got to be normal, it would have been like this."

Rovis snakes a hand up, over Tal's stomach, his chest, his collarbone, then around the back of his neck.

"I know," he says, too softly that Tal can't hear him but still manages to read his lips.

And it's so *Rovis*, elegant yet brutal, gentle yet firm, ethereal yet grounded. He's a liar who craves the truth, a demon who glows like an angel, a living paradox that Tal can't get enough of. This life, this world, all of it has always felt unreal, like Tal's creation of his own hell for never-ending suffering. And just like how every law has a loophole, Rovis is the loophole to his torment. He's always been Tal's north star, a distant hope but close enough to guide him, bouncing between harsh and lenient when he loses the light.

Maybe none of this is real. If Tal's living and dreaming in a different universe, then Rovis is the realest thing his mind has ever come up with.

He's more brilliant than anything Tal has invented for the Aconites, more enigmatic than any cipher he's broken through, more freeing than any drop of alcohol that he's ever gotten hooked on.

Using the arm he has around Rovis, Tal tugs him close.

"You are my greatest addiction," he whispers into Rovis's ear, the golden hoop sparkling under the disco lights, cold against his lips.

Fingernails dig into his neck, and Tal closes his eyes at the sparks flying between them.

"You," Rovis returns, voice rough and hot in Tal's ear, "are my most sinful temptation."

The room suddenly feels like a sauna. Sweat drips down his spine, and his red shirt feels like a thousand layers.

"Well," Tal breathes against Rovis's lips, gazing into those dark, alluring eyes through the dancing shadows. "Sin away, my beloved. We are, after all, the Damned."

Epilogue

WINTER SOLSTICE

Tal stirs when the first rays of the morning sun peeks through the curtains. His hair has grown longer, and it tickles Rovis's chest. Gentle fingers bury themselves into Tal's hair and toy with the soft curls, while Rovis stares at the ceiling of their home, his other arm folded behind his head on plush pillows. His breaths are shallow, still recovering from the lingering shock of his nightmare.

While he doesn't make much noise when his dreams take him back to the Playground, Rovis suffers paralysis every time he wakes up. It worries Tal, but at least it doesn't disturb his sleep.

With heavy lids, Tal blinks slowly as he listens to Rovis's rapid heartbeats. He reaches up a lazy hand to thread his fingers through Rovis's, his eyes falling shut again. A soft protest escapes his throat when Rovis starts shifting to get up.

Unfortunately, now that they have a regular life — free of crime, per the Council's orders — they've also discovered each other's true sleep schedules. Tal is, of course, a night owl, tinkering until dawn, while Rovis is tragically a morning person. And because he's Rovis, he's been coaxing Tal into healthier habits.

The country has now been renamed to Phlirvona, the Zessroan word for 'new day.' The Dawn Council has churned out new legislations, with a whole set of laws dedicated to a program that converts people who had to resort to crime under the Purish government to more productive jobs that ideally don't involve weapons of poison. By human nature, the black market and illicit trading still exist, but legal work has been working out pretty well for former Aconites. Hopefully with the reconstructed education system, less kids will end up among the Damned.

Rovis now works with a section of Phlirvona's government that runs public housing, and Tal has his own company of green energy technology. Both of them have flexible work hours, and they'll have more than sufficient pay for food and housing once the economy stabilizes from this political transition. The Council also let them keep half of the money they made through illicit ways as compensation for their help in capturing Marudas and Whiston, so they still live a comfortable life. Neither of them seem to miss the luxuries much, if at all.

"Do I need to get up now?" Tal mumbles.

"Soon. It's Rena's birthday."

"Yes, I remember." He shifts his head back to rest on Rovis's shoulder so he can squint up at him with bleary eyes. "You think she'll say yes?"

Rovis's chest rises and falls with a soft sigh. "I'm slightly optimistic. She hasn't said no to training as an apprentice for the international ambassadors."

"She didn't accept the job, either," Tal points out. "Maybe she's not giving them an answer because it doesn't matter to her."

"Maybe," Rovis concedes. "It's something she'd do."

Feeling Rovis's dip in mood, Tal adds, "But that's unlikely, because she wouldn't disrespect Raven's mother like that. She's come a long way, Rov. And it's only been a month since everything happened. It might just take time."

"Yeah," Rovis whispers. Then he shifts and taps Tal's shoulder. "I'm going to make breakfast."

"Wait."

Suddenly much more awake, Tal rolls over to shuffle through his clothes piled on the floor next to the bed, then turns back to Rovis with a small crystal disk, faintly glowing white and purple.

"I..." He looks up at Rovis with a searching gaze. "I found your mom's side of the family."

Rovis's heart stops. "What?"

"I tracked down the Bozyds," Tal says softly. "In Toullifuka. They're your family, and they want you to visit. This has their information in it and contacts to get across the ocean, even while international travel is prohibited right now." He smiles at Rovis's stunned expression. "You can go back to where you came from, Rov."

"Thank you," Rovis whispers, though his muscles don't feel like his own. He never thought this to be possible, when his mother was his last tie to Toullifuka. But this is Tal, who works miracles with his brain and solves any problem thrown his way. And he's gone out of his way to chase after a mystery of Rovis's past.

Rovis leans down and kisses Tal with all the words he can't speak, like he's the only tether to reality in this surreal world of new possibilities, of change, of chances they never thought they'd have.

"Us and our sisters," he murmurs against Tal's lips. "Next vacation."

"Yes," Tal agrees breathlessly and curls a hand in Rovis's hair.

Rovis sighs, then gives him a quick peck on the nose. "I really do have to get up."

Tal pouts but moves anyway. Rovis pads out of the master bedroom of the Revyxon house they've been staying in since he escaped Drokklo's Playground. A heaviness weighs down in his chest at the reminder, and fragments of his latest nightmare flash through his mind. Sometimes, his brain grants him the mercy of a dreamless night. But most of the time, his brain recreates every terrible thing that he experienced down there and builds more petrifying twists off of his memories.

In the kitchen, Avery's already sitting at the island counter, sipping from a mug.

Many of the former Aconites have grown used to living in a mansion together, so they've been sticking around. As for the rest of their 'safe houses,' Rovis has repurposed them into public housing that he keeps tabs on weekly, or bed and breakfast lodgings if a former Aconite prefers living there than here in Gezrya.

"Have you eaten?" Rovis asks.

Avery nods. "Thank you, though."

Rovis cooks up some scrambled eggs and makes a smoothie for Rena. Eyeing the pink drink, Avery asks, "When's the party?"

"Mid-afternoon."

Although Dziye tried to convince Rena to do something special for her eighteenth, she insisted on just having the gift exchange for Passing Reset to happen on her birthday so that no one drowns her in gifts. A set date to mark the new year, Passing Reset isn't here for another week. Then, of course, Kagiso came up with the brilliant idea to party every night with different themes through the end of the year.

Rena's curled up in her bed reading again. Her collection of books now towering stacks by every wall, the margins of each page clear of encoded spy notes. She sits up when Rovis knocks and opens the door.

"Oh," she says. "You didn't need to make me breakfast."

"You're too lazy to do it yourself, and I'm not going to let you starve." Rovis sets down a plate of eggs on her nightstand and hands her the cup, which she gulps down half of as soon as her fingers close around the glass. He chuckles. "See?"

She frowns. "I should be the one making you food."

"Says who? Besides, it's your birthday." Rovis sits down next to Rena. "You don't have to go downstairs today. I'm sure Kagiso has a way to spin it into a different party."

"No." She rubs her eyes. "I should get out of bed at some point."

They've both been struggling with the simple task, worn out from years of living in survival mode. Rovis holds out his hand, and Rena takes it.

"Anything I can do?"

Rena smiles, and the feeling of it sits oddly on her face. "You're already doing it. Just take care of yourself. Take care of Tal."

Rovis leans forward to press a kiss on the top of her head. "I am. Keep resting until the party, then. If you still can't get up for lunch, I'll bring it up to you."

In the end, he doesn't need to, because she comes down before noon to cook for the entire house, despite everyone's protests. Daleyza and Raven help her, and they all lounge around in the living room until Damian and Jordan show up at the front door, bags of excessive amounts of jewelry in h and.

"What am I supposed to do with this?" Rena grumbles at a crystal tiara that Saige is trying on for her. "Go to one of those archaic pageants, if those still exist?"

"You've been Rov's sister for a decade," Jordan says, ruffling her hair, "and we never got to get you anything."

Rena slants Damian an unimpressed look, and he only shrugs.

Then Dziye shows up with Enyo Zhao. Their relationship becomes the talk of the day, probably of the next century. A Marquess of the Water Lords and the devil that the Lords exiled, both with too much power for any government official to deal with. Rena hopes she can get the story out of them someday.

Following them are the Starcatchers, Katina and Vasily, and Alexei Federov. The first floor of the house bustles with reunions, gifts exchanged between friends while soundtracks with soft beats play throughout the sound system.

It might just be the first proper Passing Reset any of them ever had.

Rovis, Tal, and Daleyza cook for the feast, and dinner is full of hopeful smiles and a warmth that they were all too afraid to have when they were the Damned. Rena fidgets with the jade pendant that Rovis had given to her as protection when he sent her to the Skulls.

Save it for someone who loves you, she once told him.

This time she doesn't force it back into his hand.

Rena smiles at the matching braided leather bracelets on Tal's and Rovis's wrists, black with a small thread of red, an Avyrian gift for a special pair of lovers to meet each other again in the next life. Raven keeps the locket that Rena gave her hanging outside her white shirt, a fox and a black bird curled around a moon, for Jacek, her, and Lila. She knows Raven will put the last picture that all four of them took together inside. Saige grins at her with an intricate flower crown on her head, which can be preserved by a bio-enhancer box that Rena designed based off of the bio-lab flower spheres that Tal gave her ages ago.

After a few rounds of card games, Kagiso drags everyone into another dance party. No one protests, because they get to relive the night they found out the six countries signed the peace treaty. It's only a matter of time before a world leader grows ambitious again, when Riyssolx wants to take over another country, or when Avyria wants to burst out of their submarines from beneath the oceans, or when Toullifuka wants to show the world just how powerful their crystals are, or when Lasantirk wants revenge for all the years they've been tied down. Or, who knows, Phlirvona wants to integrate all cultures into one big melting pot across the entire globe.

But for the next several decades, they're safe. So they dance and drink and sing and laugh, for this night of peace, for all the years of youth that were stolen from them.

When the night winds down into the quietest hours, their guests stagger into the spare rooms, and the people who already live here drunkenly stumble back to their rooms. Rovis drags Rena into the lounge with glass ceilings, where the sky looks more purple than red as it distantly approaches dawn. He puts down a paper bag on the table between them.

Rena has already guessed what's inside, but she opens it anyway.

"This is an antiretroviral," she says.

Rovis nods, reaching out to grasp her hand. "Triple-combination therapy. I know I haven't been the best brother to you in the last several years. And maybe this is selfish of me, but I want you to live. You never searched for the medication because you didn't think you had much to live for, but I'm hoping you'll let me prove you wrong. We're in a new world now. I swear to you, I will do right by you from this day on to make up for all the time we've lost."

"I don't think it's selfish." Rena looks away to watch Tal, who still lingers, dancing and laughing with the former Skulls by the lake outside, masks off and shielded by the Starcatchers dome from the poisonous air. She says, "I always knew he'd be good for you. The only relationship I've ever miscalculated after I became a Heartless is ours." She turns her gaze back on Rovis. "You did a really good job as a brother. I mean it. I was the one who kept pushing you away because of the voices in my head."

Rovis opens his mouth to argue, but Rena holds up a hand to continue.

"I never cared much for living. You know that. We met each other under awful conditions, and we powered through my mother's reign of terror, not knowing how much we lost. Somehow, we're a lot more fucked up now, the country's reeling from the revolution, and there's still so much pain for the living. I'm tired, Rozzie. I'm tired of spending all of my energy trying to keep myself afloat. I'm tired of carrying this weight. I'm tired of myself."

"I know," Rovis says softly. "It's your choice to make."

"But you were the only one who convinced me I wasn't *her*," Rena continues. "I never got to tell you this because the Agency snatched you before I could. Brother, you were the reason why I couldn't kill myself."

He flinches, but he doesn't look away. "I thought it was Kagiso."

"No," she whispers. "You called me. I heard your voice, and I couldn't drink it."

The grip on her hand tightens.

"So for you?" Rena smiles weakly. "I'll do it. I'll live for you, even though it hurts, because you're the one person on this dying planet who gives me hope that I may heal someday. I'll live for you, because you wouldn't lie to me and say that this will be easy, but I know you'd walk through seven hells with me so that I can find the light in my heart again."

Rovis's eyes shine with unshed tears, and he doesn't dare to even blink, because he's holding onto these words like it's his lifeline.

"I know I can't count on anyone but myself to live for," Rena says, voice starting to scratch. "I know it's not sustainable to rely on you forever. But all you asked of me was to try. I know that whatever I'm looking for, you'll be there to help me find it. After these months of finally tackling our problems, I know that now."

"Good," Rovis says softly. "And I know that I'm not your answer. No single person ever is. But I will give you anything you need and want, because no matter what happens between us, you'll always be my little sister."

Rena stands, and Rovis follows. She pulls him into a hug, burying her face in his soft sweater.

"I'll tell Raven I'll take that job," she says. "I still need some time to recover, but I'll take it eventually."

"Take however long you need." Rovis brushes his hand through her hair. "I'm your big brother, and I'm finally making enough money, legally, to take care of you. So only accept the offer when you're ready, okay?"

"Yeah." Rena closes her eyes, sighing, letting go of all her anxieties in one long breath, if only for a moment. It might get better; it might not. But she believes she'll be alright. Despite how far they've fallen, how much they've destroyed, how lost they've felt at times, they have a future, and they still have their friends and family.

Somedays, it might not feel enough, but today she remembers that it is.

Acknowledgements

Thank you to Gleiver Prieto for the amazing cover for this book and to Ian Wang for helping me make decisions on it even though you were pursuing other artistic interests this year. I've always felt that artists are under-appreciated, especially in this new age of AI. Many people might prefer AI art because it's cheap and easy, but it's just not the same. So thank you to all artists out there, for continuously doing what you love and for creating what we authors cannot.

Next, I'd like to thank my friends again, especially the ones who have made it this far with me in our college career. To those who have been by my side since freshman year to when this book gets published around our graduation time, I love you infinitely. This book is, in some ways, a tribute to our time together and our diverging paths ahead after graduation. In these four years, my characters grew with us, and I'm so proud of all of you for finding out who you are while trying to survive the rigorous academic life and the disappointments we faced socially. I truly believe that wherever we're going, whether that's graduate school or directly into the work force, we're all going to be okay.

Thank you once again to my therapist, for believing me even when I thought I was beyond saving. I hope you enjoyed Cacia's character, even though her system is not at all how you pick your clients. You've watched me grow from our first session together, when I knew I needed to get better even though I didn't want to. You've helped me through all of my worst friendship breakups and crying sessions about my complicated family. I wouldn't have become the person I am today without you. This book is getting published during my graduation because I need to move on from this series and enter a new chapter of both my life and my writing career, yet also because I'm graduating from all the pain and coping mechanisms that went into the creation of this duology.

Thank you to my brother (even though I told him he's not allowed to read these books) and his friends for being such a supportive group, for whisking me away to fun trips in Japan and Long Island and Montreal, for the campfires and karaoke nights and the excessive hype for my books. Rovis and Tal were important characters to Zero and to me because the feeling of being protected by a brother figure has gotten me through many rough times in life.

To any readers who relate to any of my characters, I hope the pain eases soon. I know it's hard to get through one day after another, and I just want you to know you're incredibly strong, and I'm cheering for you. From one survivor to another, I'm sending you a spiritual hug. Thank you for reading and supporting my books!

About the
Author

Astraea Long is a young adult author from Boston, Massachusetts. In elementary school, she spent four years in Sichuan, China, before returning to the United States. She currently studies astrophysics in college, and she enjoys studying foreign language such as French, Italian, German, Japanese, and Korean.

She is an avid reader of science fiction and fantasy, and her future works will include a variety of urban fantasy, dark academia, and queer themes. As an aromantic asexual, she intends to focus on sibling and platonic relationships in her writing, and to challenge the popular trends of sex and romance.

Outside of writing and reading, she's a devoted dancer who previously trained as a pre-professional and now spends many late nights choreographing for her college dance groups. Her other hobbies include painting, scrolling through Asian streetwear fashion websites, watching cooking videos of things she probably can't make, and spending too much money on boba.